SALT MAGIC

HOPE LARSON * REBECCA MOCK

MARGARET FERGUSON BOOKS
HOLIDAY HOUSE · NEW YORK

Margaret Ferguson Books
Text copyright © 2021 by Hope Larson
Illustrations copyright © 2021 by Rebecca Mock
HOLIDAY HOUSE is registered in the U.S. Patent and Trademark Office.
Printed and bound in June 2021 at C&C Offset, Shenzhen, China.
The artwork was drawn digitally with charcoal-style and ink wash-style brushes for the
line art, and watercolor-style brush for the colors.
www.holidayhouse.com
First Edition
1 3 5 7 9 10 8 6 4 2
Library of Congress Cataloging-in-Publication Data
Names: Larson, Hope, author. | Mock, Rebecca, illustrator.
Title: Salt magic / by Hope Larson ; illustrated by Rebecca Mock.
Description: First edition. | New York : Margaret Ferguson Books, [2021]
Audience: Ages 10 to 14. | Audience: Grades 7–9. | Summary:
Twelve-year-old Vonceil Taggart, willing to risk everything to set
things right, leaves her family's Oklahoma farm in 1919 seeking the salt
witch who cast a spell that turned their spring to saltwater.
Identifiers: LCCN 2020036302 | ISBN 9780823446209 (hardcover)
Subjects: LCSH: Graphic novels. | CYAC: Graphic novels. | Adventure and
adventurers—Fiction. | Witches—Fiction. | Blessing and
cursing—Fiction. | Farm life—Oklahoma—Fiction.
Oklahoma—History—20th century—Fiction.
Classification: LCC PZ7.7.L37 Sal 2021 | DDC 741.5/973—dc23
LC record available at https://lccn.loc.gov/2020036302

ISBN: 978-0-8234-4620-9 (hardcover)
ISBN: 978-0-8234-5050-3 (paperback)

For P.J.H. —H.L.

For Kate, Lauren, Susan, Christina, Taylor,
K, Laurel, and Amy —R.M.

CONTENTS

Chapter One
Homecoming

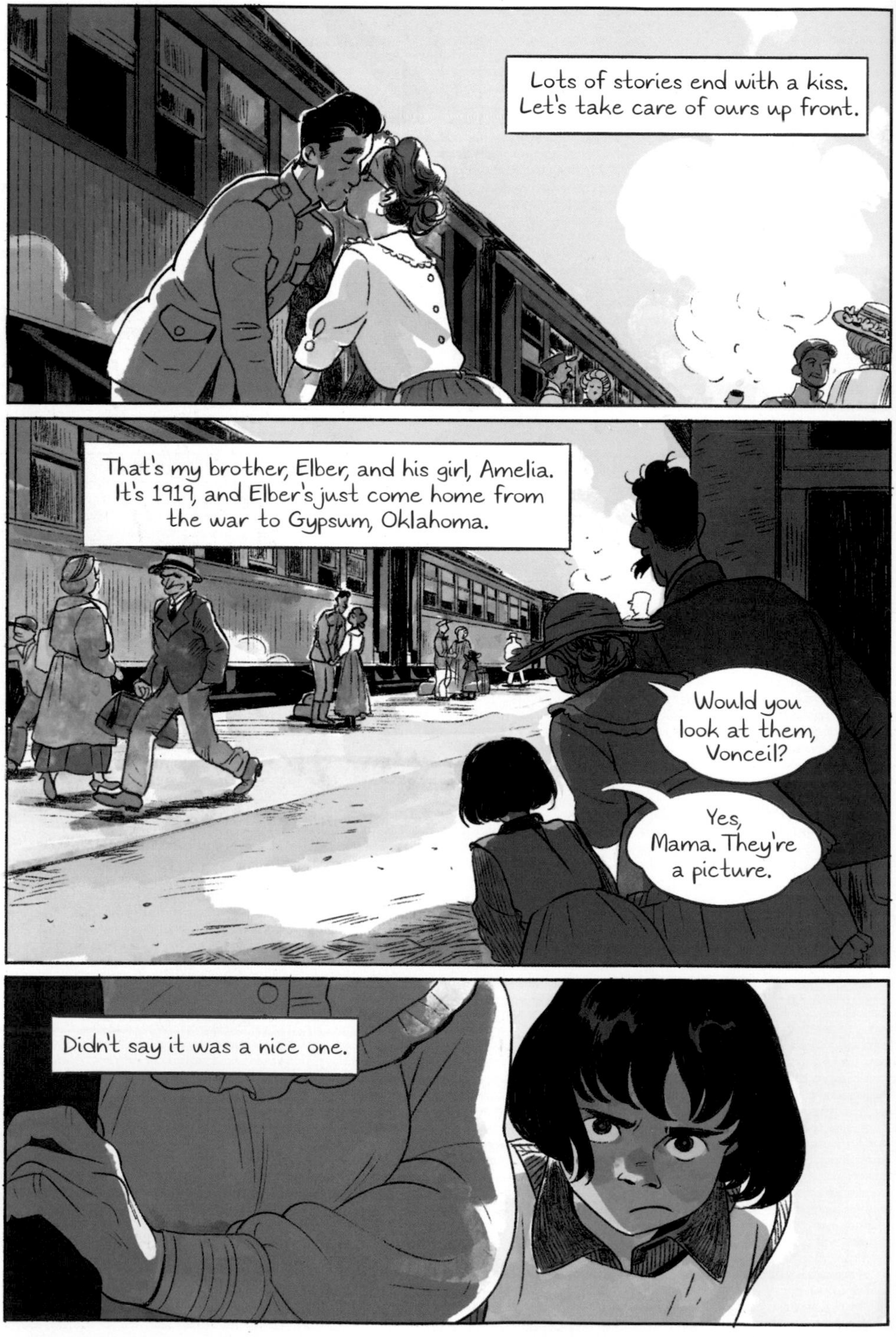
Lots of stories end with a kiss. Let's take care of ours up front.
That's my brother, Elber, and his girl, Amelia. It's 1919, and Elber's just come home from the war to Gypsum, Oklahoma.
Would you look at them, Vonceil?
Yes, Mama. They're a picture.
Didn't say it was a nice one.

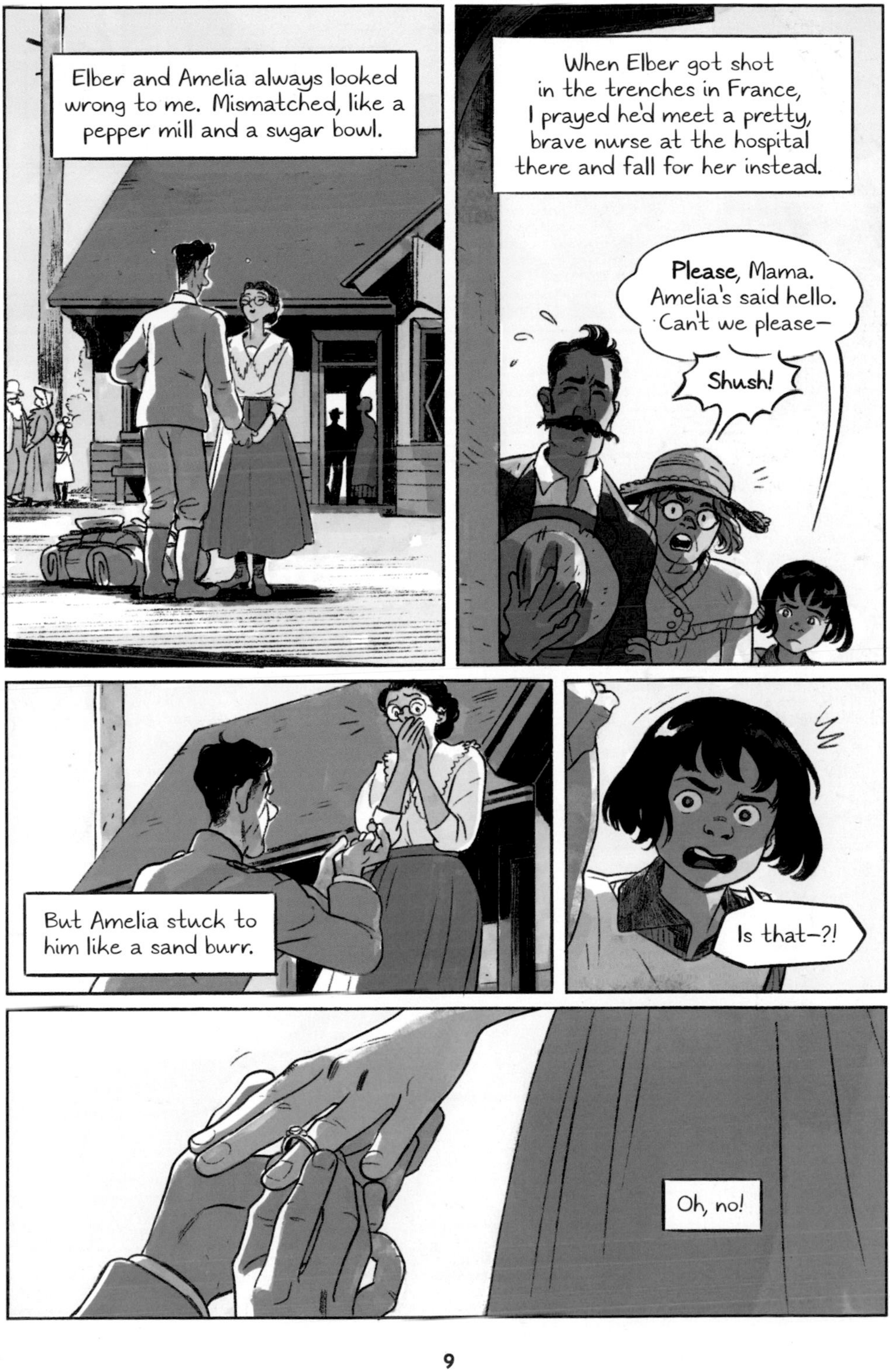

Elber and Amelia always looked wrong to me. Mismatched, like a pepper mill and a sugar bowl.
When Elber got shot in the trenches in France, I prayed he'd meet a pretty, brave nurse at the hospital there and fall for her instead.
Please, Mama. Amelia's said hello. Can't we please—
Shush!
But Amelia stuck to him like a sand burr.
Is that—?!
Oh, no!

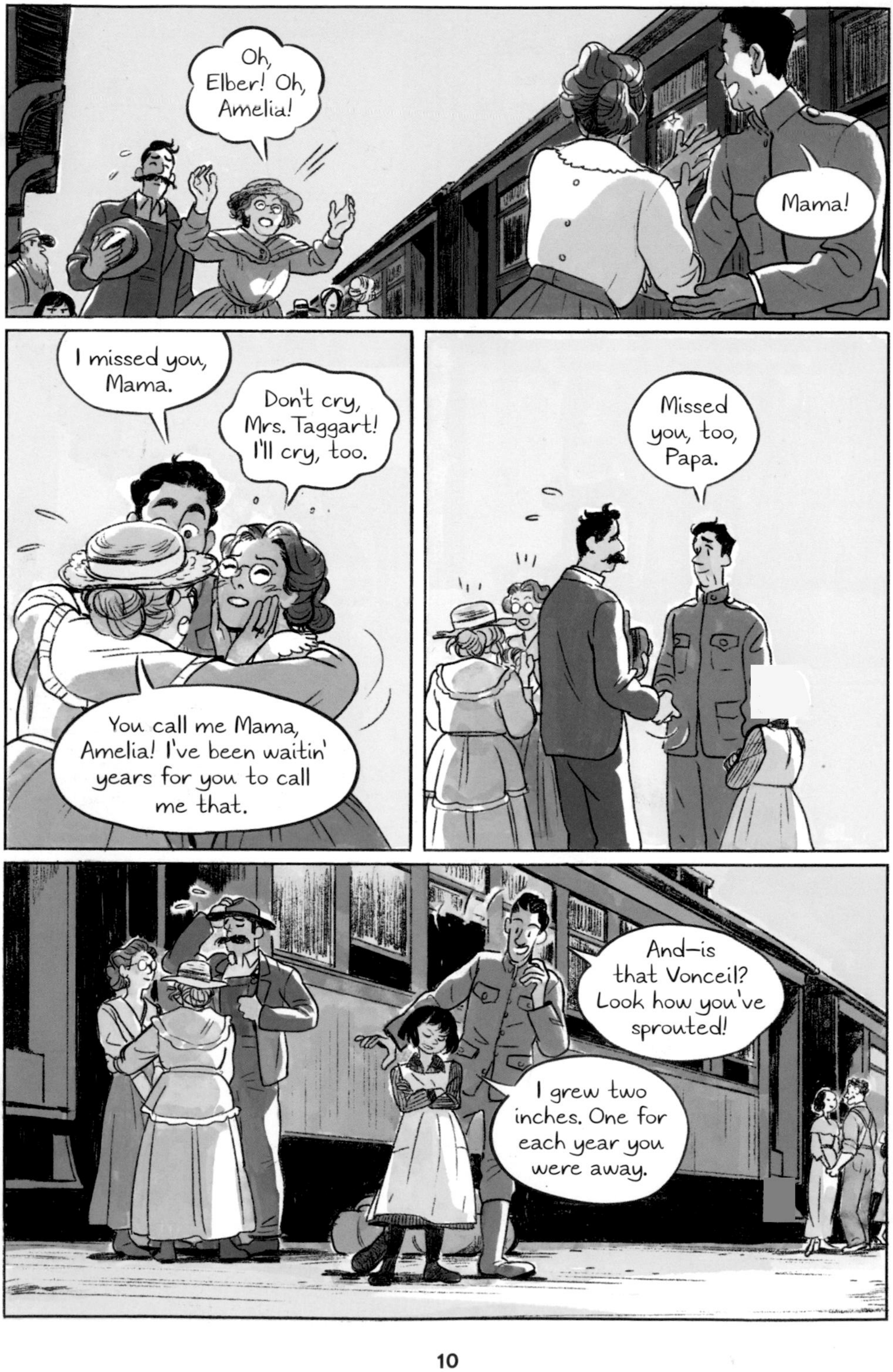
Oh, Elber! Oh, Amelia!
Mama!
I missed you, Mama.
Don't cry, Mrs. Taggart! I'll cry, too.
You call me Mama, Amelia! I've been waitin' years for you to call me that.
Missed you, too, Papa.
And—is that Vonceil? Look how you've sprouted!
I grew two inches. One for each year you were away.

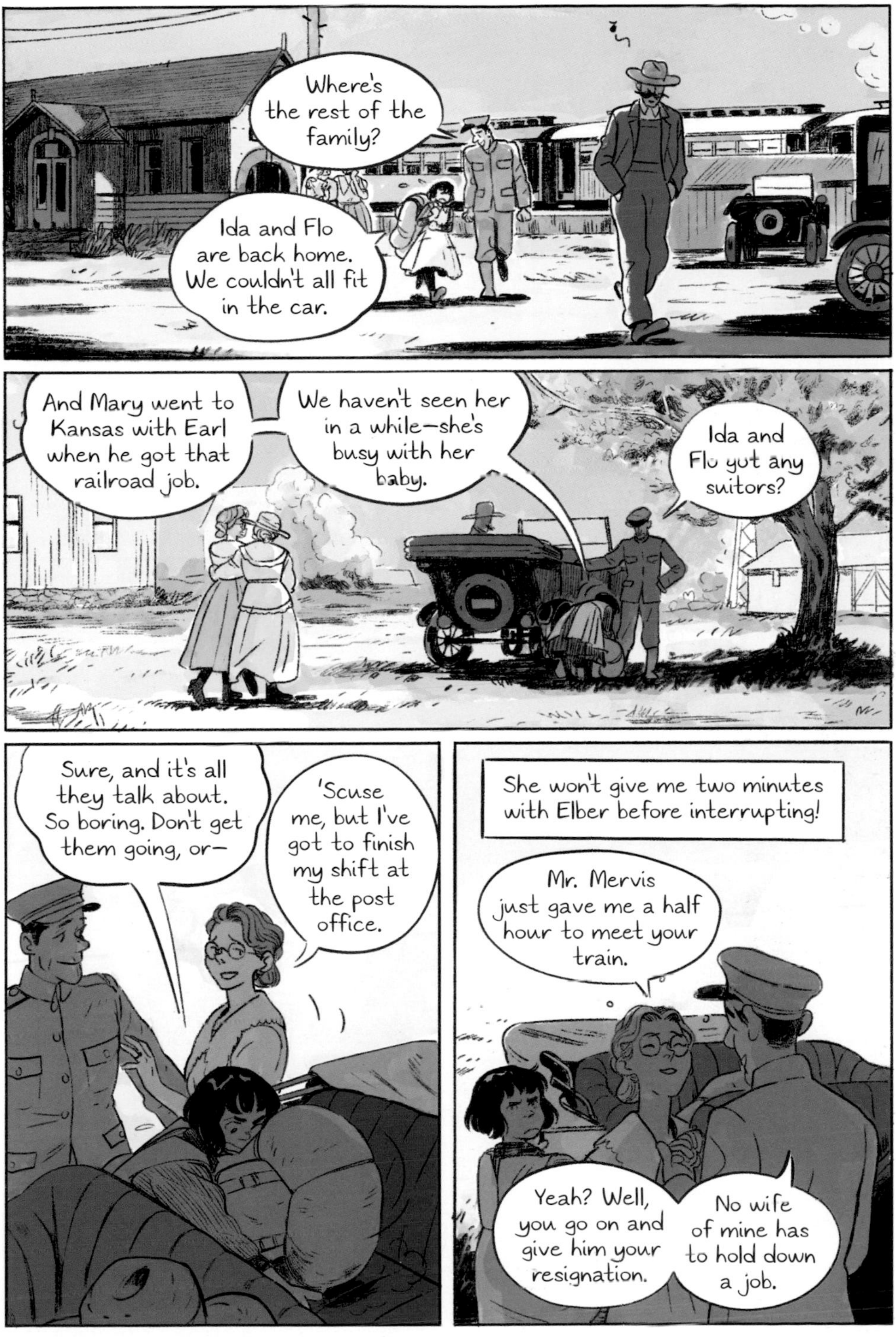
Where's the rest of the family?
Ida and Flo are back home. We couldn't all fit in the car.
And Mary went to Kansas with Earl when he got that railroad job.
We haven't seen her in a while—she's busy with her baby.
Ida and Flo got any suitors?
Sure, and it's all they talk about. So boring. Don't get them going, or—
'Scuse me, but I've got to finish my shift at the post office.
She won't give me two minutes with Elber before interrupting!
Mr. Mervis just gave me a half hour to meet your train.
Yeah? Well, you go on and give him your resignation.
No wife of mine has to hold down a job.

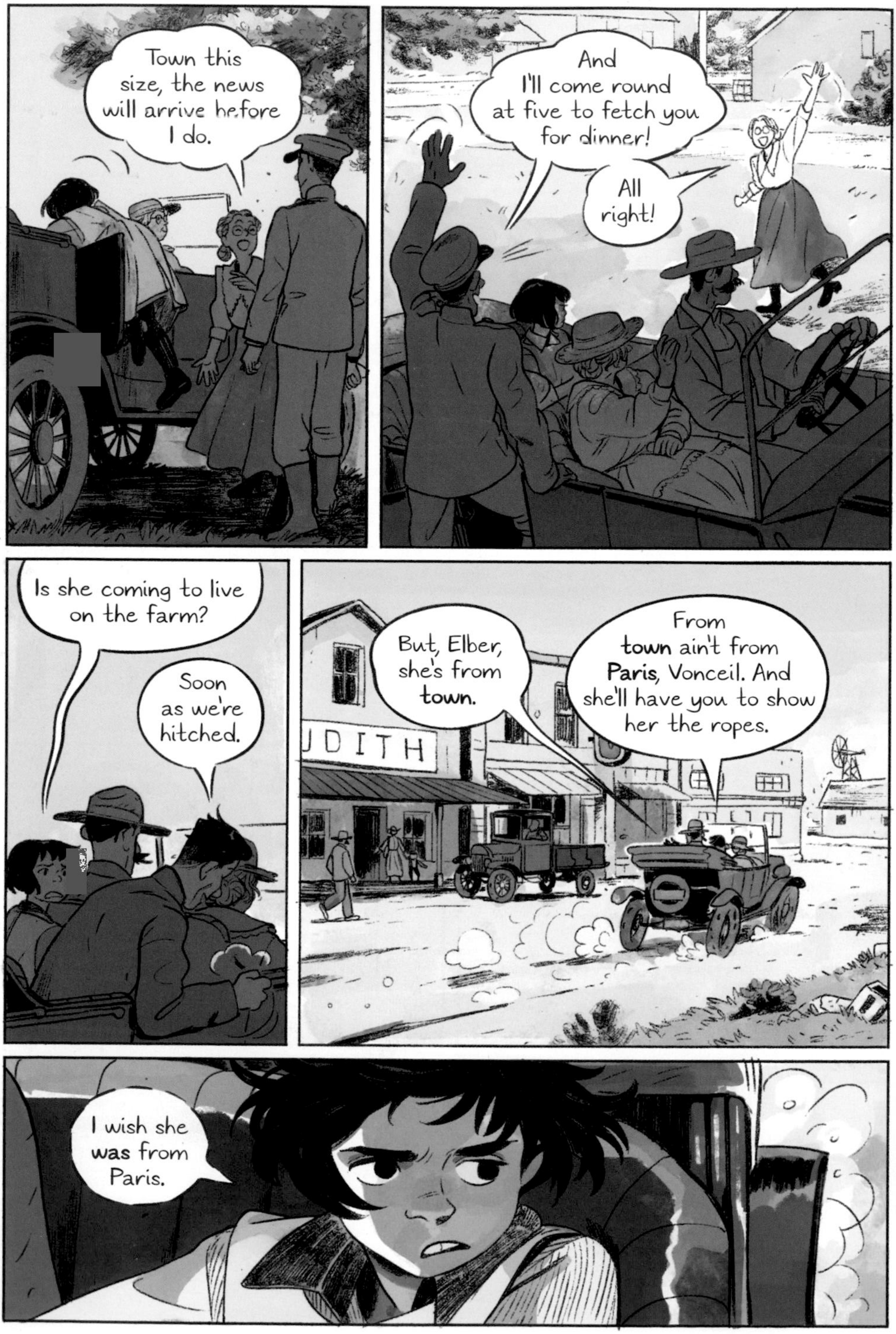
Town this size, the news will arrive before I do.
And I'll come round at five to fetch you for dinner!
All right!
Is she coming to live on the farm?
Soon as we're hitched.
UDITH
But, Elber, she's from **town.**
From **town** ain't from **Paris**, Vonceil. And she'll have you to show her the ropes.
I wish she **was** from Paris.

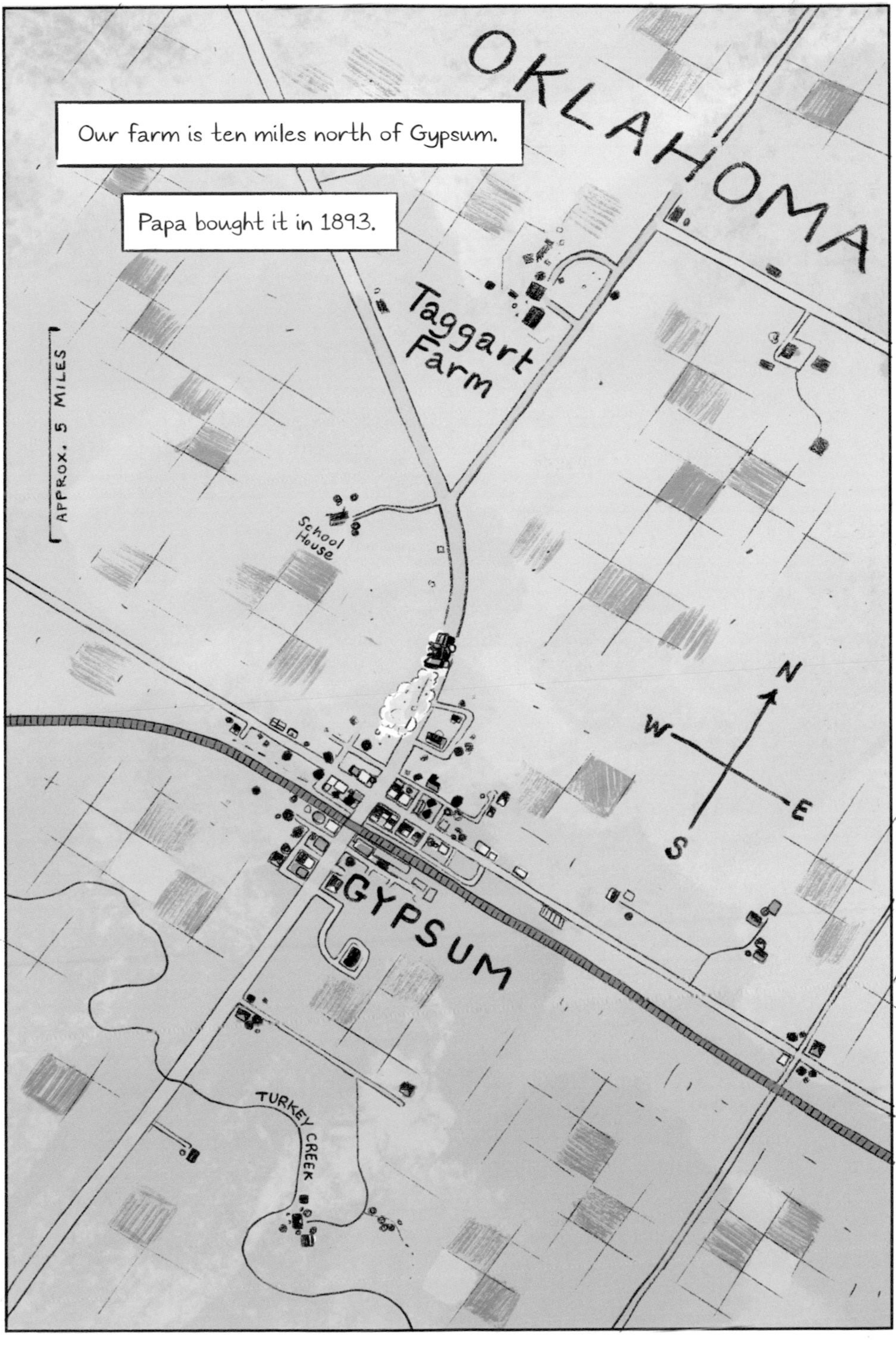
Our farm is ten miles north of Gypsum.
Papa bought it in 1893.
OKLAHOMA
Taggart Farm
School House
APPROX. 5 MILES
N
W
E
S
GYPSUM
TURKEY CREEK

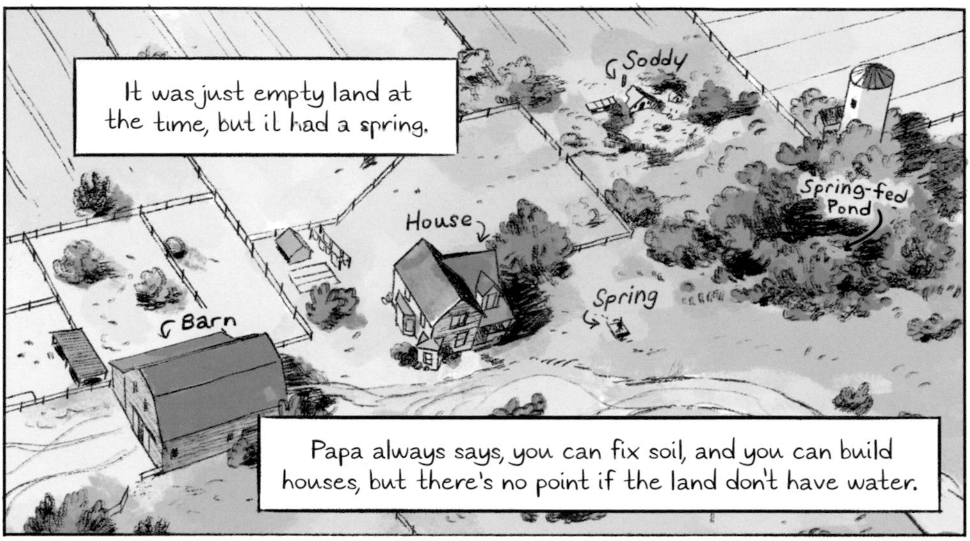
It was just empty land at the time, but it had a spring.
Soddy
Spring-fed Pond
House
Spring
Barn
Papa always says, you can fix soil, and you can build houses, but there's no point if the land don't have water.

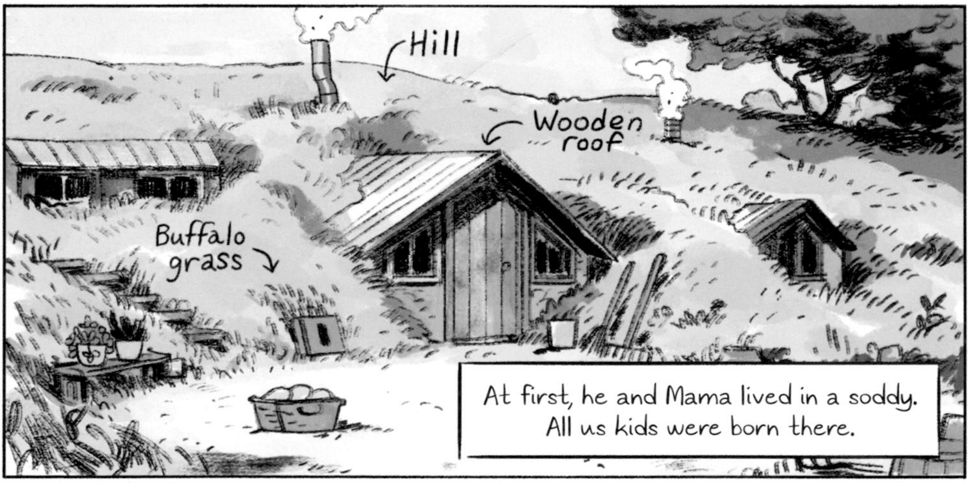
Hill
Wooden roof
Buffalo grass
At first, he and Mama lived in a soddy. All us kids were born there.

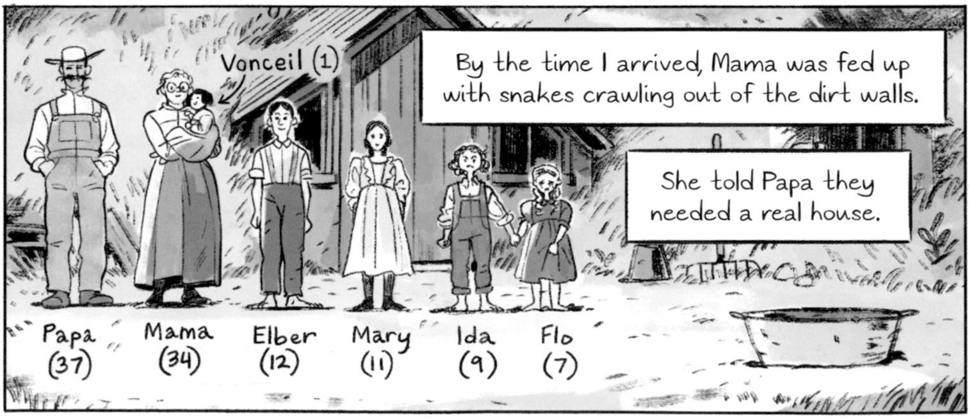
Vonceil (1)
By the time I arrived, Mama was fed up with snakes crawling out of the dirt walls.
She told Papa they needed a real house.
Papa (37)
Mama (34)
Elber (12)
Mary (11)
Ida (9)
Flo (7)

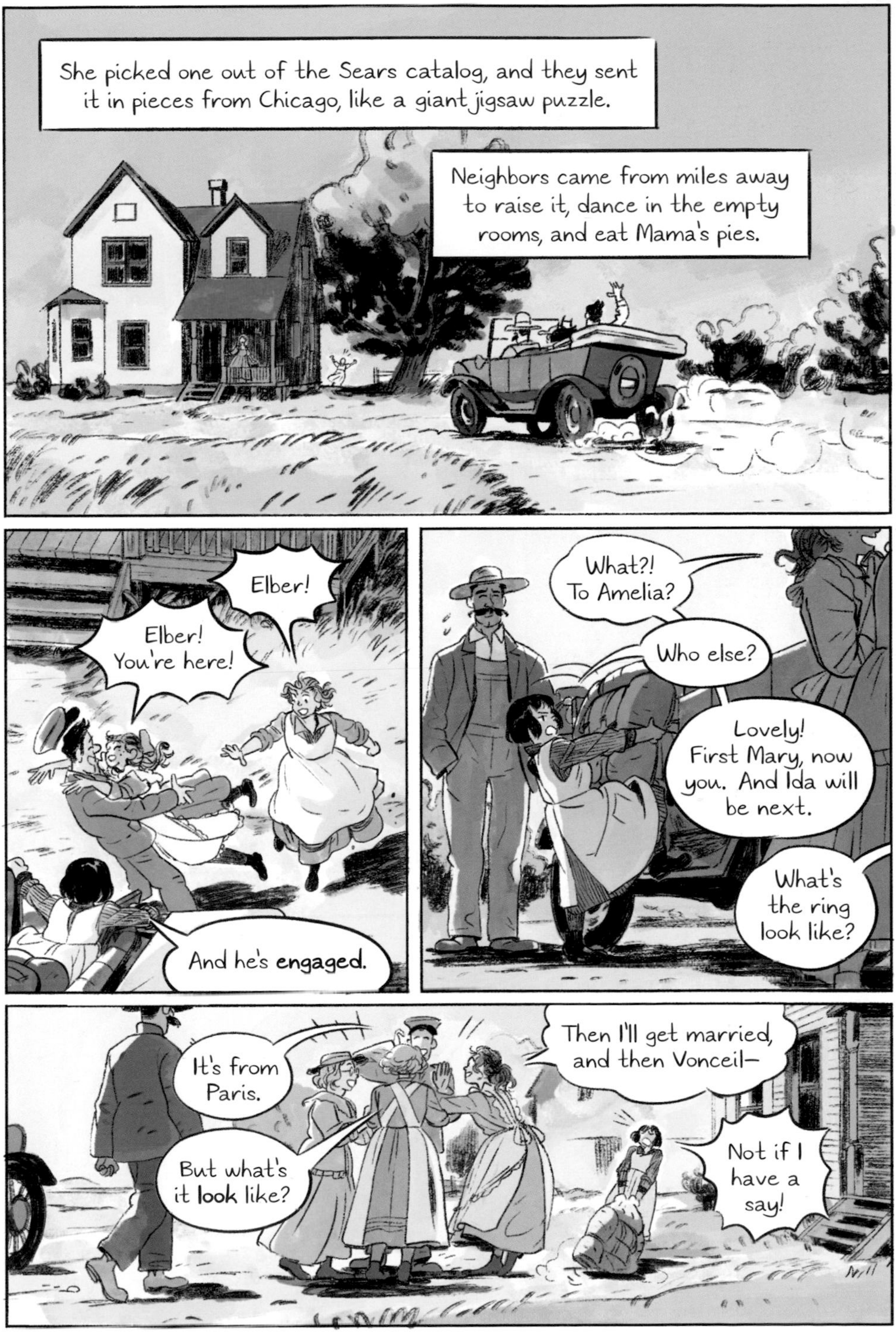
She picked one out of the Sears catalog, and they sent it in pieces from Chicago, like a giant jigsaw puzzle.
Neighbors came from miles away to raise it, dance in the empty rooms, and eat Mama's pies.
Elber!
Elber! You're here!
And he's **engaged.**
What?! To Amelia?
Who else?
Lovely! First Mary, now you. And Ida will be next.
What's the ring look like?
It's from Paris.
But what's it **look** like?
Then I'll get married, and then Vonceil—
Not if I have a say!

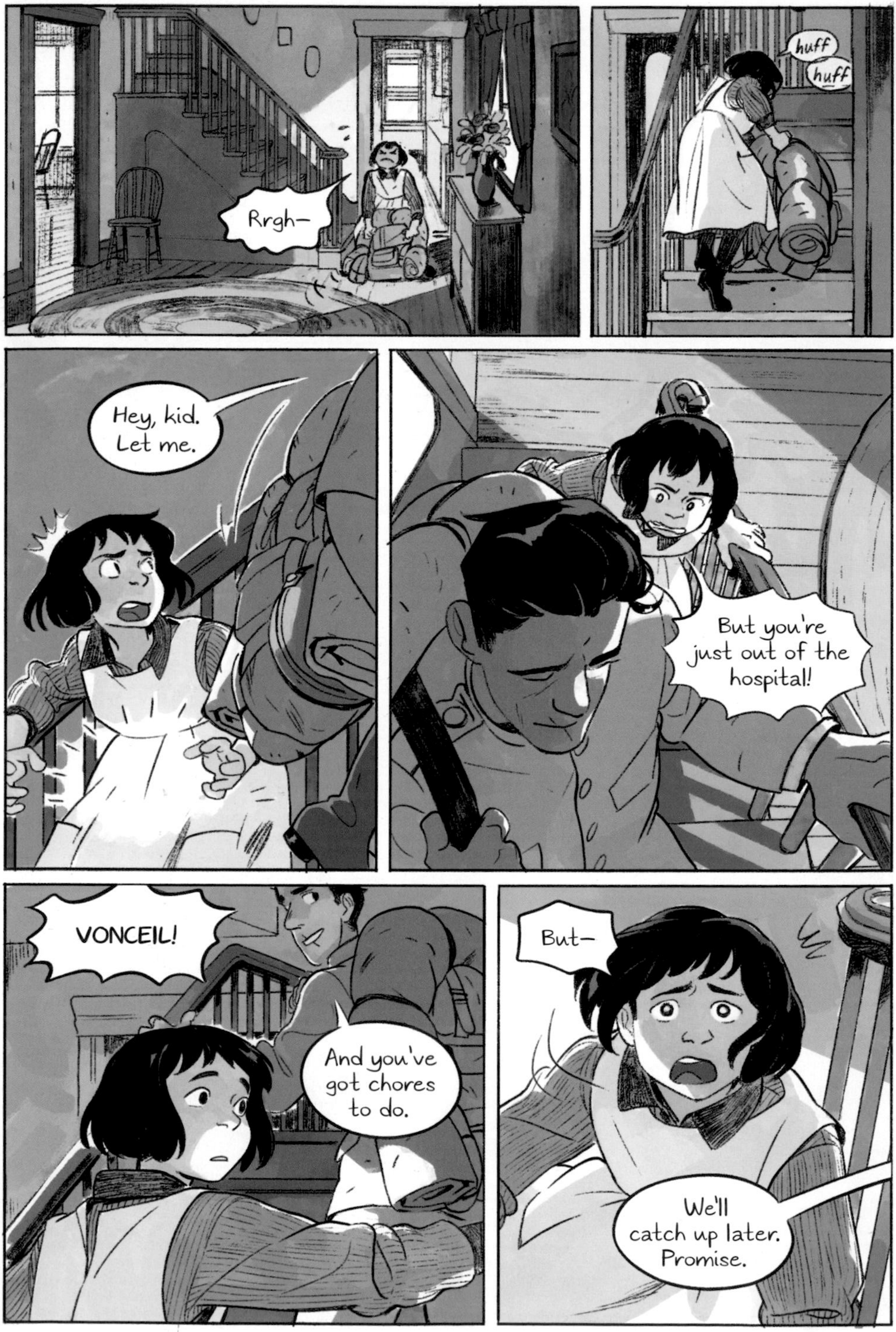
Rrgh–
huff
huff
Hey, kid. Let me.
But you're just out of the hospital!
VONCEIL!
And you've got chores to do.
But–
We'll catch up later. Promise.

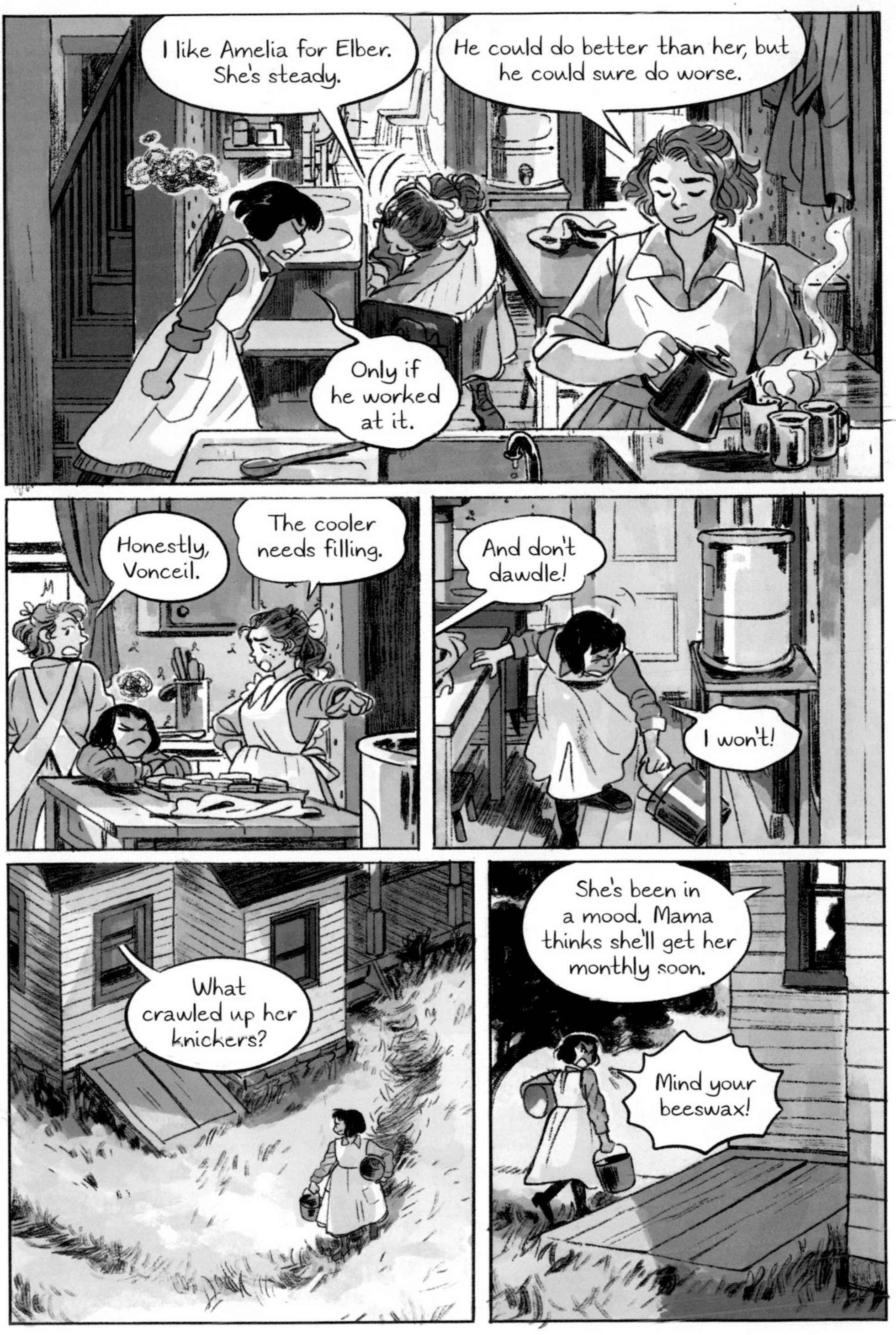
I like Amelia for Elber. She's steady.
He could do better than her, but he could sure do worse.
Only if he worked at it.
Honestly, Vonceil.
The cooler needs filling.
And don't dawdle!
I won't!
What crawled up her knickers?
She's been in a mood. Mama thinks she'll get her monthly soon.
Mind your beeswax!

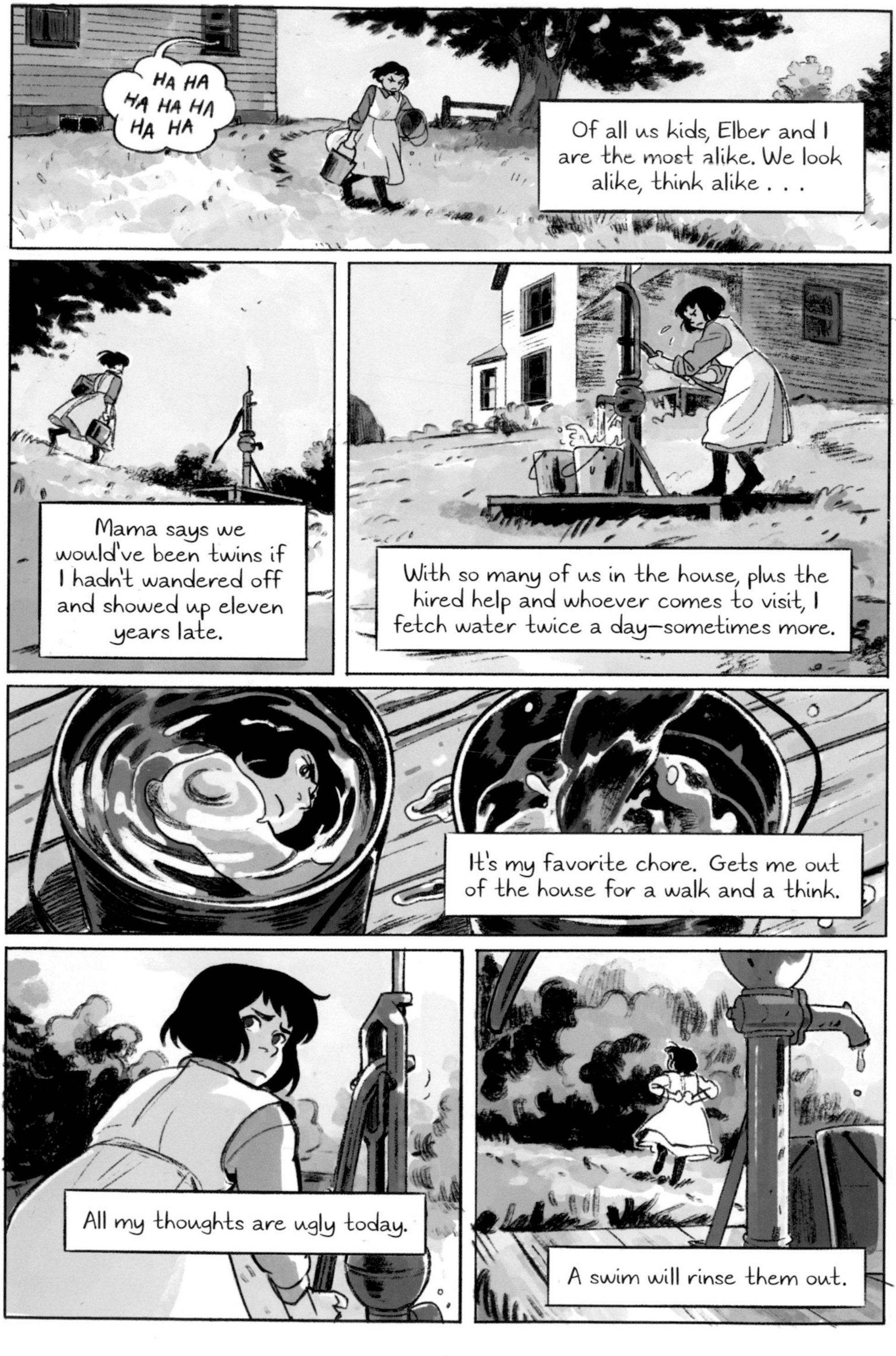
HA HA HA HA HA HA HA
Of all us kids, Elber and I are the most alike. We look alike, think alike . . .
Mama says we would've been twins if I hadn't wandered off and showed up eleven years late.
With so many of us in the house, plus the hired help and whoever comes to visit, I fetch water twice a day—sometimes more.
It's my favorite chore. Gets me out of the house for a walk and a think.
All my thoughts are ugly today.
A swim will rinse them out.

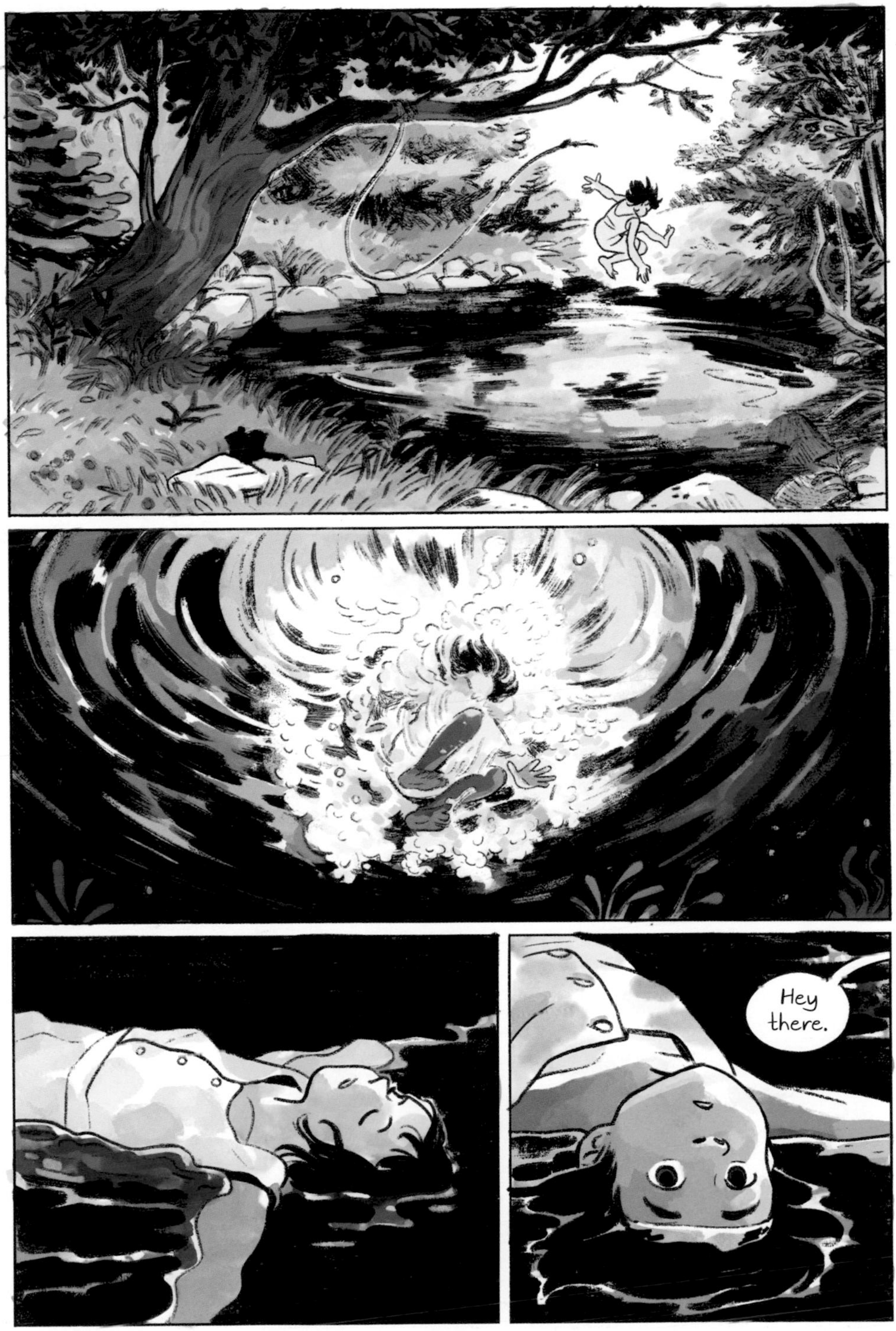
Hey there.

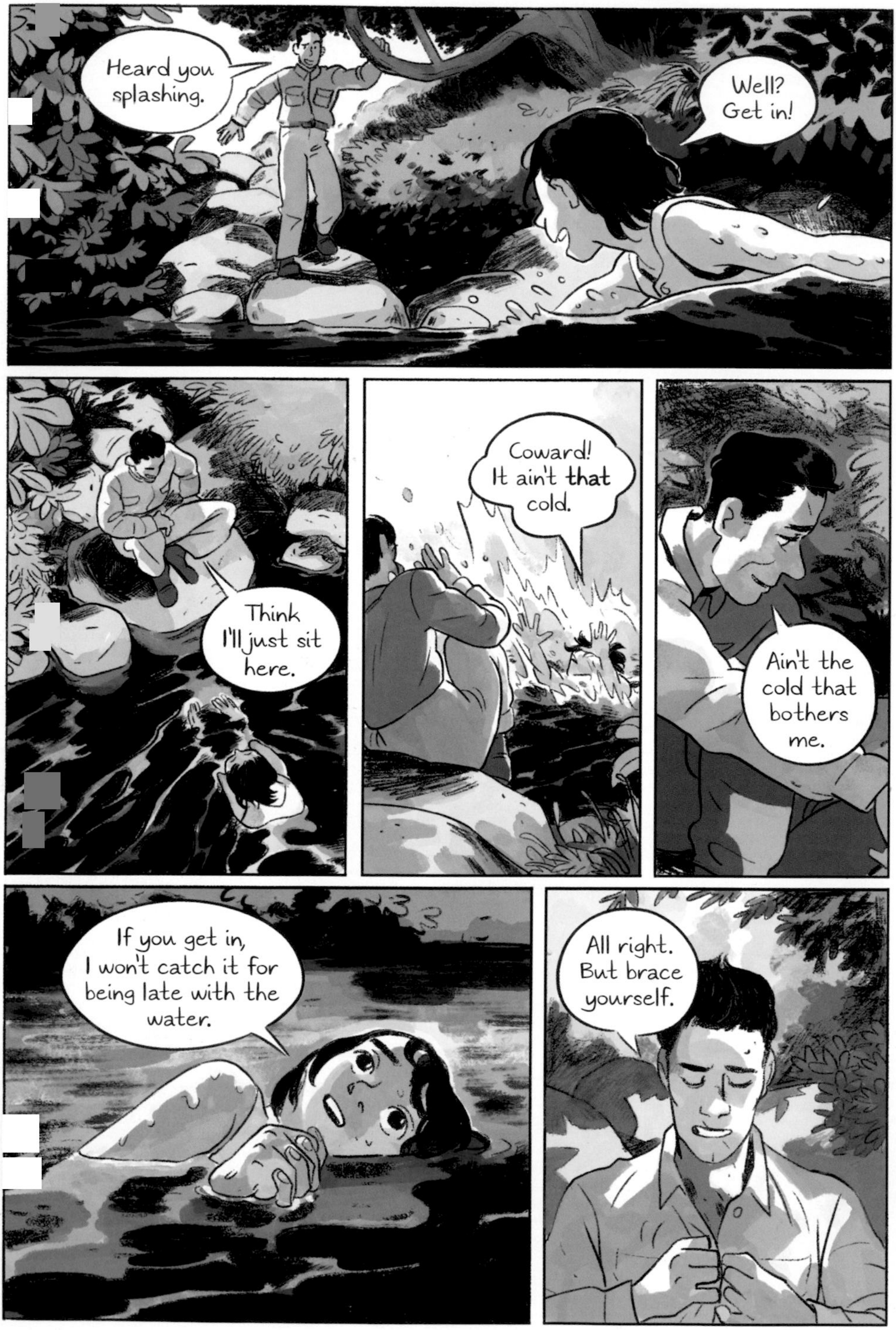
Heard you splashing.
Well? Get in!
Think I'll just sit here.
Coward! It ain't **that** cold.
Ain't the cold that bothers me.
If you get in, I won't catch it for being late with the water.
All right. But brace yourself.

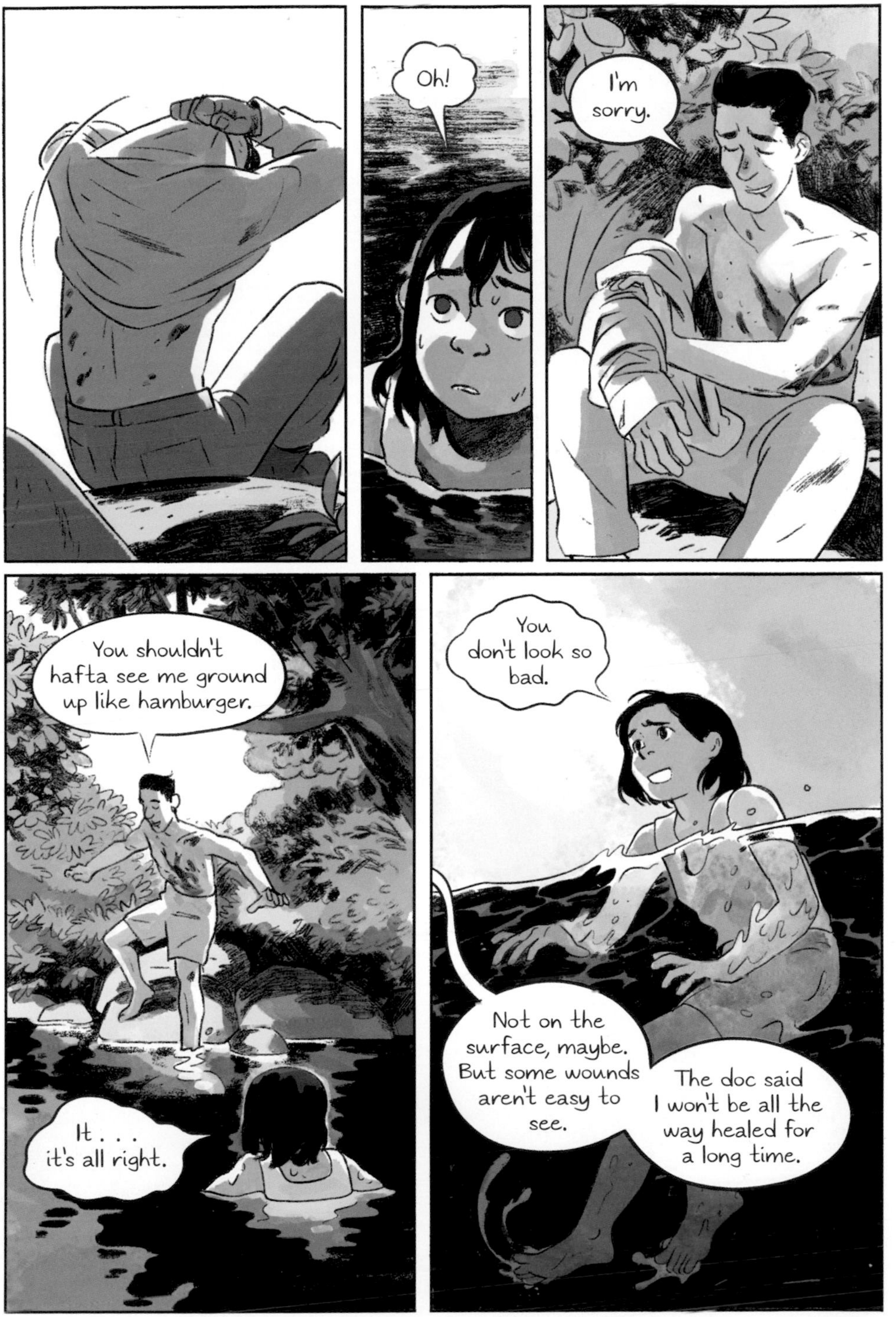
Oh!
I'm sorry.
You shouldn't hafta see me ground up like hamburger.
It . . . it's all right.
You don't look so bad.
Not on the surface, maybe. But some wounds aren't easy to see.
The doc said I won't be all the way healed for a long time.

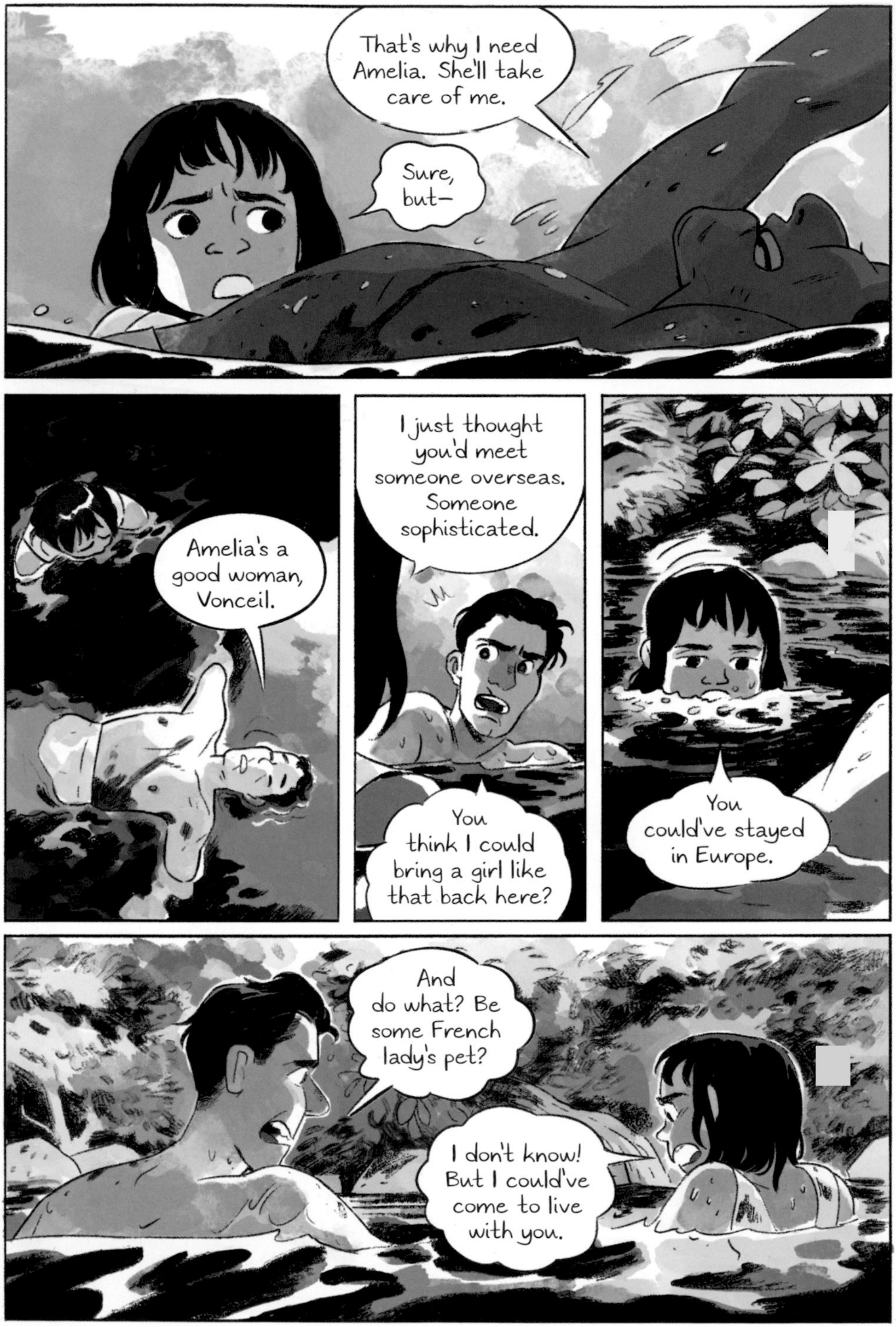
That's why I need Amelia. She'll take care of me.
Sure, but–
Amelia's a good woman, Vonceil.
I just thought you'd meet someone overseas. Someone sophisticated.
You think I could bring a girl like that back here?
You could've stayed in Europe.
And do what? Be some French lady's pet?
I don't know! But I could've come to live with you.

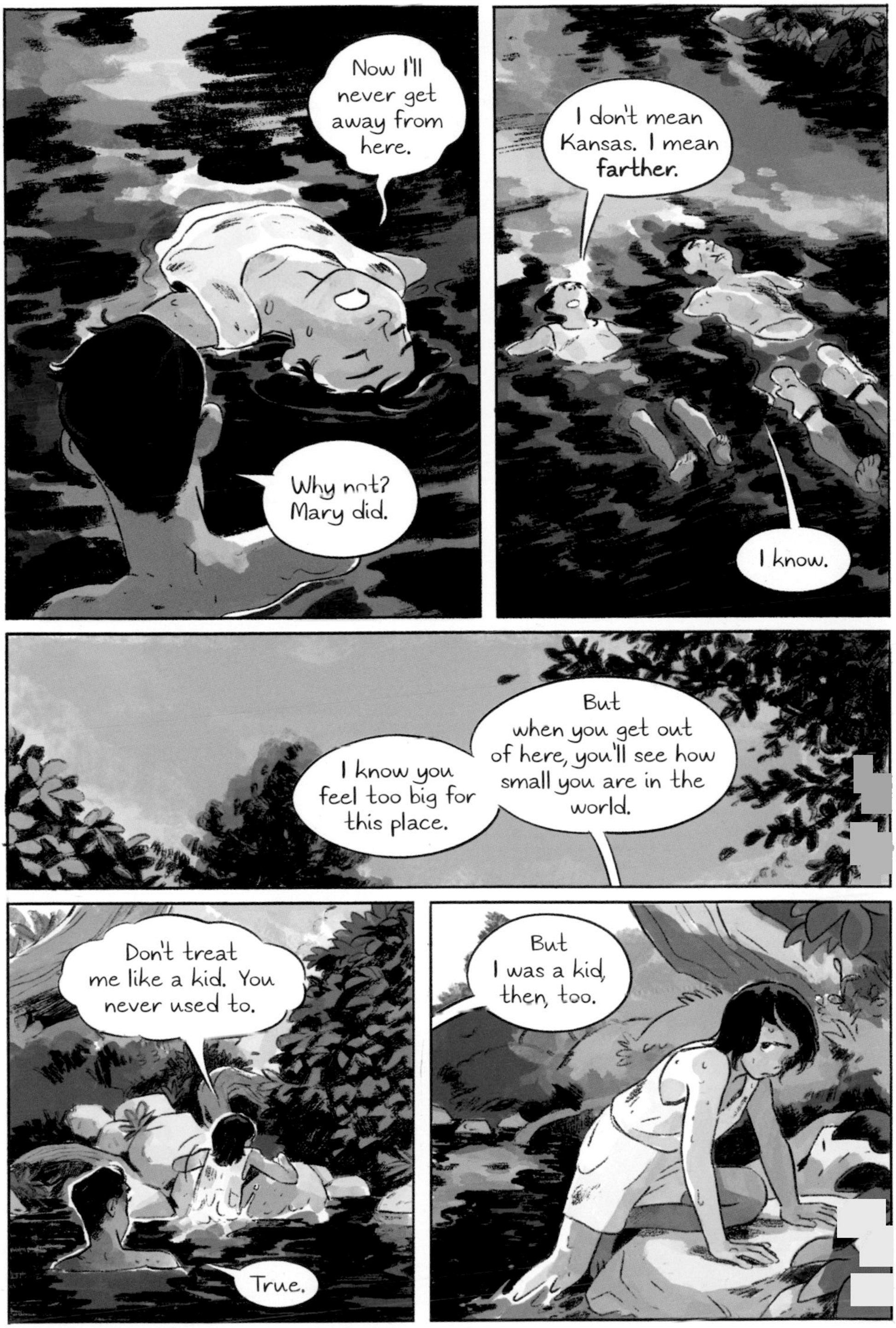

Now I'll never get away from here.
Why not? Mary did.
I don't mean Kansas. I mean **farther.**
I know.
I know you feel too big for this place.
But when you get out of here, you'll see how small you are in the world.
Don't treat me like a kid. You never used to.
True.
But I was a kid, then, too.

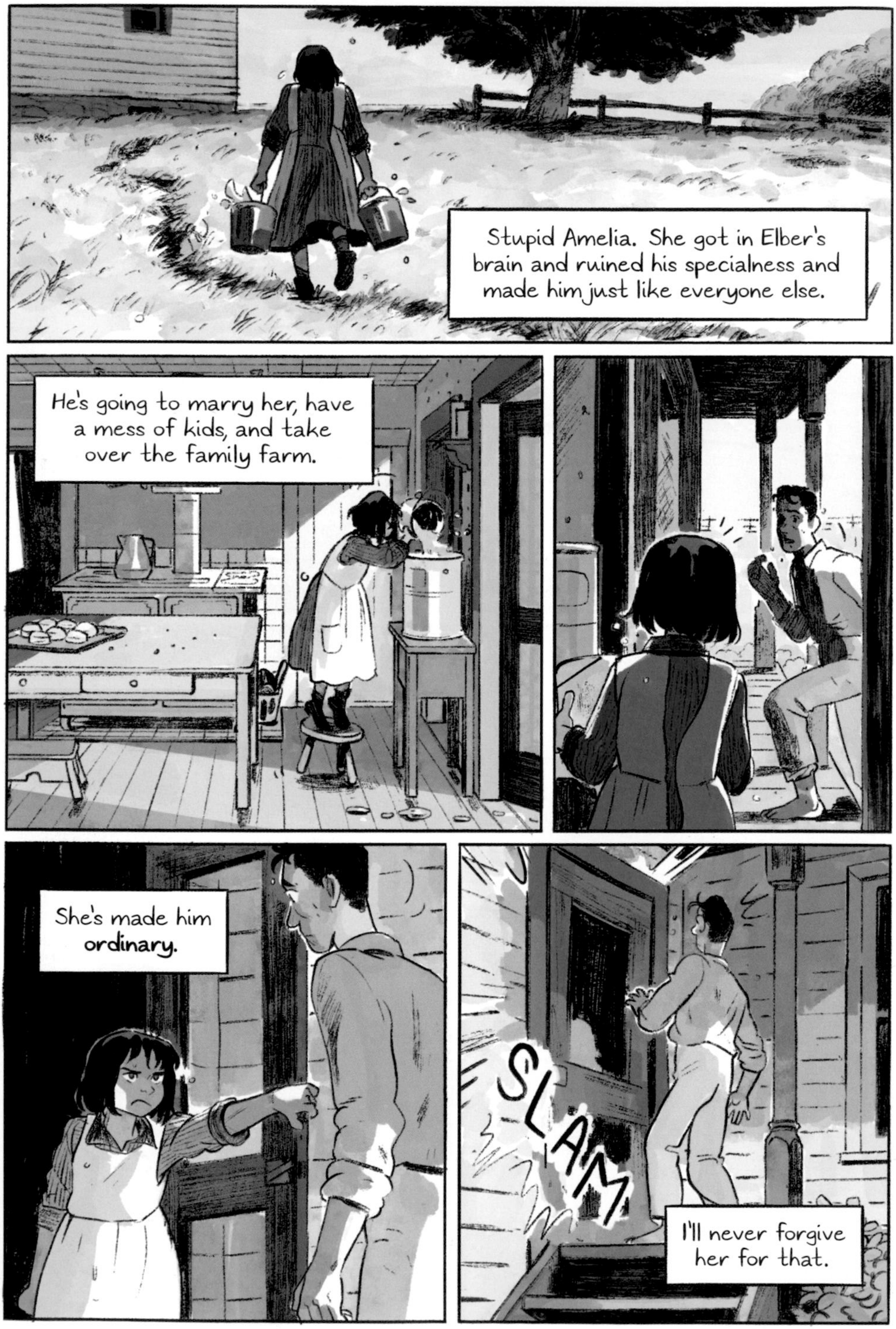
Stupid Amelia. She got in Elber's brain and ruined his specialness and made him just like everyone else.
He's going to marry her, have a mess of kids, and take over the family farm.
She's made him **ordinary.**
SLAM
I'll never forgive her for that.

Chapter Two

Old Dell

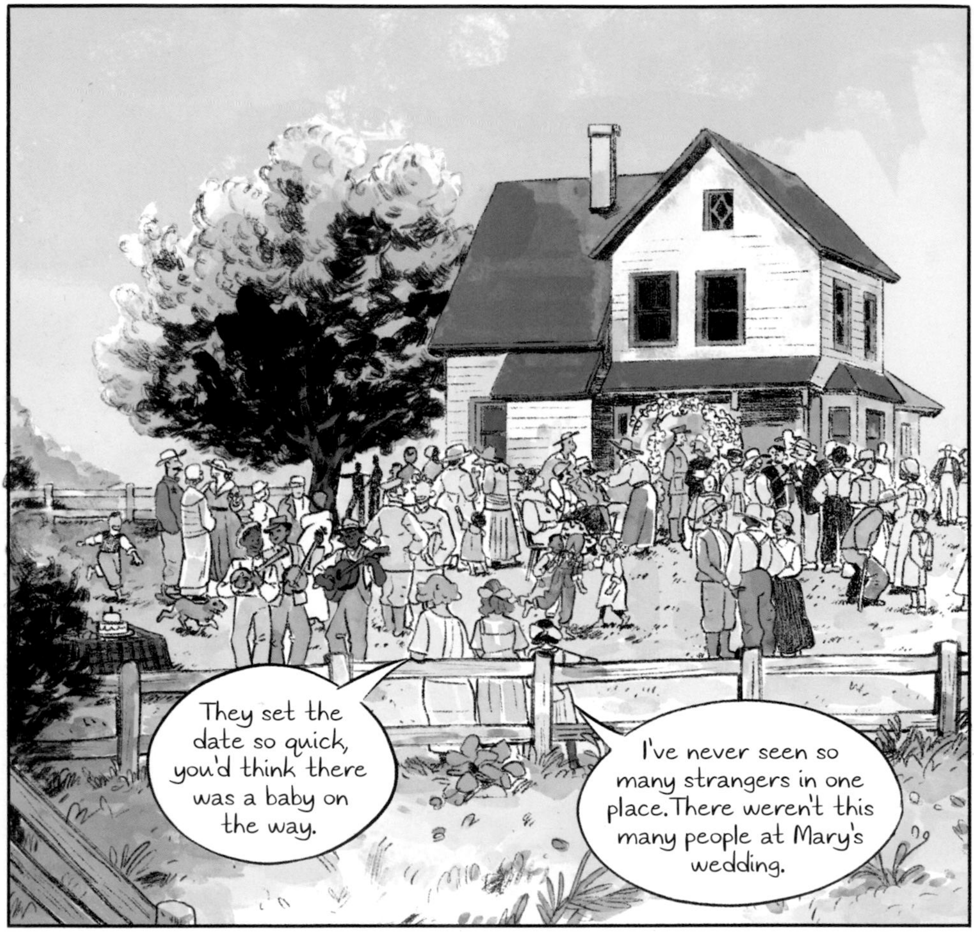
They set the date so quick, you'd think there was a baby on the way.
I've never seen so many strangers in one place. There weren't this many people at Mary's wedding.

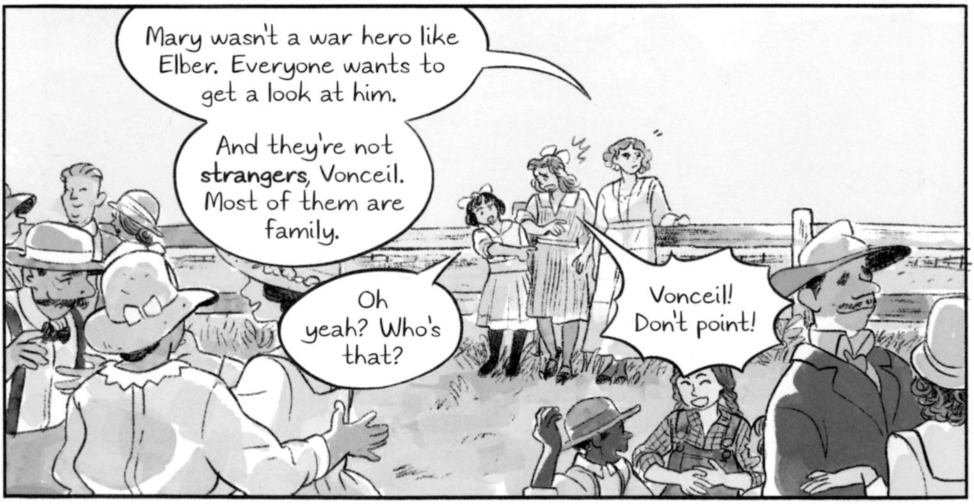
Mary wasn't a war hero like Elber. Everyone wants to get a look at him.
And they're not **strangers**, Vonceil. Most of them are family.
Oh yeah? Who's that?
Vonceil! Don't point!

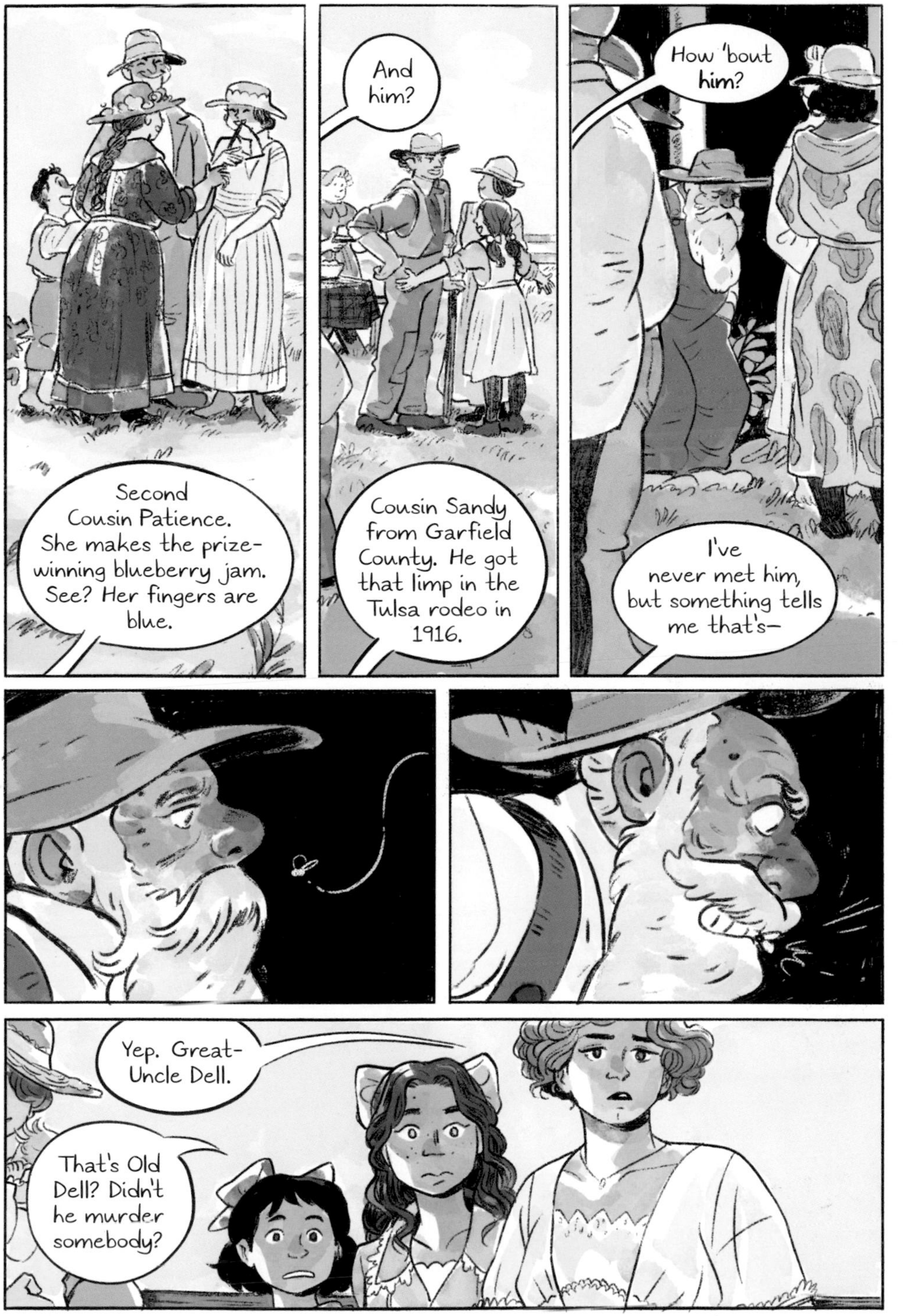

Second Cousin Patience. She makes the prize-winning blueberry jam. See? Her fingers are blue.
And him?
Cousin Sandy from Garfield County. He got that limp in the Tulsa rodeo in 1916.
How 'bout **him?**
I've never met him, but something tells me that's—
Yep. Great-Uncle Dell.
That's Old Dell? Didn't he murder somebody?

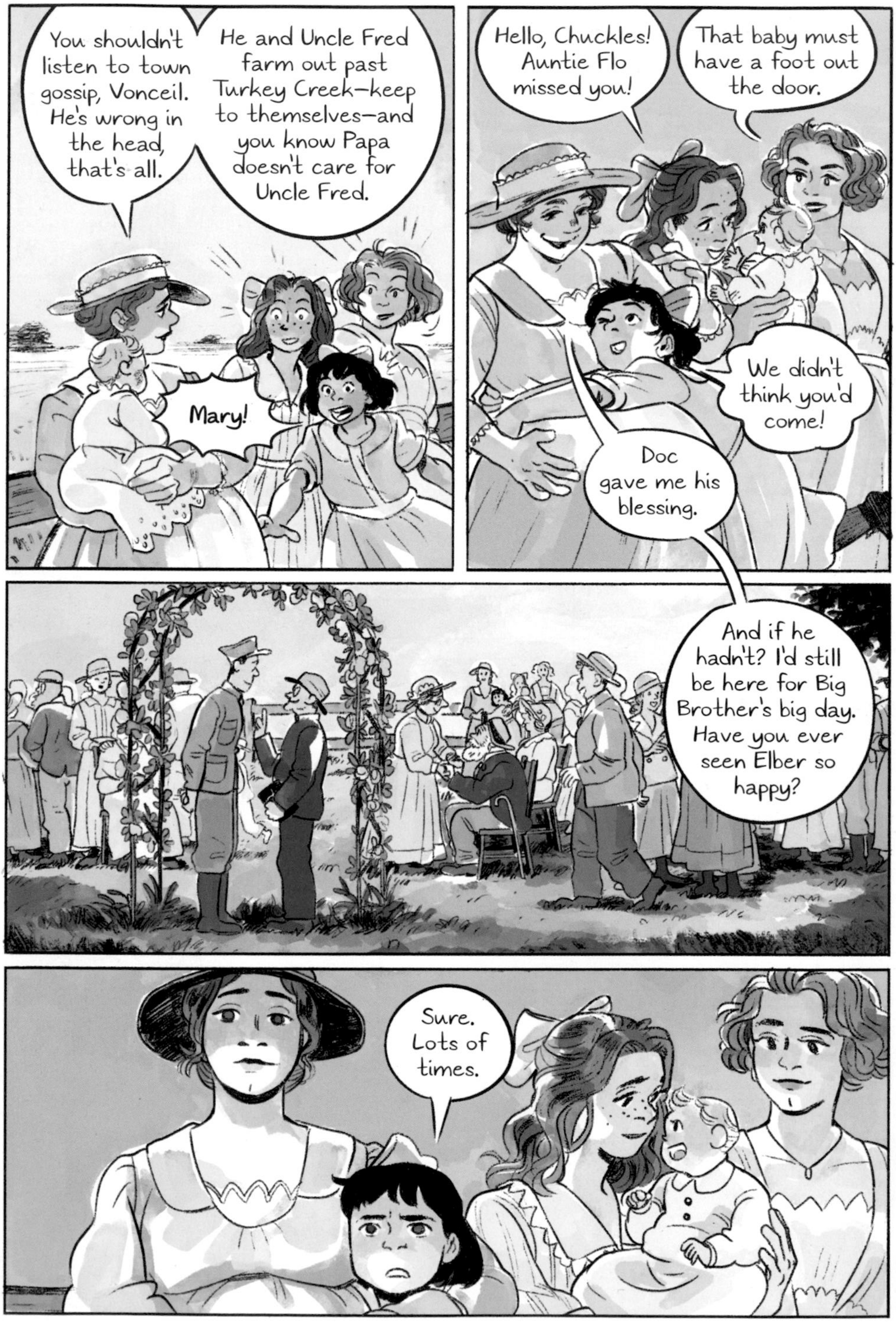
You shouldn't listen to town gossip, Vonceil. He's wrong in the head, that's all.
He and Uncle Fred farm out past Turkey Creek—keep to themselves—and you know Papa doesn't care for Uncle Fred.
Mary!
Hello, Chuckles! Auntie Flo missed you!
That baby must have a foot out the door.
We didn't think you'd come!
Doc gave me his blessing.
And if he hadn't? I'd still be here for Big Brother's big day. Have you ever seen Elber so happy?
Sure. Lots of times.

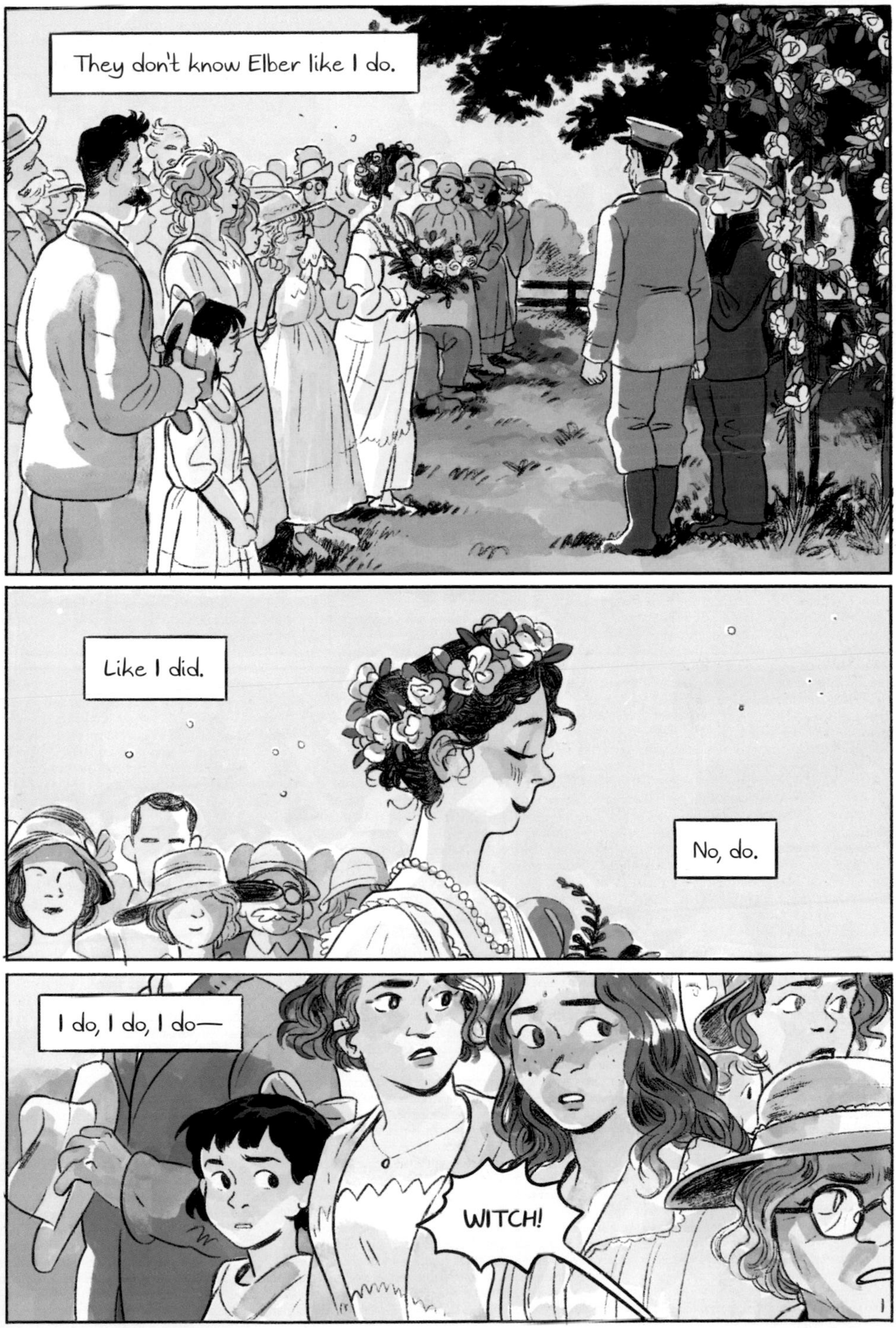
They don't know Elber like I do.
Like I did.
No, do.
I do, I do, I do—
WITCH!

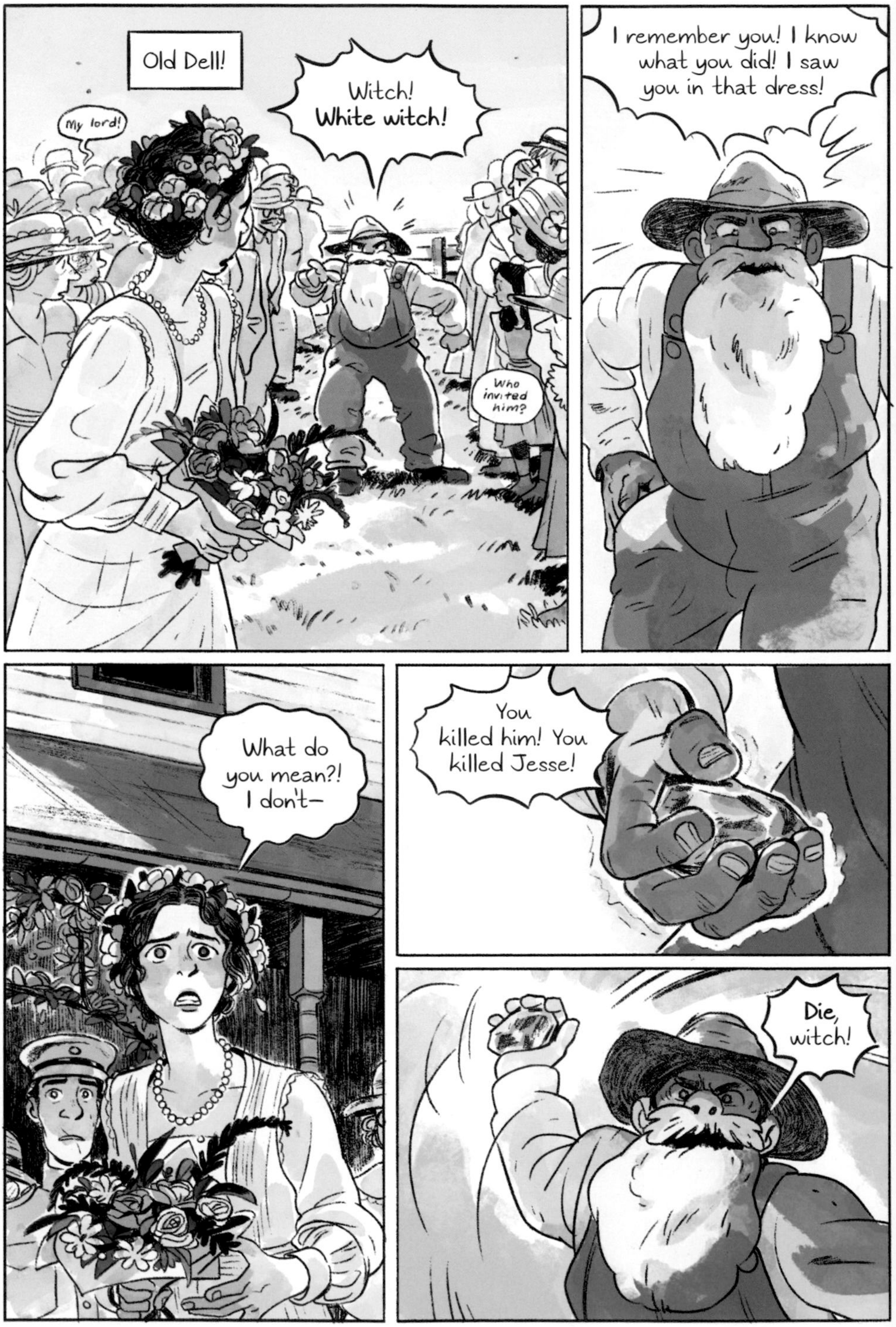
Old Dell!
My lord!
Witch! White witch!
Who invited him?
I remember you! I know what you did! I saw you in that dress!
What do you mean?! I don't—
You killed him! You killed Jesse!
Die, witch!

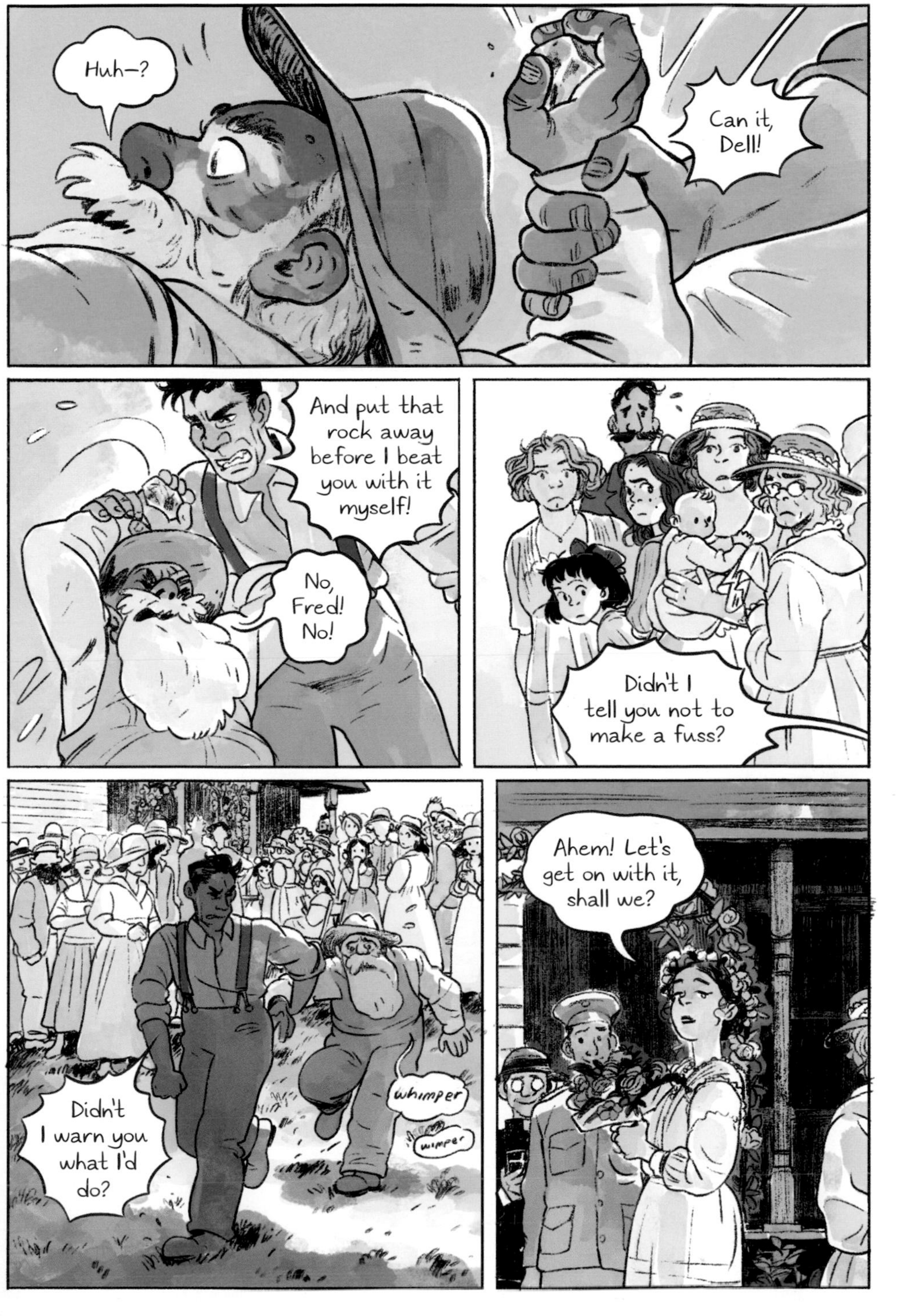
Huh–?
Can it, Dell!
And put that rock away before I beat you with it myself!
No, Fred! No!
Didn't I tell you not to make a fuss?
Didn't I warn you what I'd do?
whimper
wimper
Ahem! Let's get on with it, shall we?

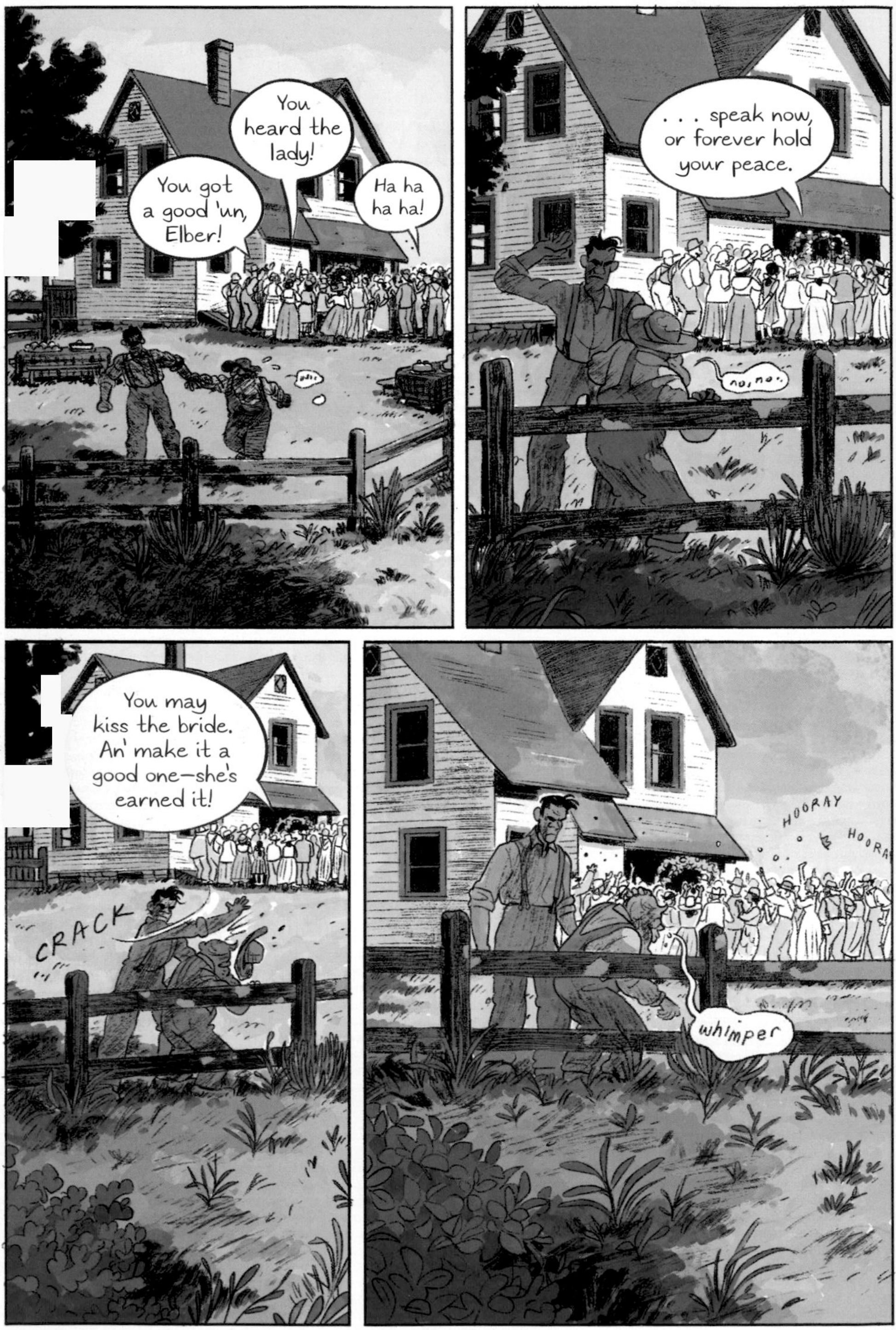

You heard the lady!
You got a good 'un, Elber!
Ha ha ha ha!
. . . speak now, or forever hold your peace.
no, no.
You may kiss the bride. An' make it a good one—she's earned it!
CRACK
HOORAY
HOORAY
whimper

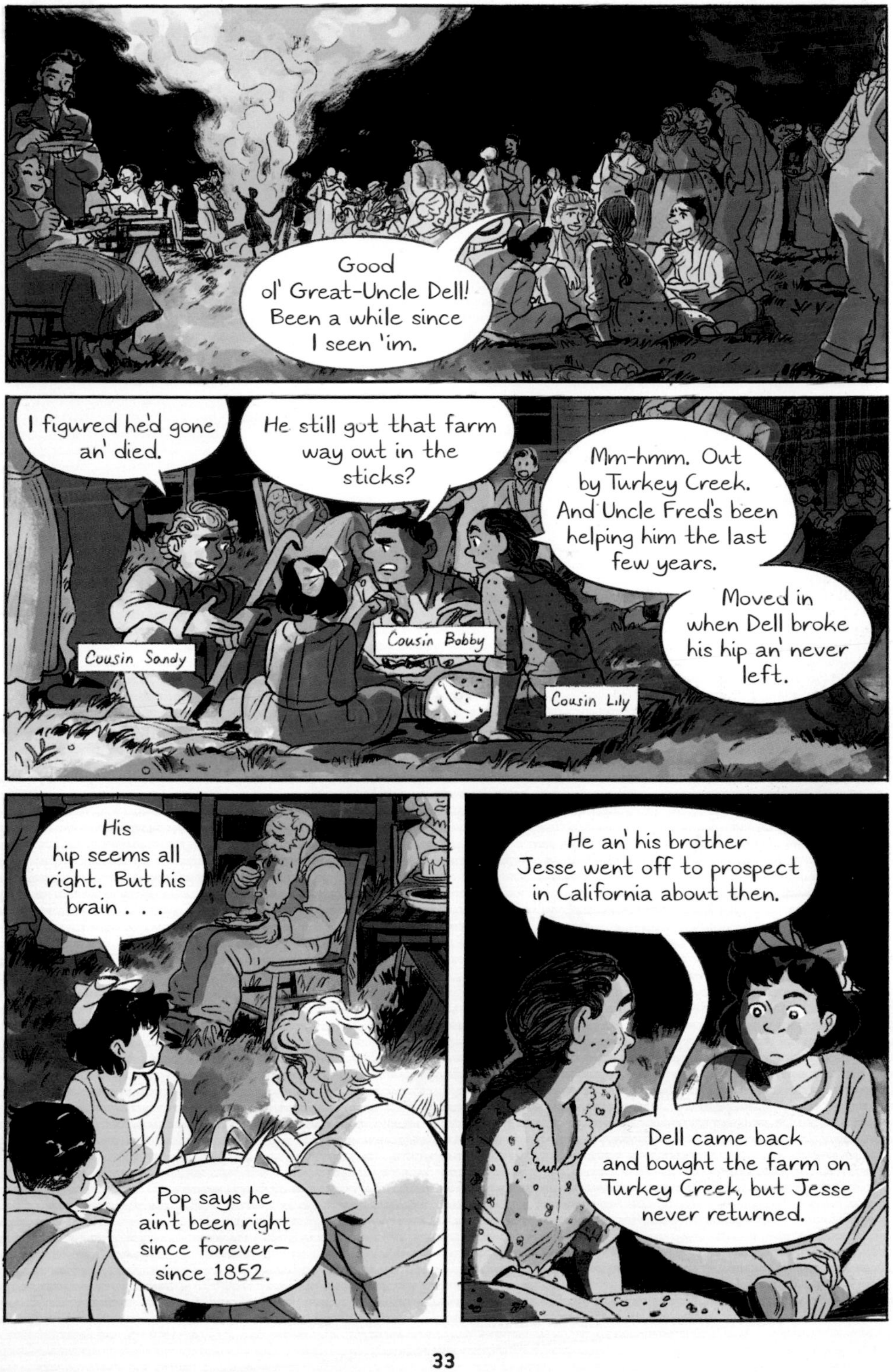
Good ol' Great-Uncle Dell! Been a while since I seen 'im.
I figured he'd gone an' died.
He still got that farm way out in the sticks?
Mm-hmm. Out by Turkey Creek. And Uncle Fred's been helping him the last few years.
Moved in when Dell broke his hip an' never left.
Cousin Sandy
Cousin Bobby
Cousin Lily
His hip seems all right. But his brain . . .
Pop says he ain't been right since forever— since 1852.
He an' his brother Jesse went off to prospect in California about then.
Dell came back and bought the farm on Turkey Creek, but Jesse never returned.

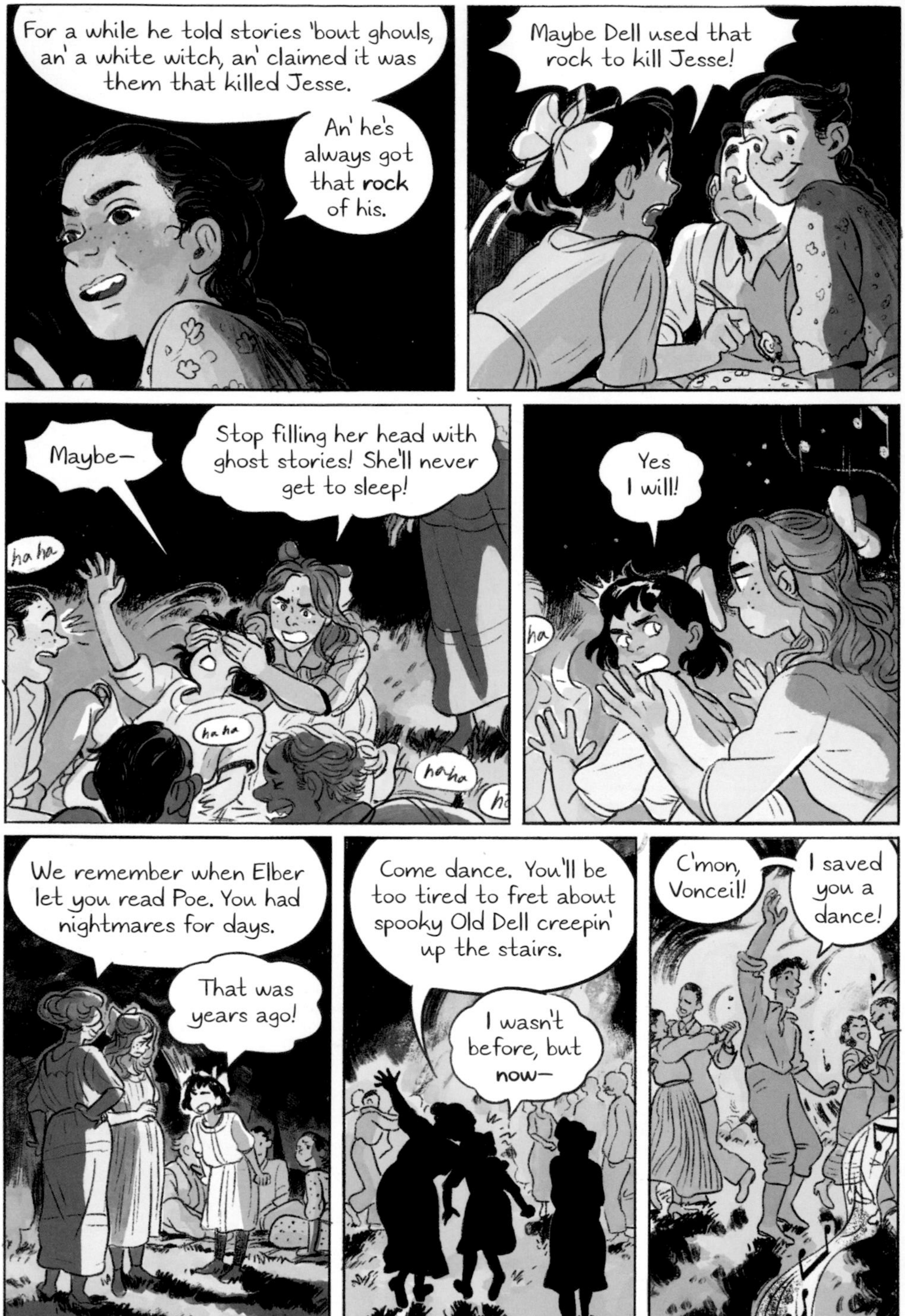
For a while he told stories 'bout ghouls, an' a white witch, an' claimed it was them that killed Jesse.
An' he's always got that **rock** of his.
Maybe Dell used that rock to kill Jesse!
Maybe—
Stop filling her head with ghost stories! She'll never get to sleep!
ha ha
ha ha
ha ha
Yes I will!
ha
We remember when Elber let you read Poe. You had nightmares for days.
That was years ago!
Come dance. You'll be too tired to fret about spooky Old Dell creepin' up the stairs.
I wasn't before, but **now**—
C'mon, Vonceil!
I saved you a dance!

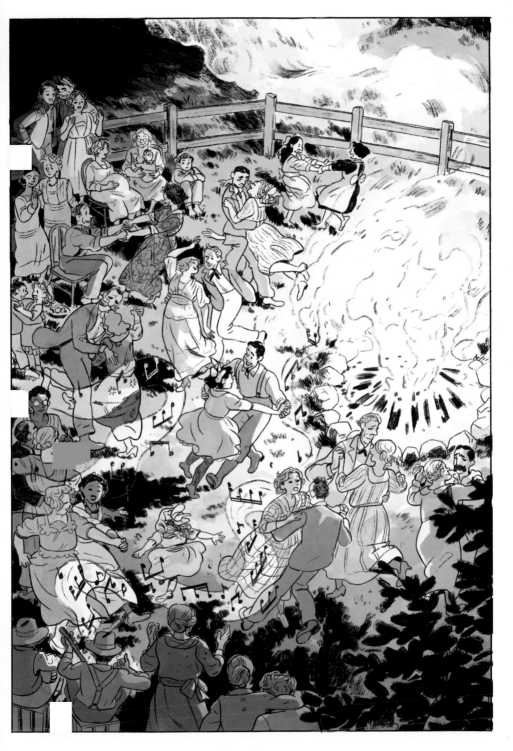

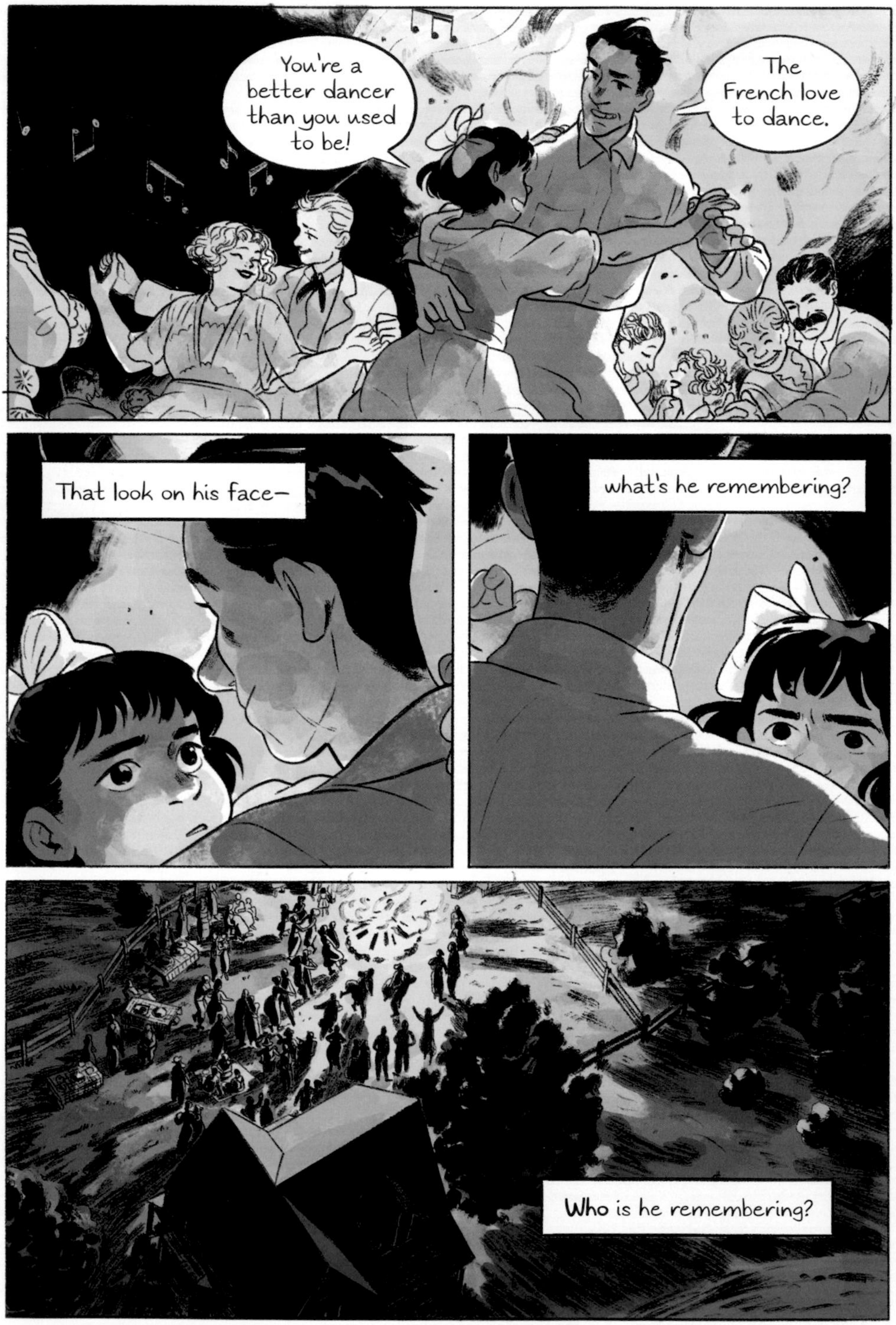
You're a better dancer than you used to be!
The French love to dance.
That look on his face—
what's he remembering?
Who is he remembering?

Chapter Three

The Lady in White

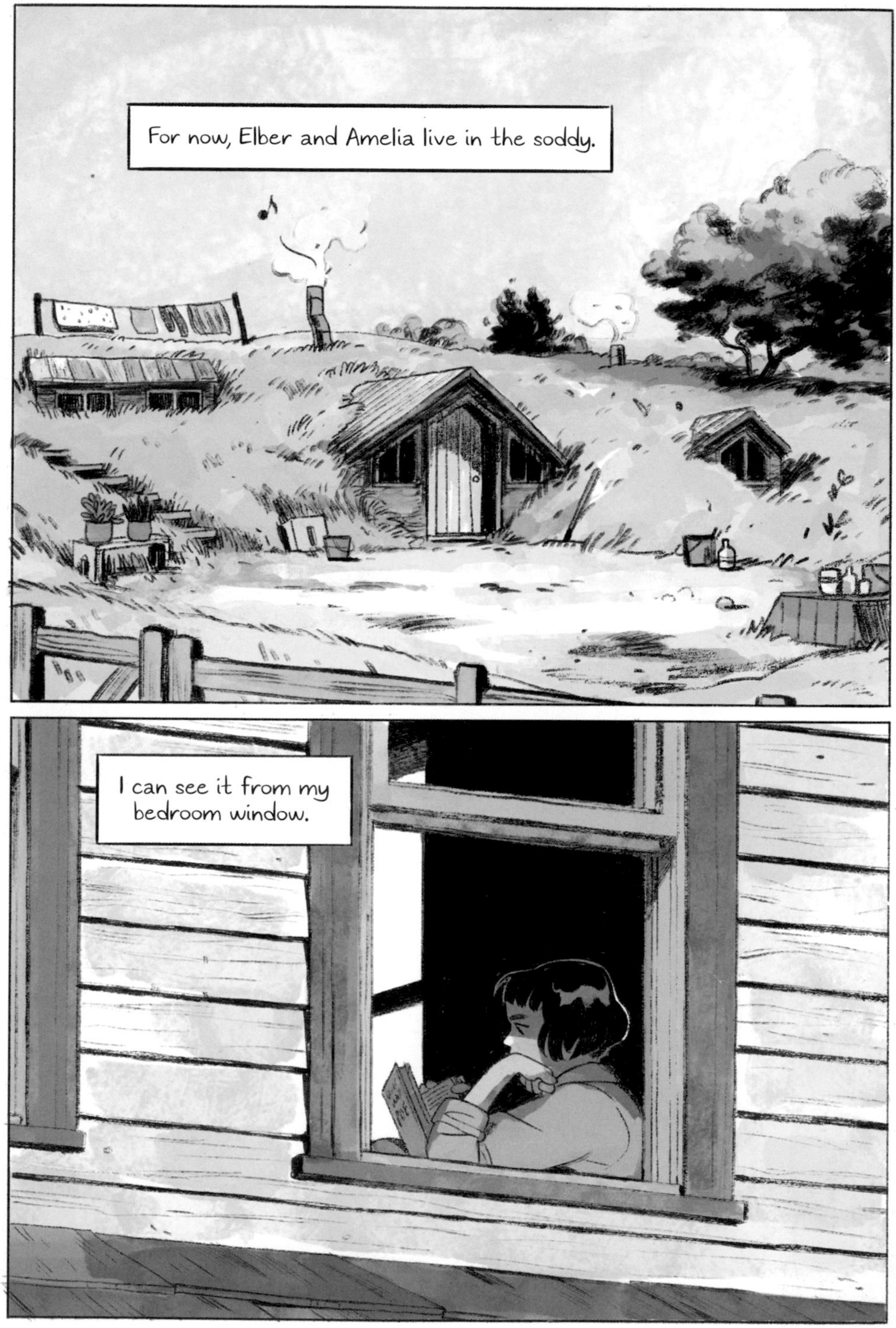
For now, Elber and Amelia live in the soddy.
I can see it from my bedroom window.

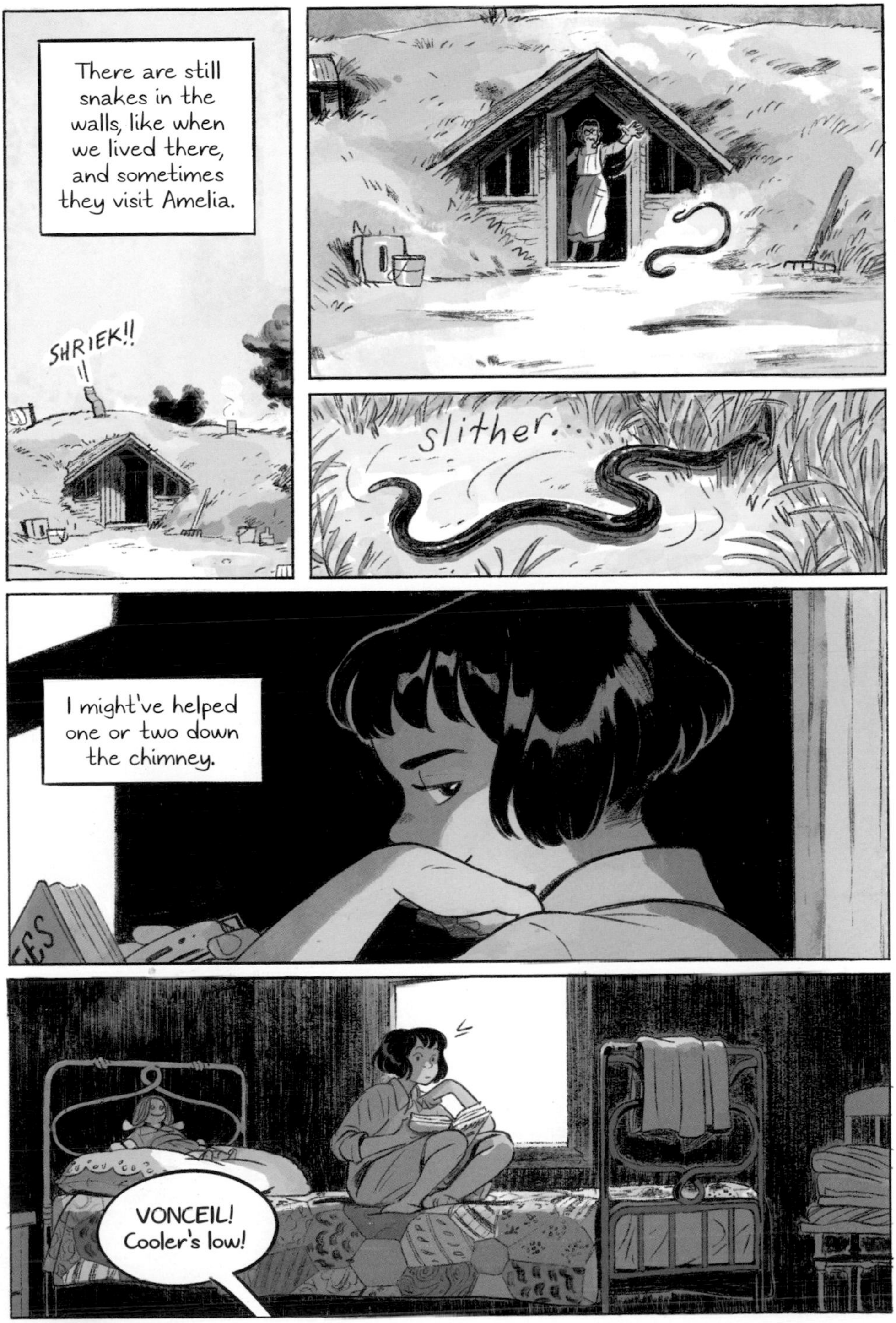
There are still snakes in the walls, like when we lived there, and sometimes they visit Amelia.
SHRIEK!!
slither...
I might've helped one or two down the chimney.
VONCEIL! Cooler's low!

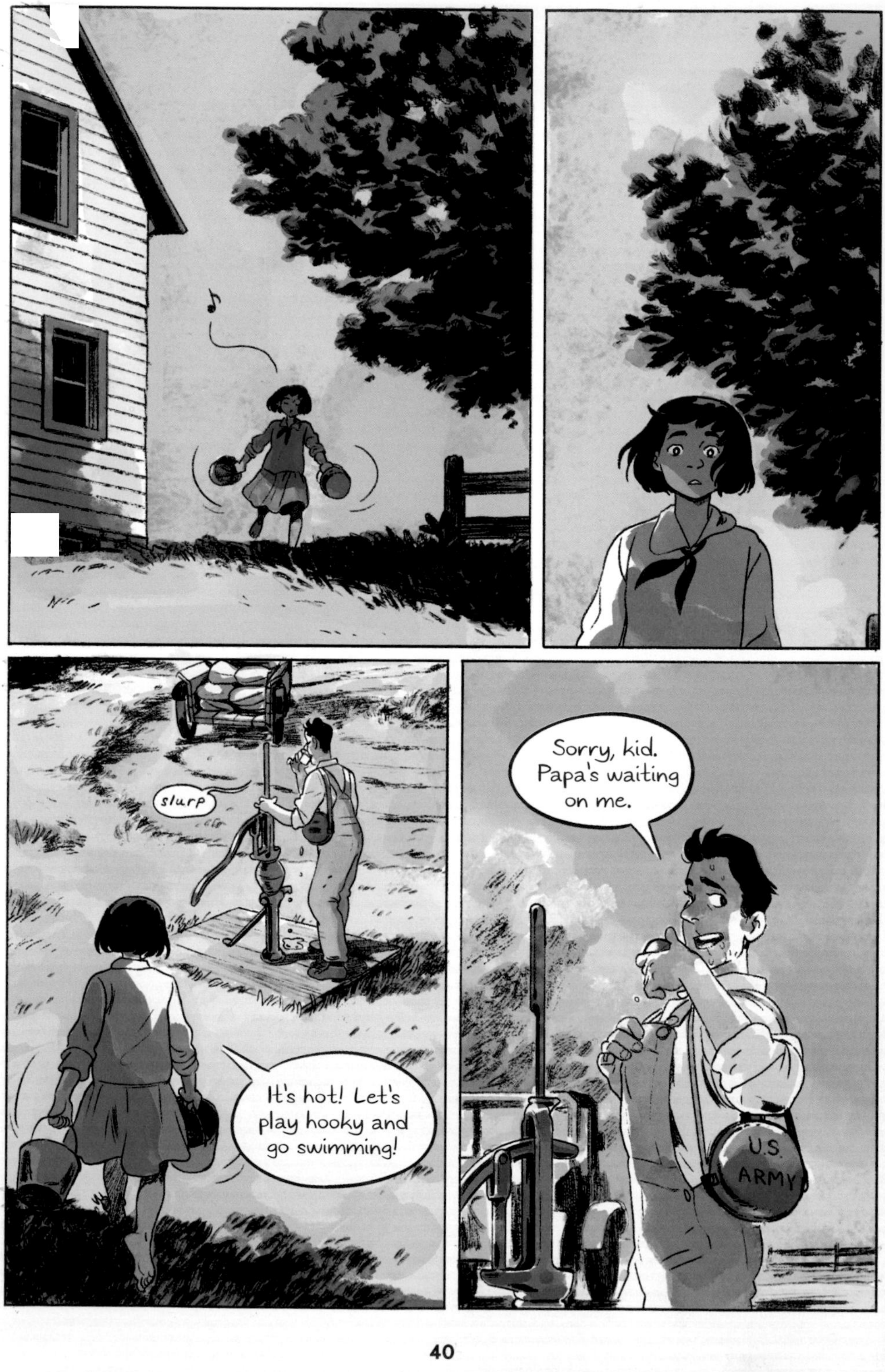
slurp
It's hot! Let's play hooky and go swimming!
Sorry, kid. Papa's waiting on me.
U.S. ARMY

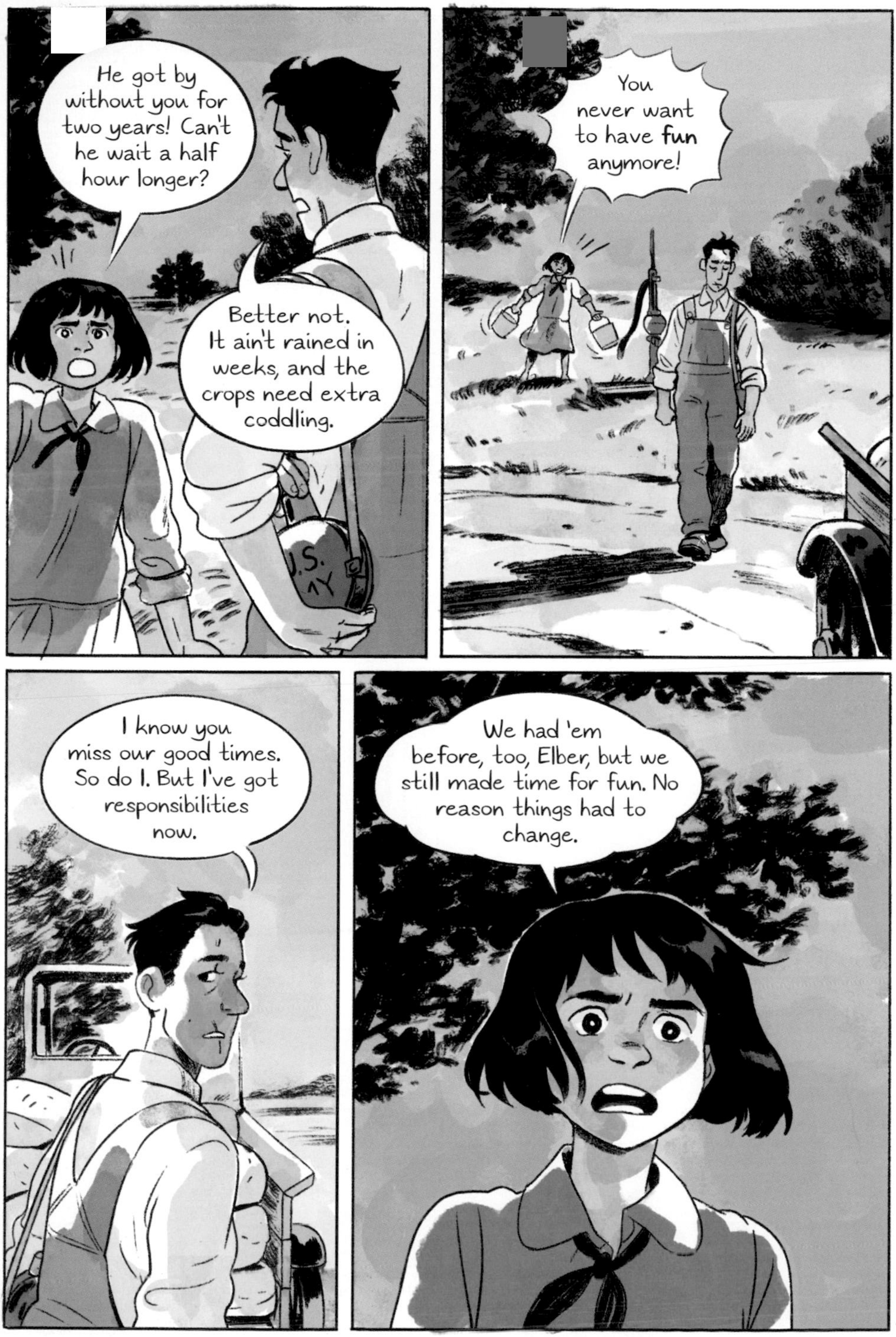
He got by without you for two years! Can't he wait a half hour longer?
Better not. It ain't rained in weeks, and the crops need extra coddling.
U.S.
You never want to have **fun** anymore!
I know you miss our good times. So do I. But I've got responsibilities now.
We had 'em before, too, Elber, but we still made time for fun. No reason things had to change.

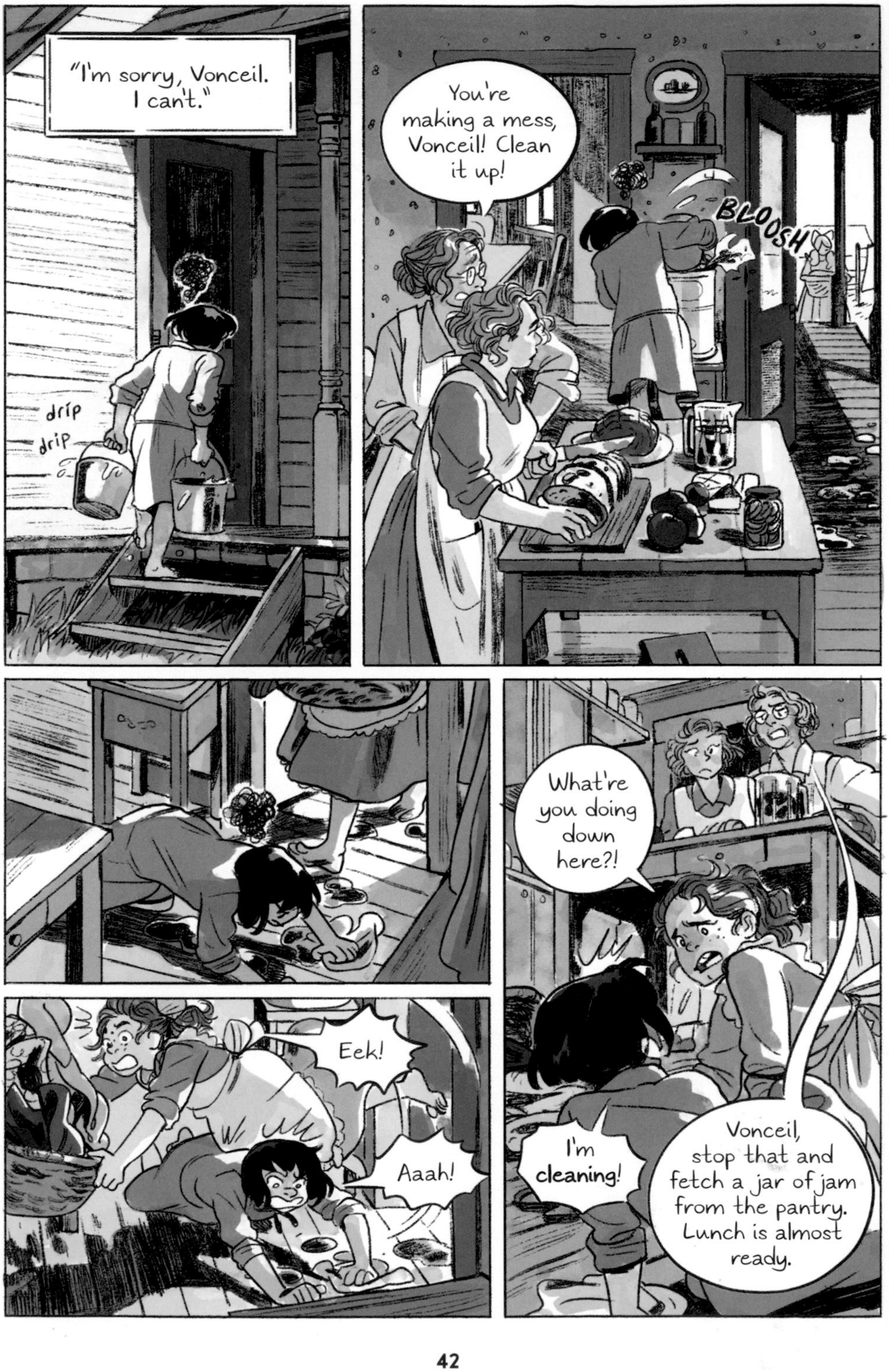
"I'm sorry, Vonceil. I can't."
drip
drip
You're making a mess, Vonceil! Clean it up!
BLOOSH
What're you doing down here?!
Eek!
Aaah!
I'm **cleaning**!
Vonceil, stop that and fetch a jar of jam from the pantry. Lunch is almost ready.

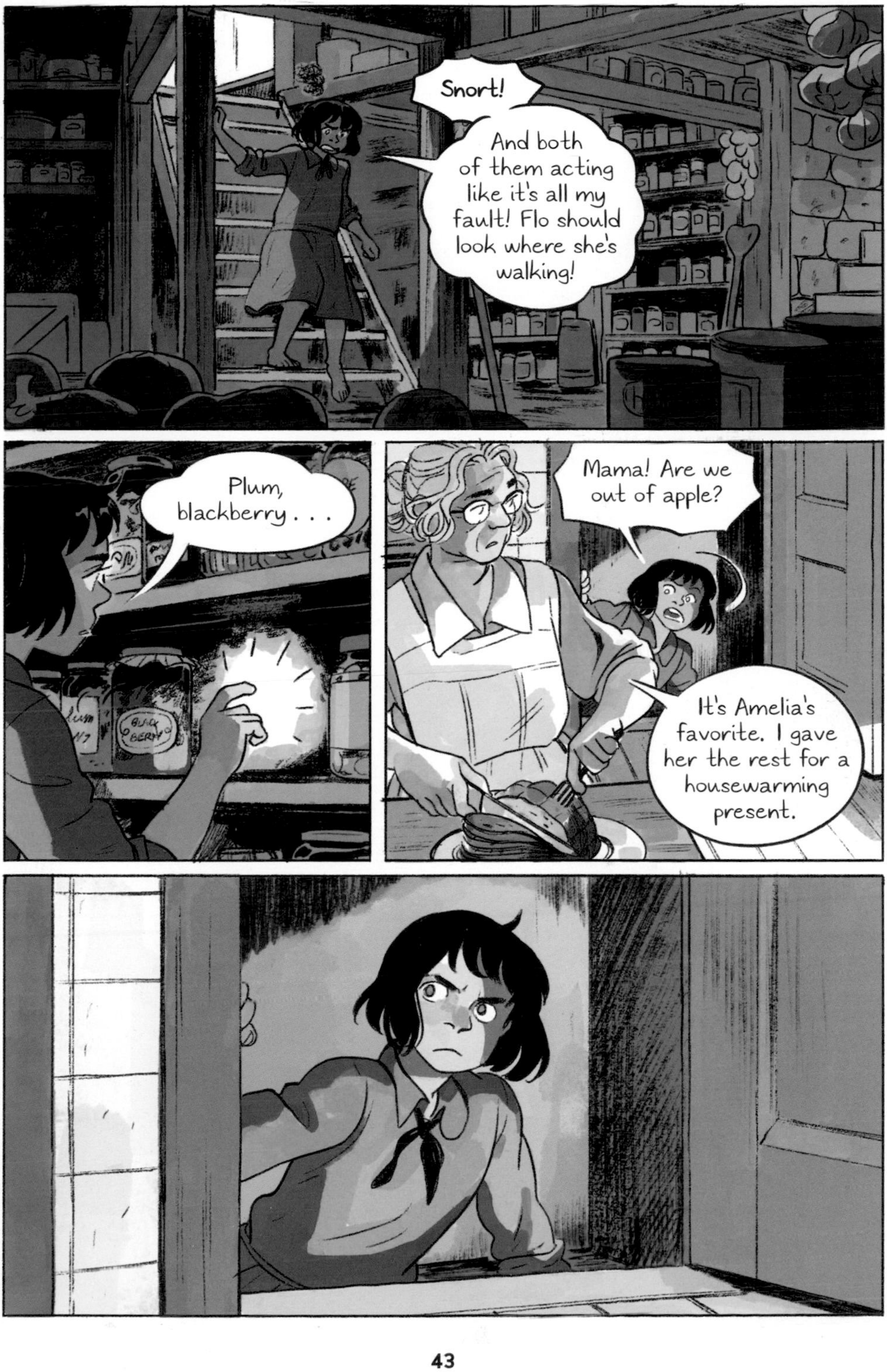
Snort!
And both of them acting like it's all my fault! Flo should look where she's walking!
Plum, blackberry . . .
Mama! Are we out of apple?
It's Amelia's favorite. I gave her the rest for a housewarming present.

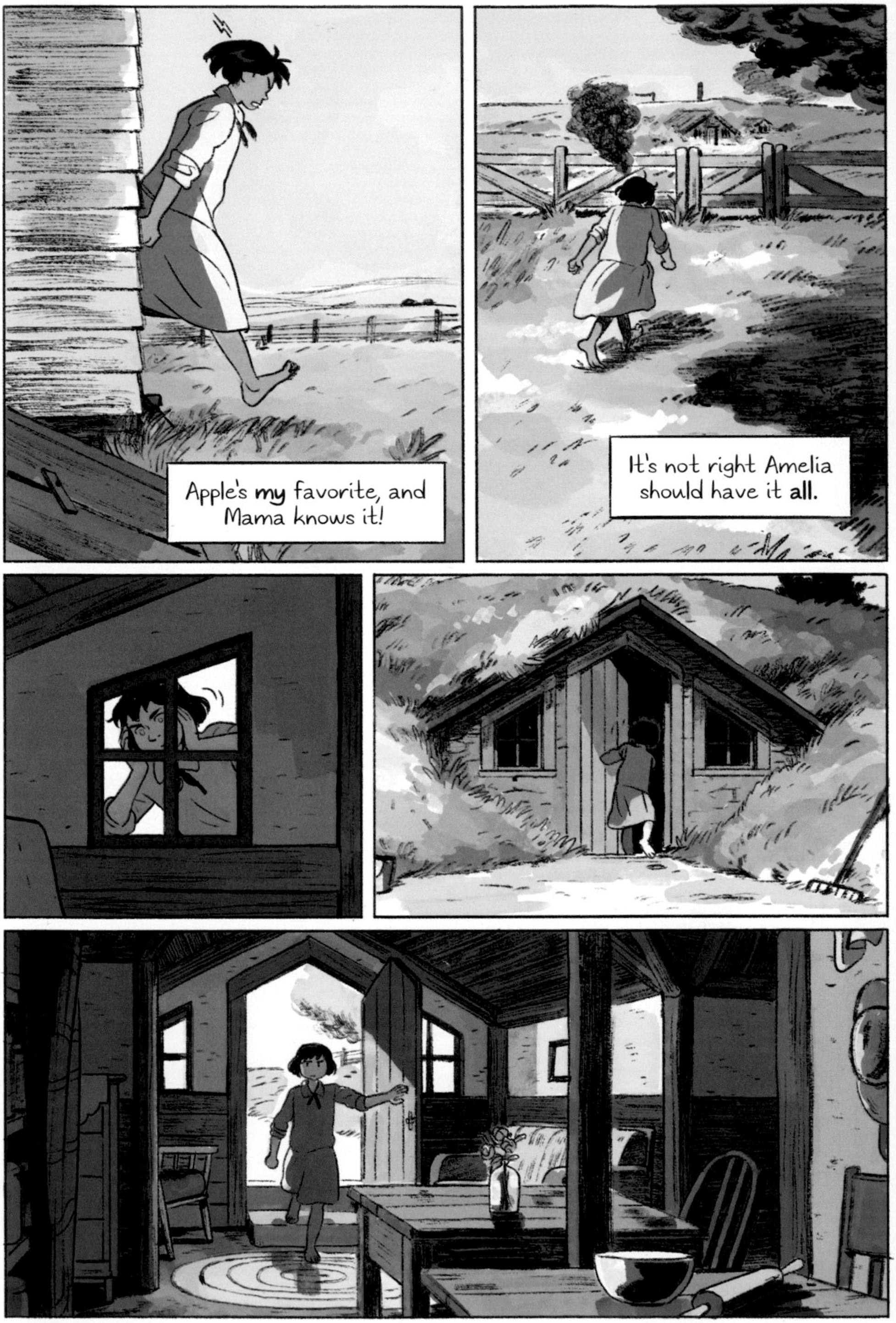
Apple's **my** favorite, and Mama knows it!
It's not right Amelia should have it **all.**

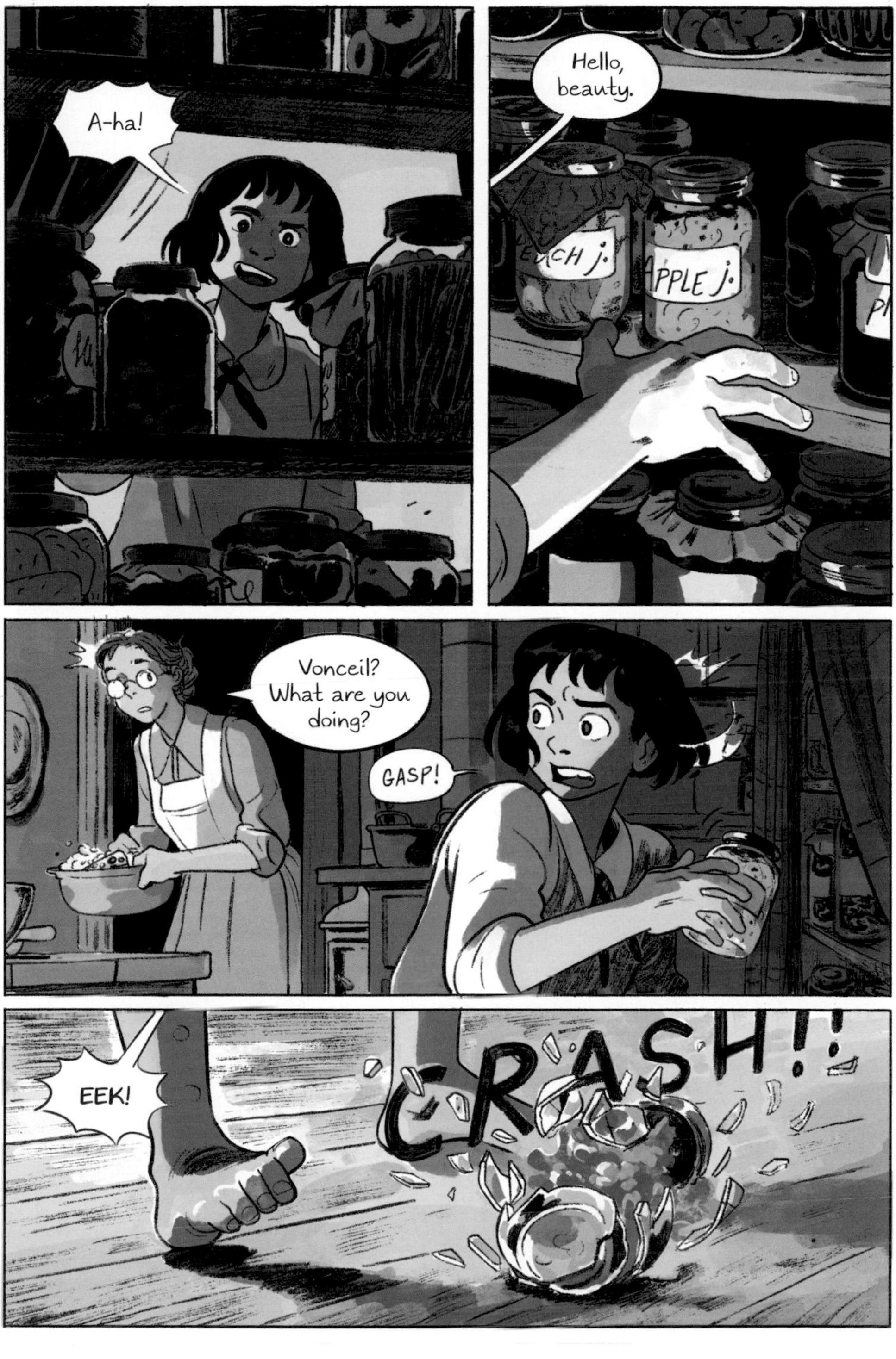
A-ha!
Hello, beauty.
PEACH j.
APPLE j.
Vonceil? What are you doing?
GASP!
EEK!
CRASH!!

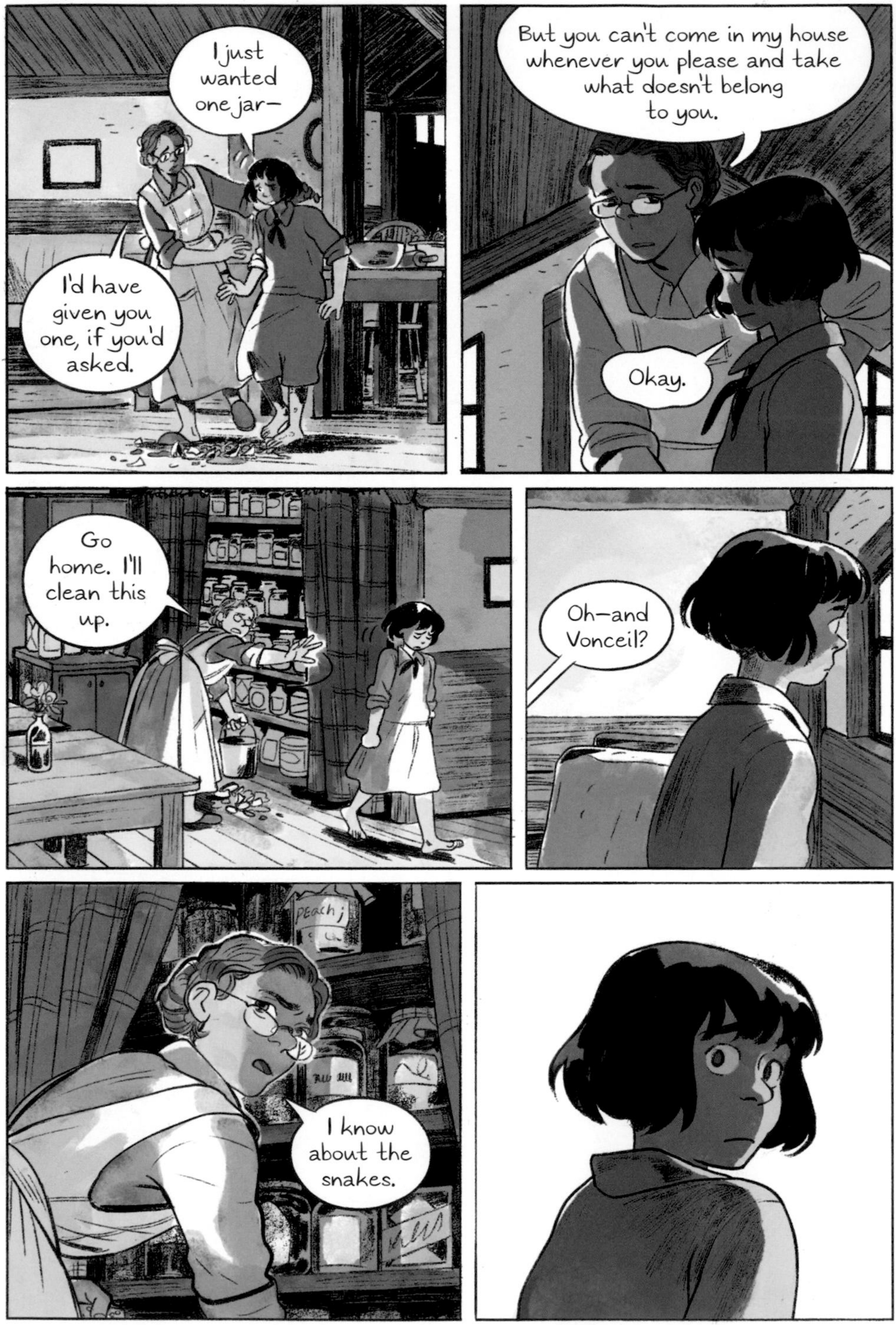
I just wanted one jar—
I'd have given you one, if you'd asked.
But you can't come in my house whenever you please and take what doesn't belong to you.
Okay.
Go home. I'll clean this up.
Oh—and Vonceil?
I know about the snakes.

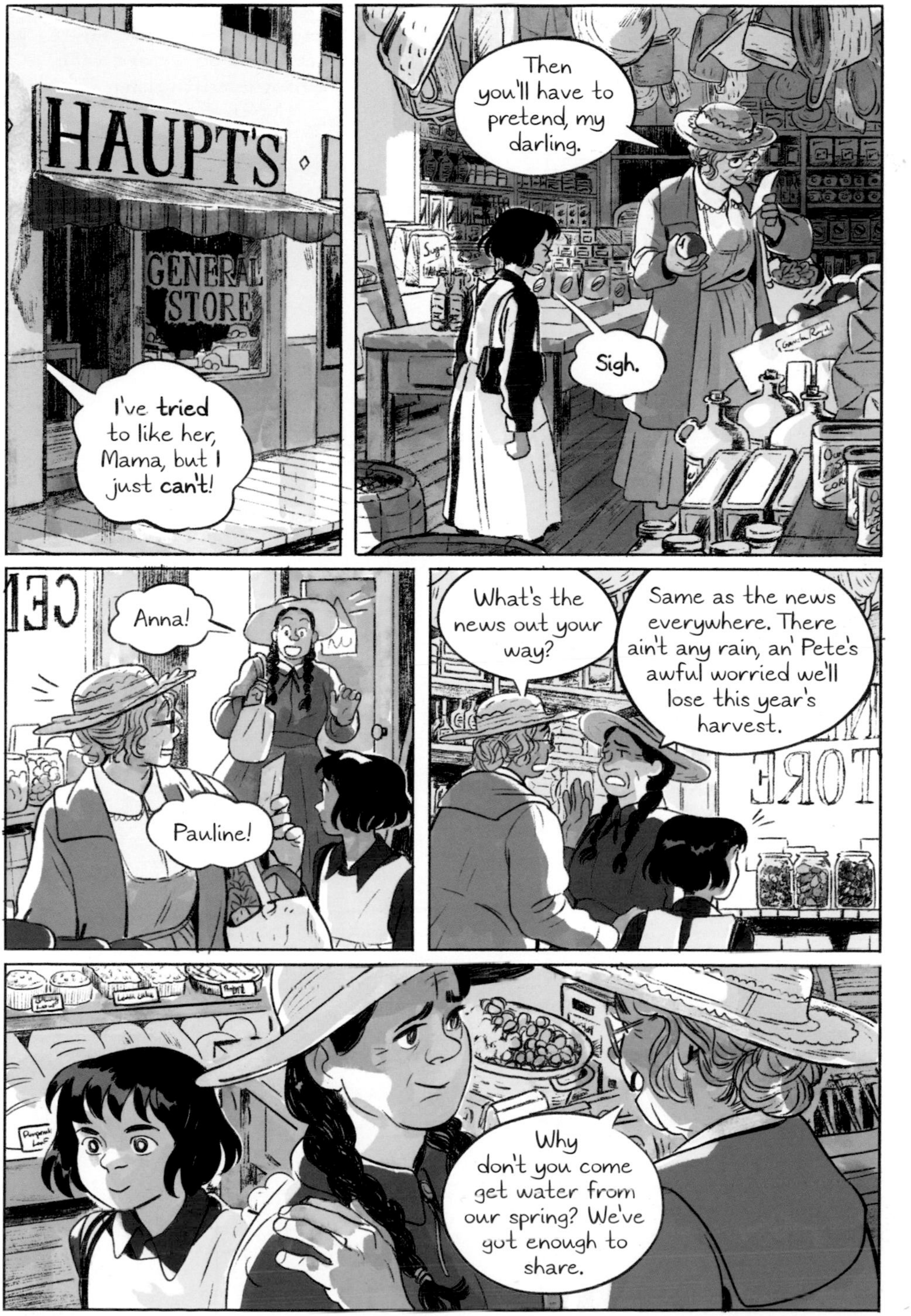
HAUPT'S
GENERAL STORE
I've **tried** to like her, Mama, but I just **can't**!
Then you'll have to pretend, my darling.
Sigh.
Anna!
Pauline!
What's the news out your way?
Same as the news everywhere. There ain't any rain, an' Pete's awful worried we'll lose this year's harvest.
Why don't you come get water from our spring? We've got enough to share.

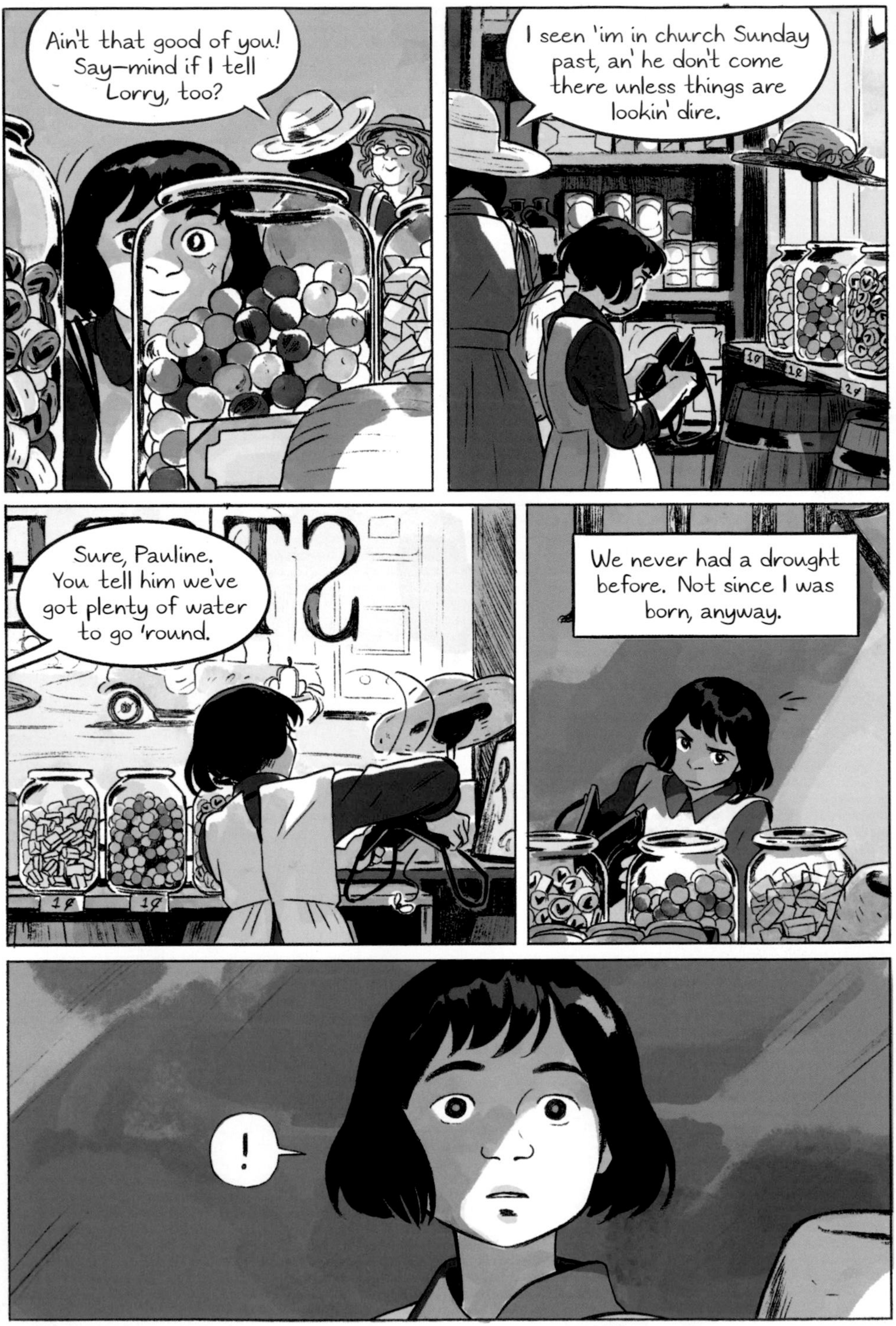
Ain't that good of you! Say—mind if I tell Lorry, too?
I seen 'im in church Sunday past, an' he don't come there unless things are lookin' dire.
Sure, Pauline. You tell him we've got plenty of water to go 'round.
We never had a drought before. Not since I was born, anyway.
!

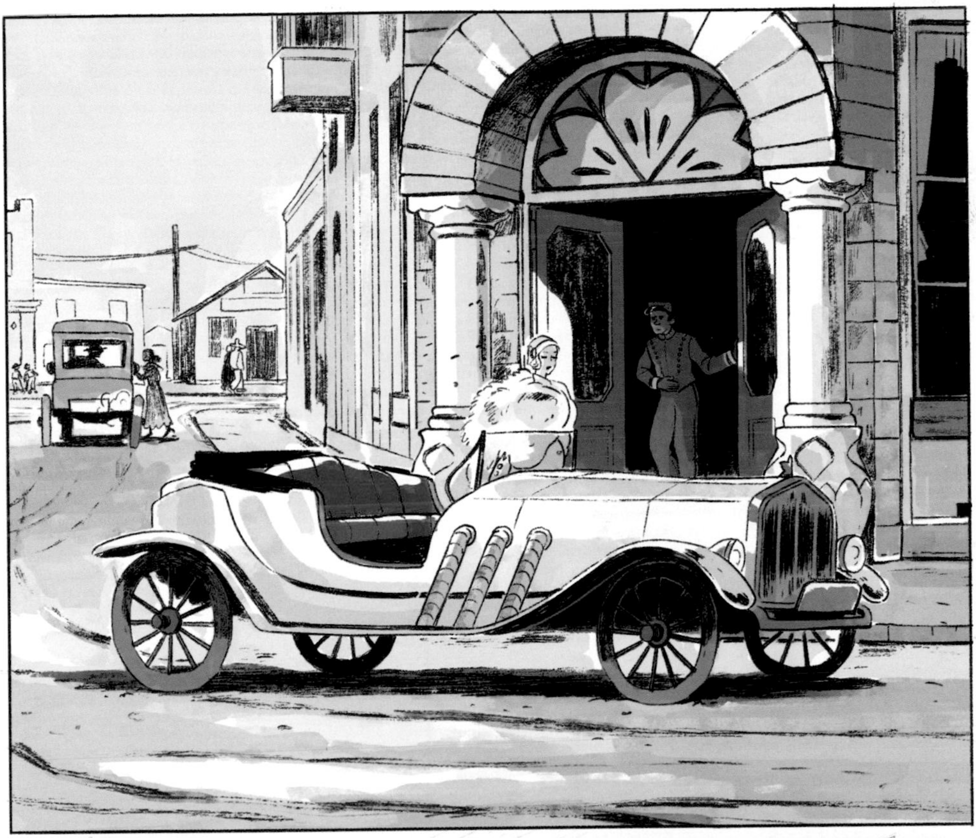

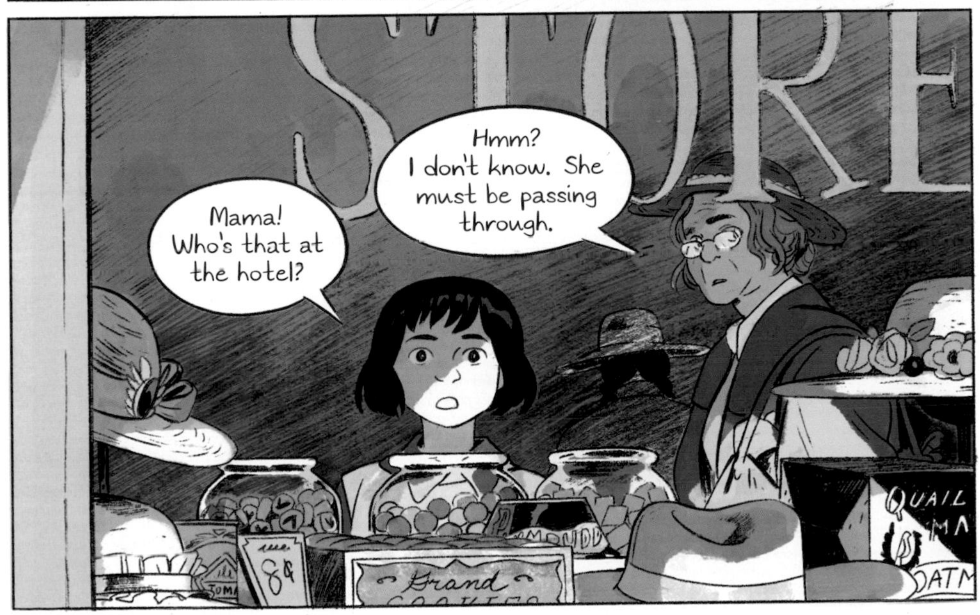
Mama! Who's that at the hotel?
Hmm? I don't know. She must be passing through.

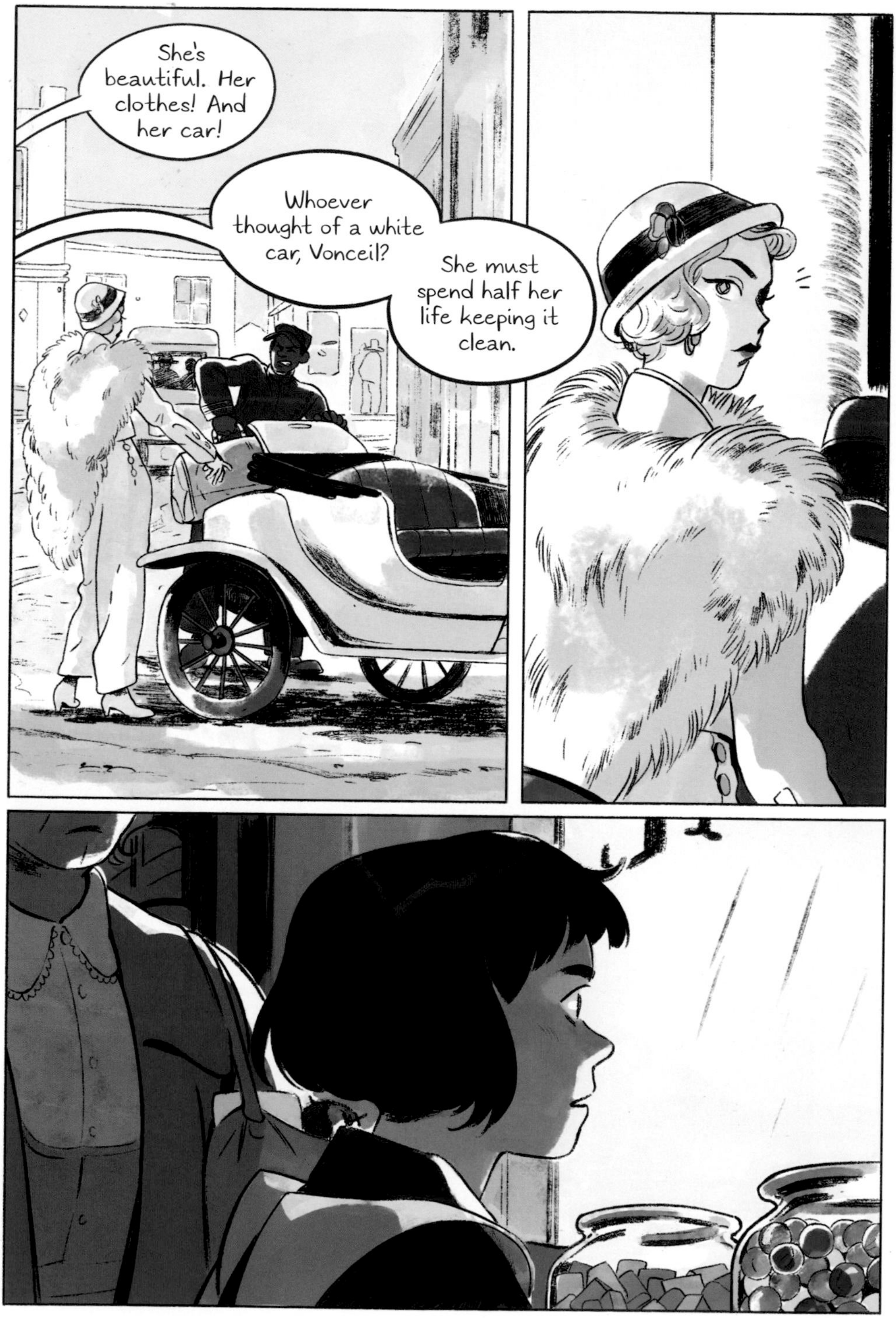
She's beautiful. Her clothes! And her car!
Whoever thought of a white car, Vonceil?
She must spend half her life keeping it clean.

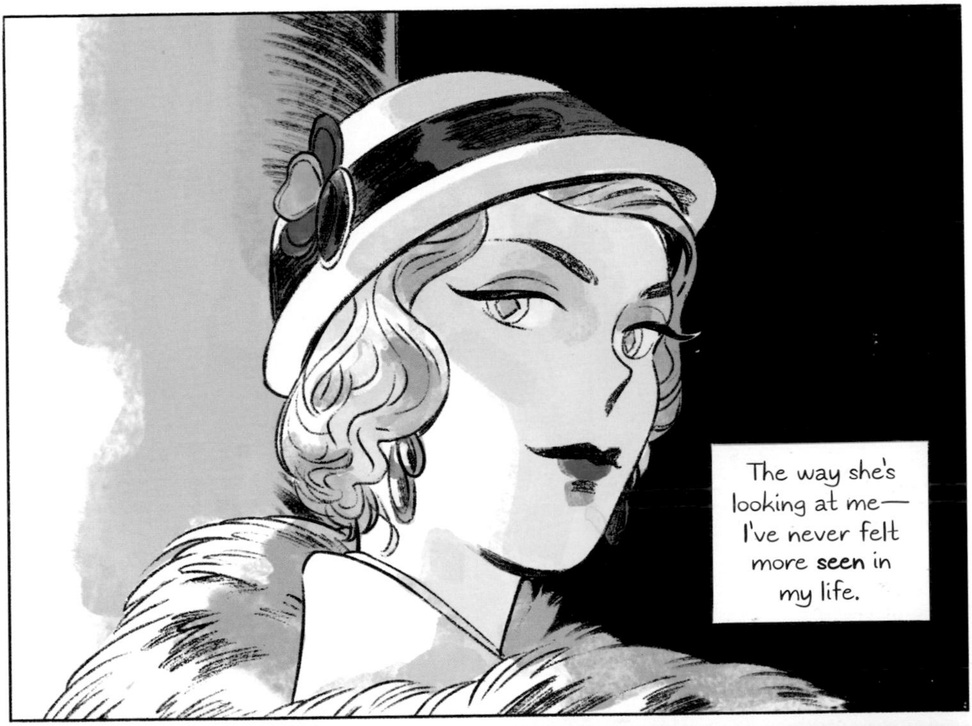
The way she's looking at me— I've never felt more **seen** in my life.

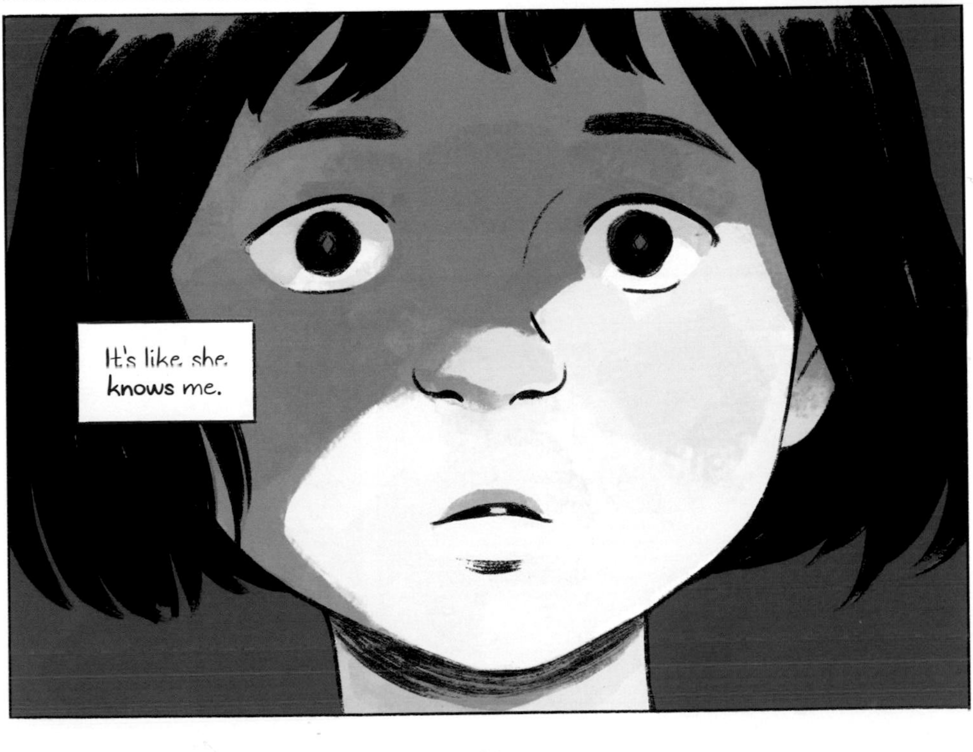
It's like she **knows** me.

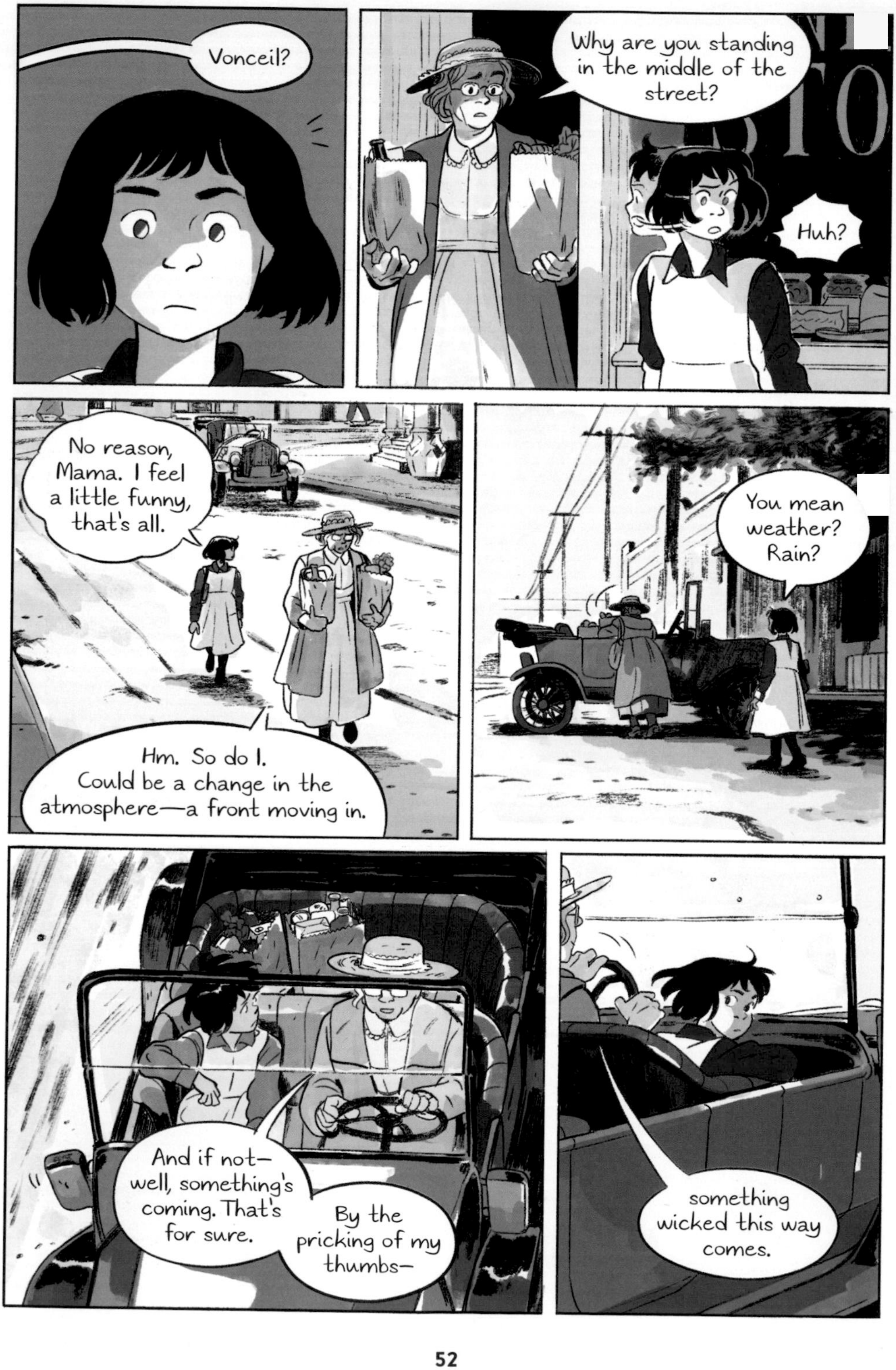
Vonceil?
Why are you standing in the middle of the street?
Huh?
No reason, Mama. I feel a little funny, that's all.
Hm. So do I. Could be a change in the atmosphere—a front moving in.
You mean weather? Rain?
And if not—well, something's coming. That's for sure.
By the pricking of my thumbs—
something wicked this way comes.

Chapter Four

Salt Water

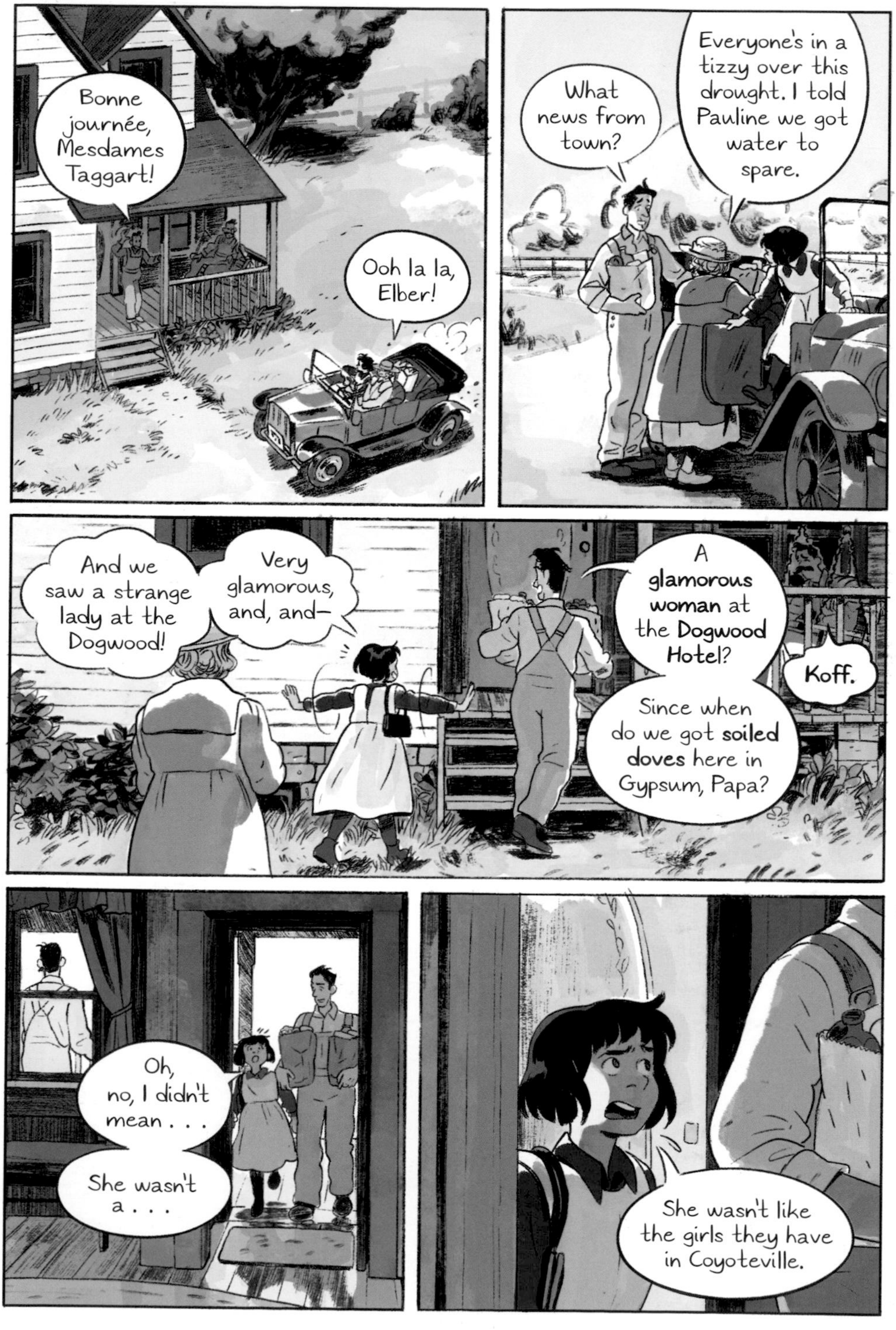

Bonne journée, Mesdames Taggart!
Ooh la la, Elber!
What news from town?
Everyone's in a tizzy over this drought. I told Pauline we got water to spare.
And we saw a strange lady at the Dogwood!
Very glamorous, and, and—
A **glamorous woman** at the **Dogwood Hotel**?
Since when do we got **soiled doves** here in Gypsum, Papa?
Koff.
Oh, no, I didn't mean . . .
She wasn't a . . .
She wasn't like the girls they have in Coyoteville.

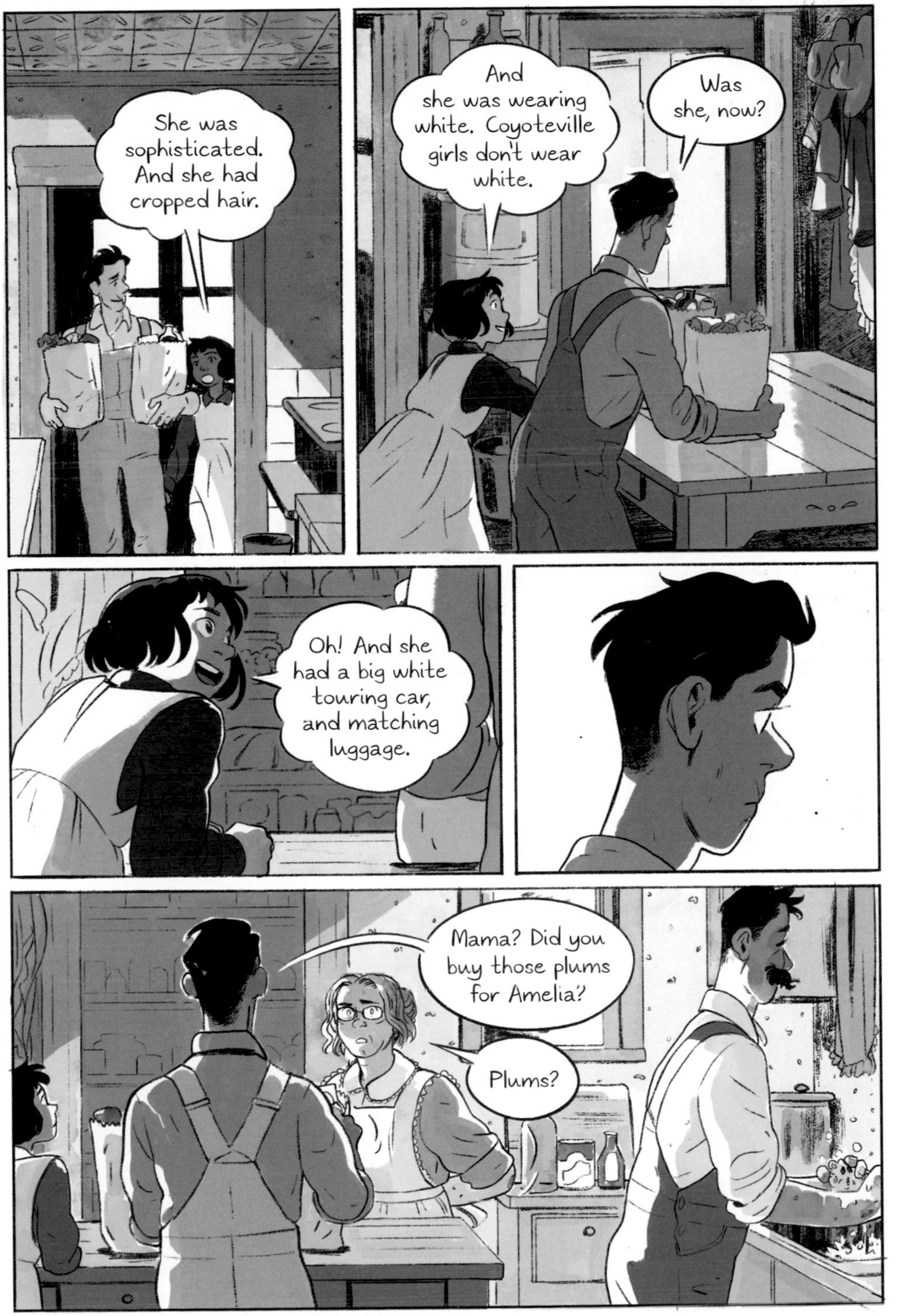
She was sophisticated. And she had cropped hair.
And she was wearing white. Coyoteville girls don't wear white.
Was she, now?
Oh! And she had a big white touring car, and matching luggage.
Mama? Did you buy those plums for Amelia?
Plums?

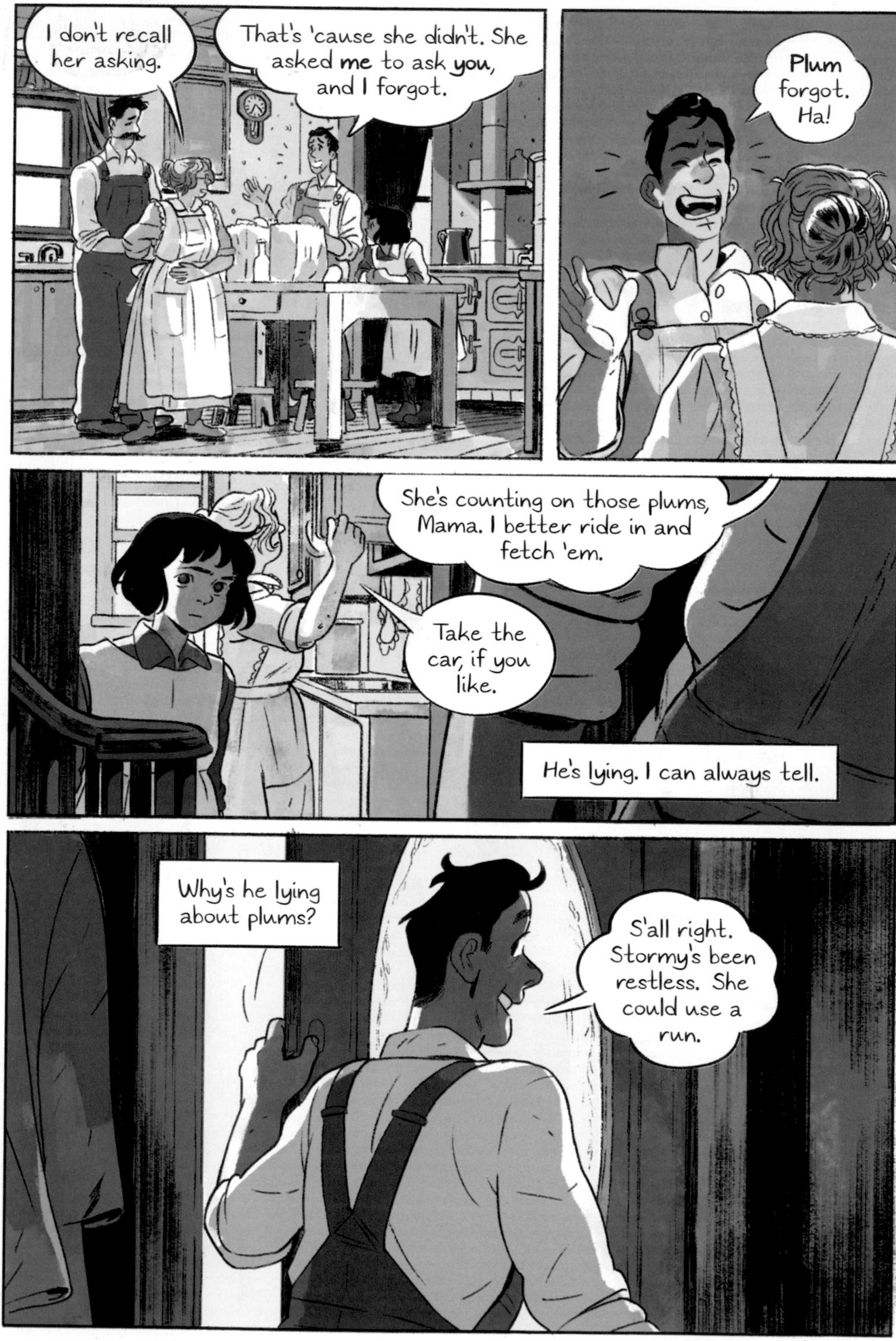
I don't recall her asking.
That's 'cause she didn't. She asked **me** to ask **you**, and I forgot.
Plum forgot. Ha!
She's counting on those plums, Mama. I better ride in and fetch 'em.
Take the car, if you like.
He's lying. I can always tell.
Why's he lying about plums?
S'all right. Stormy's been restless. She could use a run.

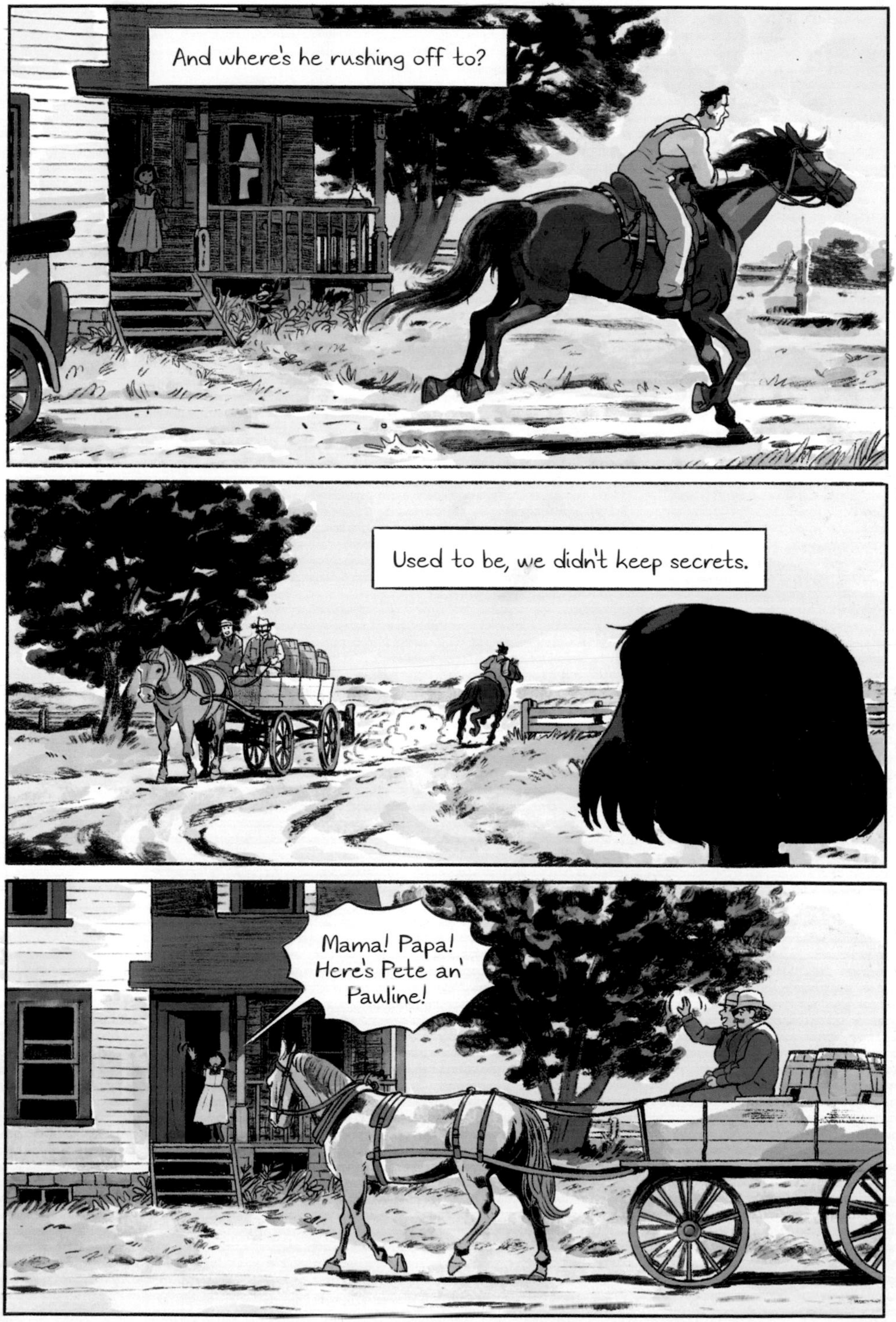
And where's he rushing off to?
Used to be, we didn't keep secrets.
Mama! Papa! Here's Pete an' Pauline!

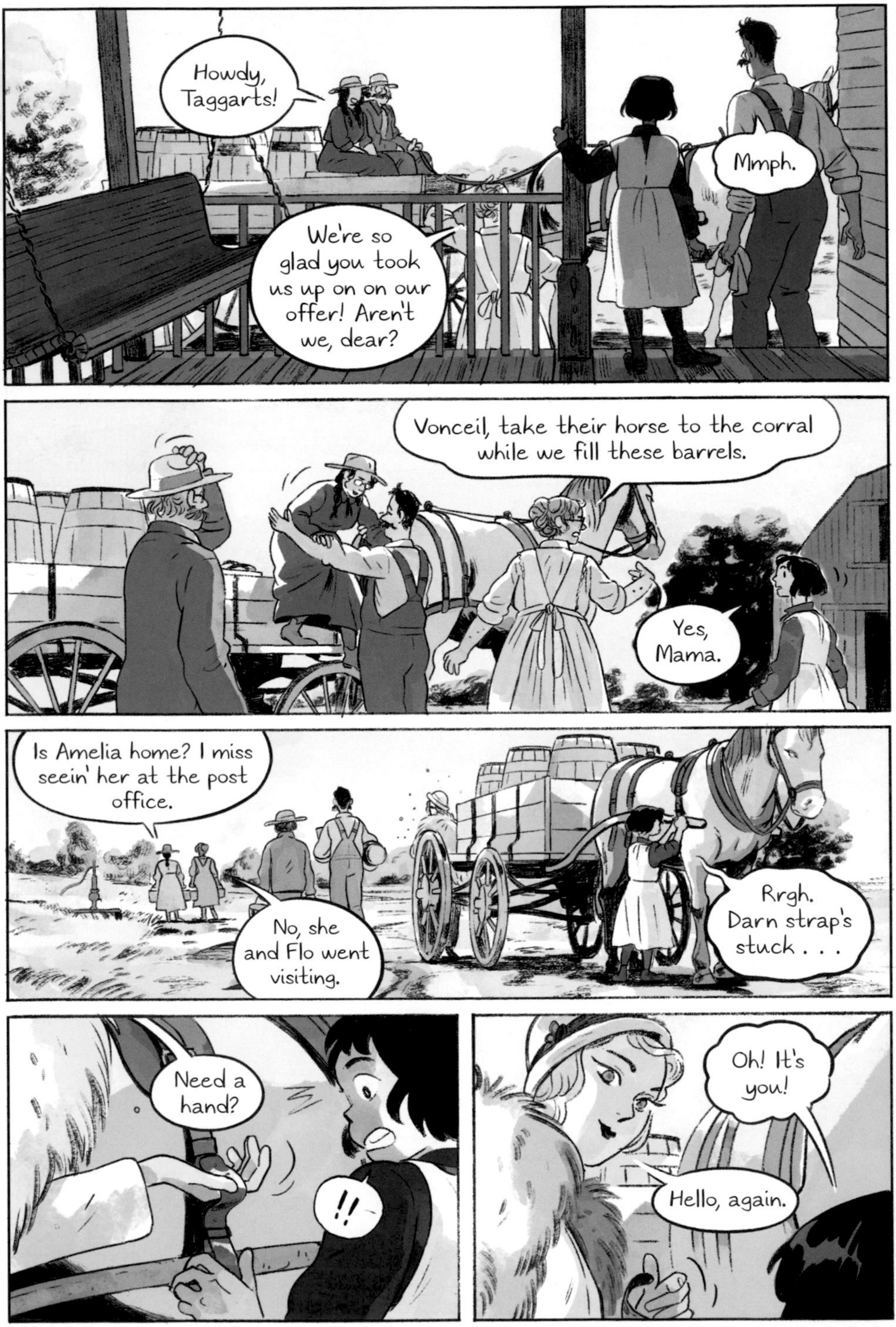
Howdy, Taggarts!
Mmph.
We're so glad you took us up on on our offer! Aren't we, dear?
Vonceil, take their horse to the corral while we fill these barrels.
Yes, Mama.
Is Amelia home? I miss seein' her at the post office.
No, she and Flo went visiting.
Rrgh. Darn strap's stuck . . .
Need a hand?
!!
Oh! It's you!
Hello, again.

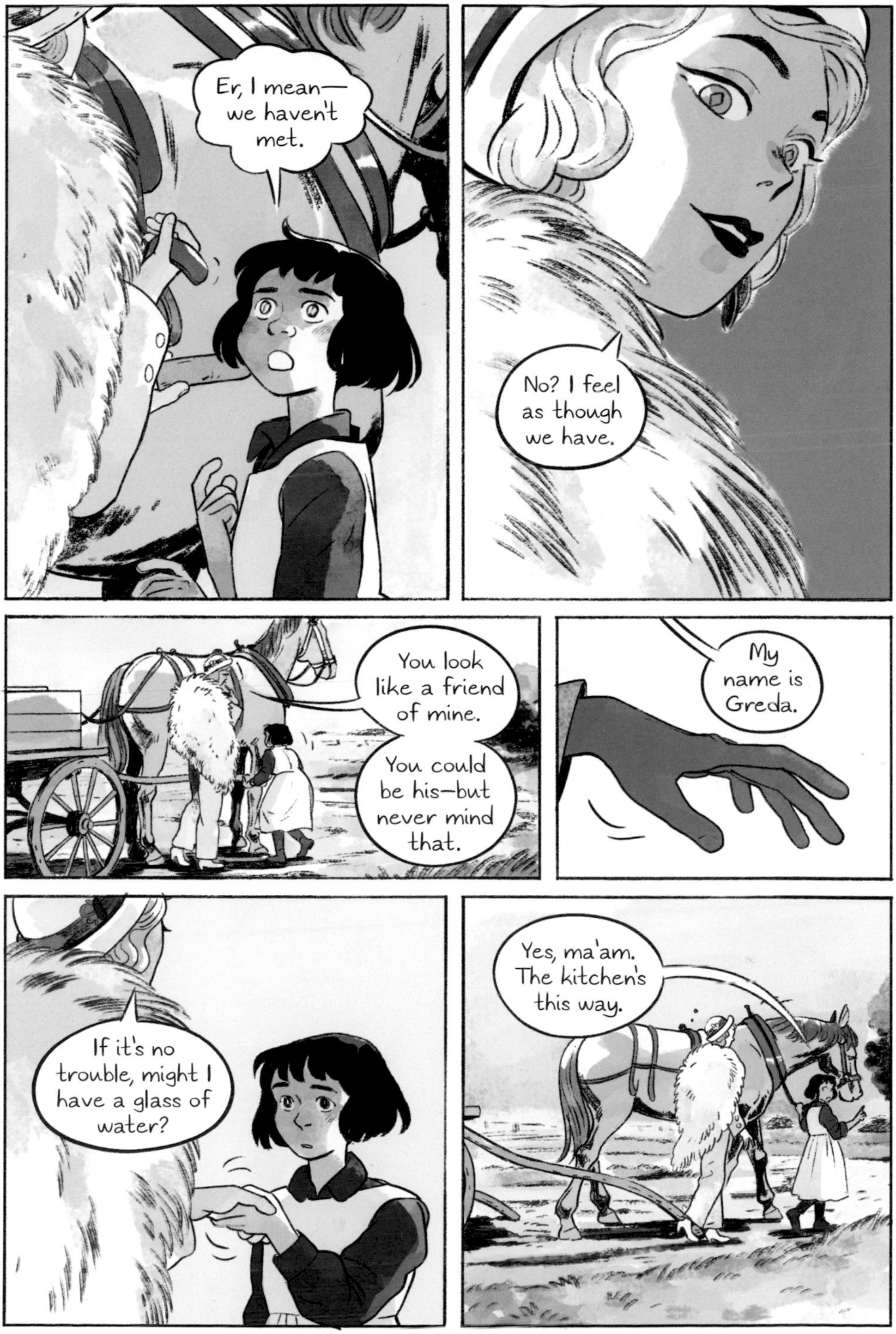
Er, I mean—we haven't met.
No? I feel as though we have.
You look like a friend of mine.
You could be his—but never mind that.
My name is Greda.
If it's no trouble, might I have a glass of water?
Yes, ma'am. The kitchen's this way.

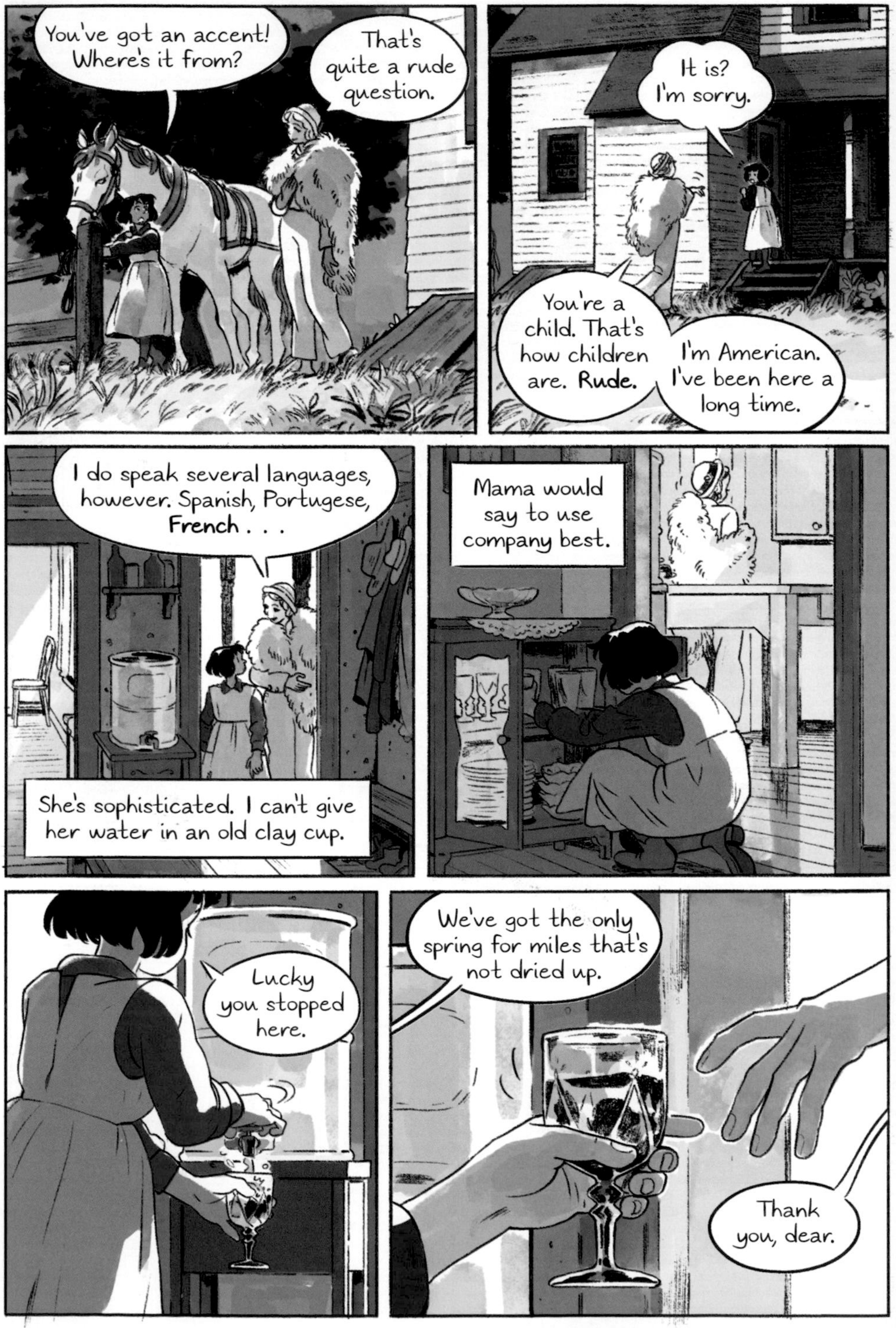
You've got an accent! Where's it from?
That's quite a rude question.
It is? I'm sorry.
You're a child. That's how children are. **Rude.**
I'm American. I've been here a long time.
I do speak several languages, however. Spanish, Portugese, **French** . . .
She's sophisticated. I can't give her water in an old clay cup.
Mama would say to use company best.
Lucky you stopped here.
We've got the only spring for miles that's not dried up.
Thank you, dear.

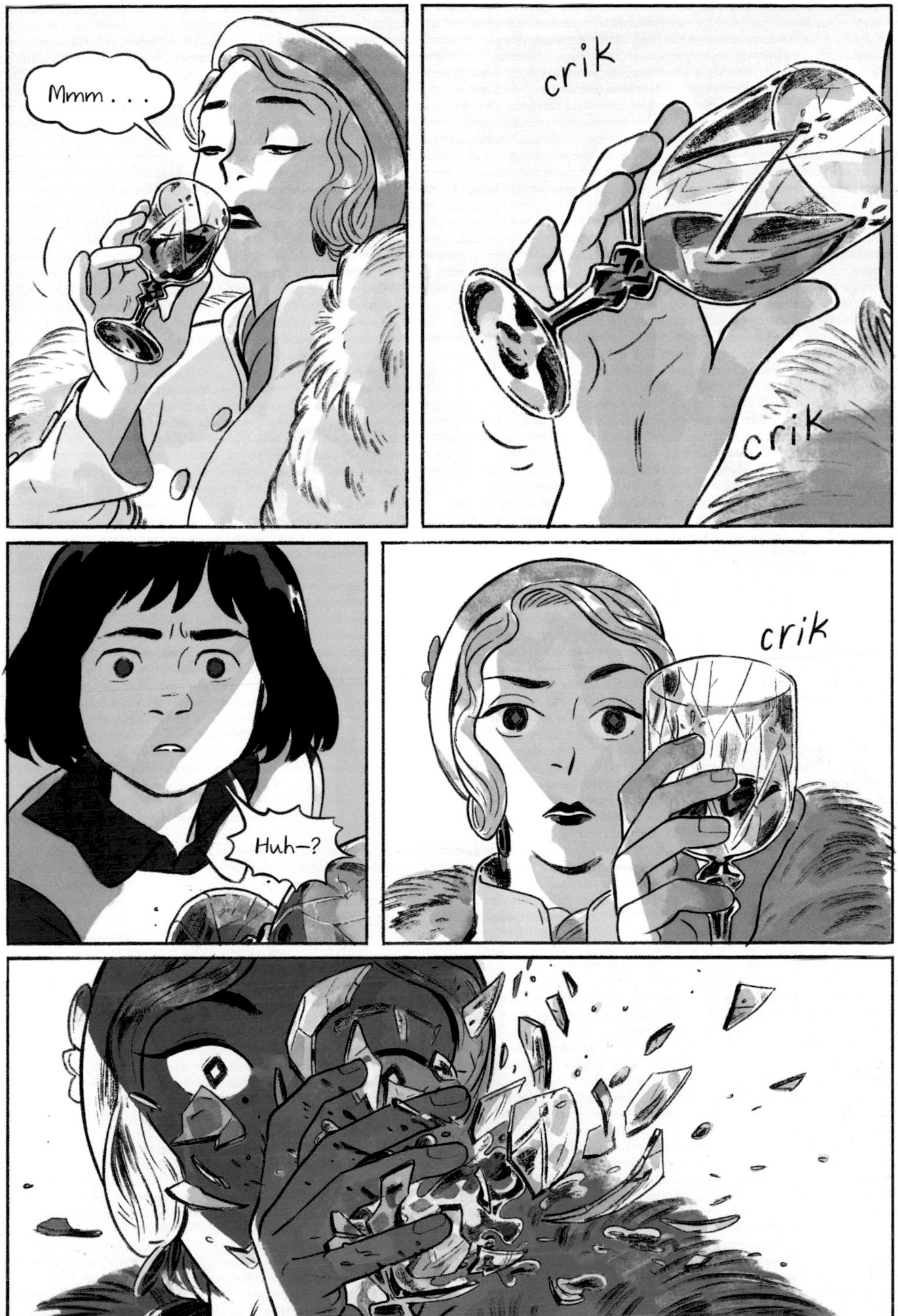
Mmm . . .
crik
crik
Huh–?
crik

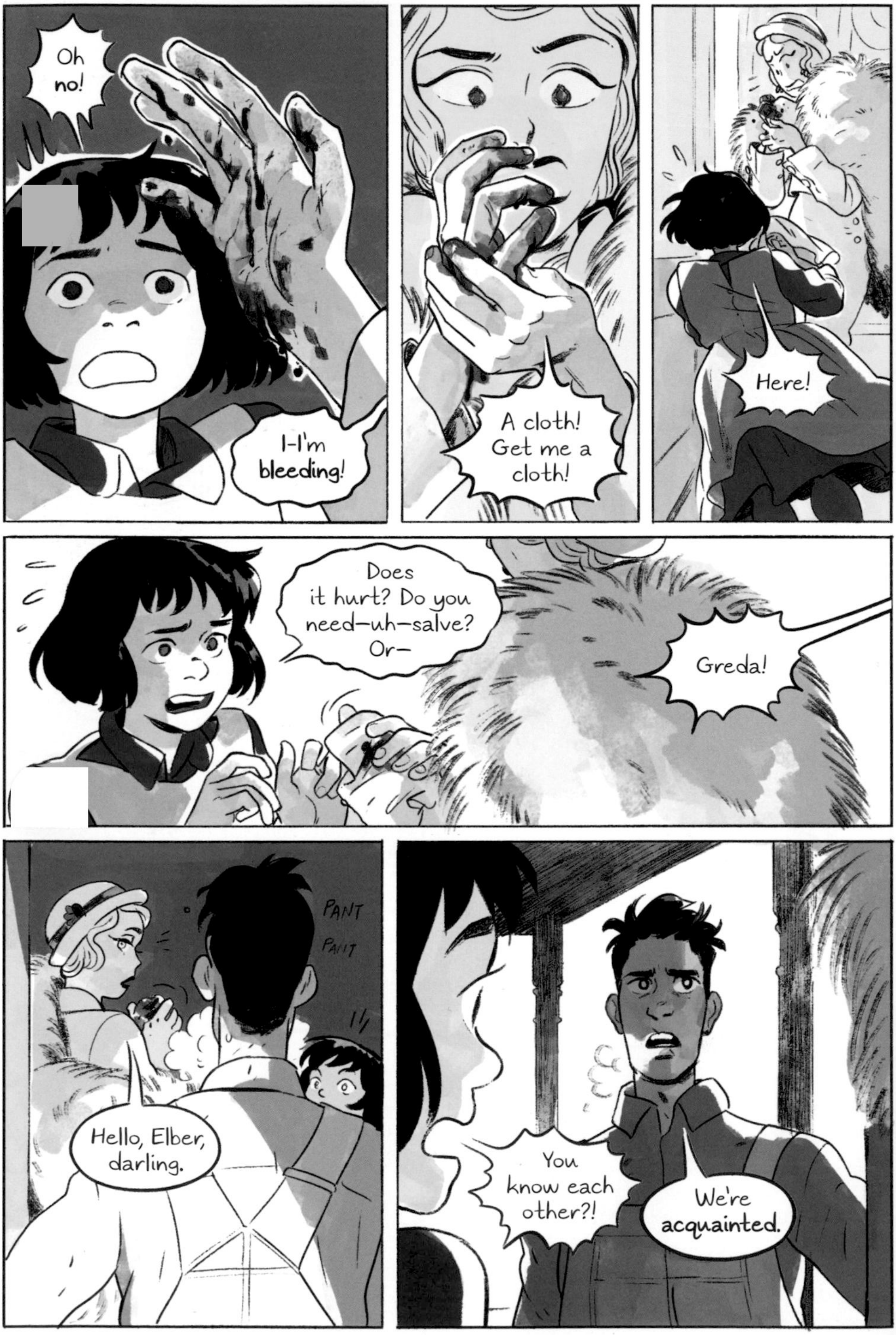
Oh no!
I-I'm bleeding!
A cloth! Get me a cloth!
Here!
Does it hurt? Do you need—uh—salve? Or—
Greda!
PANT
PANT
Hello, Elber, darling.
You know each other?!
We're acquainted.

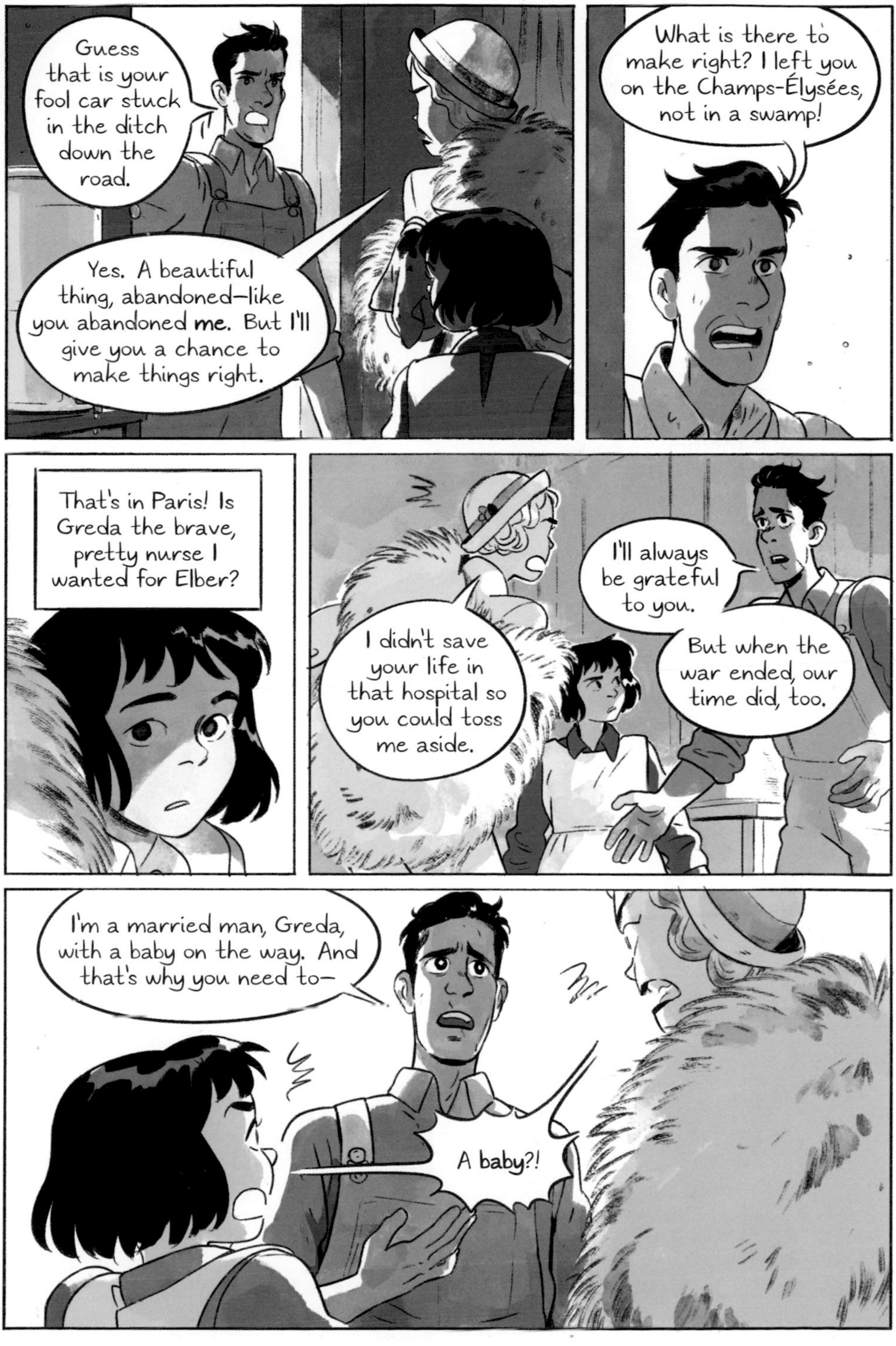
Guess that is your fool car stuck in the ditch down the road.
Yes. A beautiful thing, abandoned—like you abandoned **me.** But I'll give you a chance to make things right.
What is there to make right? I left you on the Champs-Élysées, not in a swamp!
That's in Paris! Is Greda the brave, pretty nurse I wanted for Elber?
I'll always be grateful to you.
I didn't save your life in that hospital so you could toss me aside.
But when the war ended, our time did, too.
I'm a married man, Greda, with a baby on the way. And that's why you need to—
A baby?!

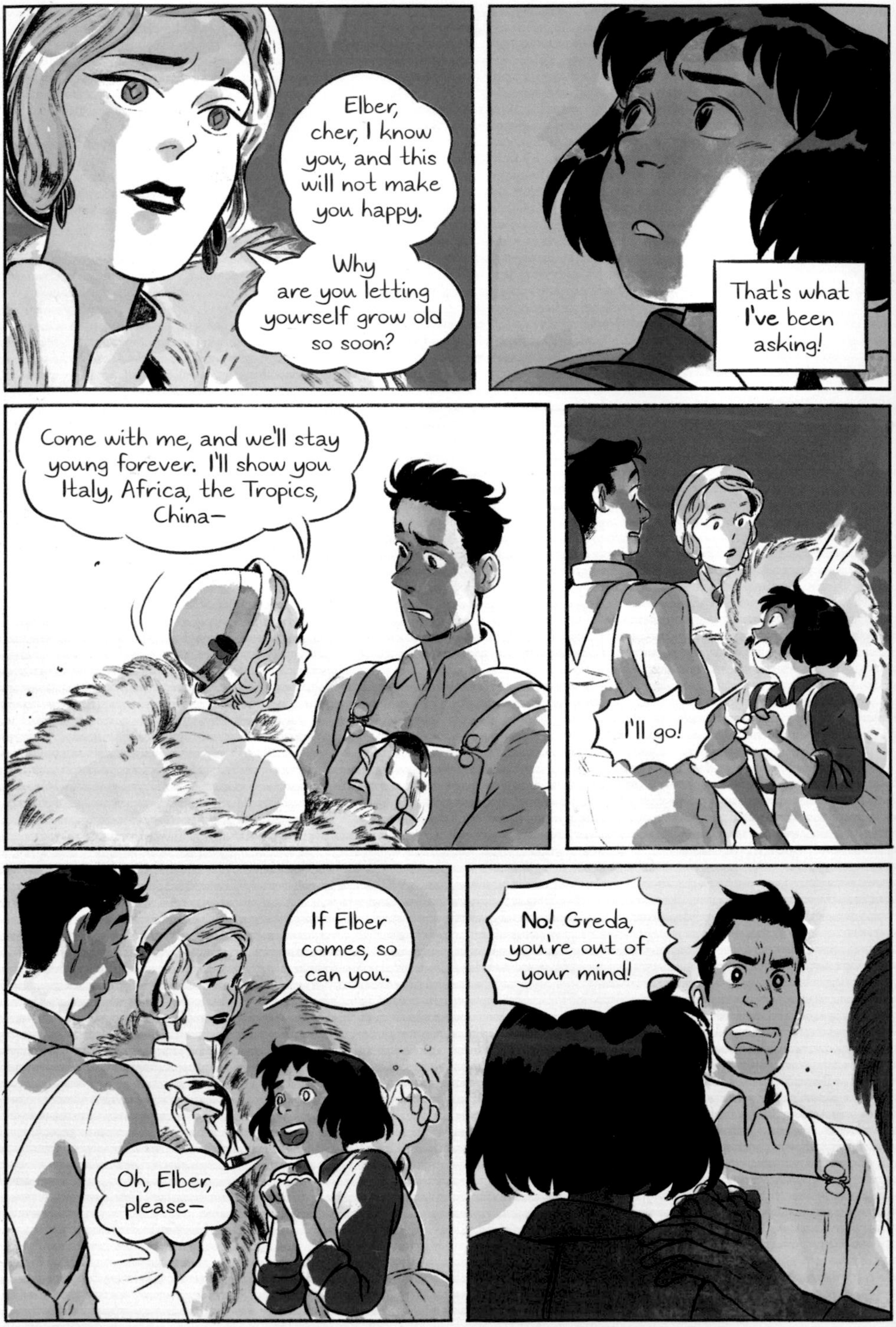
Elber, cher, I know you, and this will not make you happy.
Why are you letting yourself grow old so soon?
That's what **I've** been asking!
Come with me, and we'll stay young forever. I'll show you Italy, Africa, the Tropics, China—
I'll go!
If Elber comes, so can you.
Oh, Elber, please—
No! Greda, you're out of your mind!

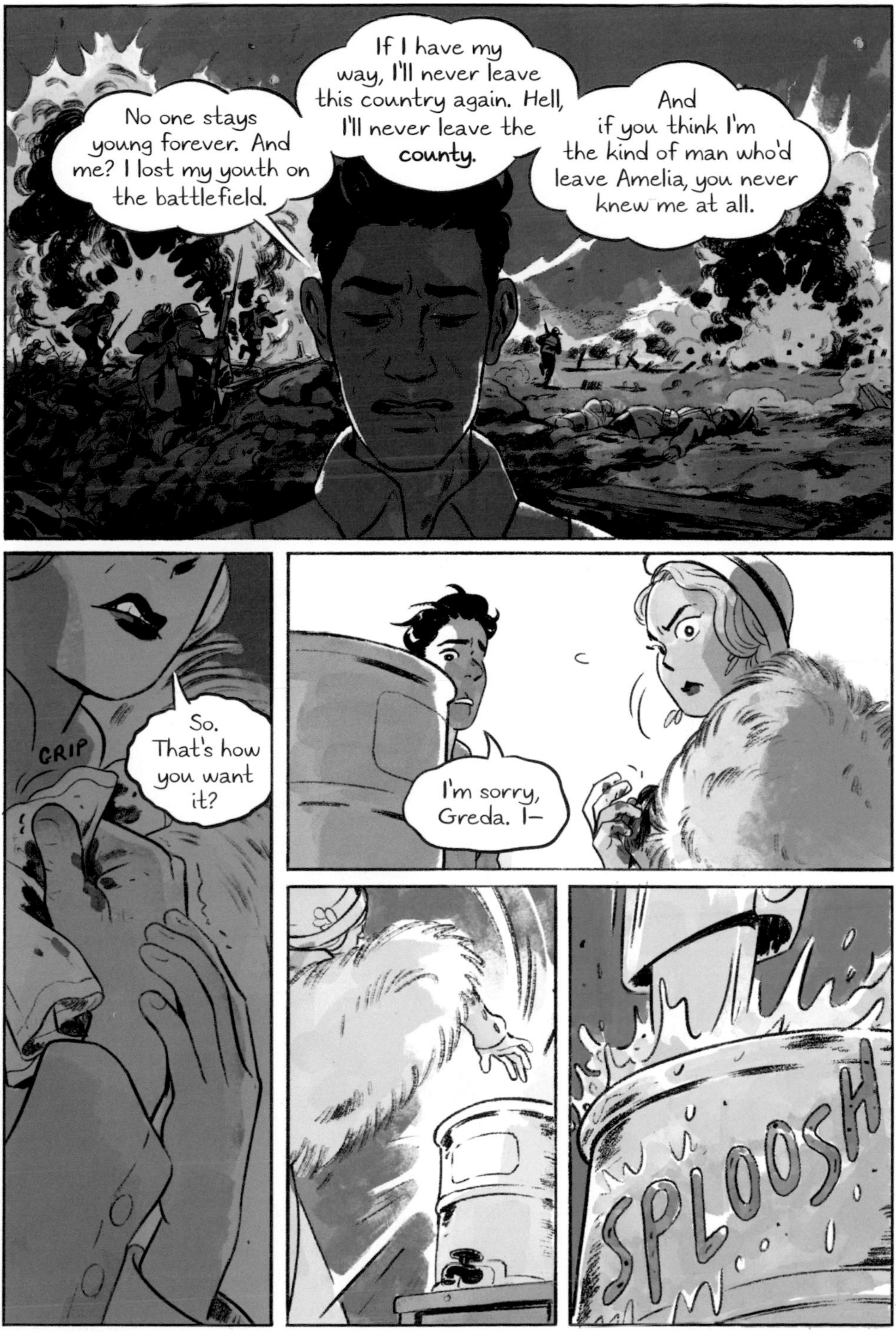
No one stays young forever. And me? I lost my youth on the battlefield.
If I have my way, I'll never leave this country again. Hell, I'll never leave the **county.**
And if you think I'm the kind of man who'd leave Amelia, you never knew me at all.
GRIP
So. That's how you want it?
I'm sorry, Greda. I—
SPLOOSH

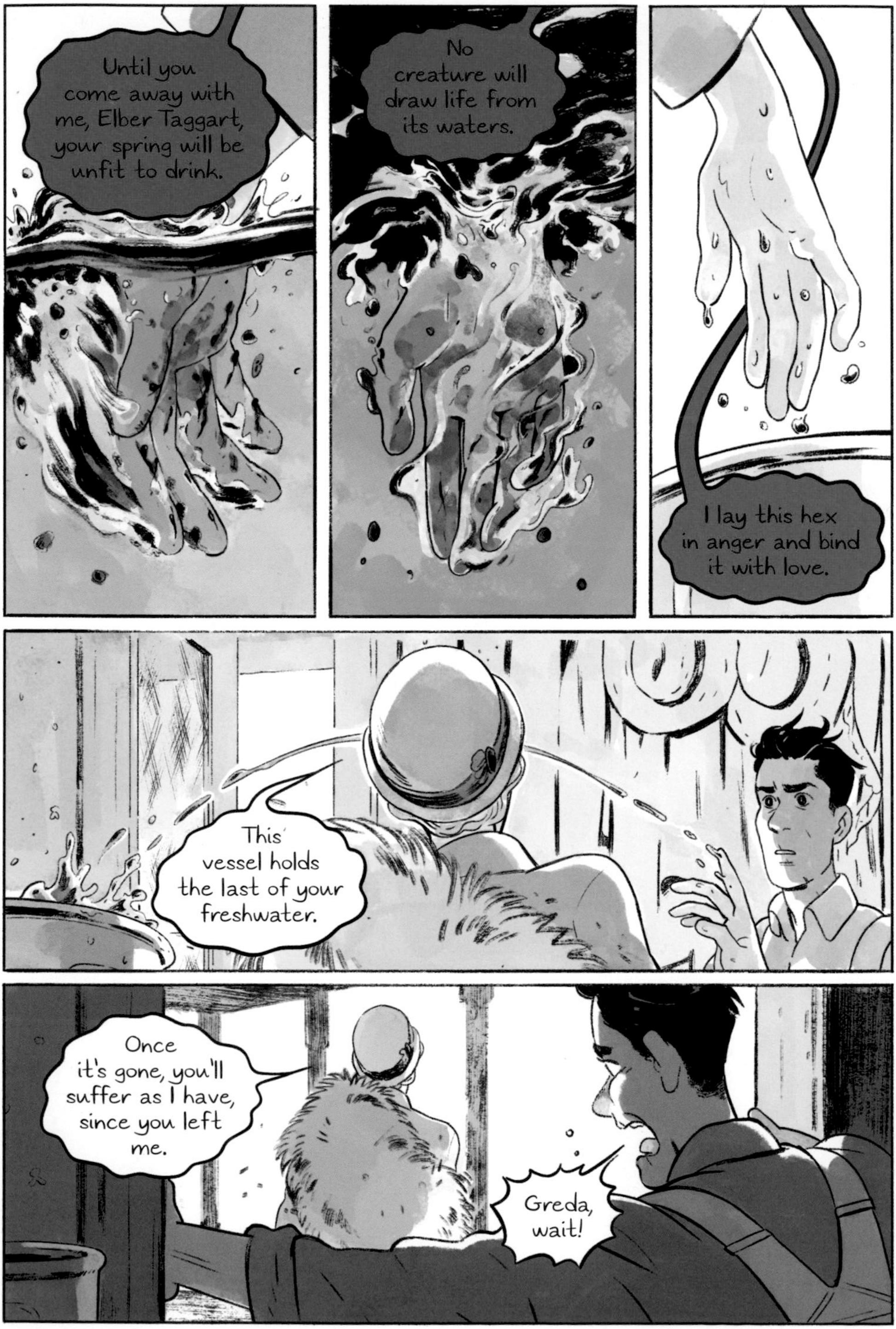
Until you come away with me, Elber Taggart, your spring will be unfit to drink.
No creature will draw life from its waters.
I lay this hex in anger and bind it with love.
This vessel holds the last of your freshwater.
Once it's gone, you'll suffer as I have, since you left me.
Greda, wait!

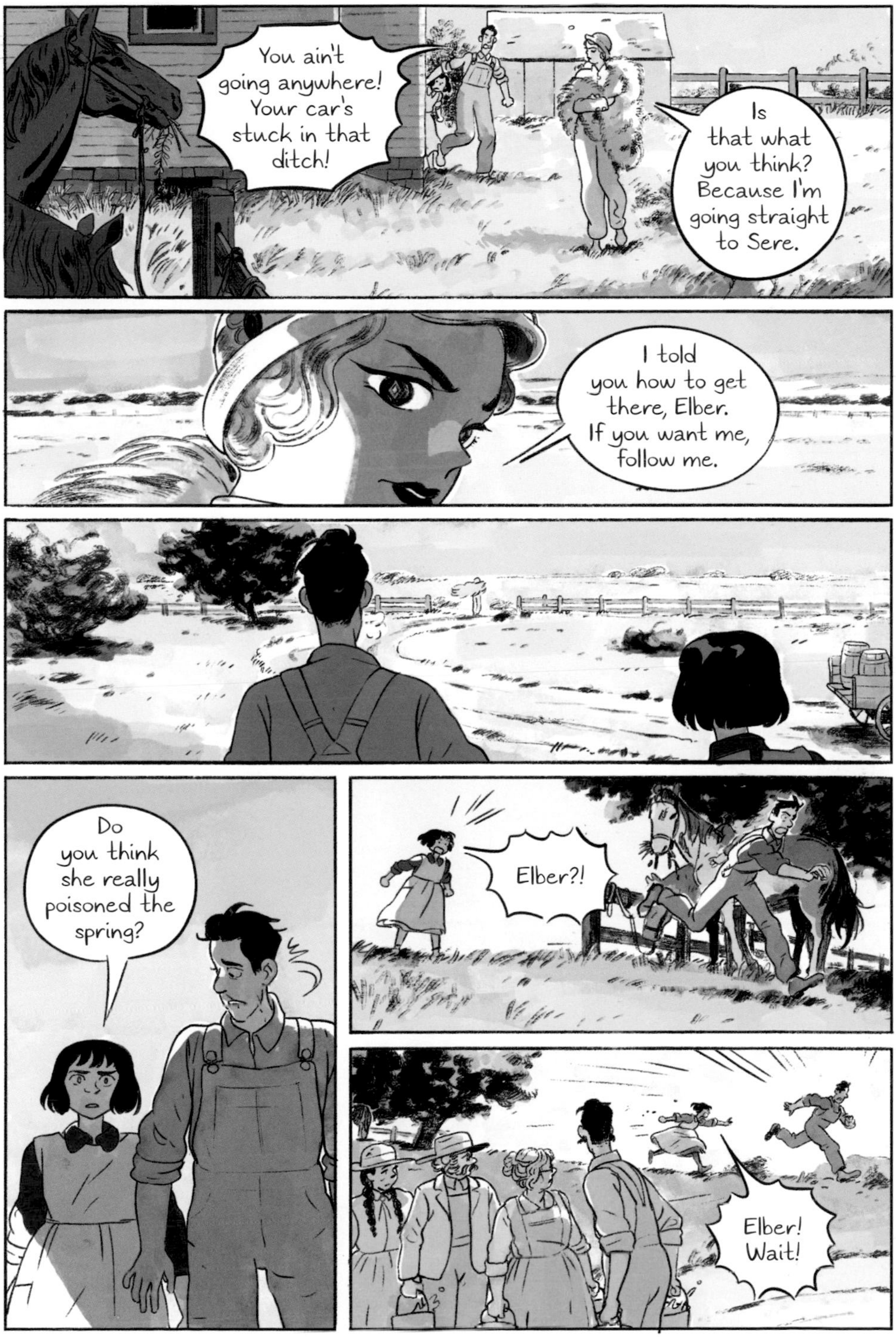
You ain't going anywhere! Your car's stuck in that ditch!
Is that what you think? Because I'm going straight to Sere.
I told you how to get there, Elber. If you want me, follow me.
Do you think she really poisoned the spring?
Elber?!
Elber! Wait!

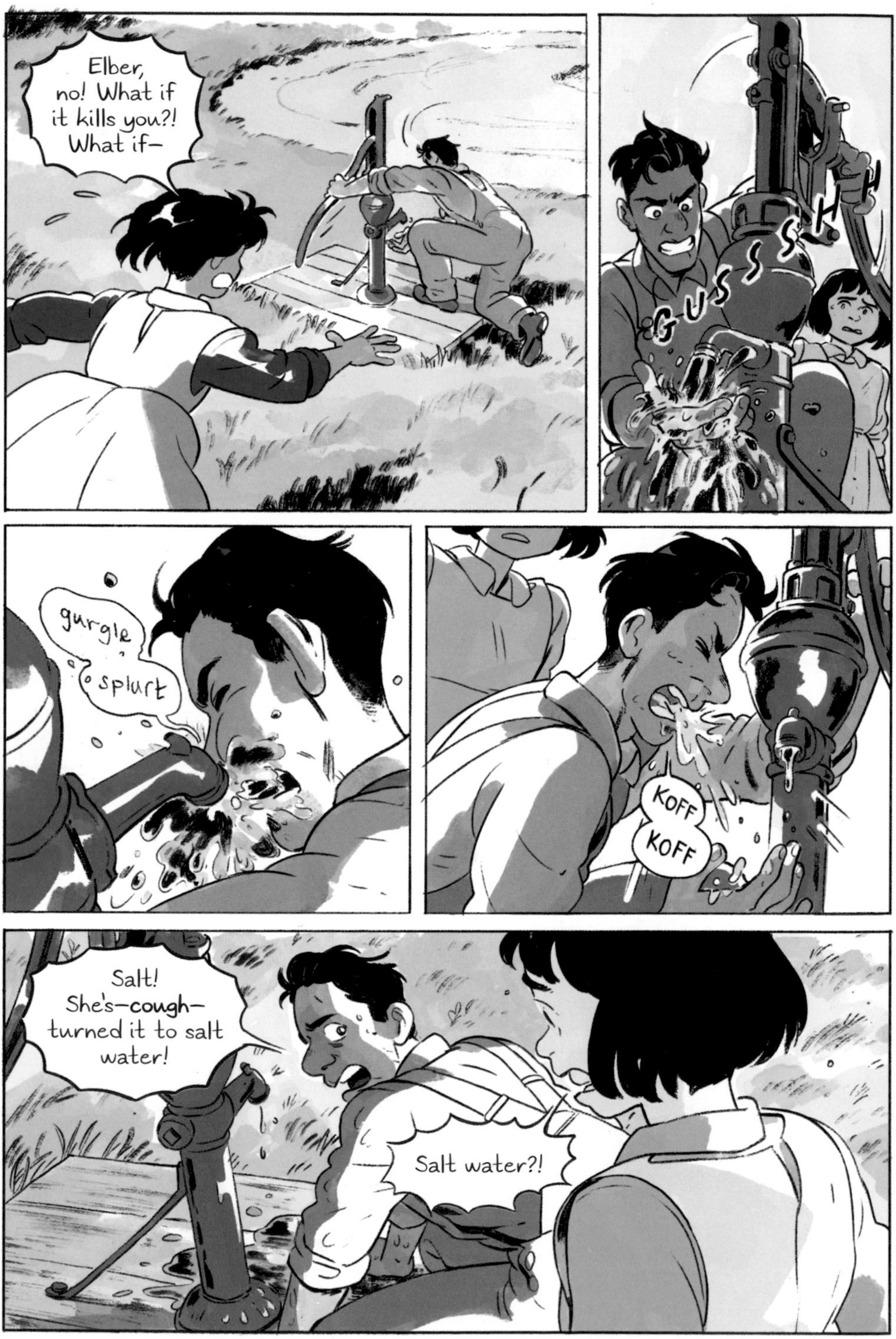
Elber, no! What if it kills you?! What if–
GUSSSHH
gurgle
splurt
KOFF
KOFF
Salt! She's–**cough**– turned it to salt water!
Salt water?!

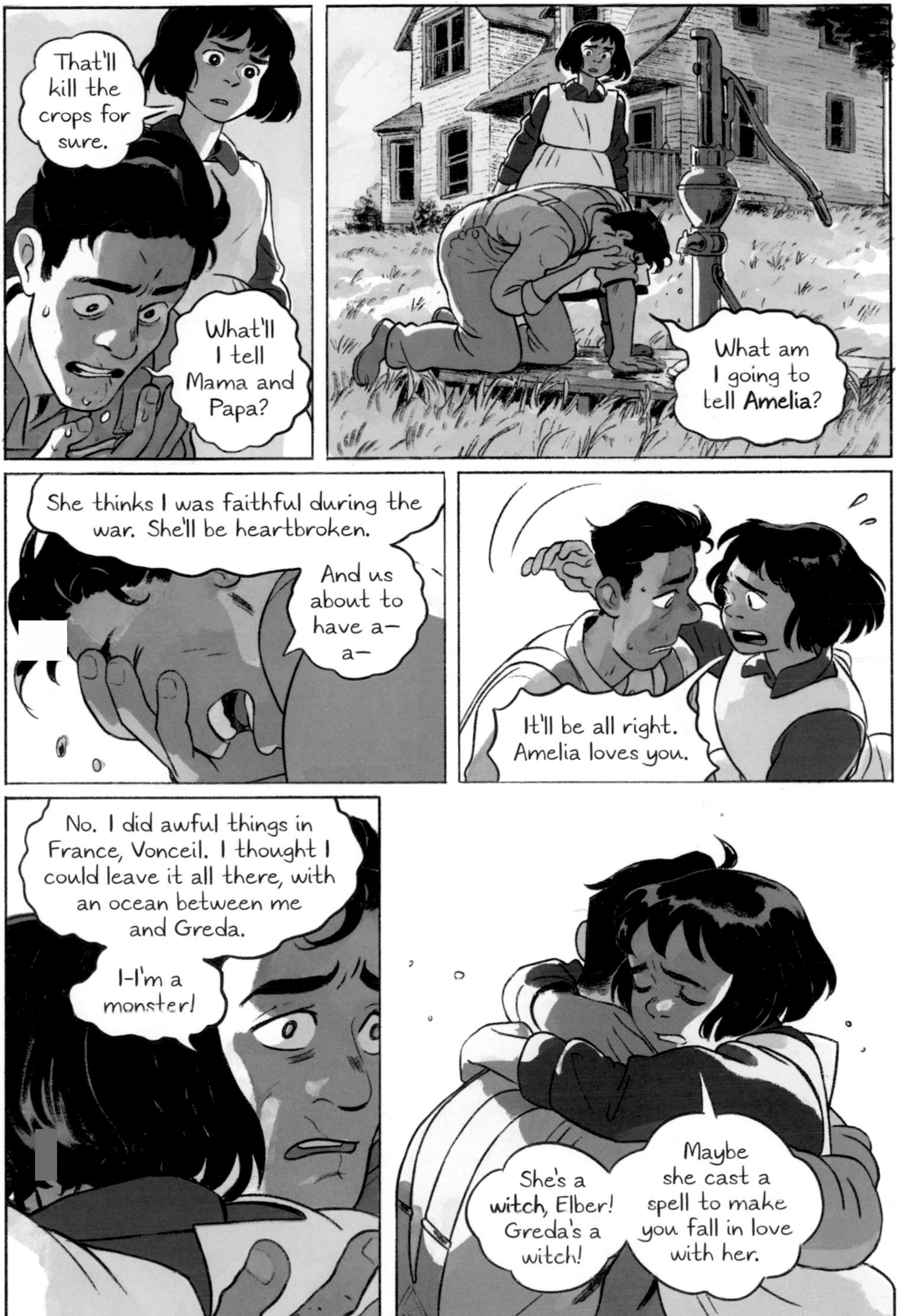
That'll kill the crops for sure.
What'll I tell Mama and Papa?
What am I going to tell **Amelia**?
She thinks I was faithful during the war. She'll be heartbroken.
And us about to have a— a—
It'll be all right. Amelia loves you.
No. I did awful things in France, Vonceil. I thought I could leave it all there, with an ocean between me and Greda.
I-I'm a monster!
She's a **witch**, Elber! Greda's a witch!
Maybe she cast a spell to make you fall in love with her.

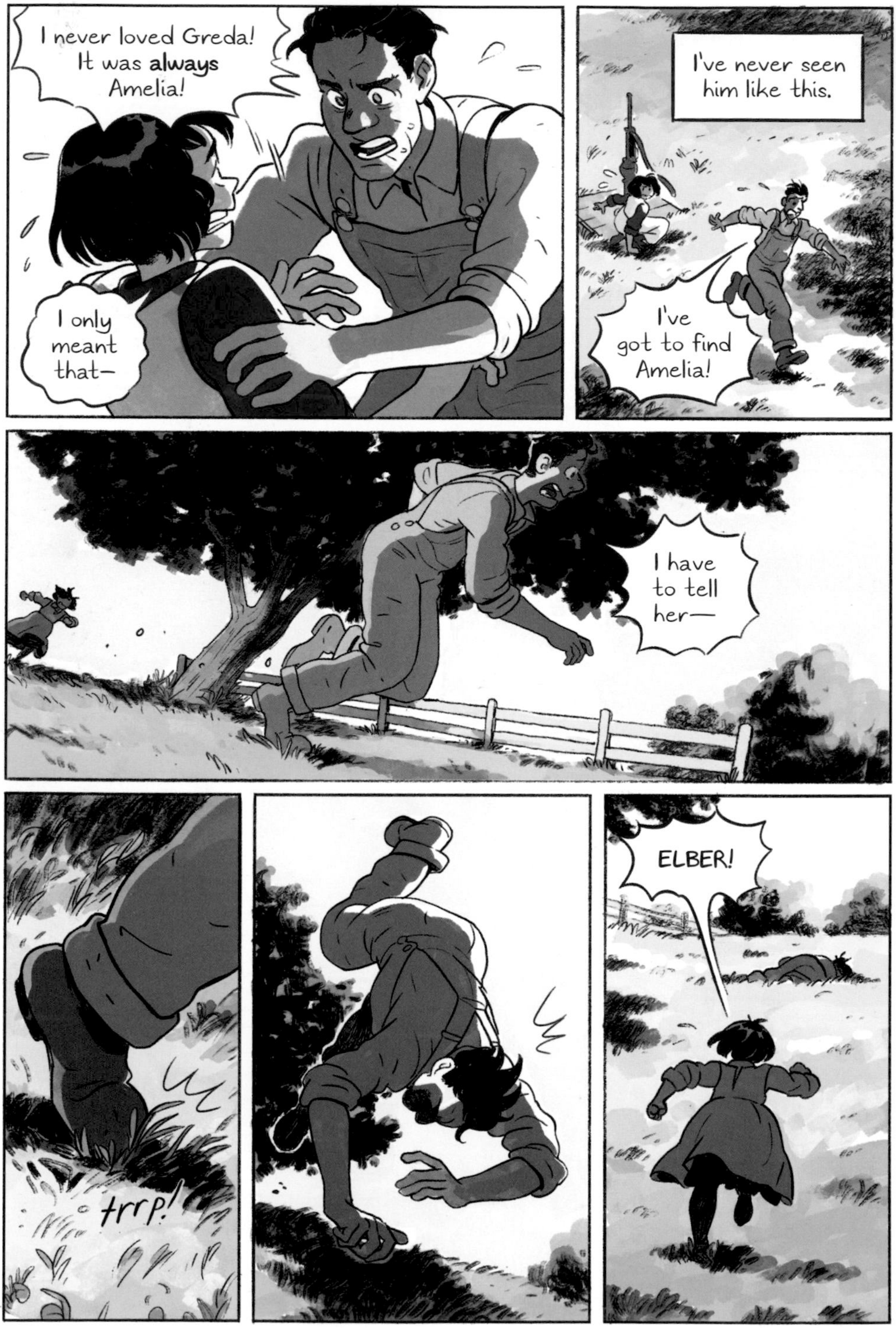
I never loved Greda! It was **always** Amelia!
I only meant that—
I've never seen him like this.
I've got to find Amelia!
I have to tell her—
trrp!
ELBER!

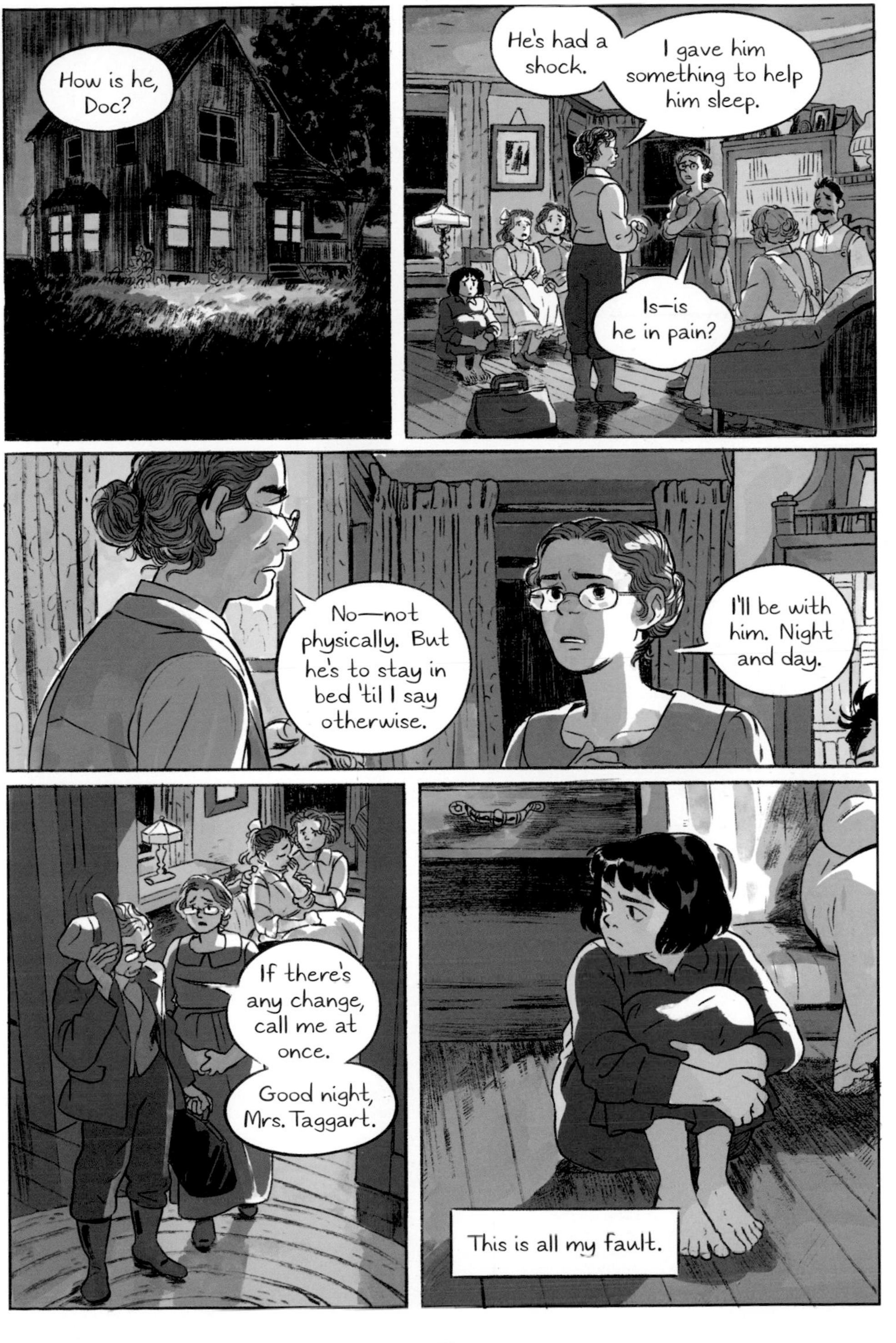
How is he, Doc?
He's had a shock.
I gave him something to help him sleep.
Is—is he in pain?
No—not physically. But he's to stay in bed 'til I say otherwise.
I'll be with him. Night and day.
If there's any change, call me at once.
Good night, Mrs. Taggart.
This is all my fault.

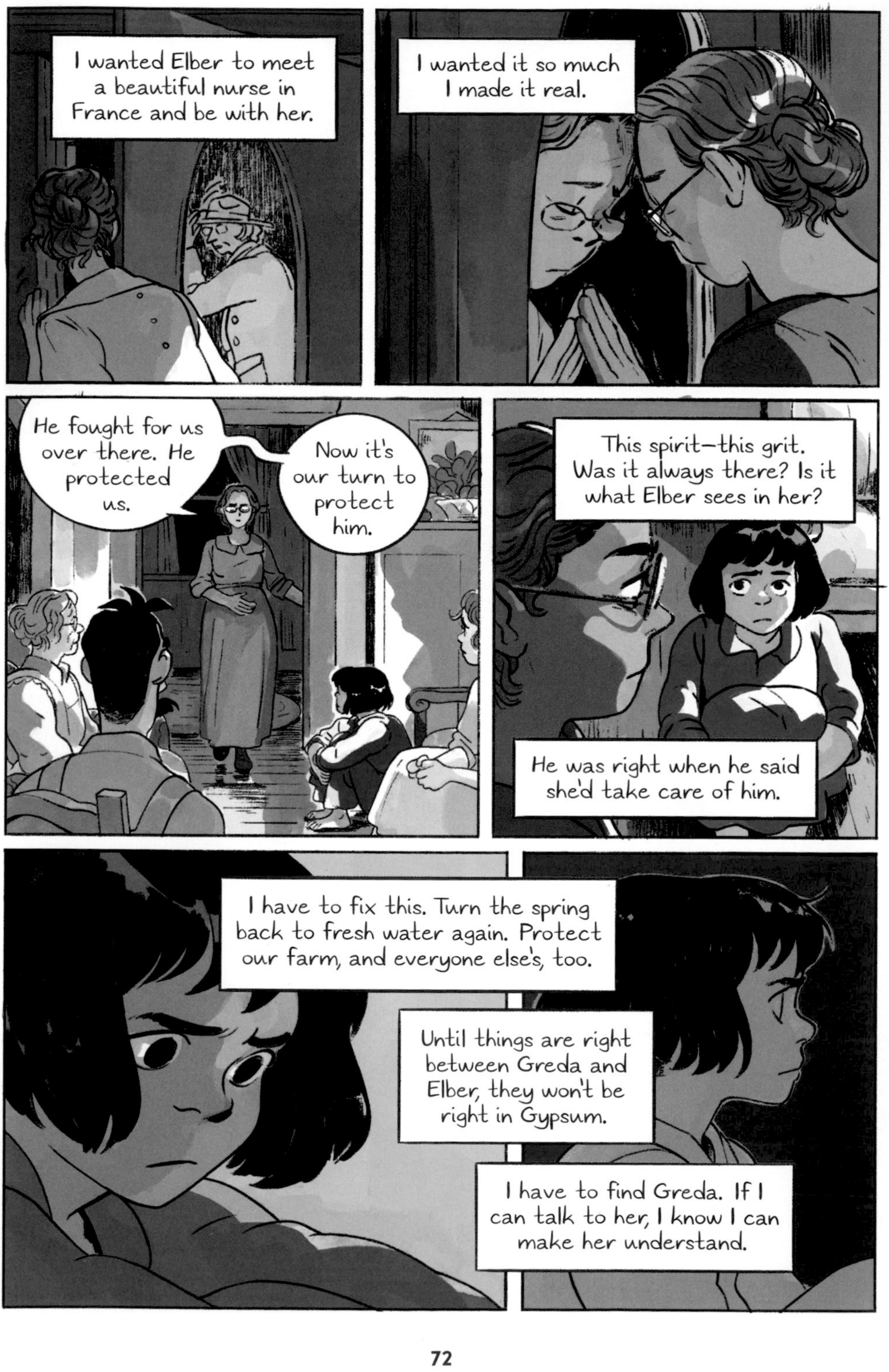
I wanted Elber to meet a beautiful nurse in France and be with her.
I wanted it so much I made it real.
He fought for us over there. He protected us.
Now it's our turn to protect him.
This spirit—this grit. Was it always there? Is it what Elber sees in her?
He was right when he said she'd take care of him.
I have to fix this. Turn the spring back to fresh water again. Protect our farm, and everyone else's, too.
Until things are right between Greda and Elber, they won't be right in Gypsum.
I have to find Greda. If I can talk to her, I know I can make her understand.

Chapter Five

A Sacrificial Pawn

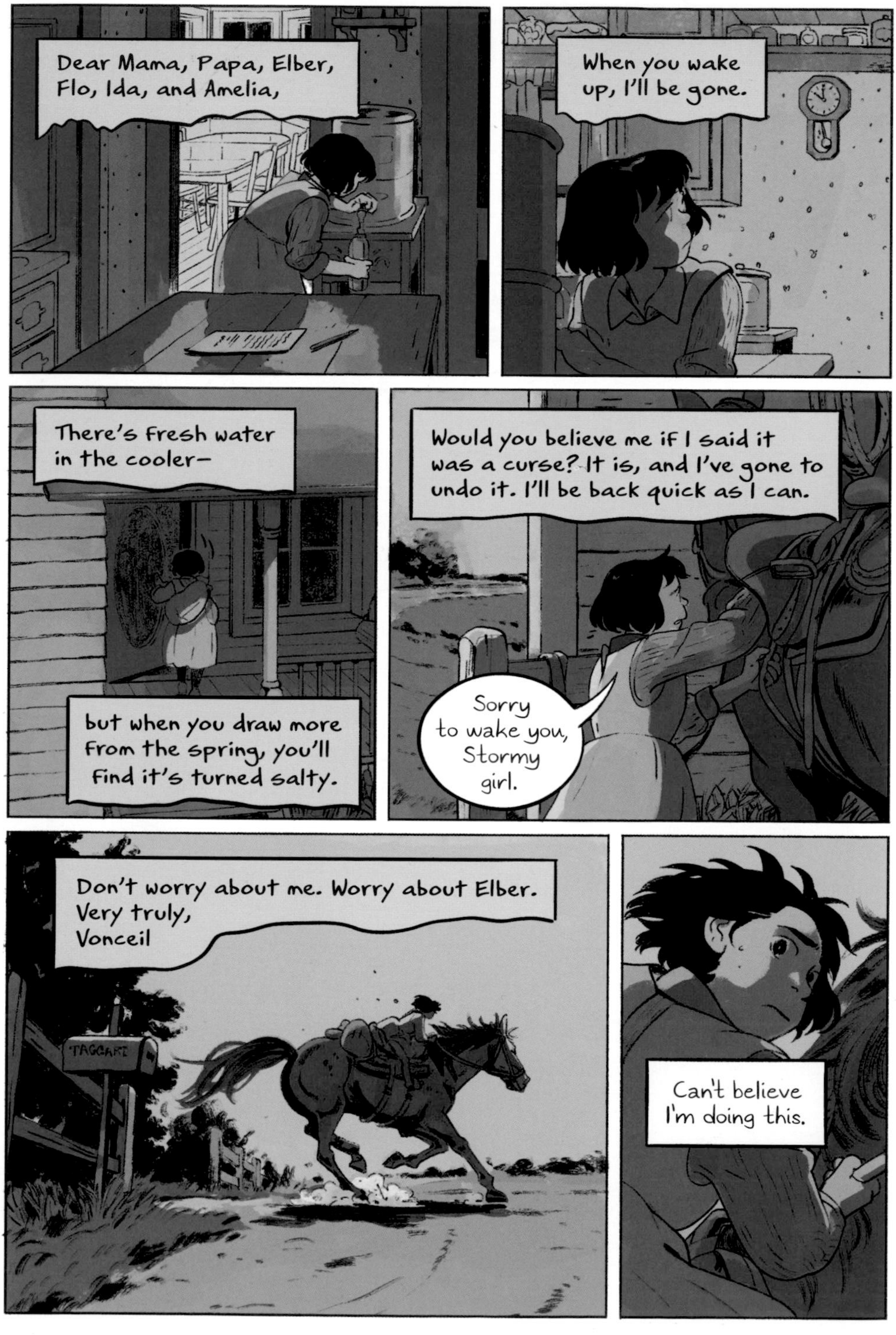
Dear Mama, Papa, Elber, Flo, Ida, and Amelia,
When you wake up, I'll be gone.
There's fresh water in the cooler—
but when you draw more from the spring, you'll find it's turned salty.
Would you believe me if I said it was a curse? It is, and I've gone to undo it. I'll be back quick as I can.
Sorry to wake you, Stormy girl.
Don't worry about me. Worry about Elber.
Very truly,
Vonceil
TAGGART
Can't believe I'm doing this.

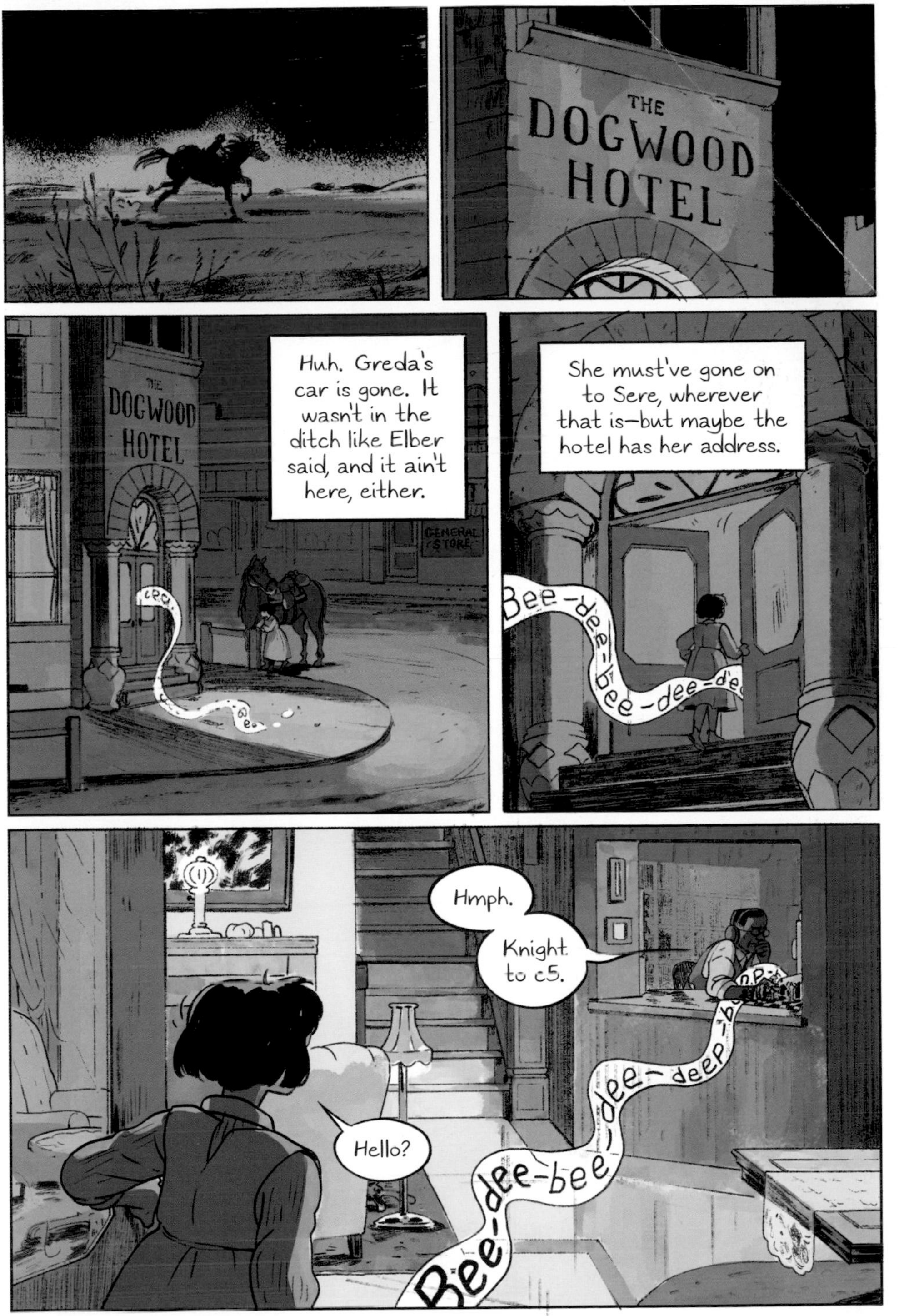
THE DOGWOOD HOTEL
THE DOGWOOD HOTEL
Huh. Greda's car is gone. It wasn't in the ditch like Elber said, and it ain't here, either.
GENERAL STORE
She must've gone on to Sere, wherever that is—but maybe the hotel has her address.
Bee-dee-bee-dee-dee
Hmph.
Knight to c5.
Hello?
Bee-dee-bee-dee-dee-deep

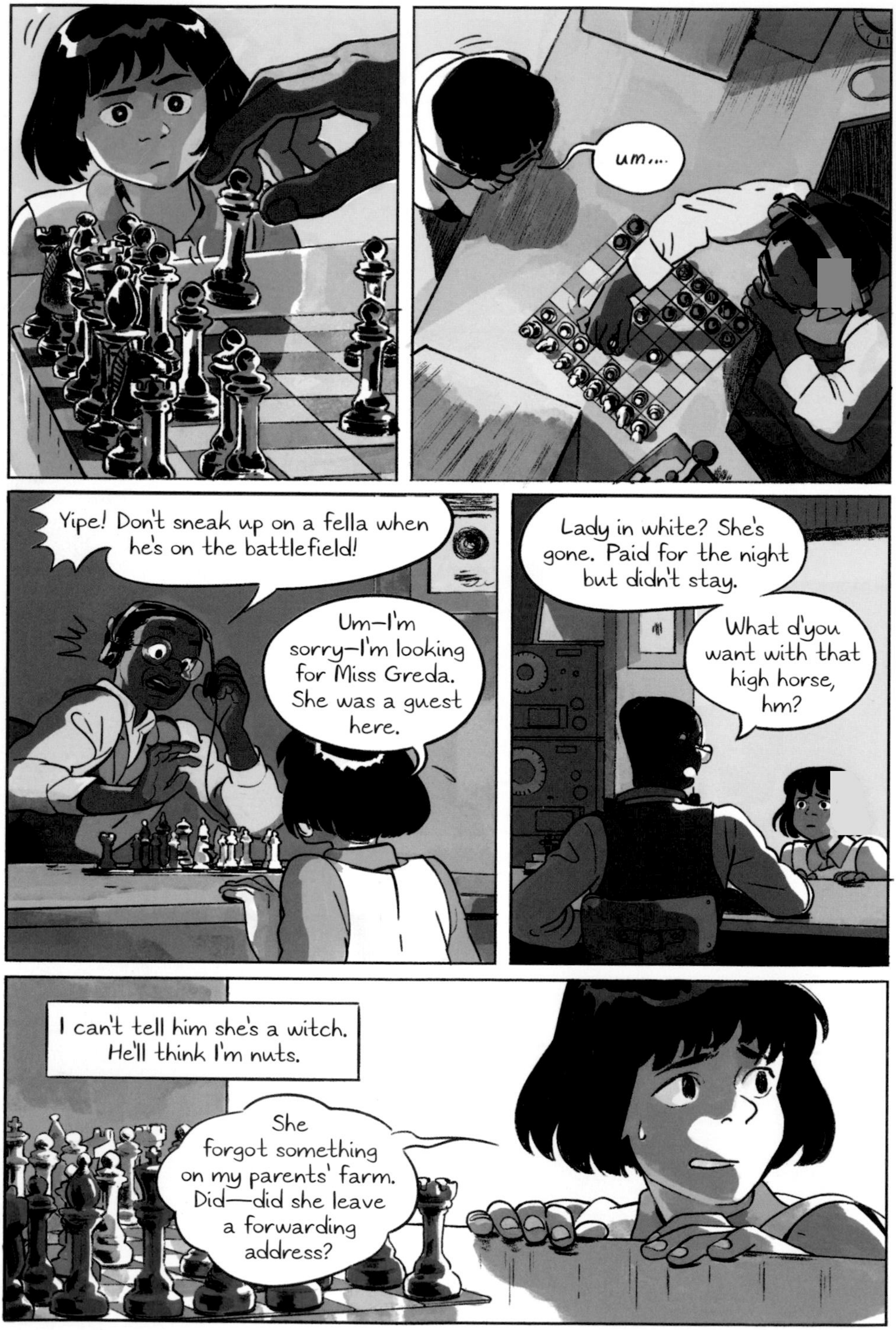
um....
Yipe! Don't sneak up on a fella when he's on the battlefield!
Um—I'm sorry—I'm looking for Miss Greda. She was a guest here.
Lady in white? She's gone. Paid for the night but didn't stay.
What d'you want with that high horse, hm?
I can't tell him she's a witch. He'll think I'm nuts.
She forgot something on my parents' farm. Did—did she leave a forwarding address?

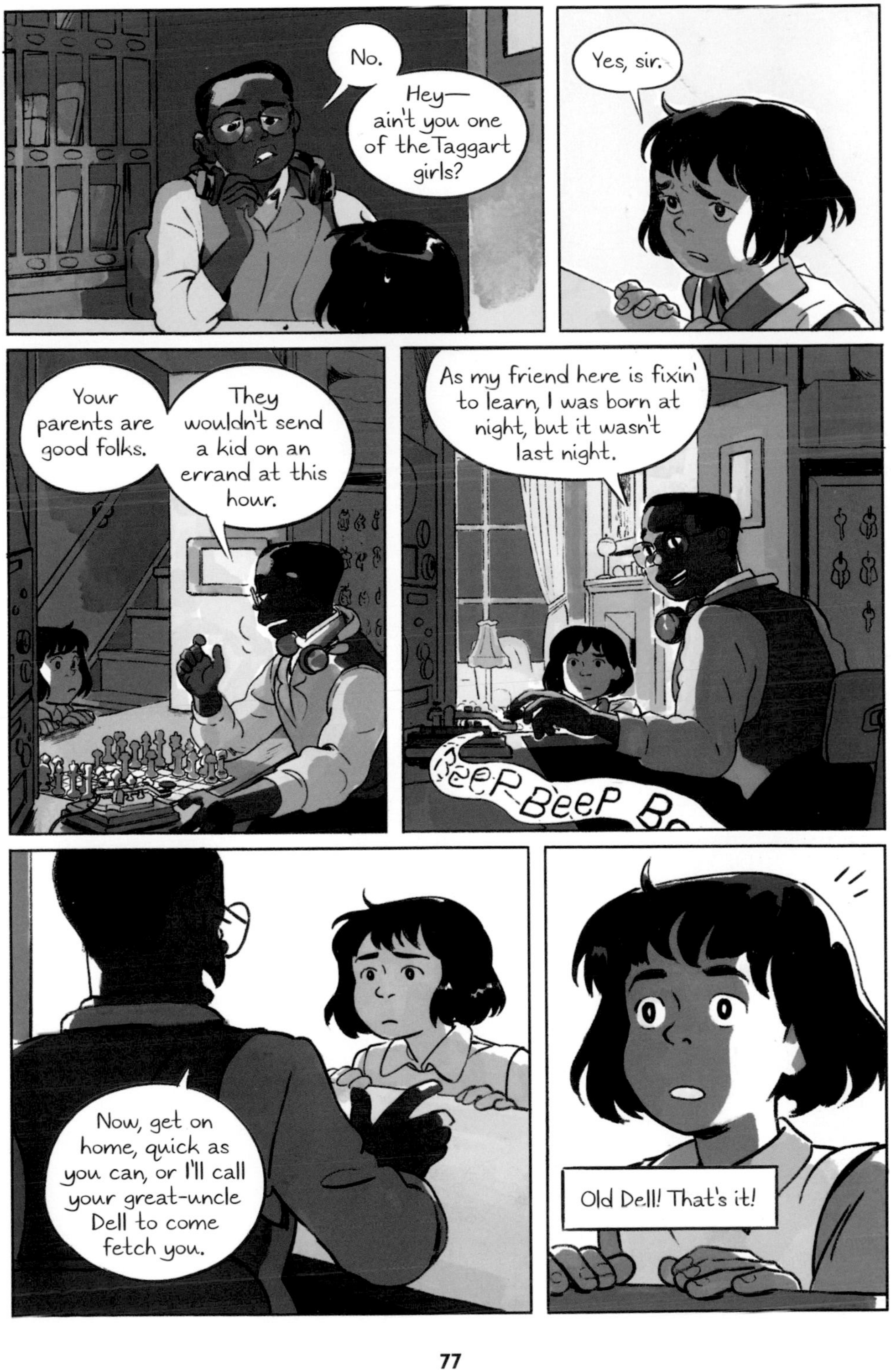
No.
Hey—ain't you one of the Taggart girls?
Yes, sir.
Your parents are good folks.
They wouldn't send a kid on an errand at this hour.
As my friend here is fixin' to learn, I was born at night, but it wasn't last night.
BEEP BEEP
Now, get on home, quick as you can, or I'll call your great-uncle Dell to come fetch you.
Old Dell! That's it!

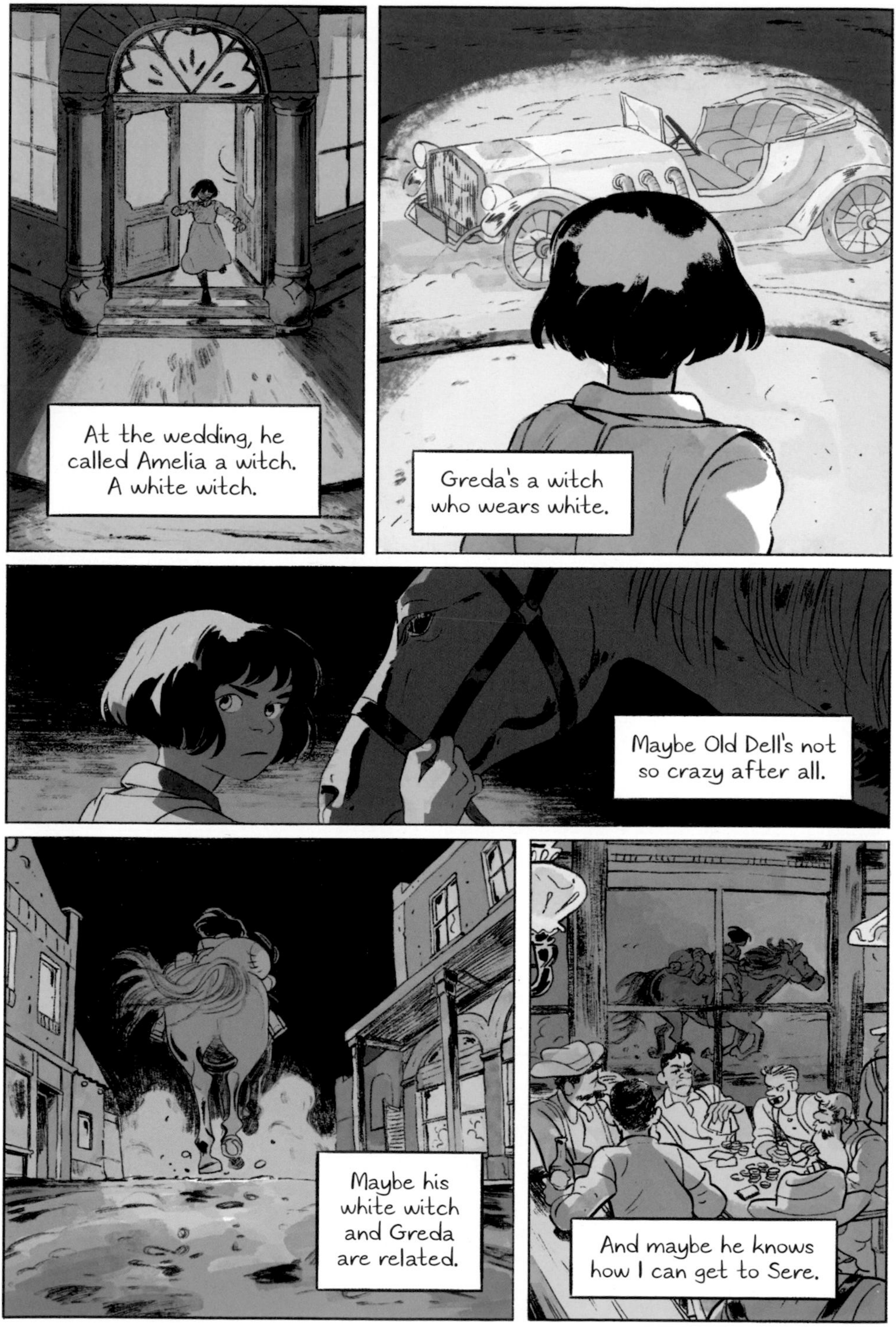
At the wedding, he called Amelia a witch. A white witch.
Greda's a witch who wears white.
Maybe Old Dell's not so crazy after all.
Maybe his white witch and Greda are related.
And maybe he knows how I can get to Sere.

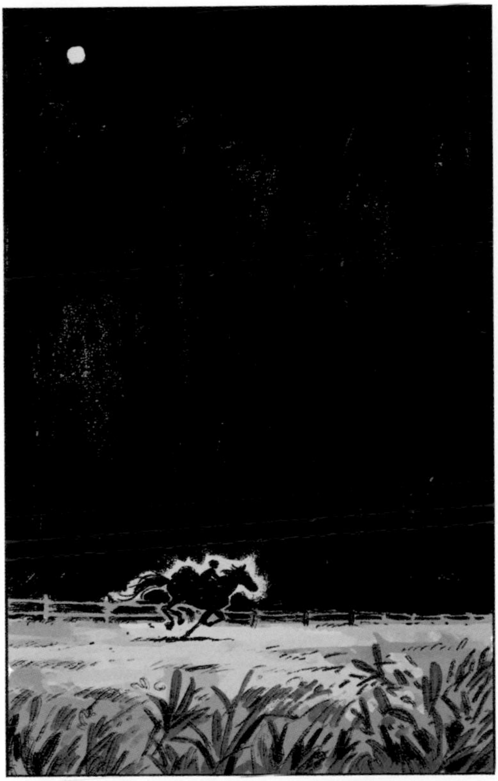

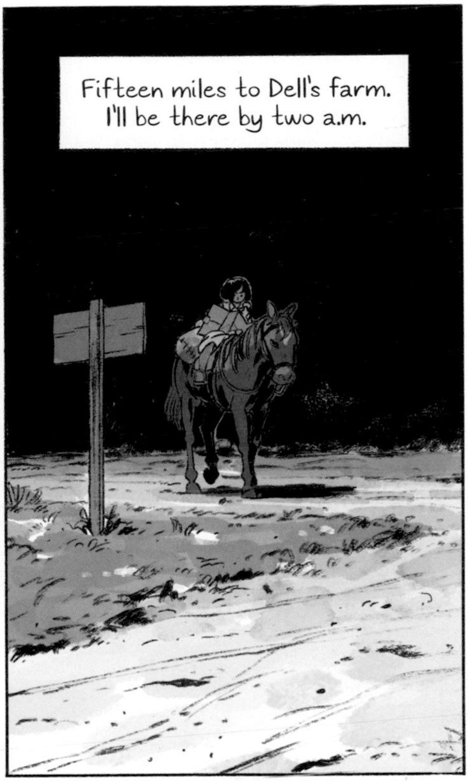
Fifteen miles to Dell's farm.
I'll be there by two a.m.

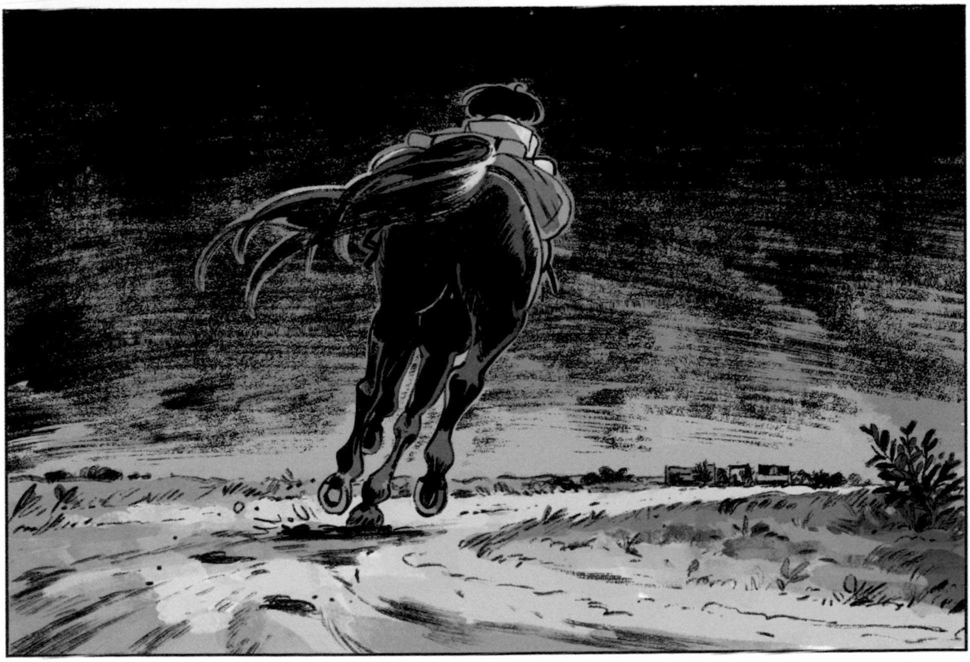

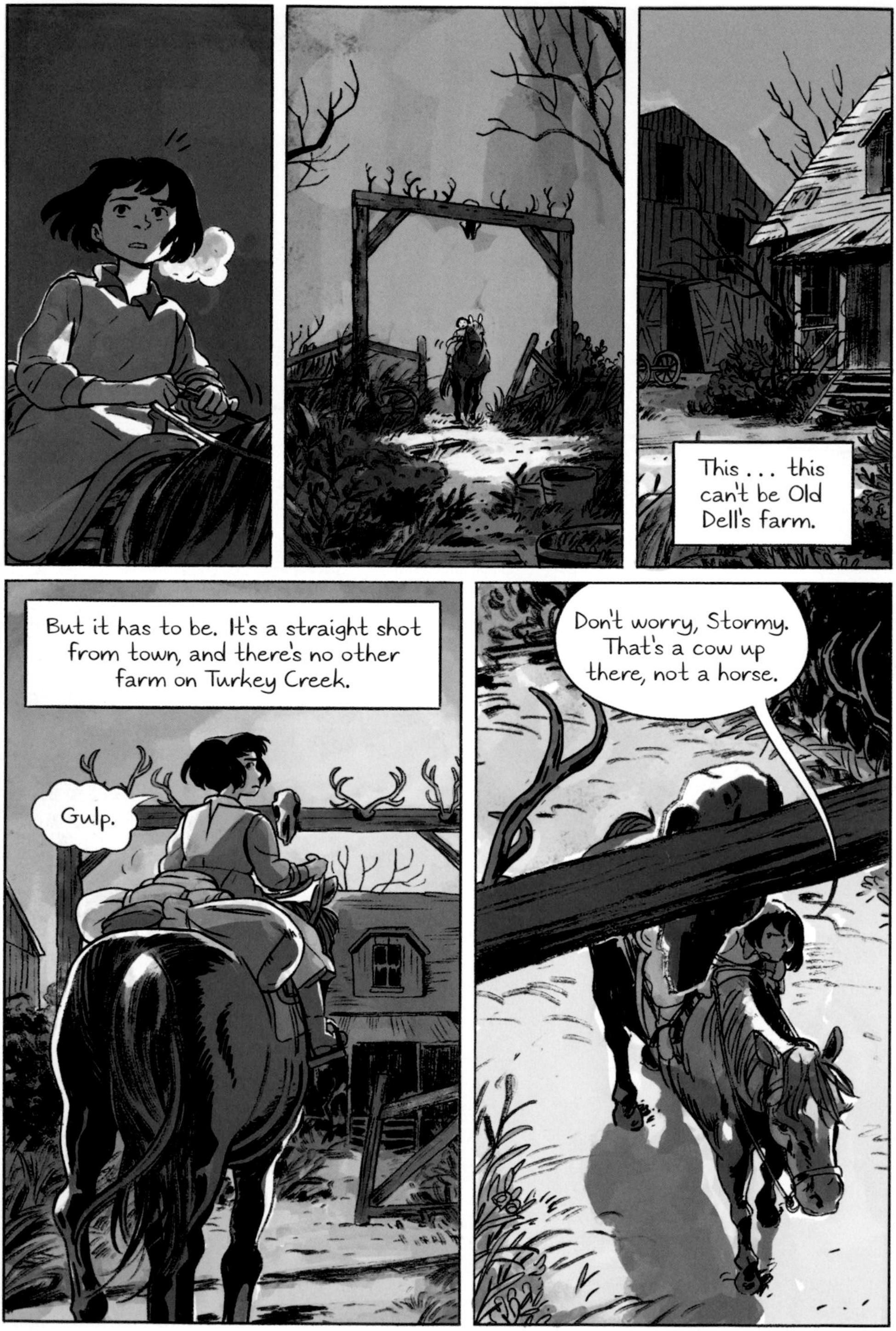
This . . . this can't be Old Dell's farm.
But it has to be. It's a straight shot from town, and there's no other farm on Turkey Creek.
Gulp.
Don't worry, Stormy. That's a cow up there, not a horse.

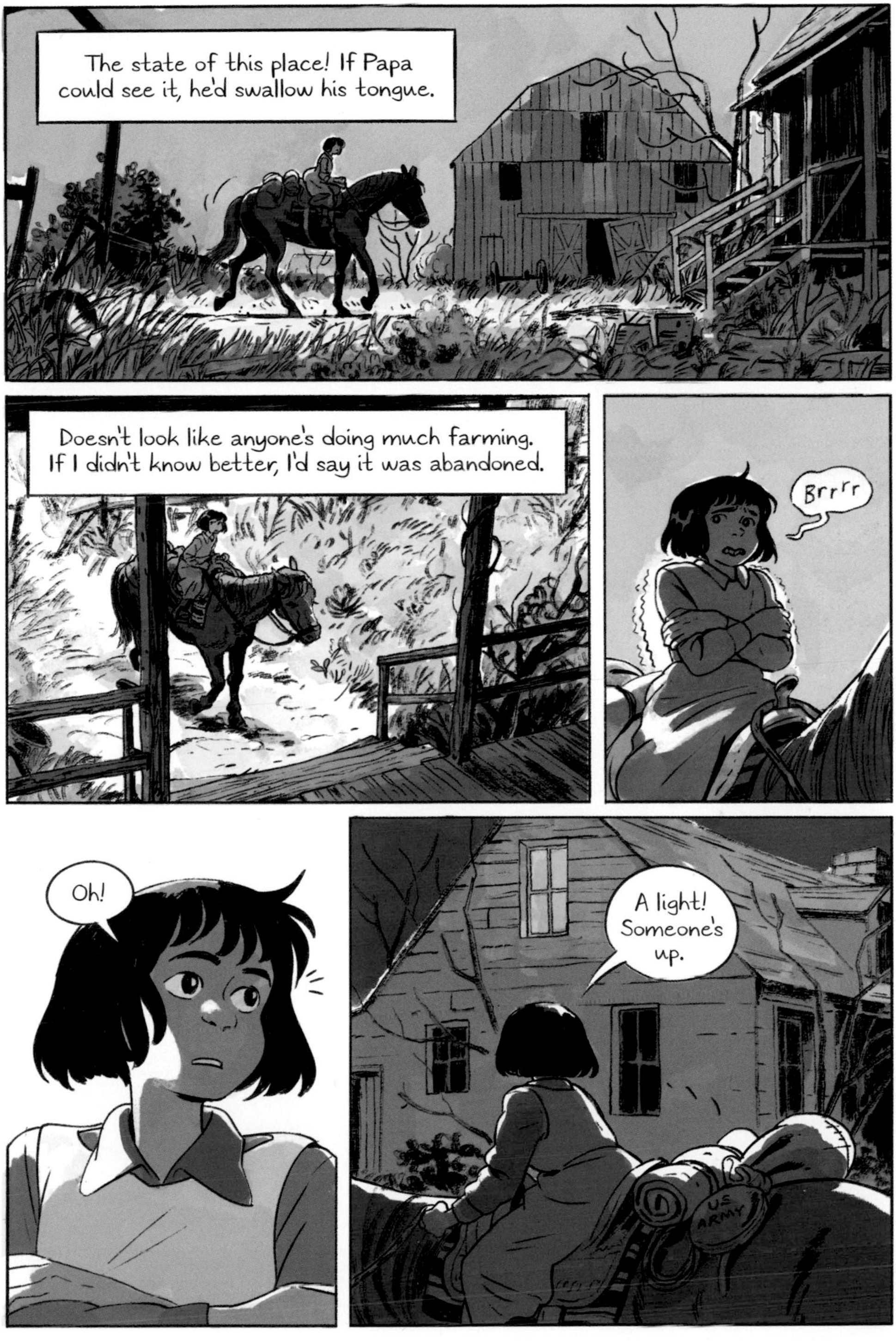
The state of this place! If Papa could see it, he'd swallow his tongue.
Doesn't look like anyone's doing much farming. If I didn't know better, I'd say it was abandoned.
Brrrr
Oh!
A light! Someone's up.
US ARMY

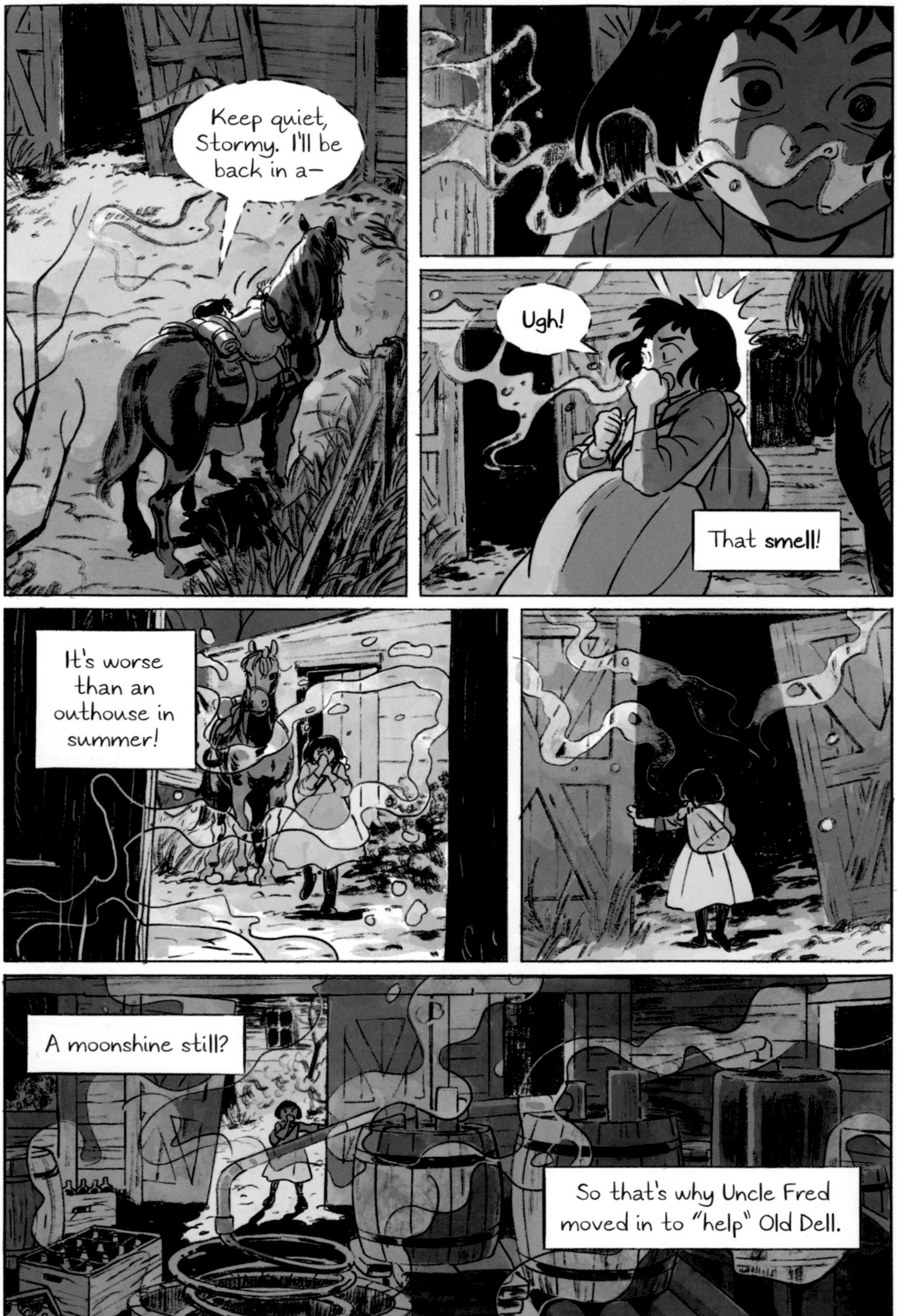
Keep quiet, Stormy. I'll be back in a—
Ugh!
That smell!
It's worse than an outhouse in summer!
A moonshine still?
So that's why Uncle Fred moved in to "help" Old Dell.

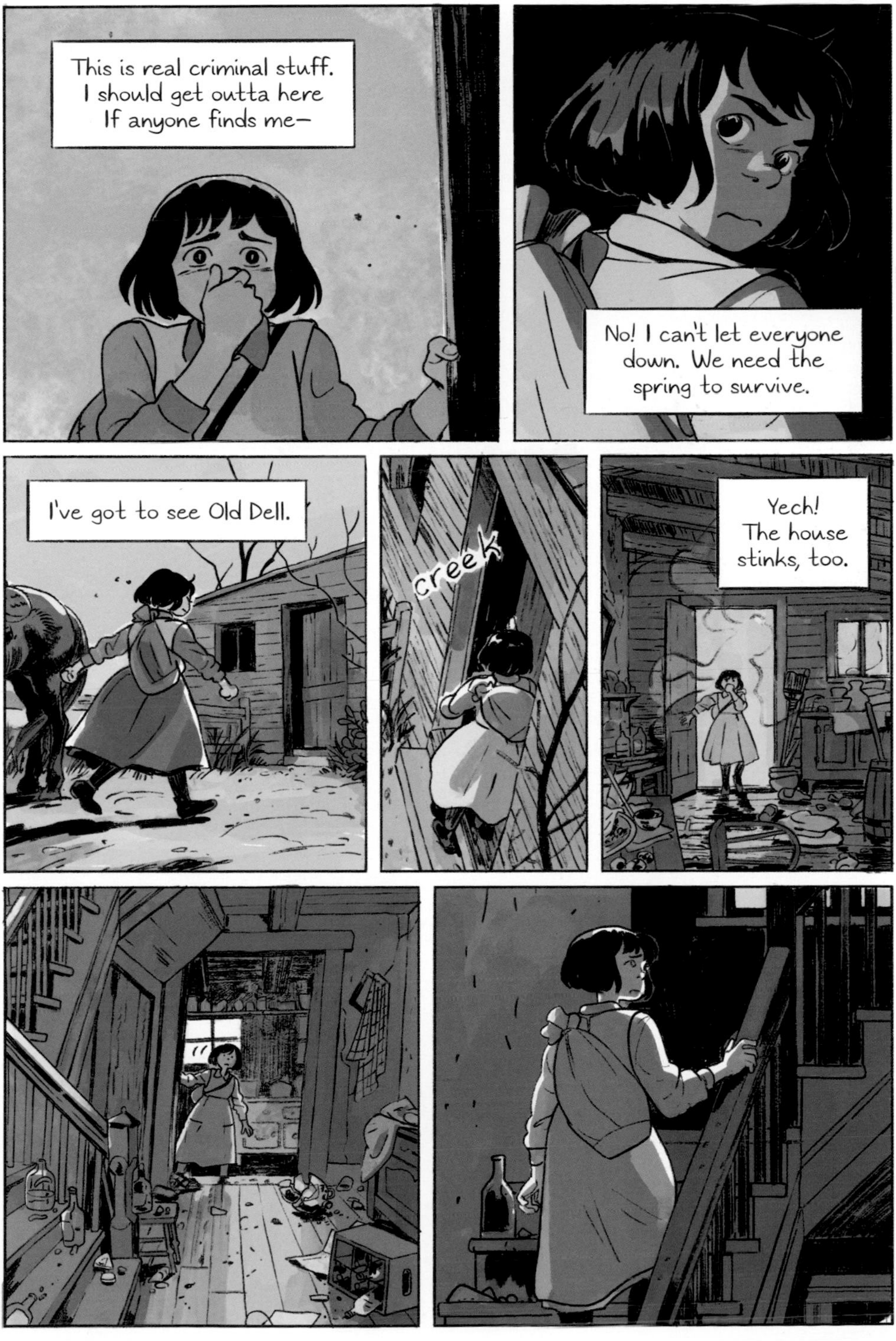

This is real criminal stuff. I should get outta here If anyone finds me—
No! I can't let everyone down. We need the spring to survive.
I've got to see Old Dell.
creek
Yech! The house stinks, too.

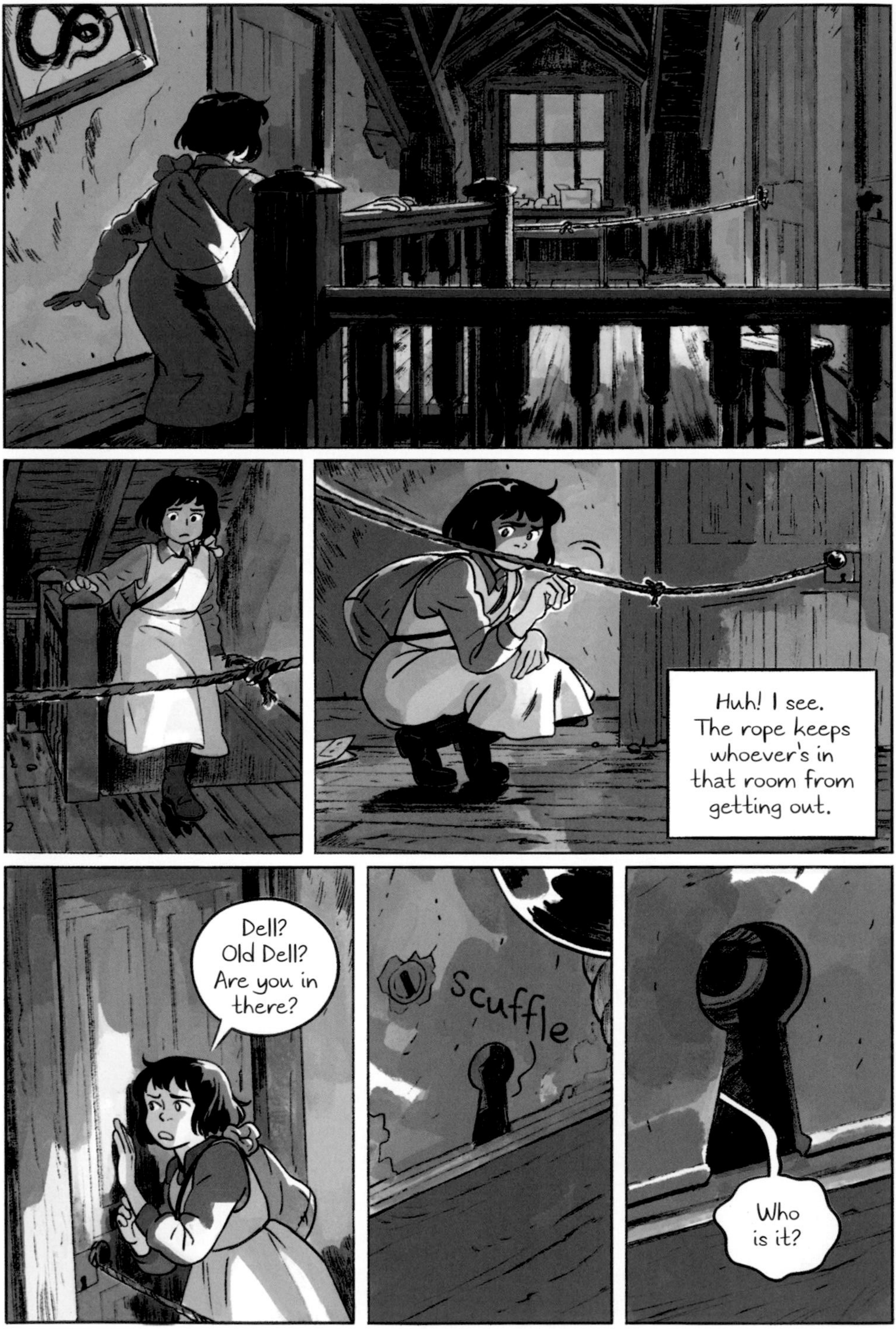
Huh! I see. The rope keeps whoever's in that room from getting out.
Dell? Old Dell? Are you in there?
scuffle
Who is it?

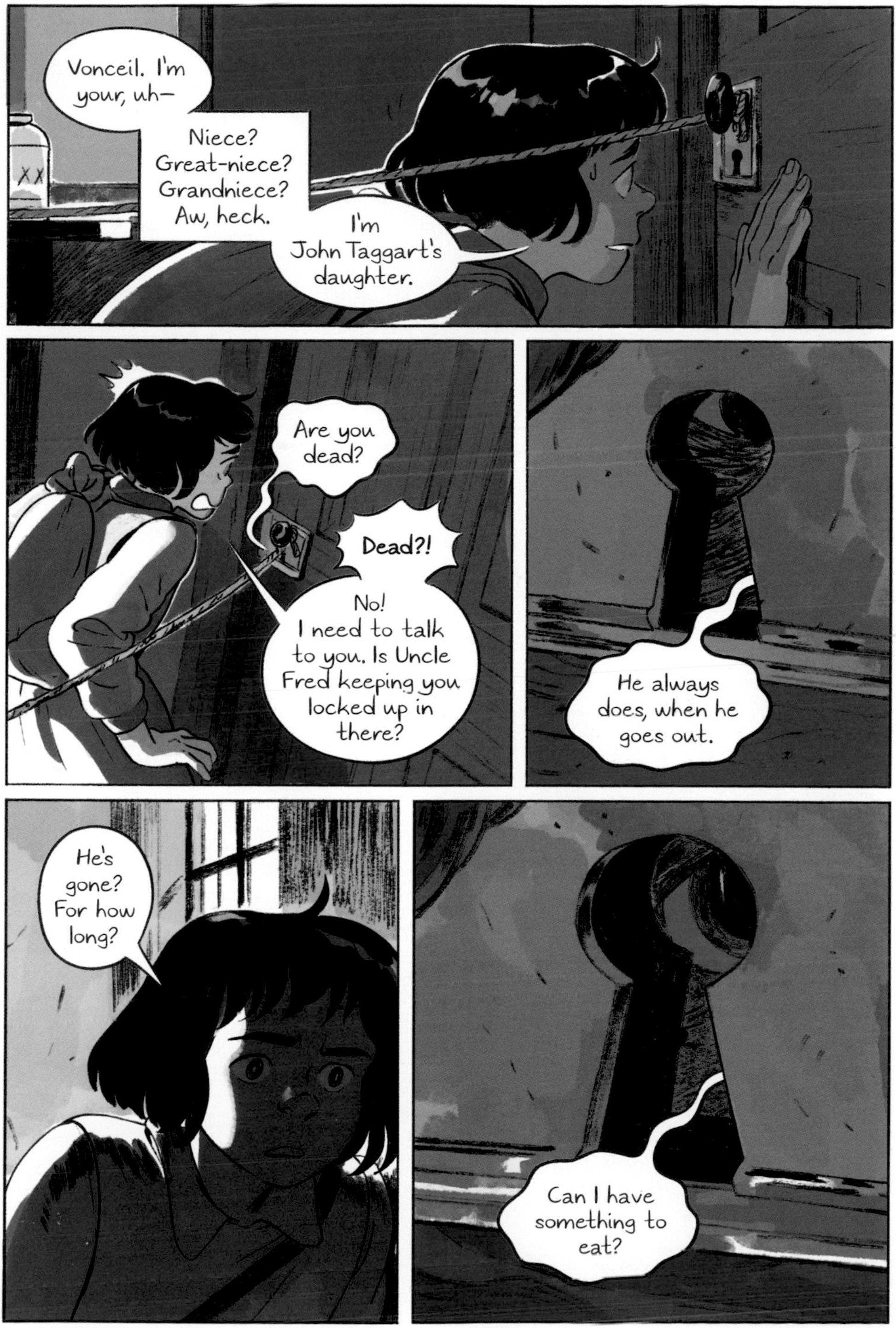
Vonceil. I'm your, uh—
Niece? Great-niece? Grandniece? Aw, heck.
I'm John Taggart's daughter.
Are you dead?
Dead?!
No! I need to talk to you. Is Uncle Fred keeping you locked up in there?
He always does, when he goes out.
He's gone? For how long?
Can I have something to eat?

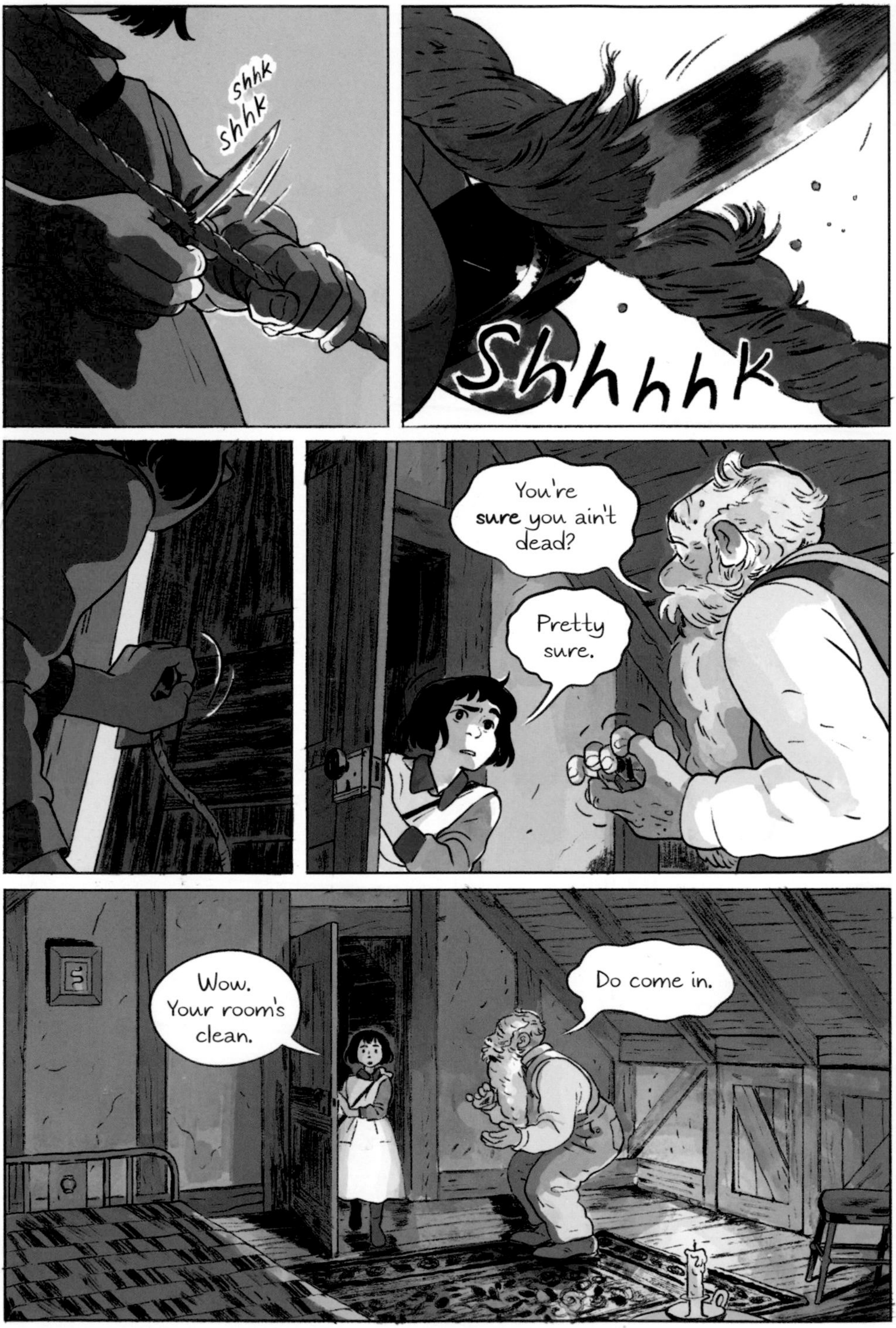
shhk
shhk
Shhhhk
You're **sure** you ain't dead?
Pretty sure.
Wow. Your room's clean.
Do come in.

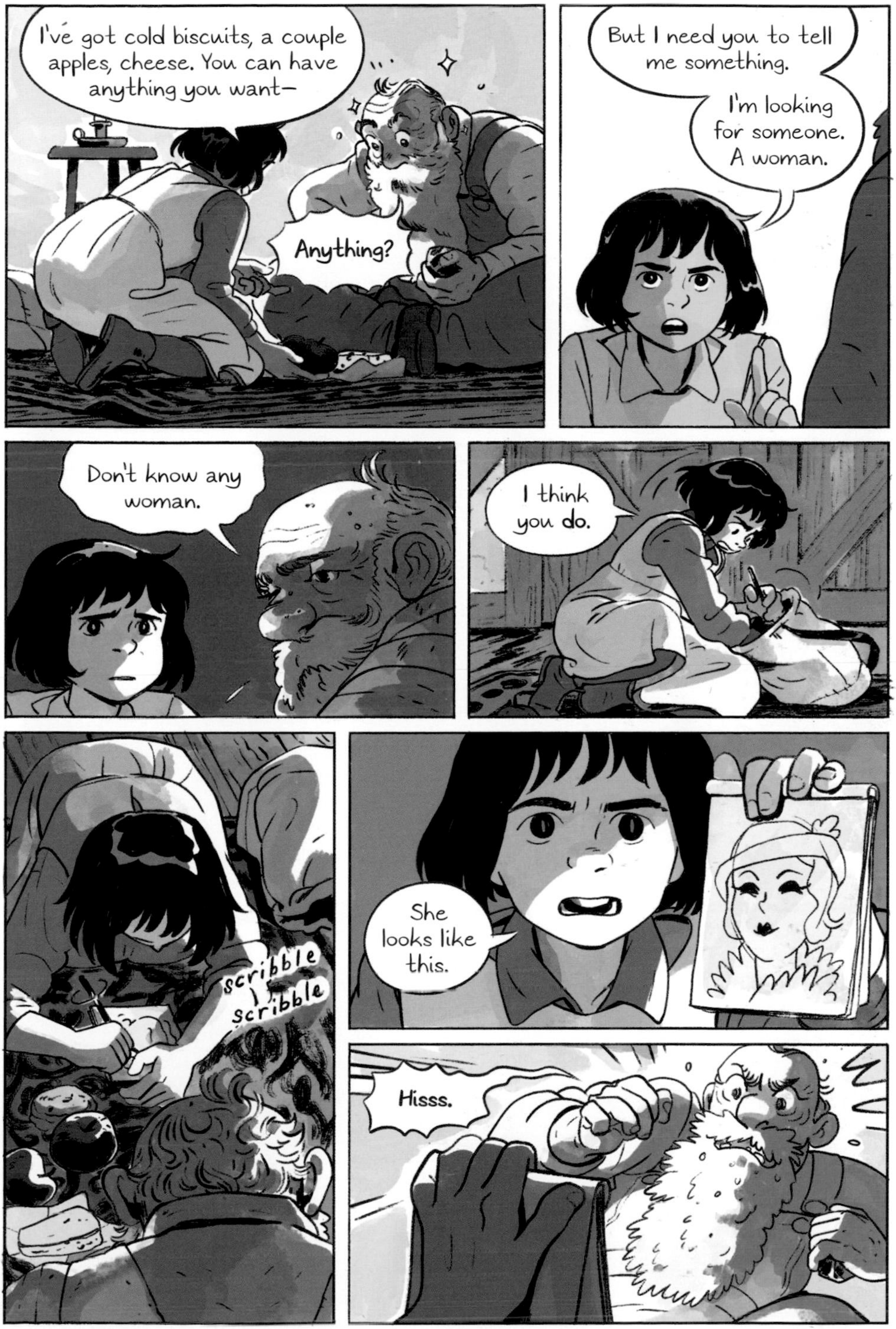
I've got cold biscuits, a couple apples, cheese. You can have anything you want—
Anything?
But I need you to tell me something.
I'm looking for someone. A woman.
Don't know any woman.
I think you do.
scribble scribble
She looks like this.
Hisss.

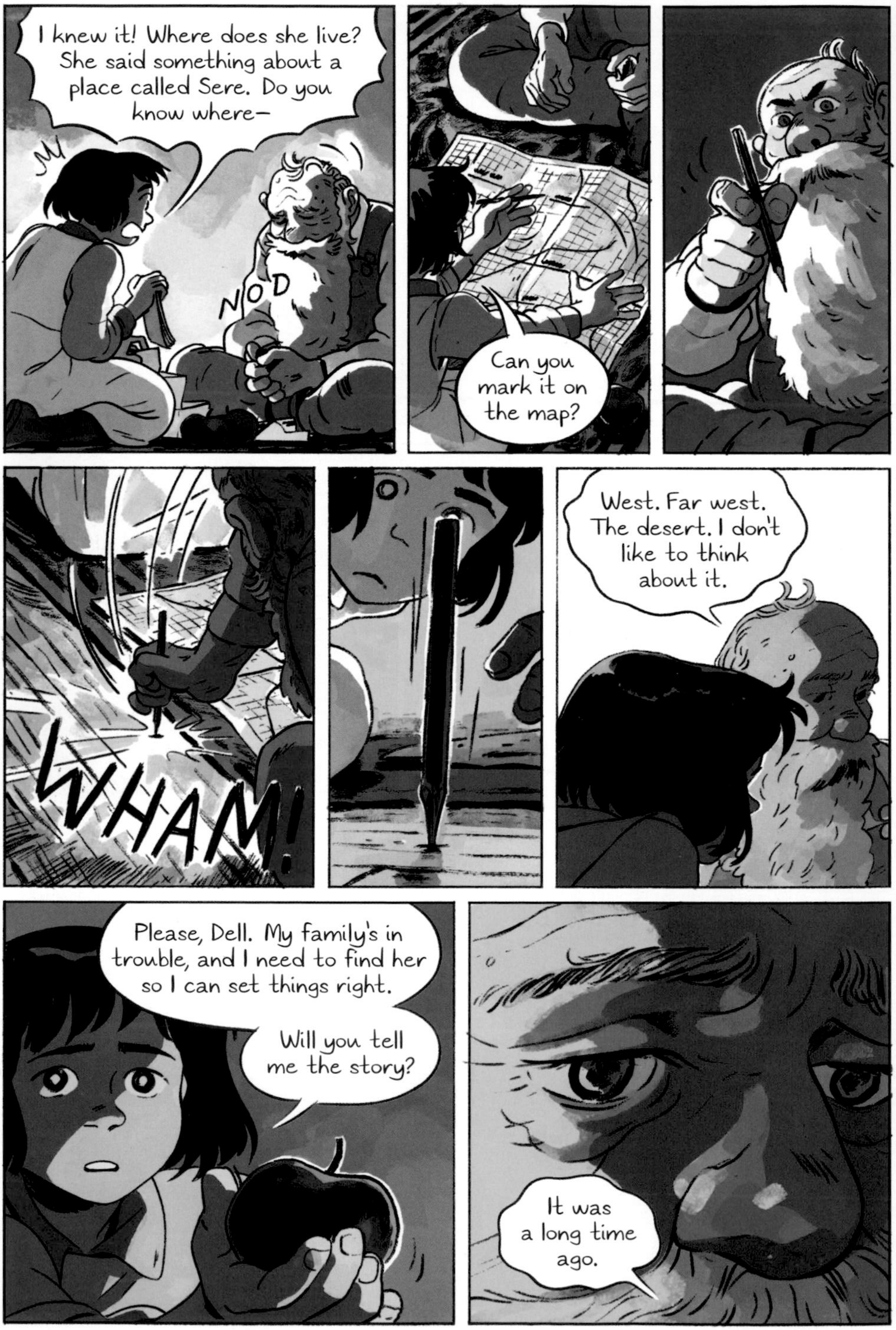

I knew it! Where does she live? She said something about a place called Sere. Do you know where—
NOD
Can you mark it on the map?
WHAM!
West. Far west. The desert. I don't like to think about it.
Please, Dell. My family's in trouble, and I need to find her so I can set things right.
Will you tell me the story?
It was a long time ago.

Chapter Six

The Lady of Sere

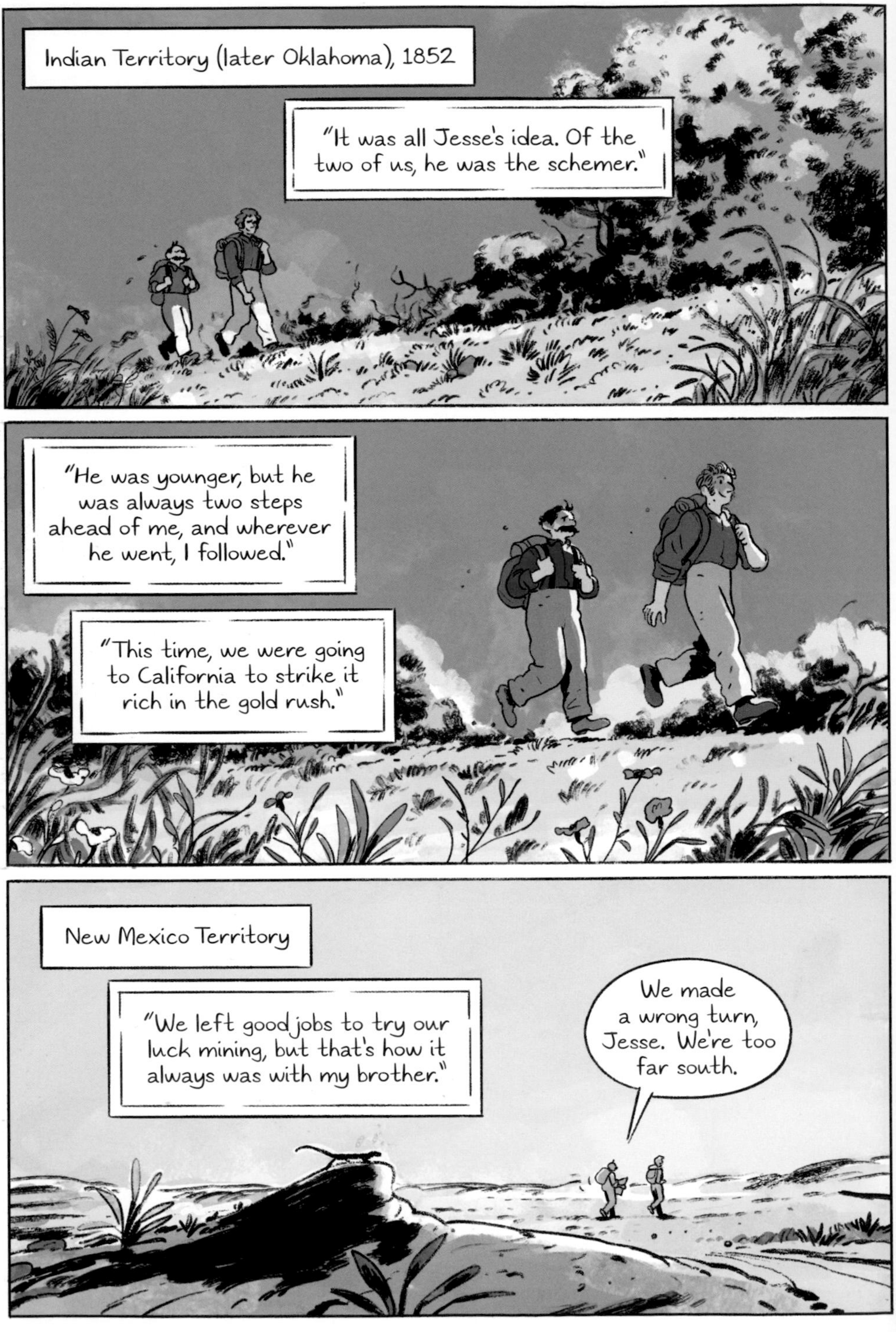
Indian Territory (later Oklahoma), 1852
"It was all Jesse's idea. Of the two of us, he was the schemer."
"He was younger, but he was always two steps ahead of me, and wherever he went, I followed."
"This time, we were going to California to strike it rich in the gold rush."
New Mexico Territory
"We left good jobs to try our luck mining, but that's how it always was with my brother."
We made a wrong turn, Jesse. We're too far south.

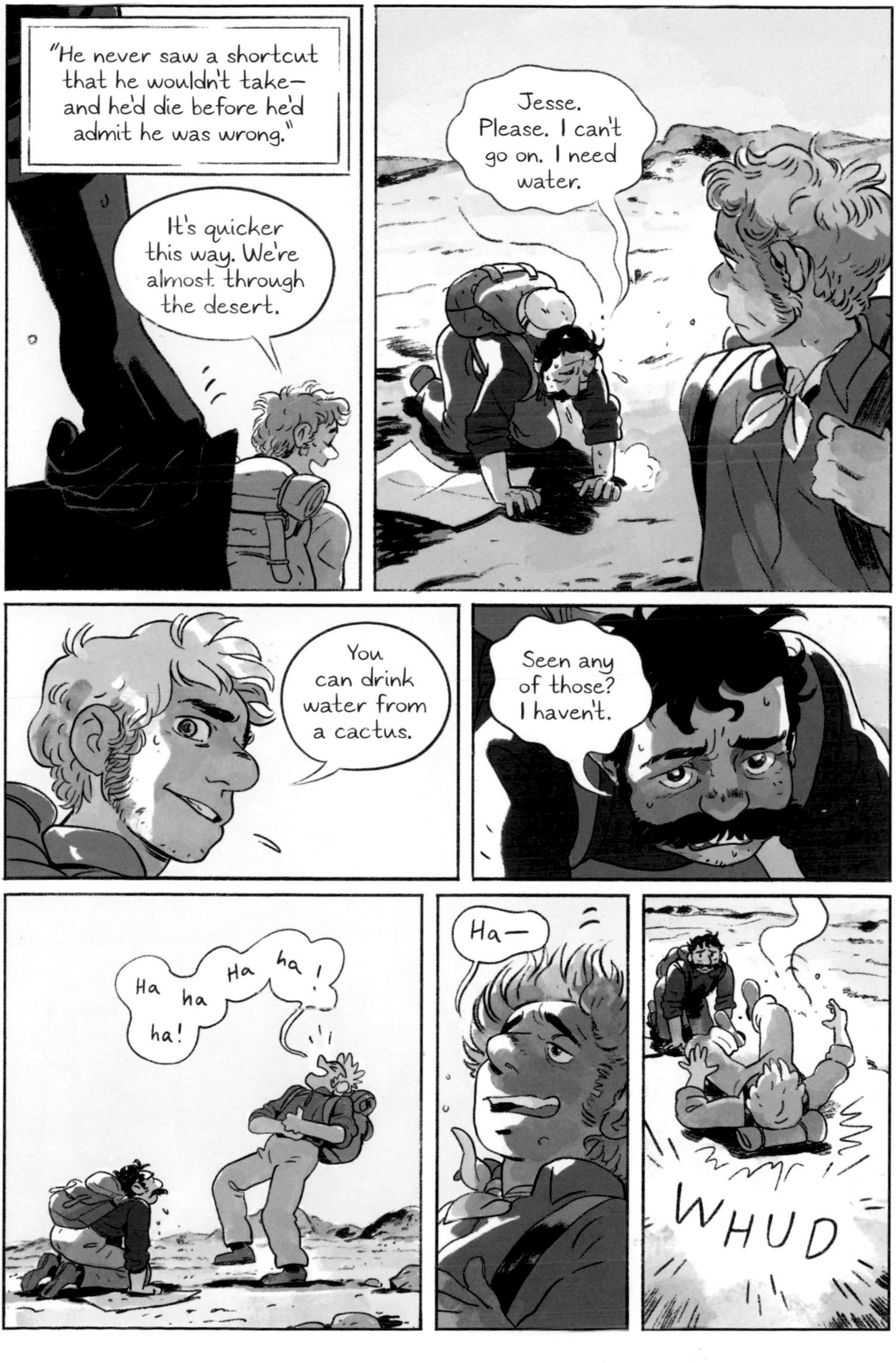
"He never saw a shortcut that he wouldn't take—and he'd die before he'd admit he was wrong."
It's quicker this way. We're almost through the desert.
Jesse. Please. I can't go on. I need water.
You can drink water from a cactus.
Seen any of those? I haven't.
Ha ha Ha ha! ha!
Ha—
WHUD

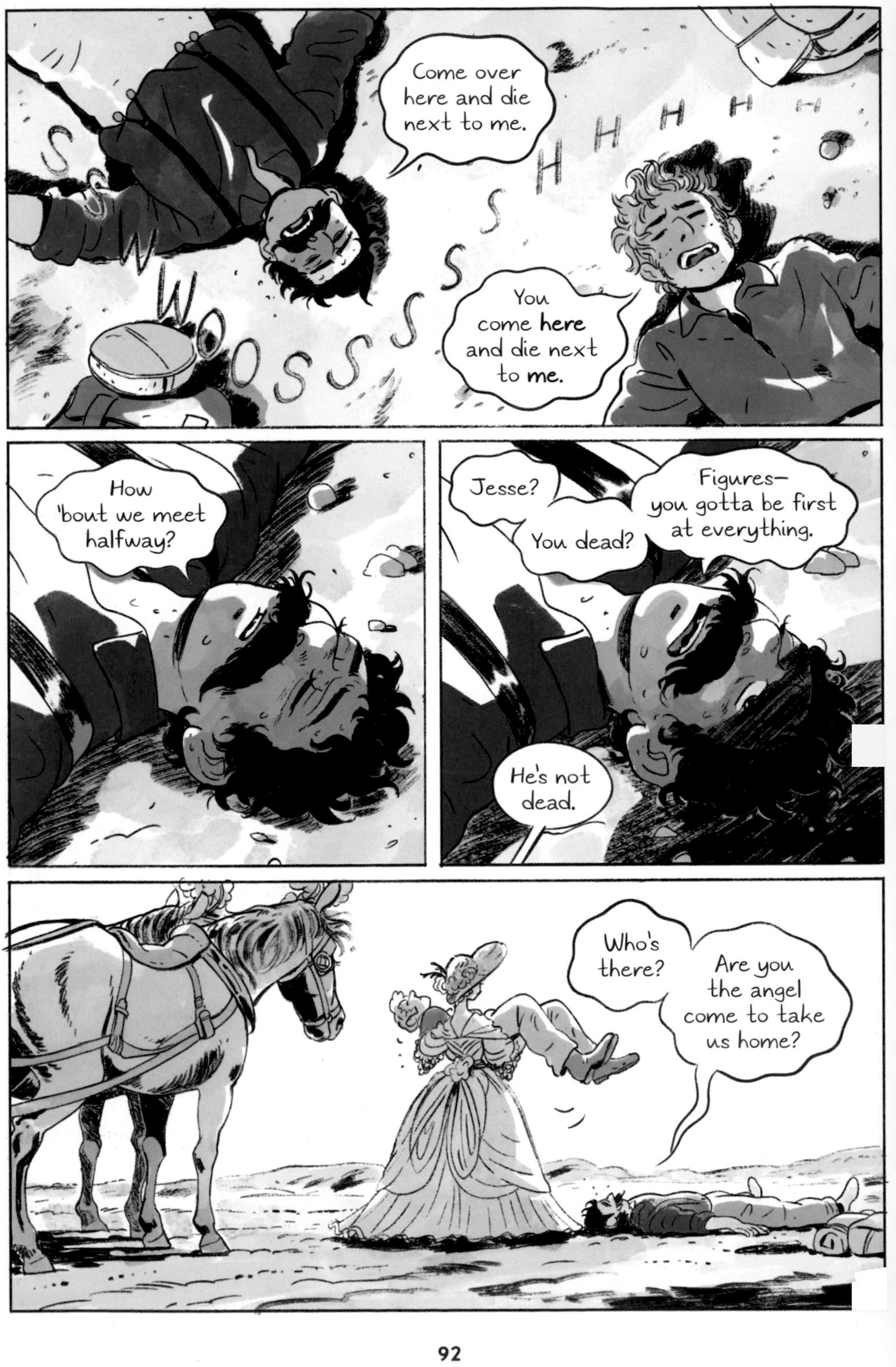
Come over here and die next to me.
SSWWOOSSSSSHHHHHH
You come **here** and die next to **me.**
How 'bout we meet halfway?
Jesse?
You dead?
Figures— you gotta be first at everything.
He's not dead.
Who's there?
Are you the angel come to take us home?

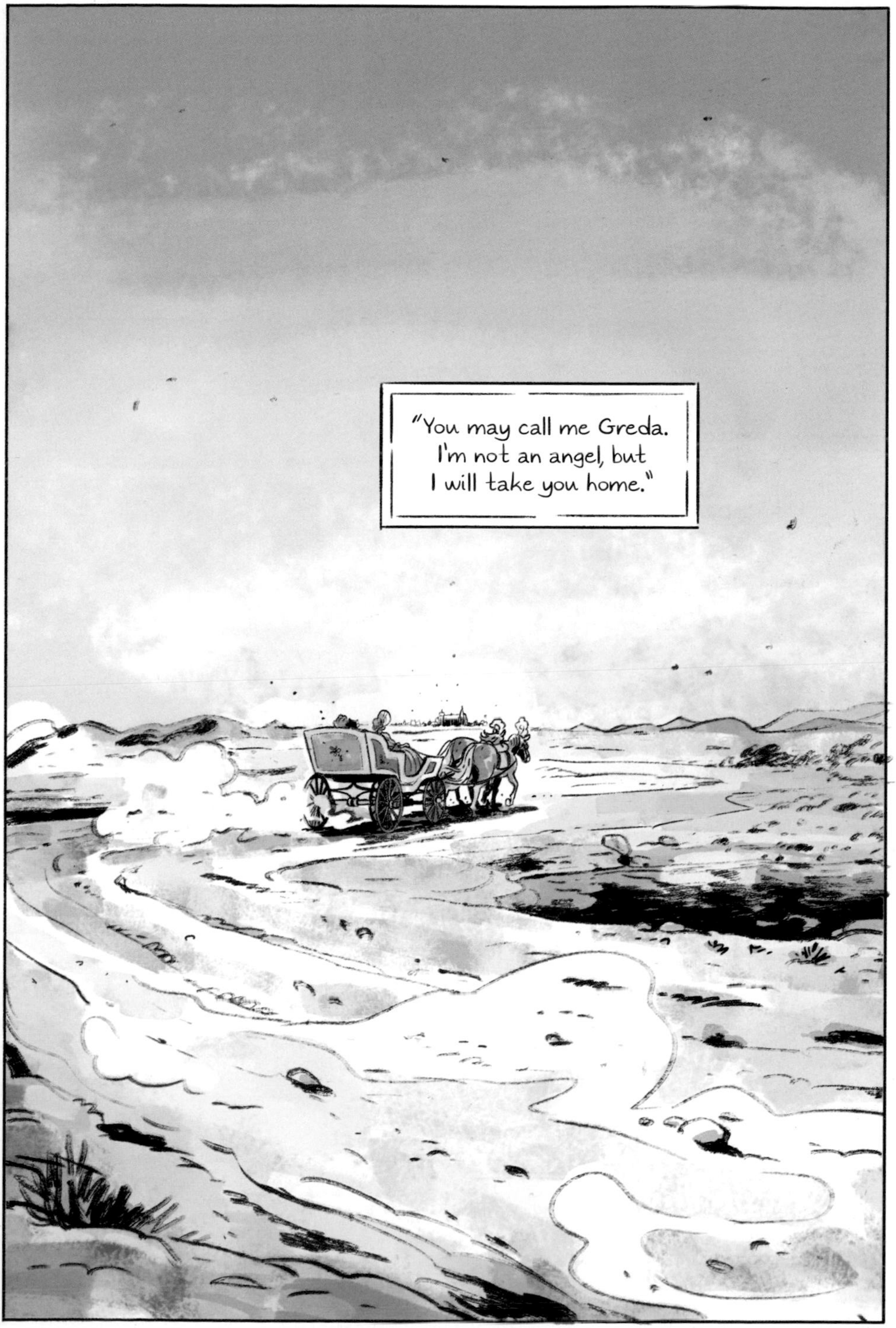
"You may call me Greda. I'm not an angel, but I will take you home."

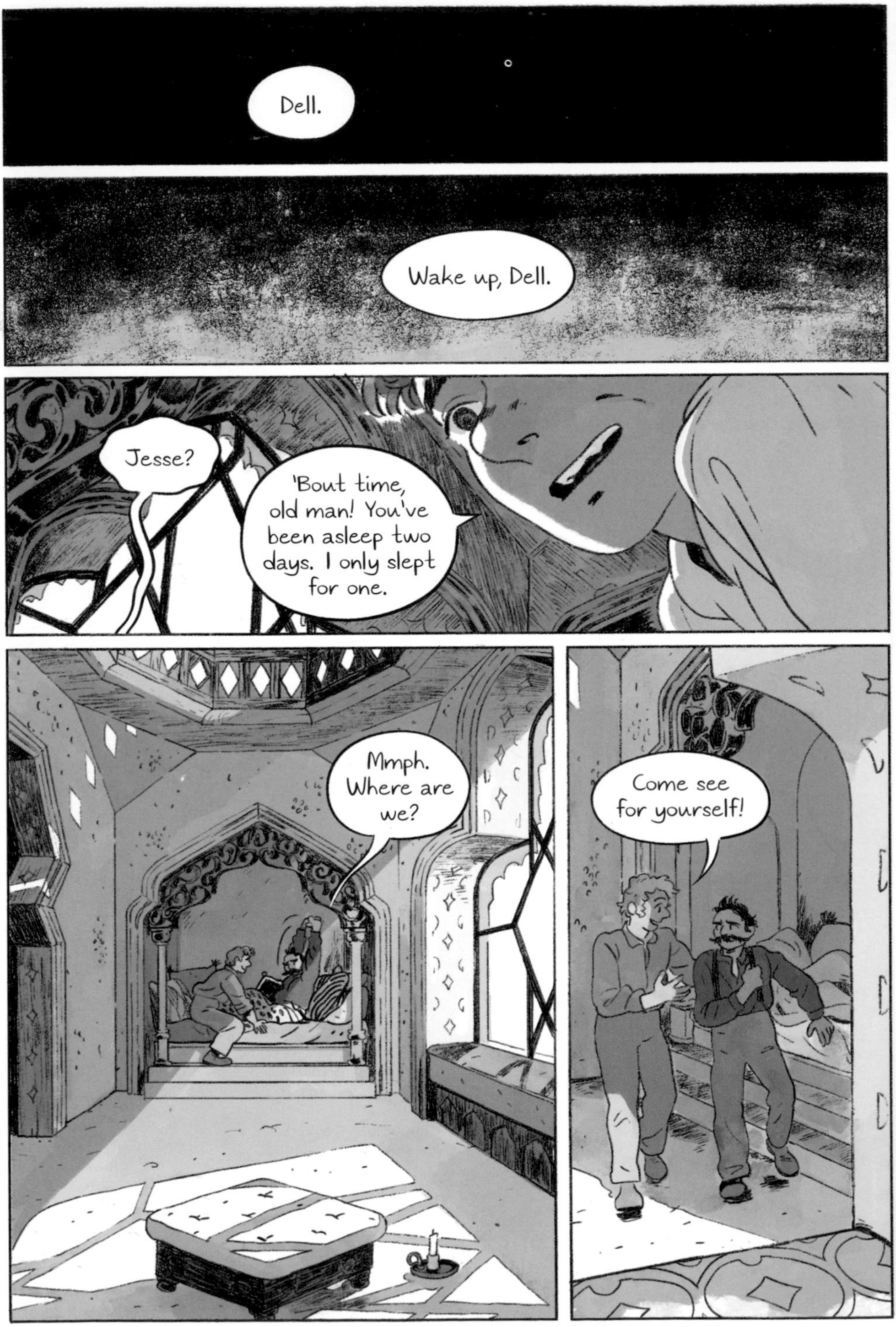
Dell.
Wake up, Dell.
Jesse?
'Bout time, old man! You've been asleep two days. I only slept for one.
Mmph. Where are we?
Come see for yourself!

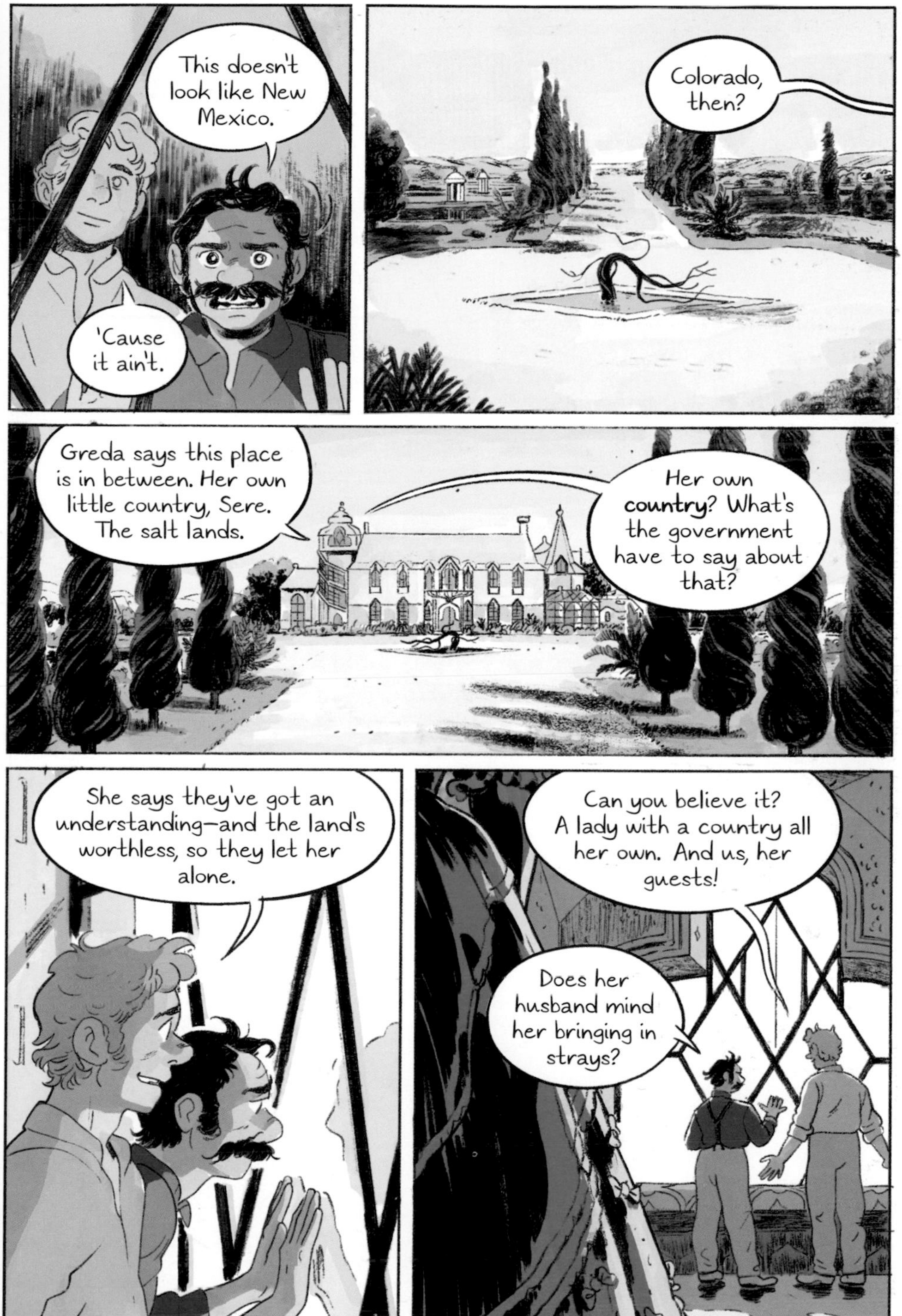
This doesn't look like New Mexico.
'Cause it ain't.
Colorado, then?
Greda says this place is in between. Her own little country, Sere. The salt lands.
Her own **country**? What's the government have to say about that?
She says they've got an understanding—and the land's worthless, so they let her alone.
Can you believe it? A lady with a country all her own. And us, her guests!
Does her husband mind her bringing in strays?

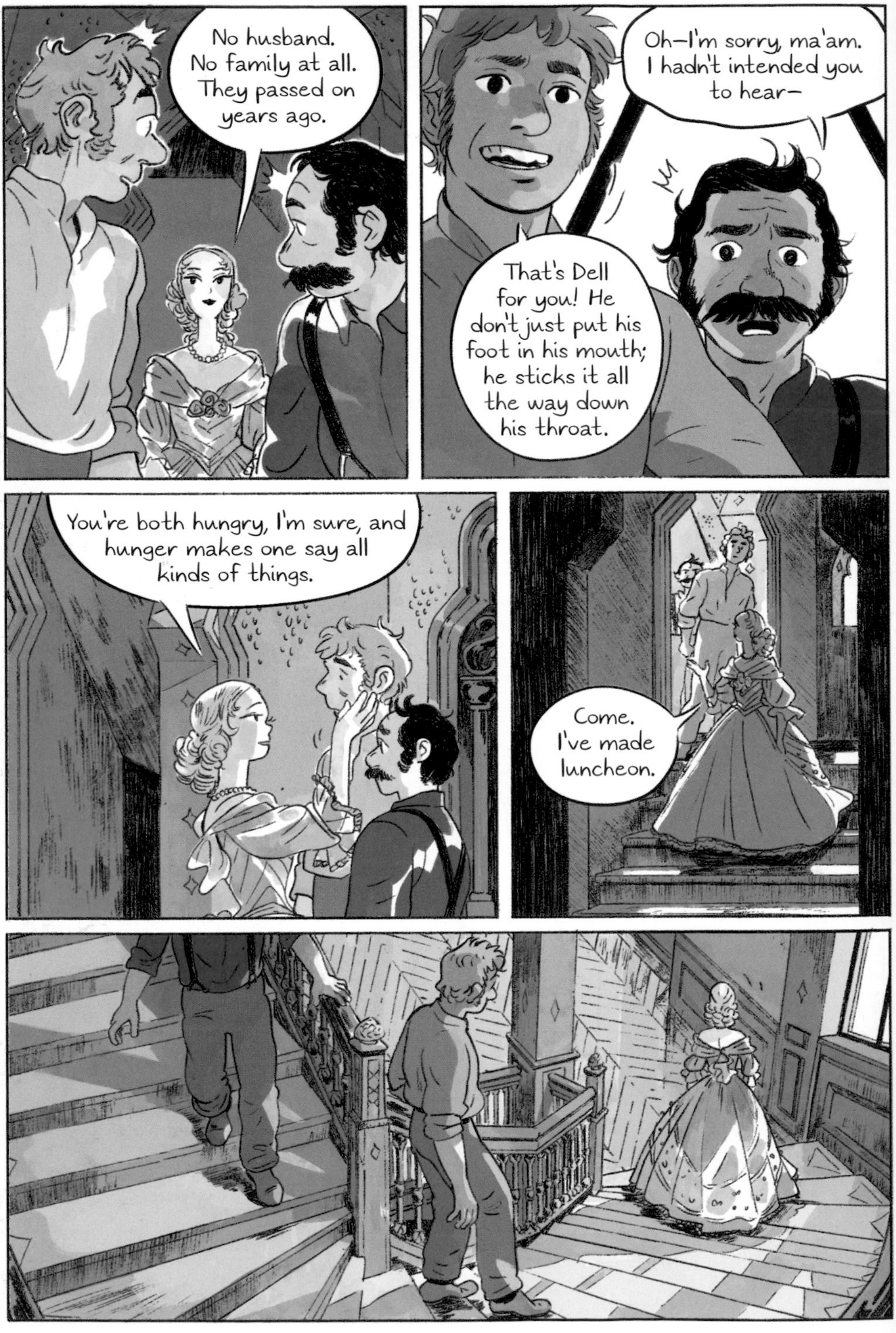
No husband. No family at all. They passed on years ago.
Oh—I'm sorry, ma'am. I hadn't intended you to hear—
That's Dell for you! He don't just put his foot in his mouth; he sticks it all the way down his throat.
You're both hungry, I'm sure, and hunger makes one say all kinds of things.
Come. I've made luncheon.

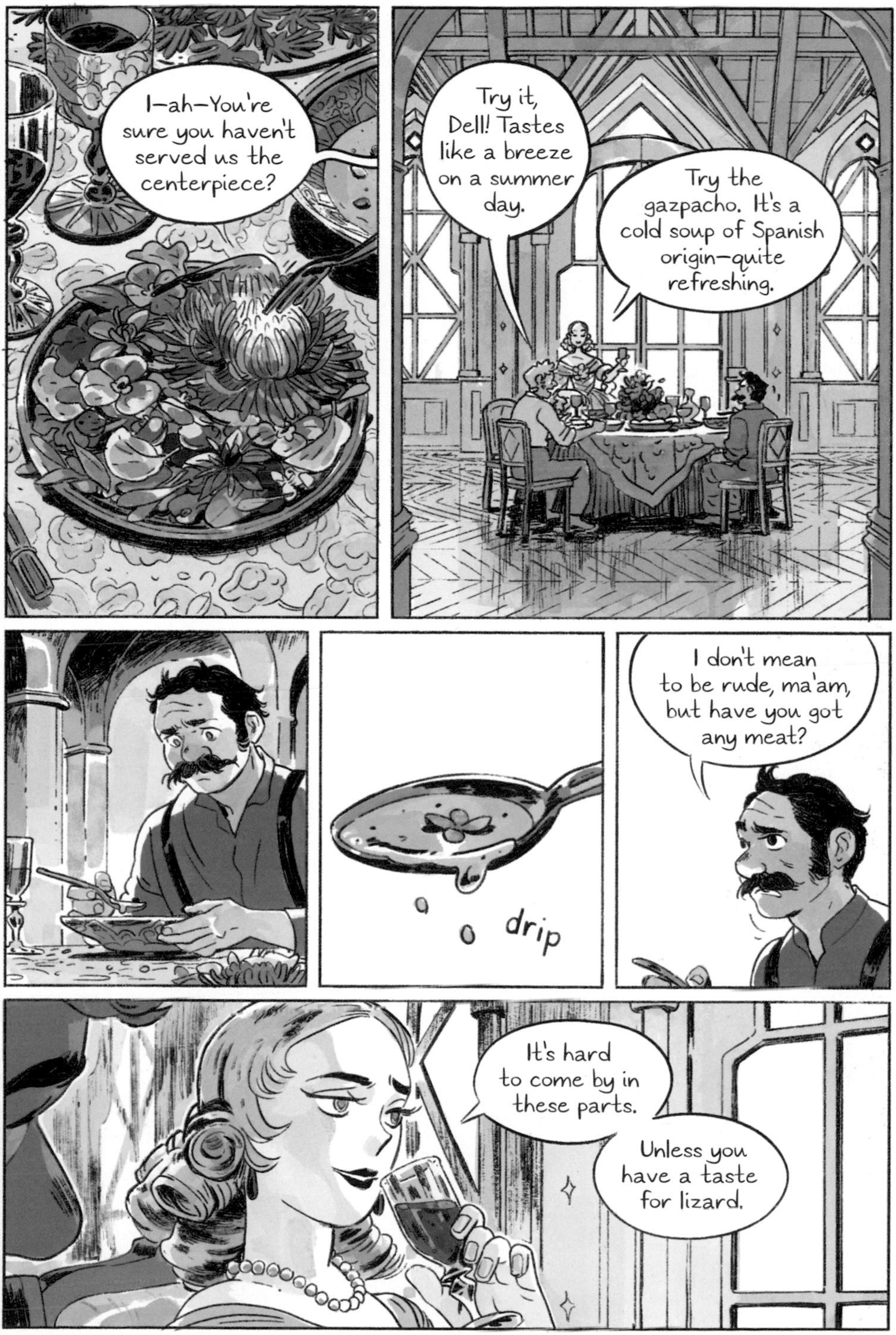
I—ah—You're sure you haven't served us the centerpiece?
Try it, Dell! Tastes like a breeze on a summer day.
Try the gazpacho. It's a cold soup of Spanish origin—quite refreshing.
drip
I don't mean to be rude, ma'am, but have you got any meat?
It's hard to come by in these parts.
Unless you have a taste for lizard.

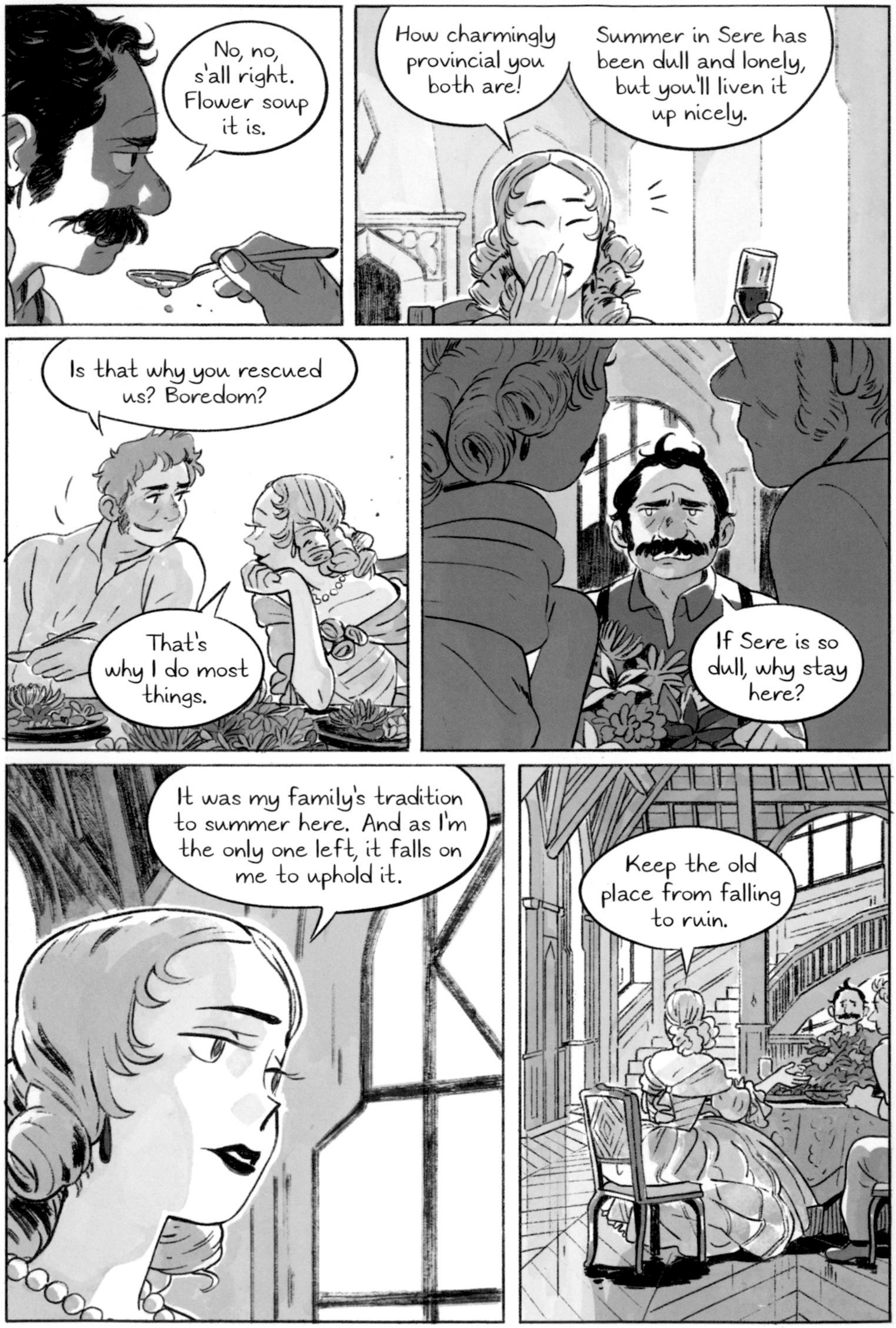

No, no, s'all right. Flower soup it is.
How charmingly provincial you both are!
Summer in Sere has been dull and lonely, but you'll liven it up nicely.
Is that why you rescued us? Boredom?
That's why I do most things.
If Sere is so dull, why stay here?
It was my family's tradition to summer here. And as I'm the only one left, it falls on me to uphold it.
Keep the old place from falling to ruin.

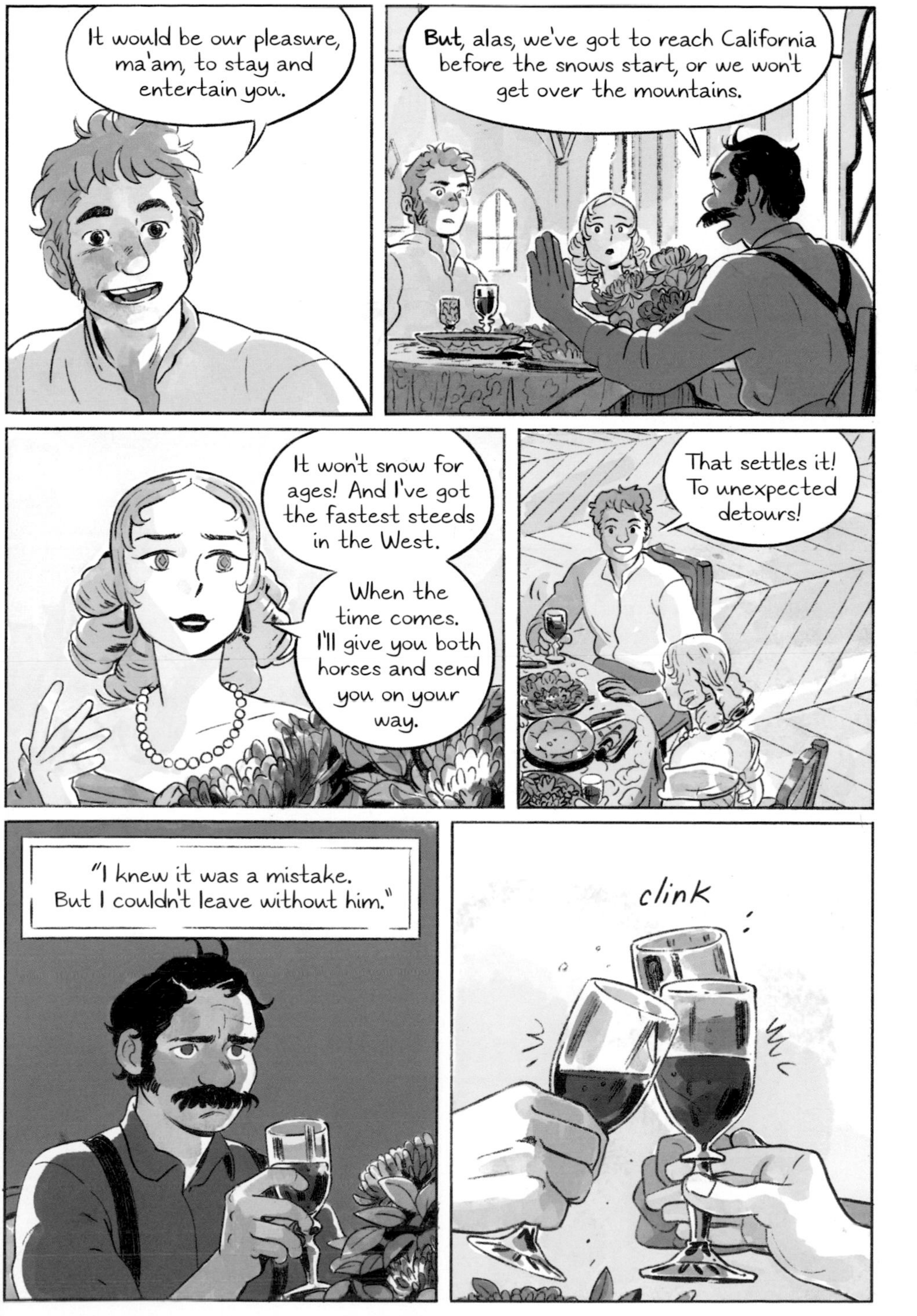
It would be our pleasure, ma'am, to stay and entertain you.
But, alas, we've got to reach California before the snows start, or we won't get over the mountains.
It won't snow for ages! And I've got the fastest steeds in the West.
When the time comes. I'll give you both horses and send you on your way.
That settles it! To unexpected detours!
"I knew it was a mistake. But I couldn't leave without him."
clink

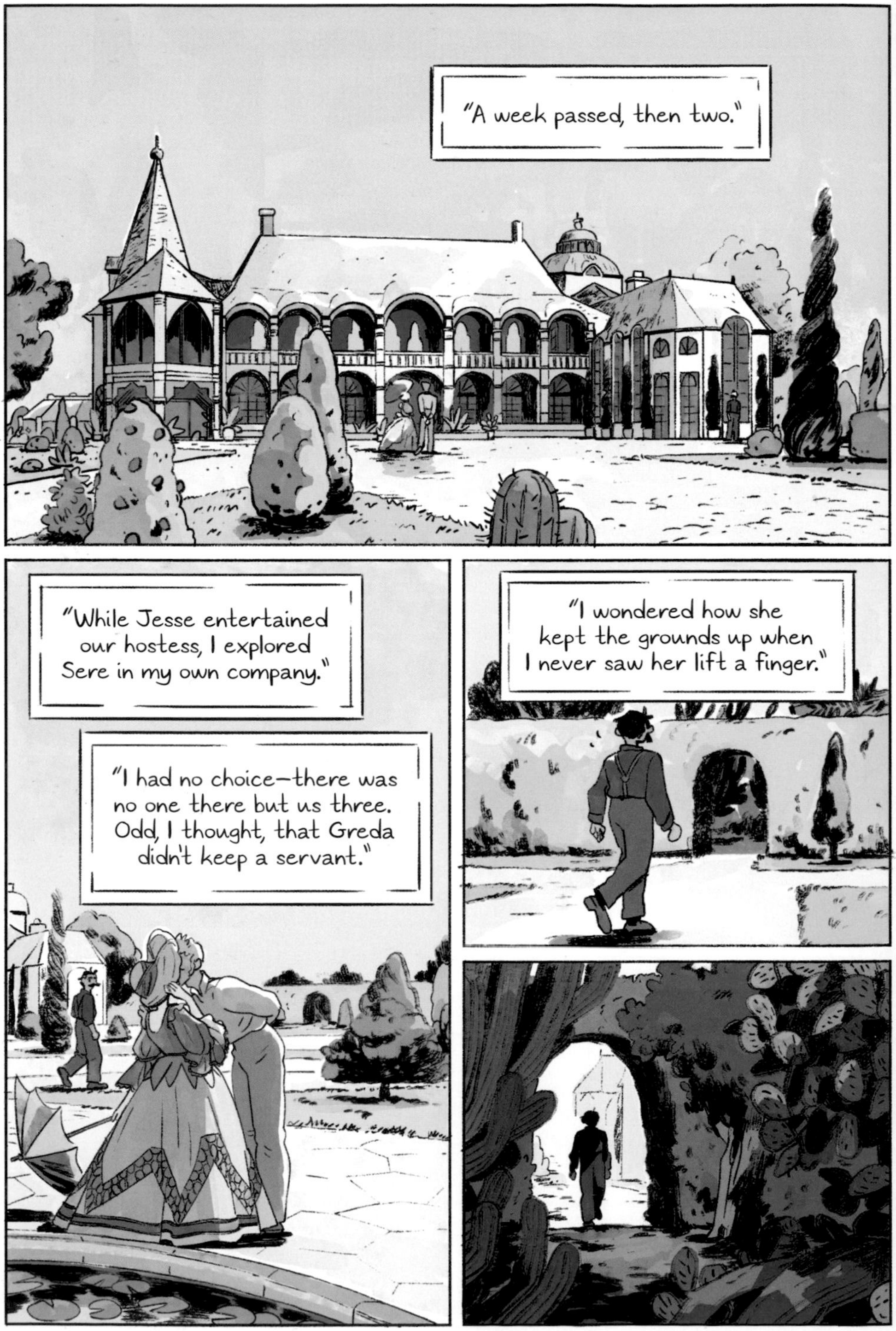
"A week passed, then two."
"While Jesse entertained our hostess, I explored Sere in my own company."
"I had no choice—there was no one there but us three. Odd, I thought, that Greda didn't keep a servant."
"I wondered how she kept the grounds up when I never saw her lift a finger."

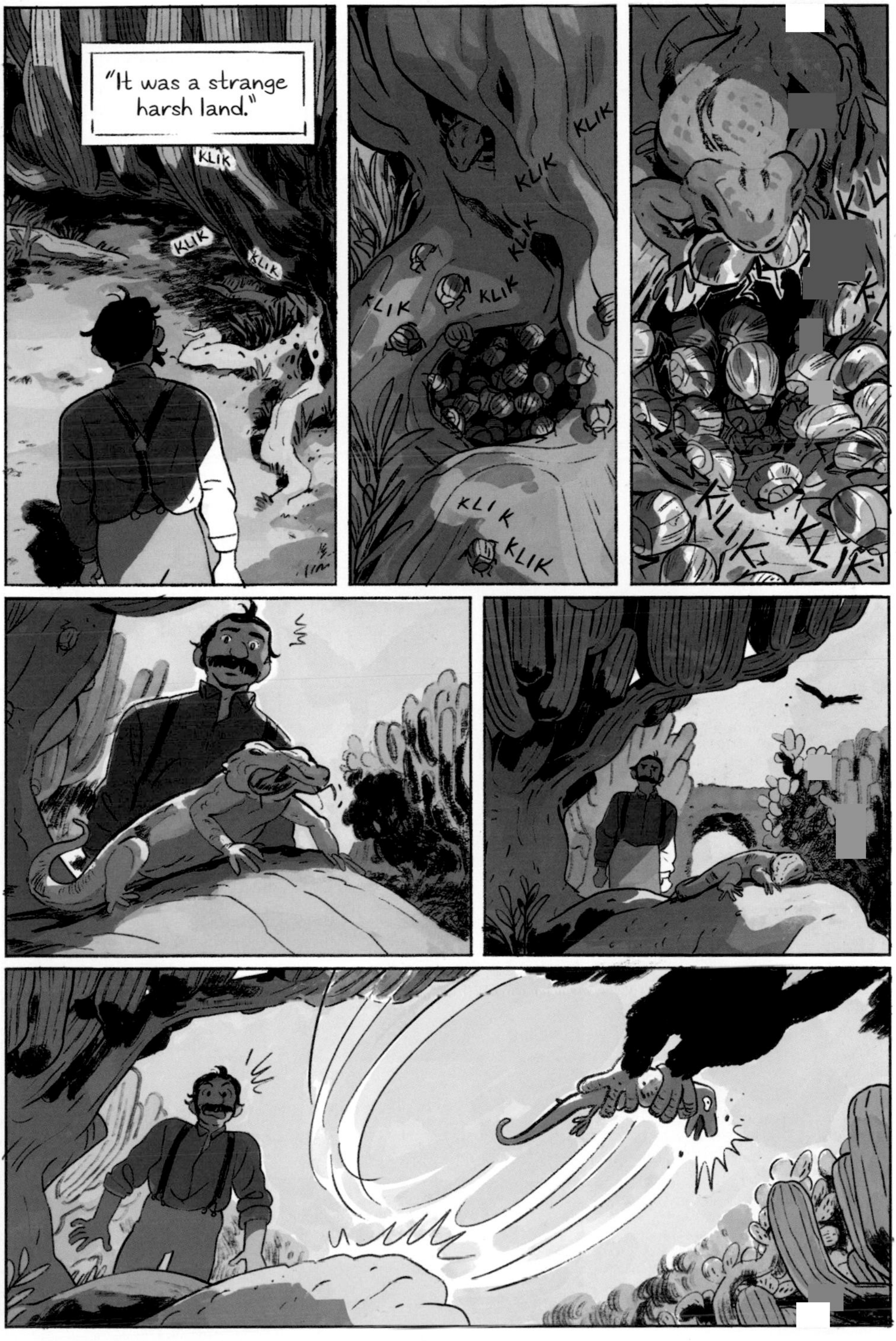
"It was a strange harsh land."
KLIK
KLIK
KLIK
KLIK
KLIK
KLIK
KLIK
KLIK
KLIK
KLIK

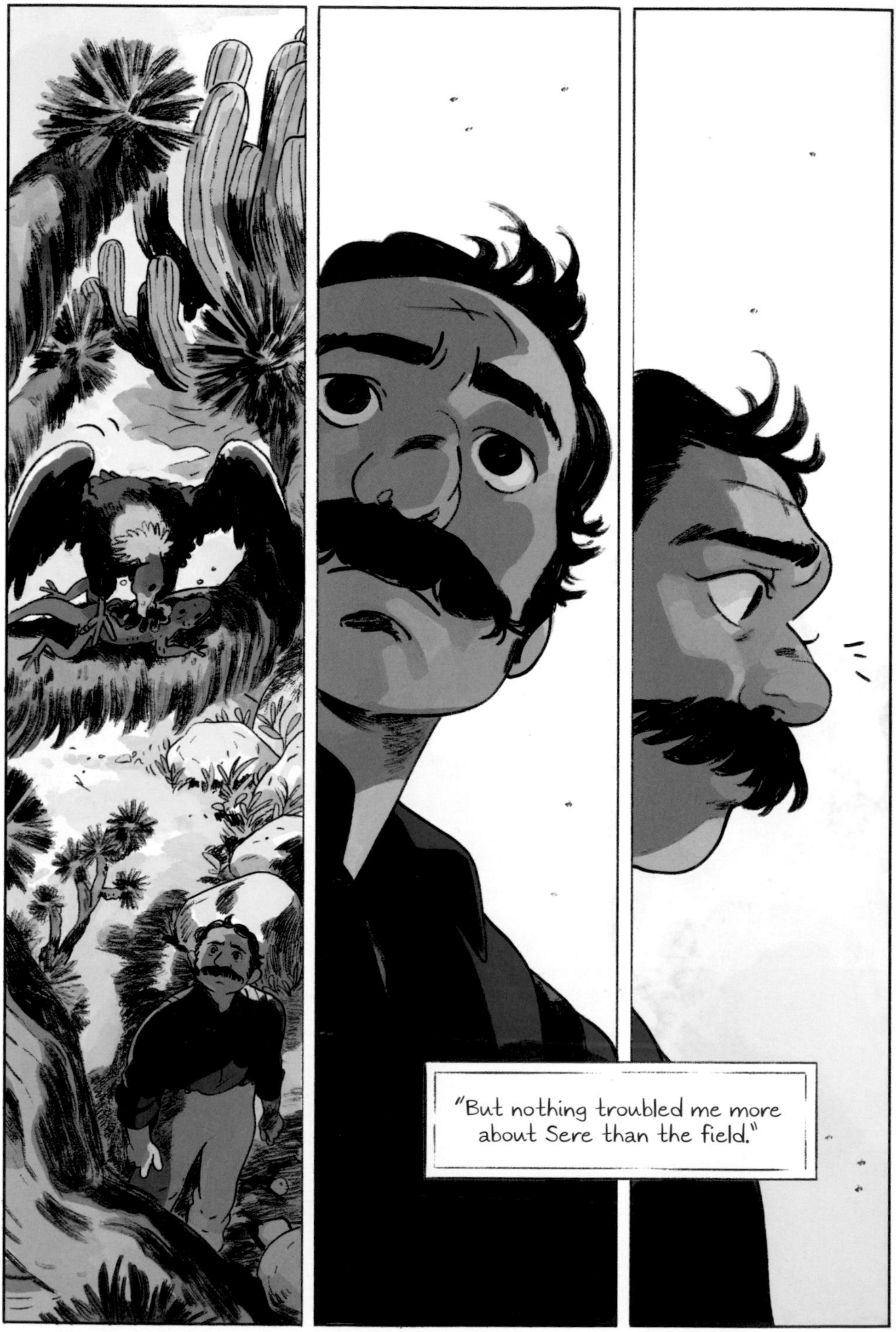
"But nothing troubled me more about Sere than the field."

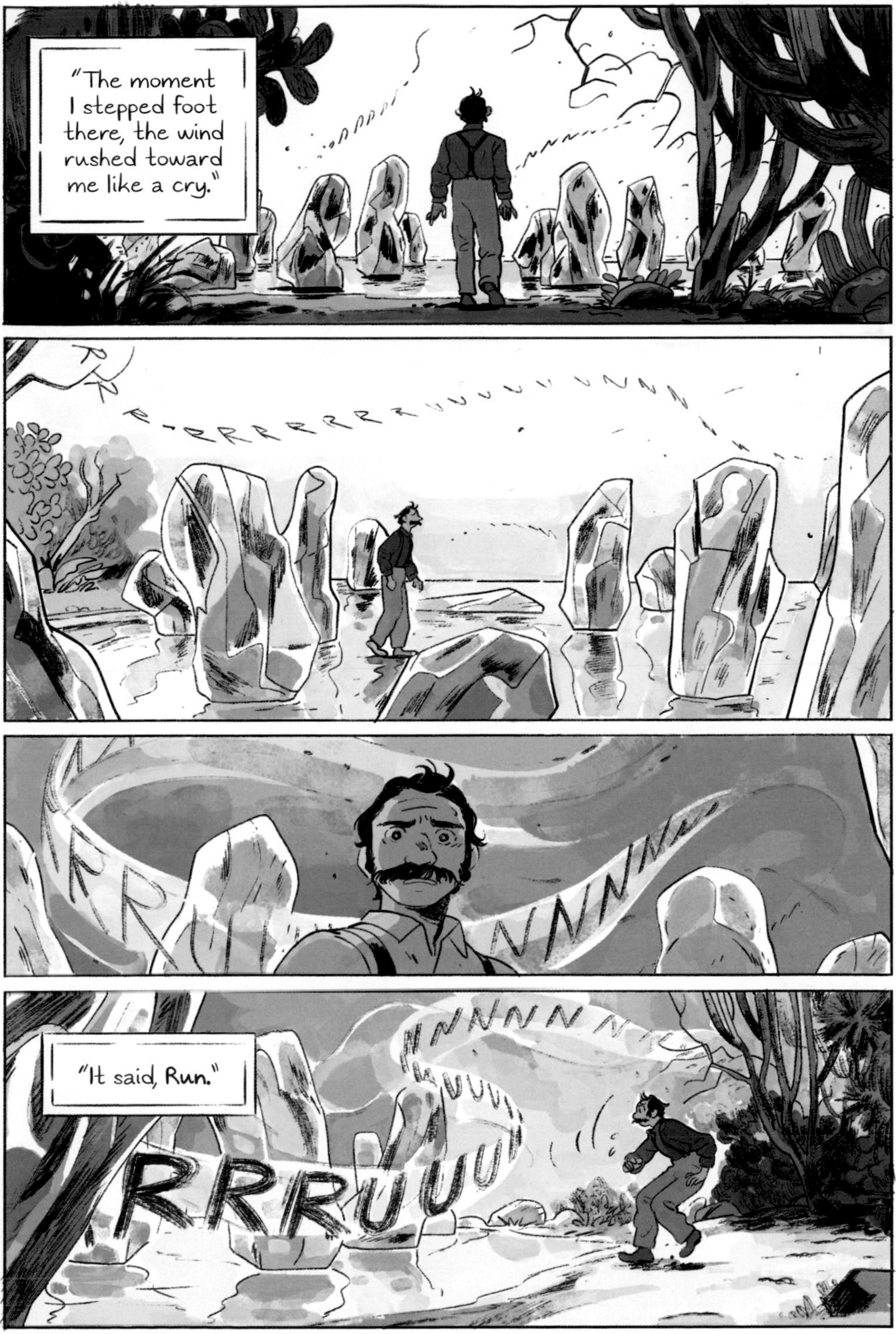
"The moment I stepped foot there, the wind rushed toward me like a cry."
"It said, **Run.**"
RRRU

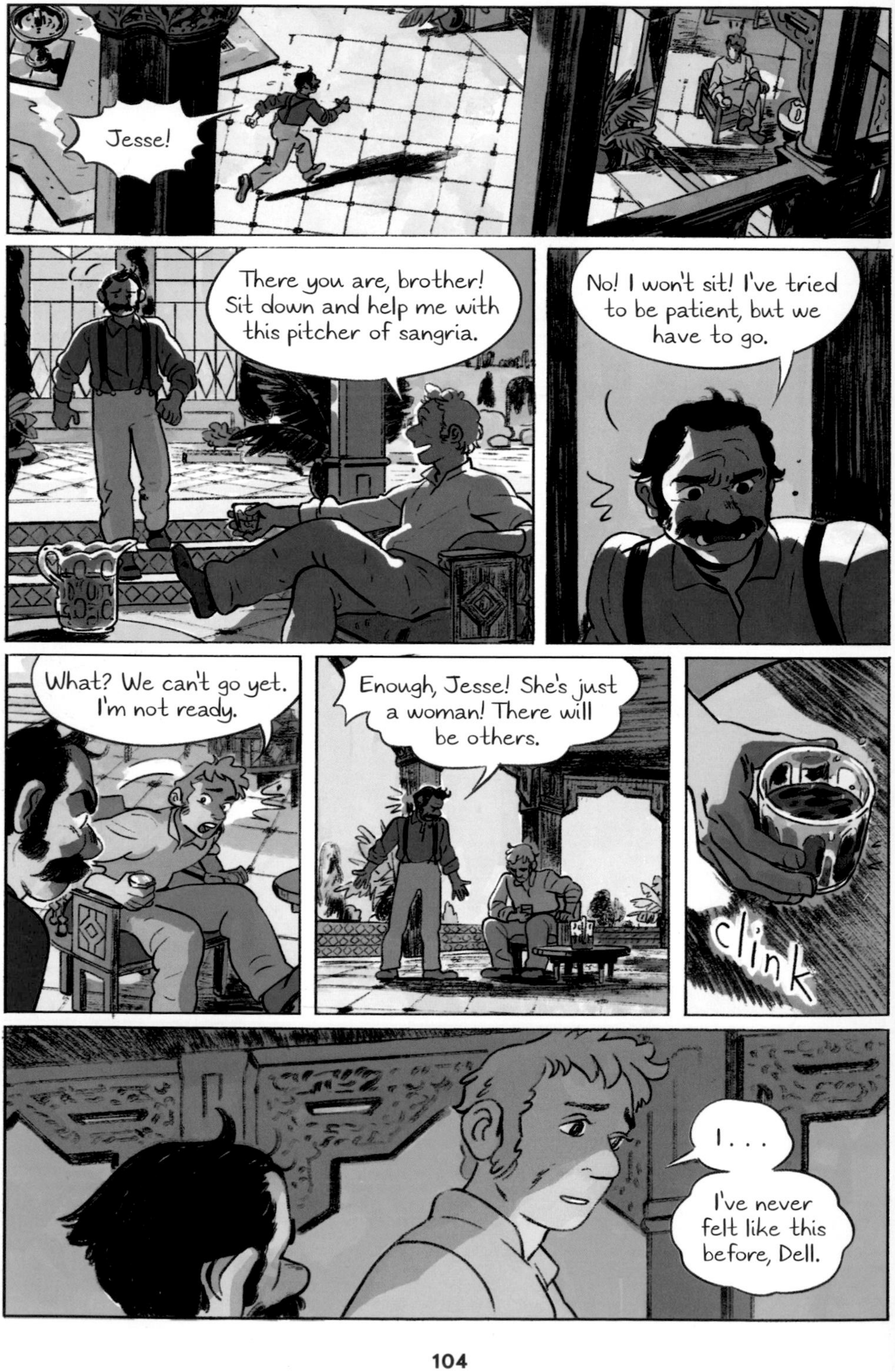
Jesse!
There you are, brother! Sit down and help me with this pitcher of sangria.
No! I won't sit! I've tried to be patient, but we have to go.
What? We can't go yet. I'm not ready.
Enough, Jesse! She's just a woman! There will be others.
clink
I . . .
I've never felt like this before, Dell.

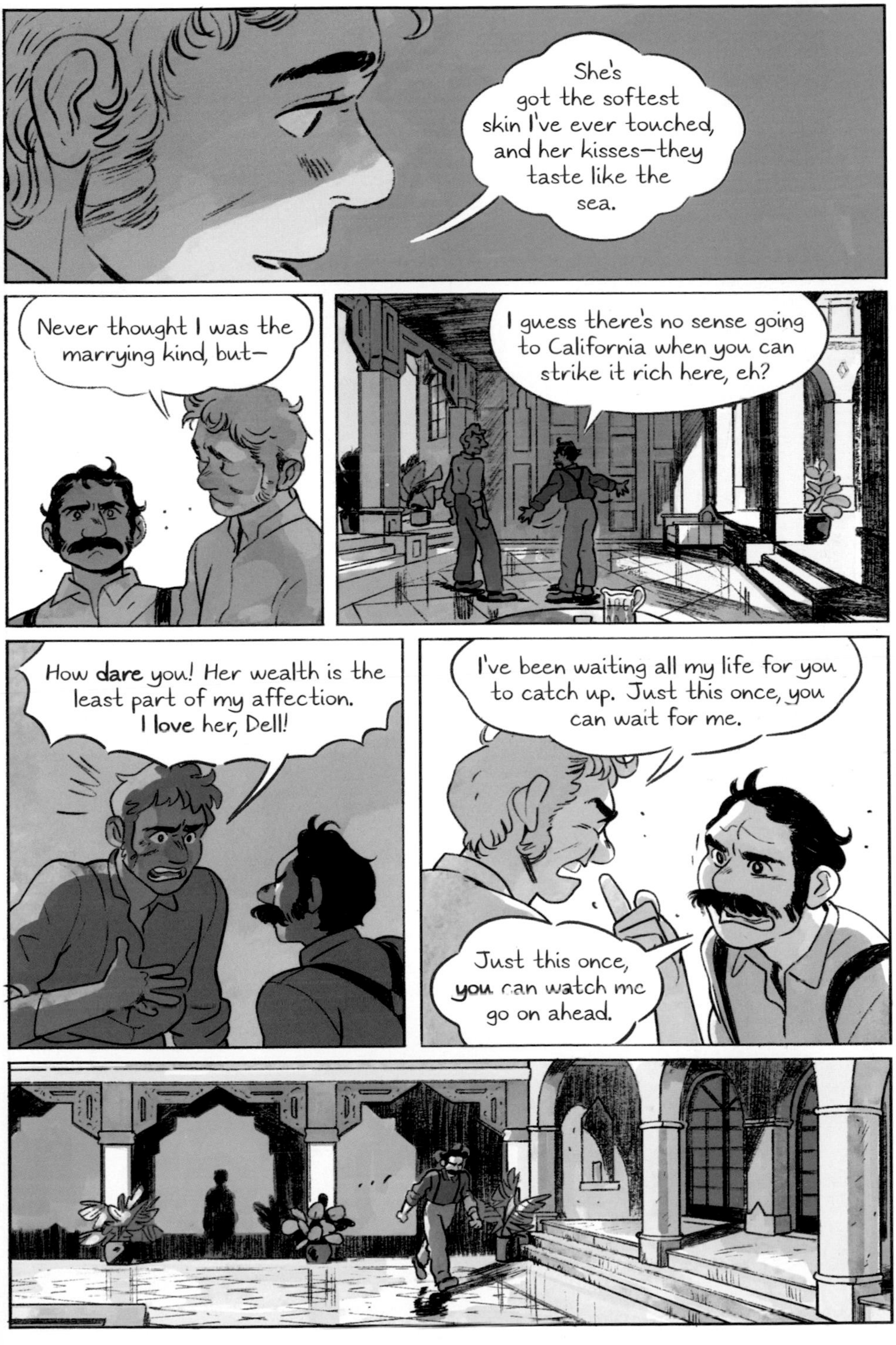
She's got the softest skin I've ever touched, and her kisses—they taste like the sea.
Never thought I was the marrying kind, but—
I guess there's no sense going to California when you can strike it rich here, eh?
How **dare** you! Her wealth is the least part of my affection. I **love** her, Dell!
I've been waiting all my life for you to catch up. Just this once, you can wait for me.
Just this once, **you** can watch me go on ahead.

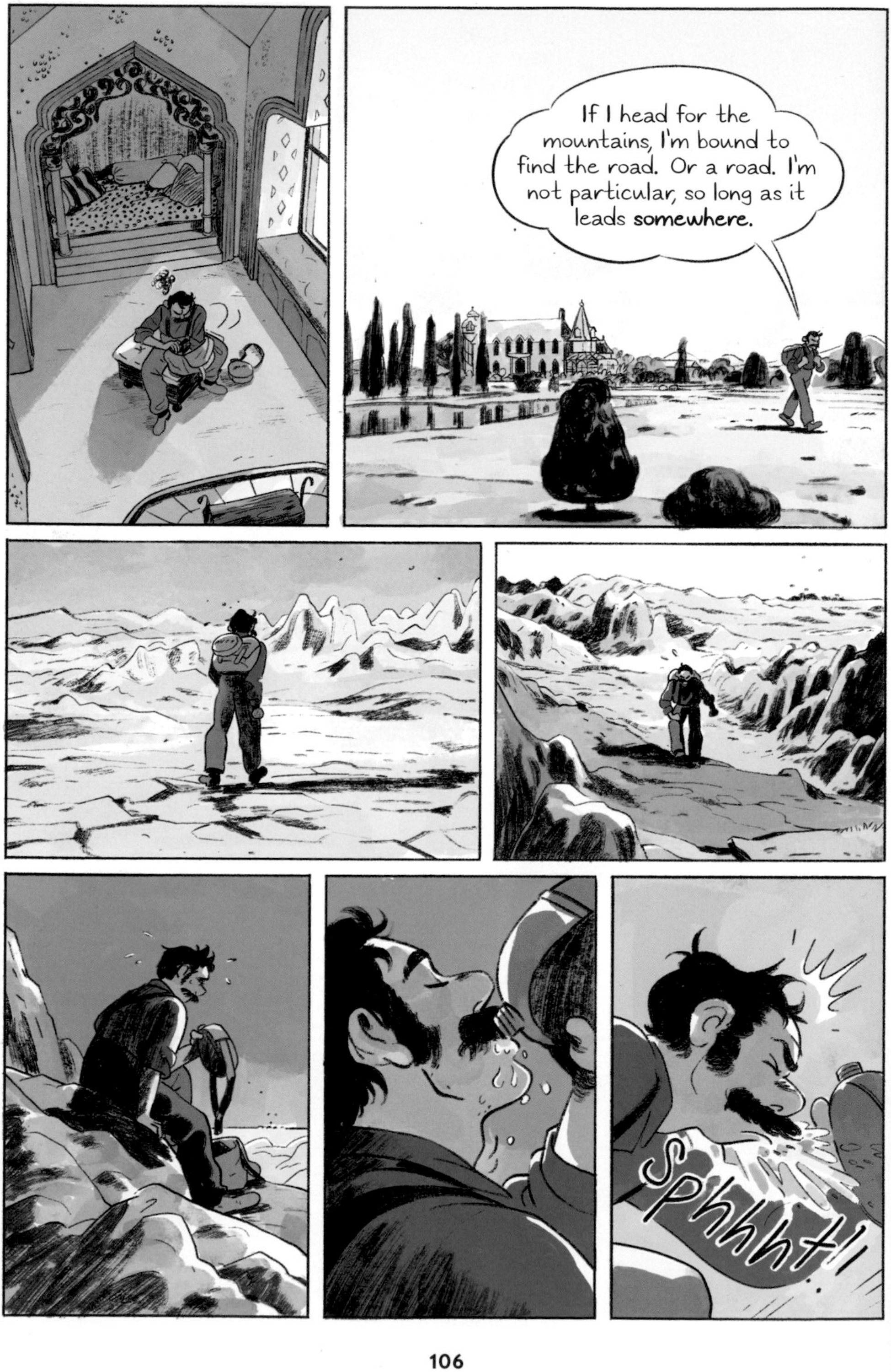
If I head for the mountains, I'm bound to find the road. Or a road. I'm not particular, so long as it leads **somewhere.**
Sphhht!

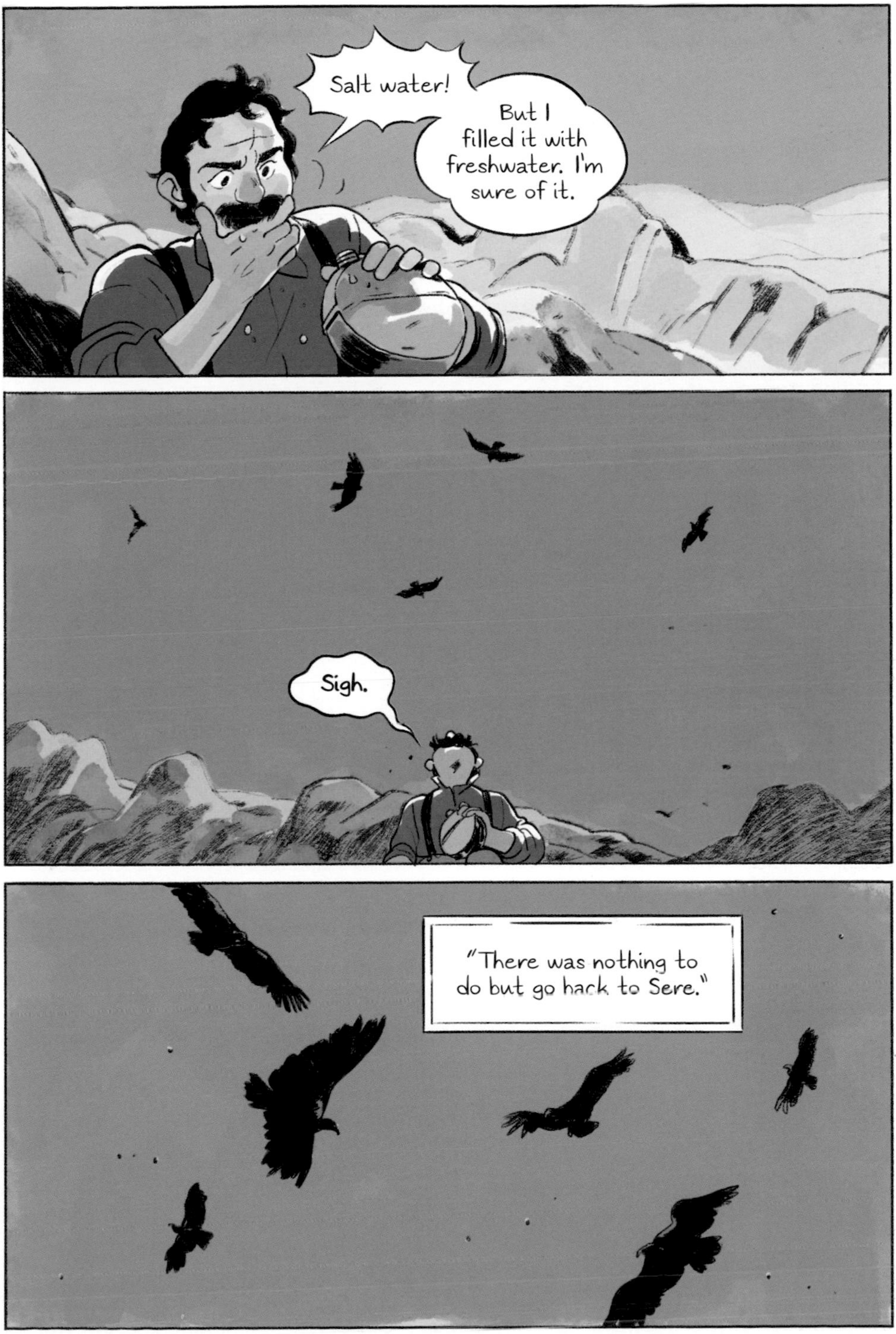
Salt water!
But I filled it with freshwater. I'm sure of it.
Sigh.
"There was nothing to do but go back to Sere."

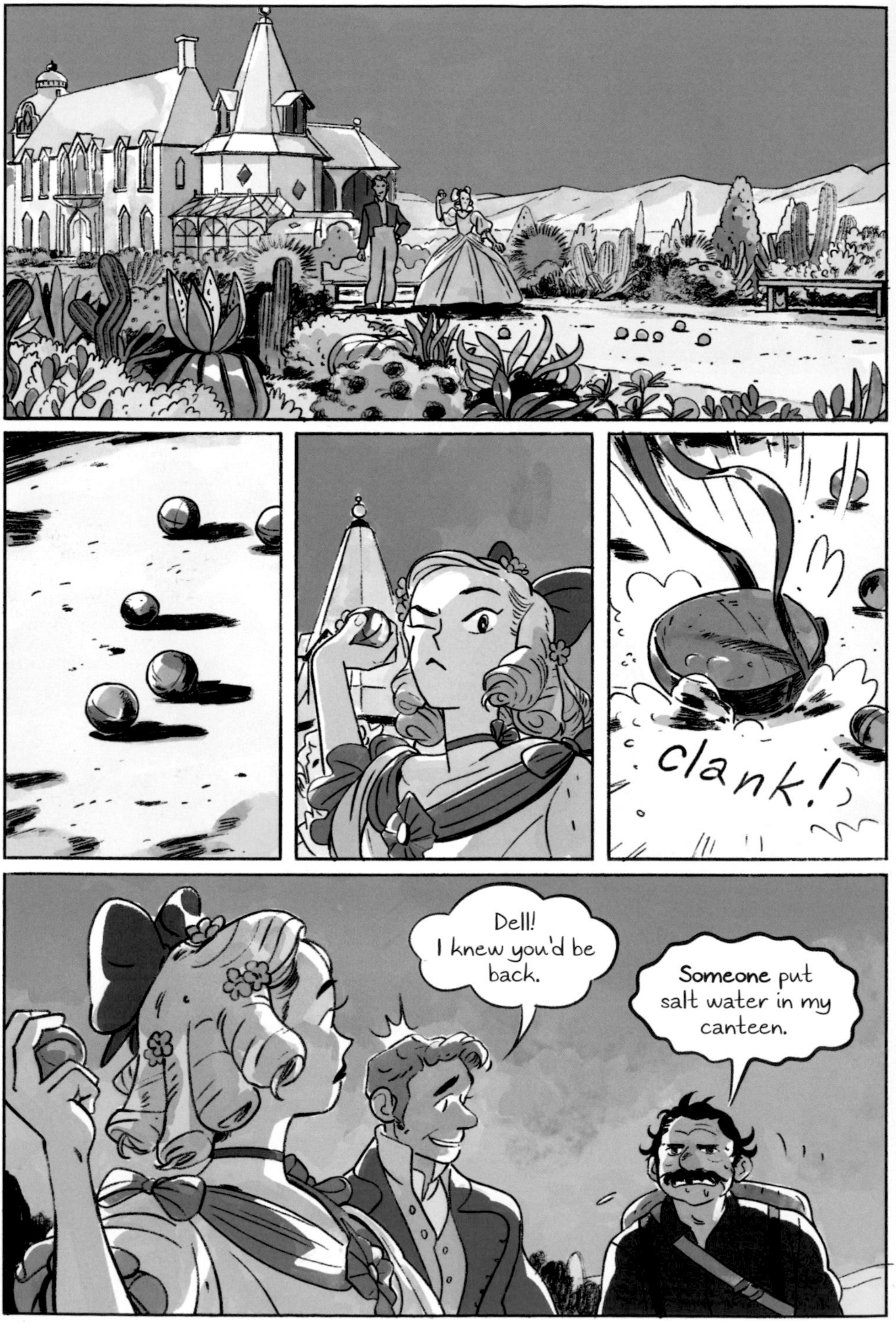
clank!
Dell! I knew you'd be back.
Someone put salt water in my canteen.

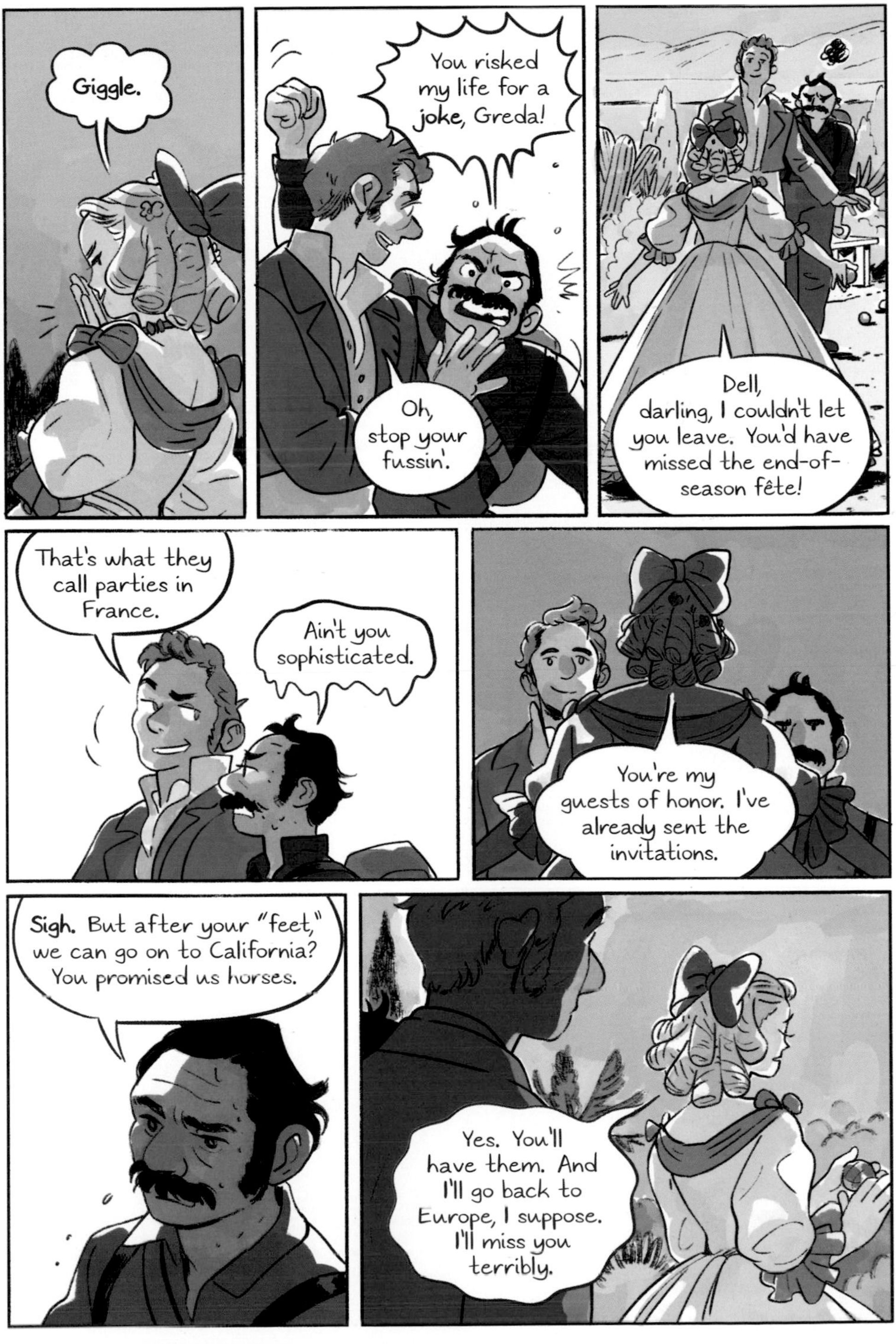
Giggle.
You risked my life for a joke, Greda!
Oh, stop your fussin'.
Dell, darling, I couldn't let you leave. You'd have missed the end-of-season fête!
That's what they call parties in France.
Ain't you sophisticated.
You're my guests of honor. I've already sent the invitations.
Sigh. But after your "feet," we can go on to California? You promised us horses.
Yes. You'll have them. And I'll go back to Europe, I suppose. I'll miss you terribly.

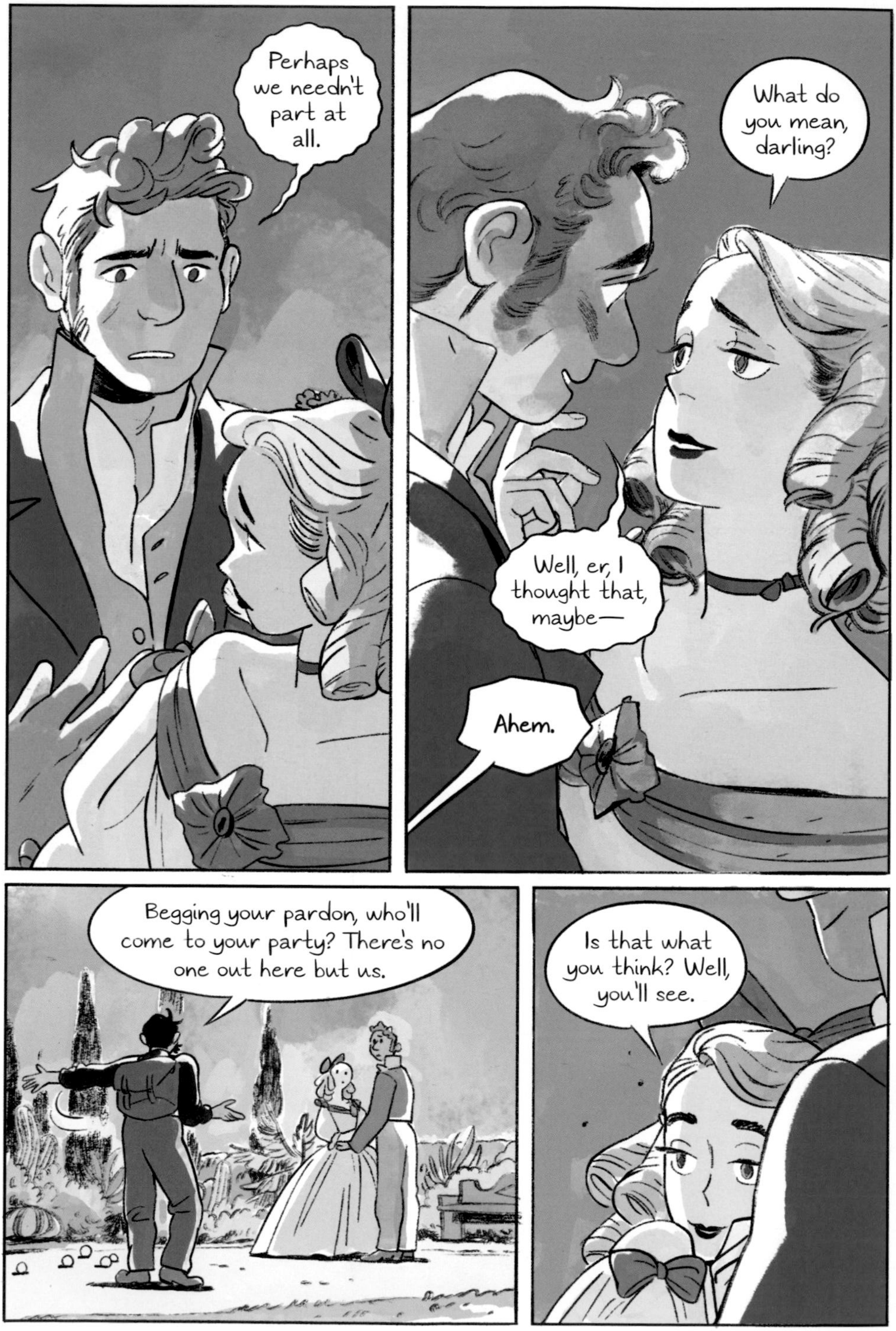
Perhaps we needn't part at all.
What do you mean, darling?
Well, er, I thought that, maybe—
Ahem.
Begging your pardon, who'll come to your party? There's no one out here but us.
Is that what you think? Well, you'll see.

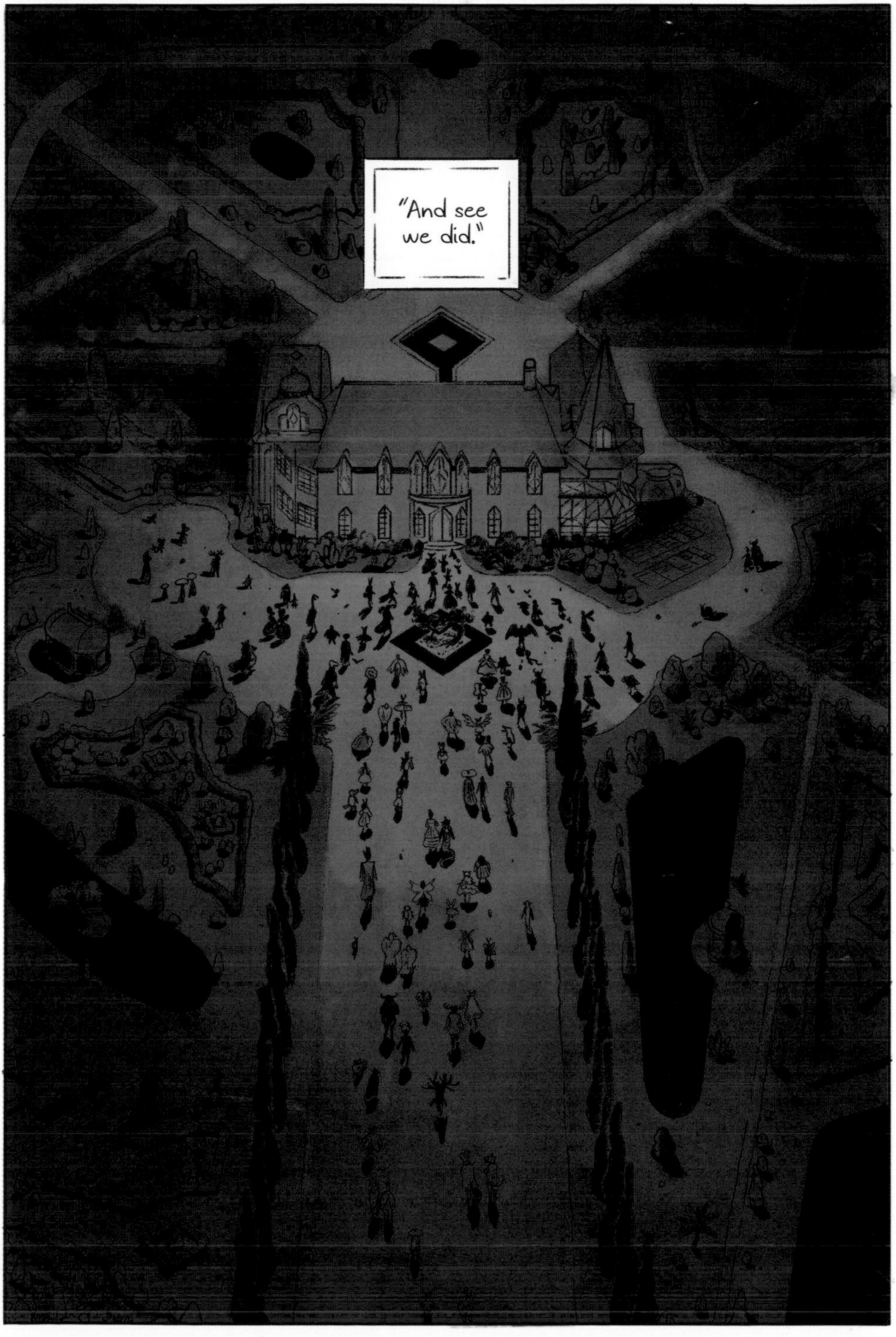
"And see we did."

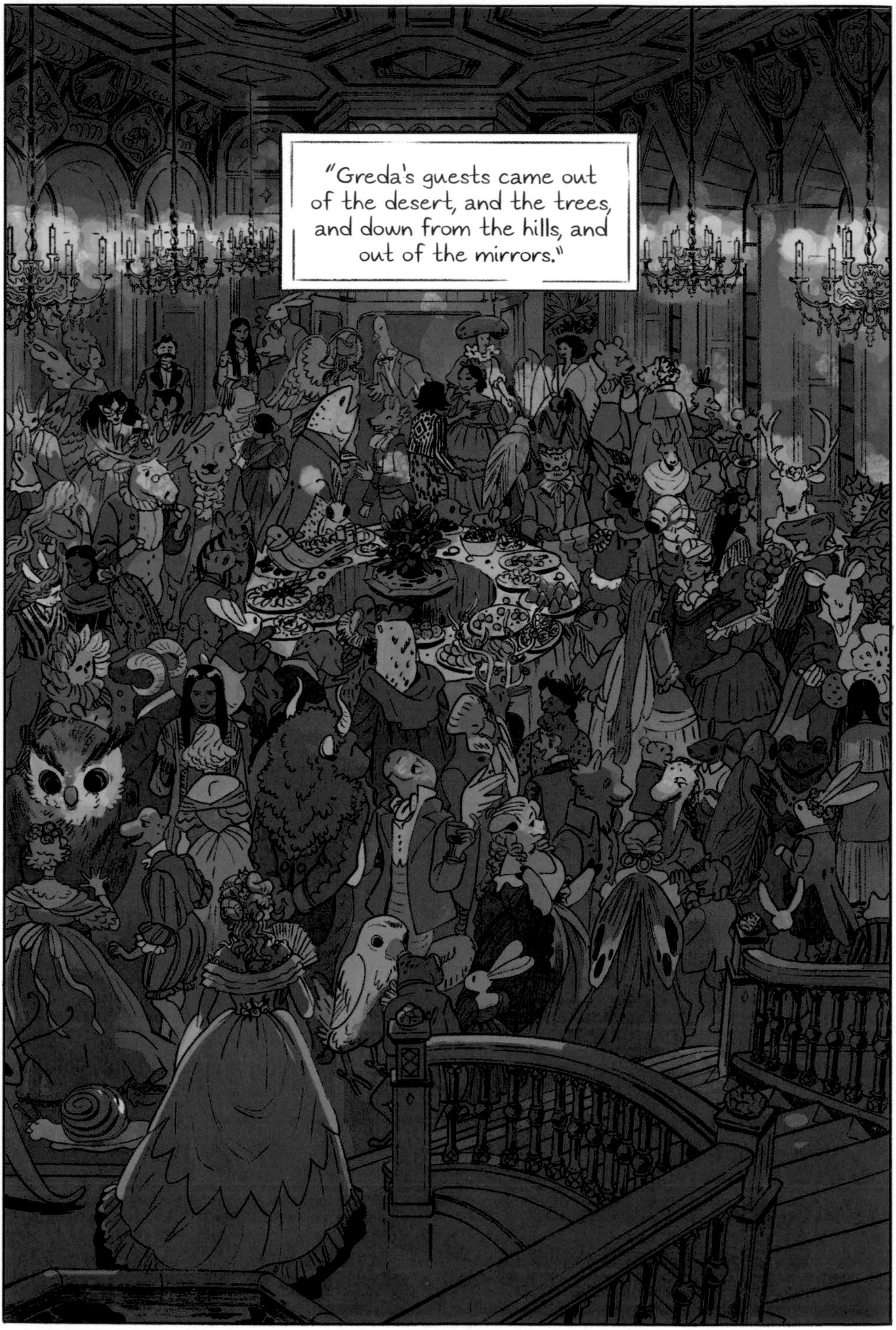
"Greda's guests came out of the desert, and the trees, and down from the hills, and out of the mirrors."

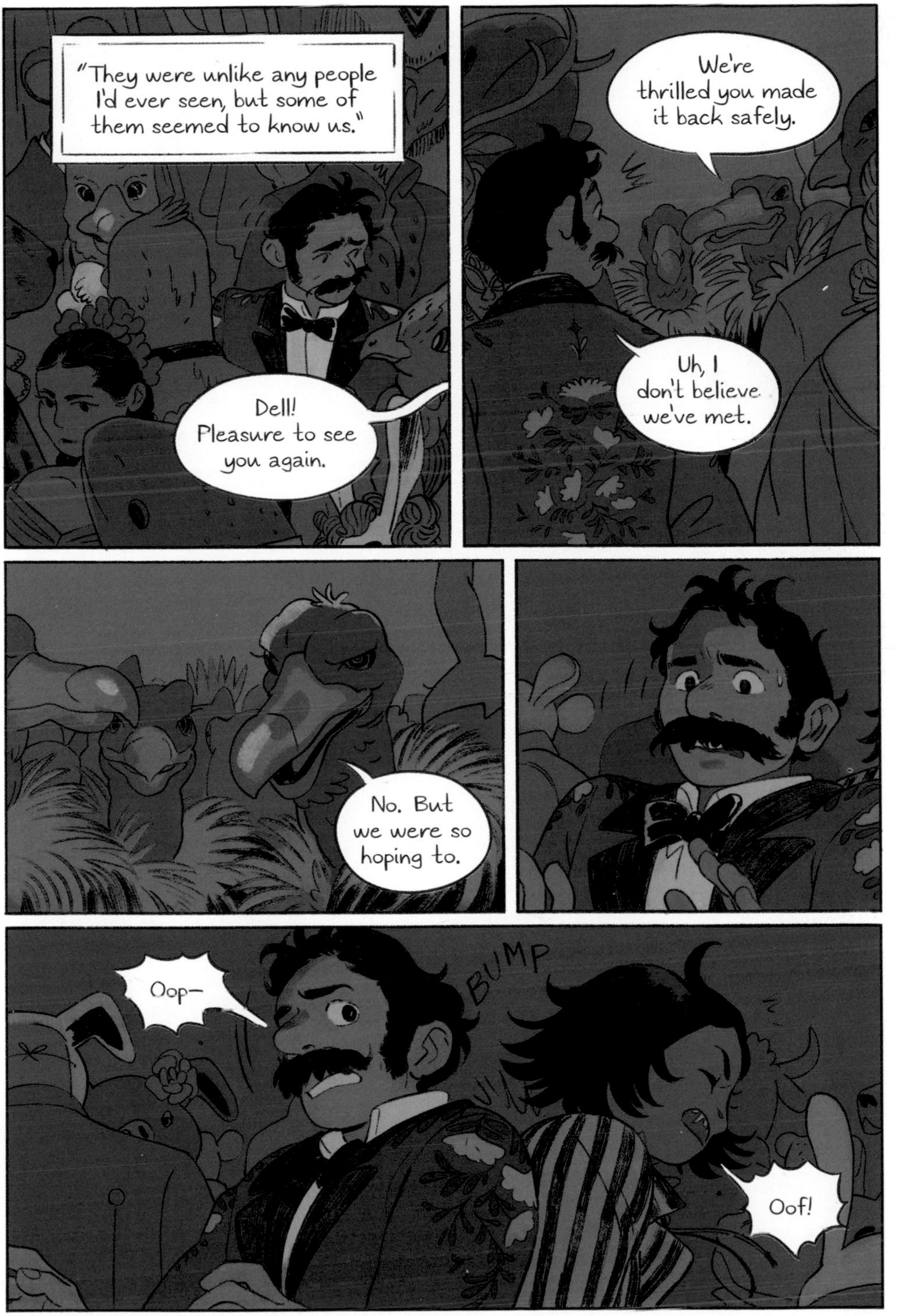
"They were unlike any people I'd ever seen, but some of them seemed to know us."
Dell! Pleasure to see you again.
We're thrilled you made it back safely.
Uh, I don't believe we've met.
No. But we were so hoping to.
Oop–
BUMP
Oof!

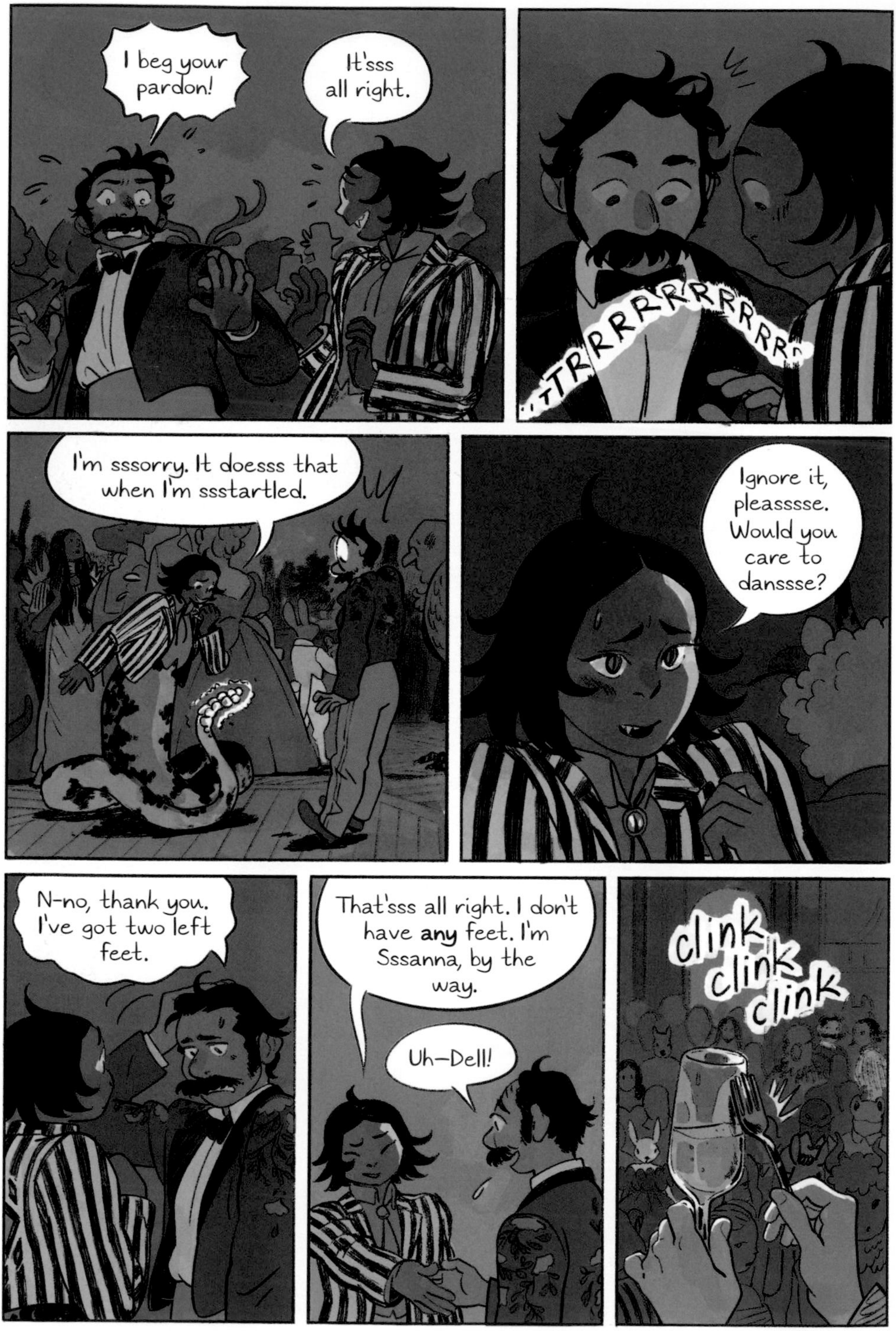
I beg your pardon!
It'sss all right.
...TRRRRRRRRRRR
I'm sssorry. It doesss that when I'm ssstartled.
Ignore it, pleasssse. Would you care to dansssse?
N-no, thank you. I've got two left feet.
That'sss all right. I don't have **any** feet. I'm Sssanna, by the way.
Uh—Dell!
clink clink clink

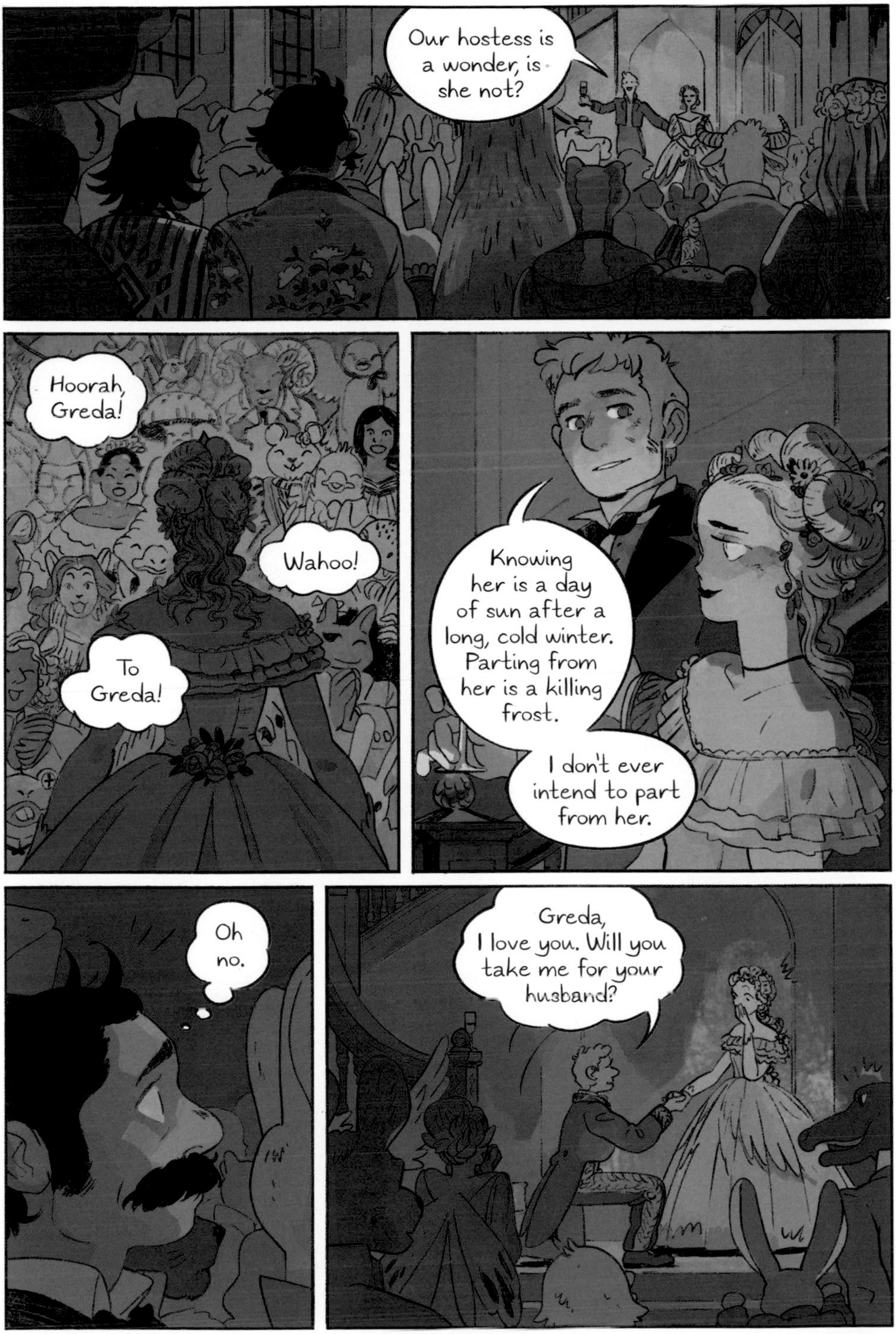
Our hostess is a wonder, is she not?
Hoorah, Greda!
Wahoo!
To Greda!
Knowing her is a day of sun after a long, cold winter. Parting from her is a killing frost.
I don't ever intend to part from her.
Oh no.
Greda, I love you. Will you take me for your husband?

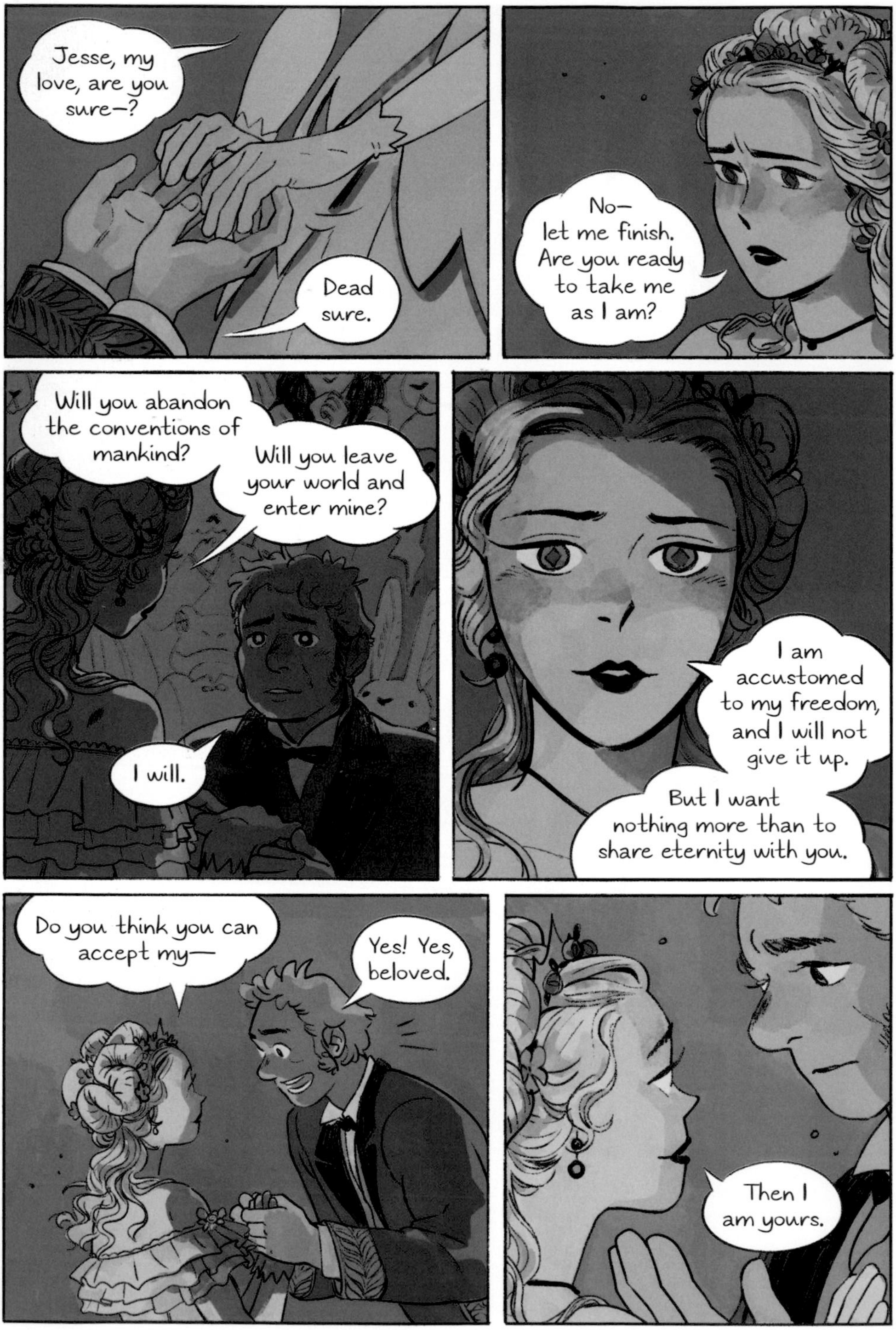
Jesse, my love, are you sure—?
Dead sure.
No— let me finish. Are you ready to take me as I am?
Will you abandon the conventions of mankind?
Will you leave your world and enter mine?
I will.
I am accustomed to my freedom, and I will not give it up.
But I want nothing more than to share eternity with you.
Do you think you can accept my—
Yes! Yes, beloved.
Then I am yours.

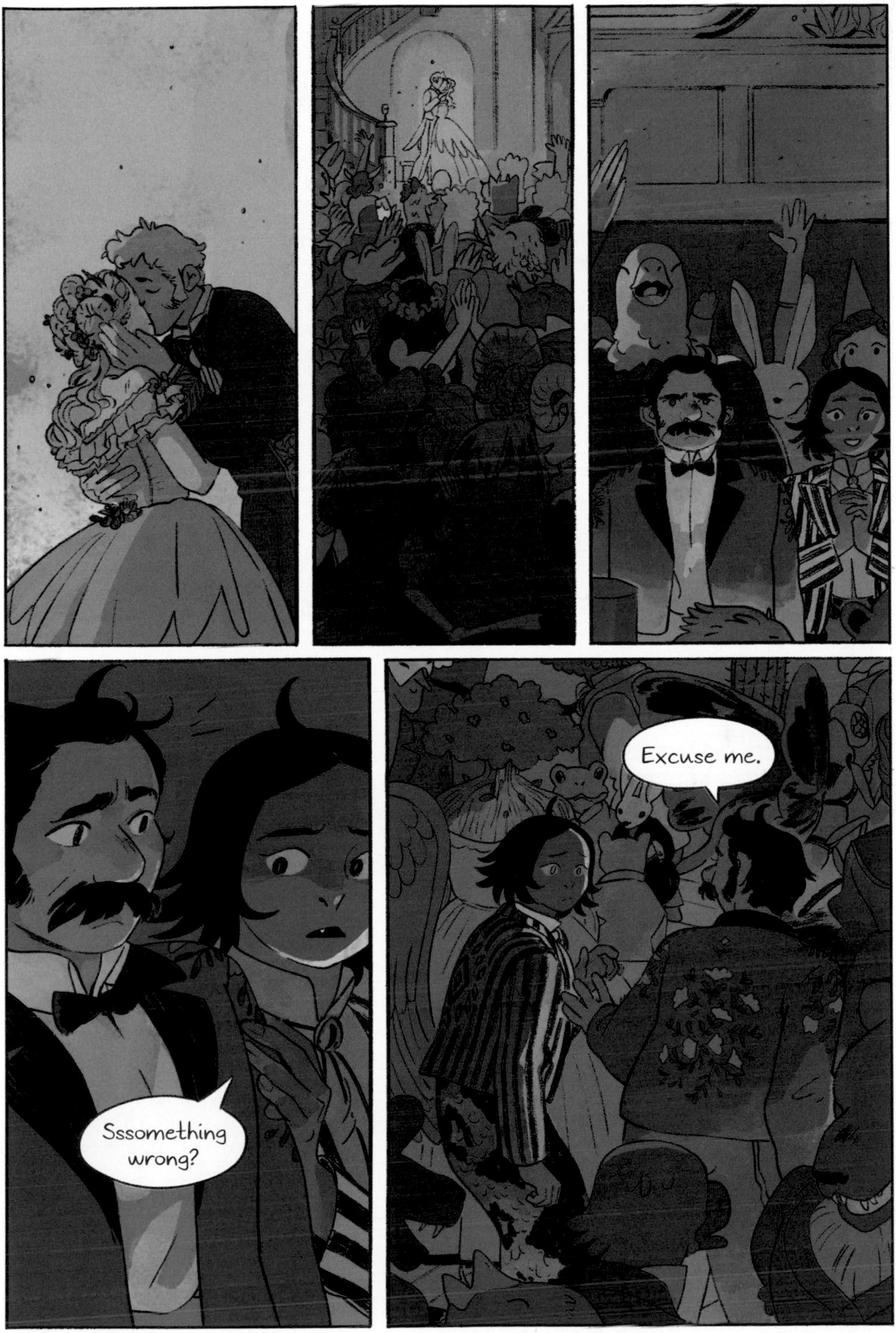
Sssomething wrong?
Excuse me.

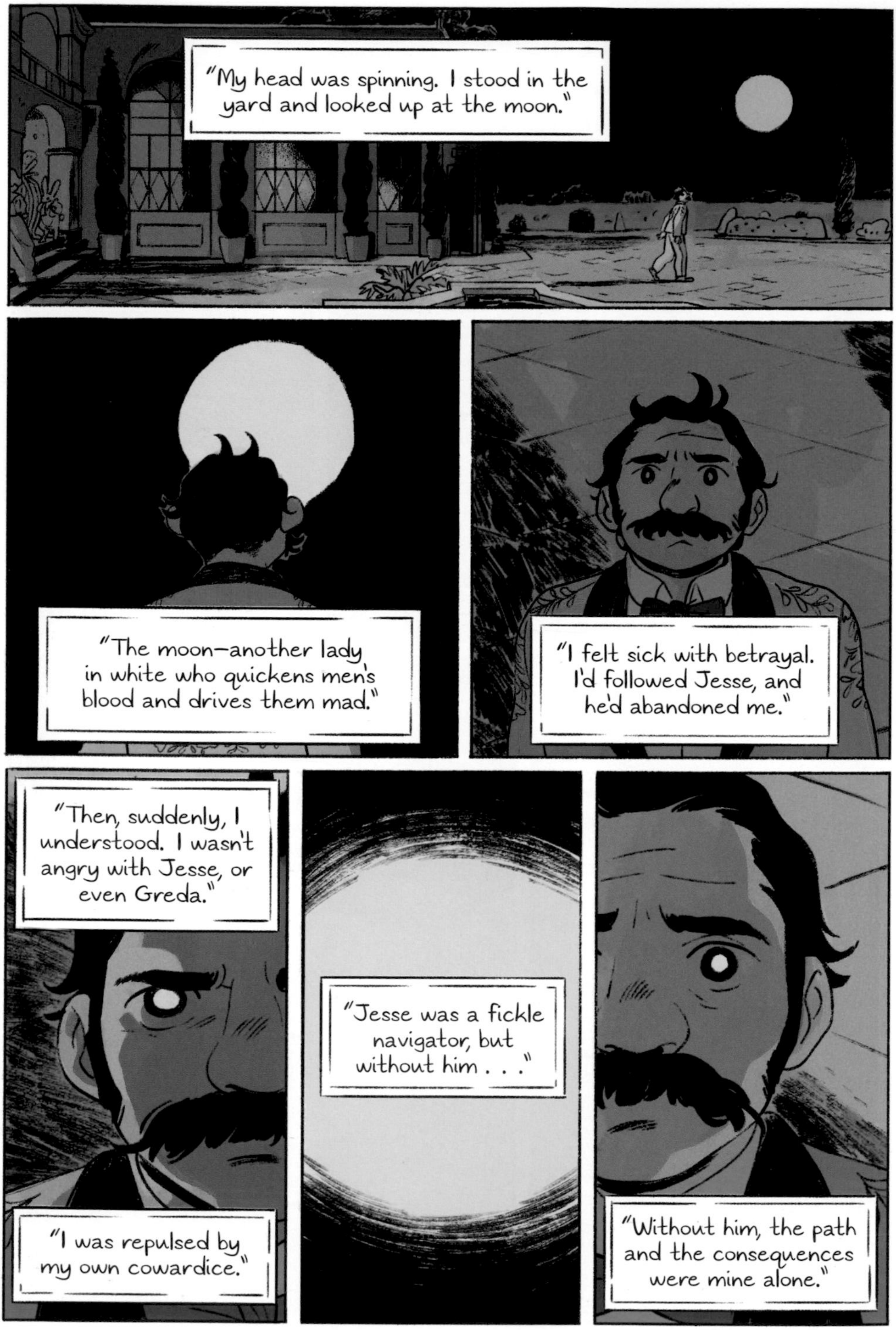
"My head was spinning. I stood in the yard and looked up at the moon."
"The moon—another lady in white who quickens men's blood and drives them mad."
"I felt sick with betrayal. I'd followed Jesse, and he'd abandoned me."
"Then, suddenly, I understood. I wasn't angry with Jesse, or even Greda."
"I was repulsed by my own cowardice."
"Jesse was a fickle navigator, but without him . . ."
"Without him, the path and the consequences were mine alone."

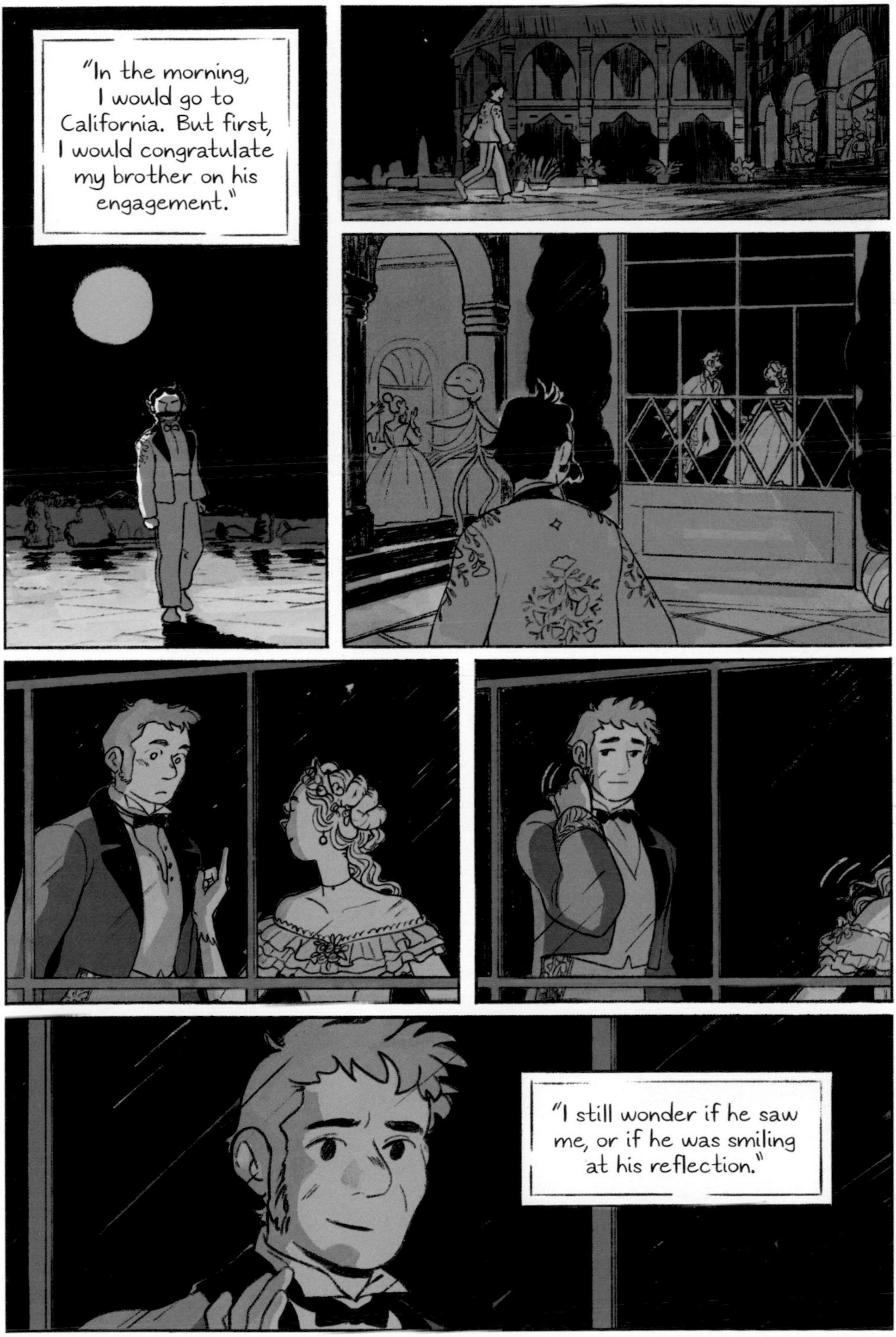
"In the morning, I would go to California. But first, I would congratulate my brother on his engagement."
"I still wonder if he saw me, or if he was smiling at his reflection."

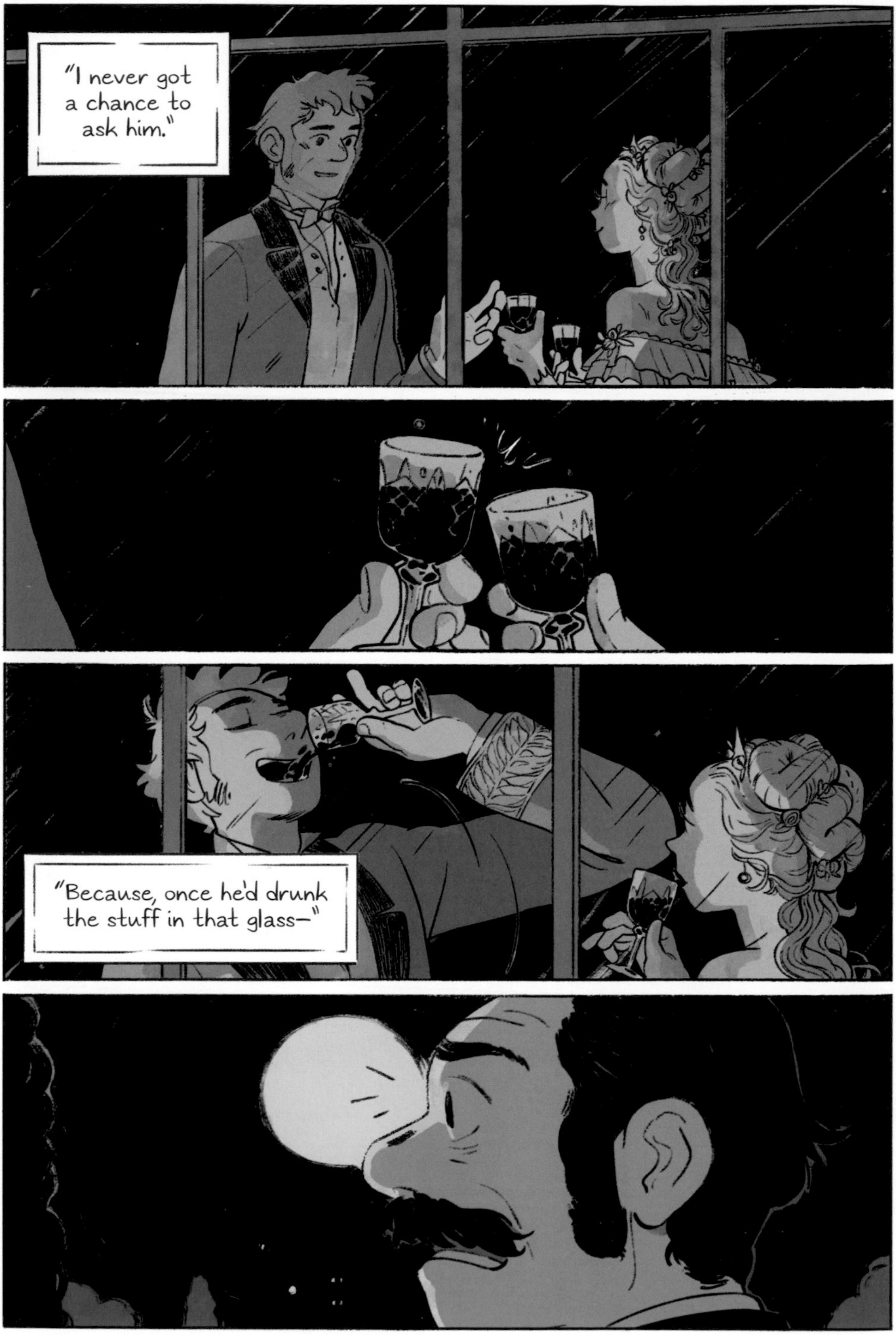
"I never got a chance to ask him."
"Because, once he'd drunk the stuff in that glass—"

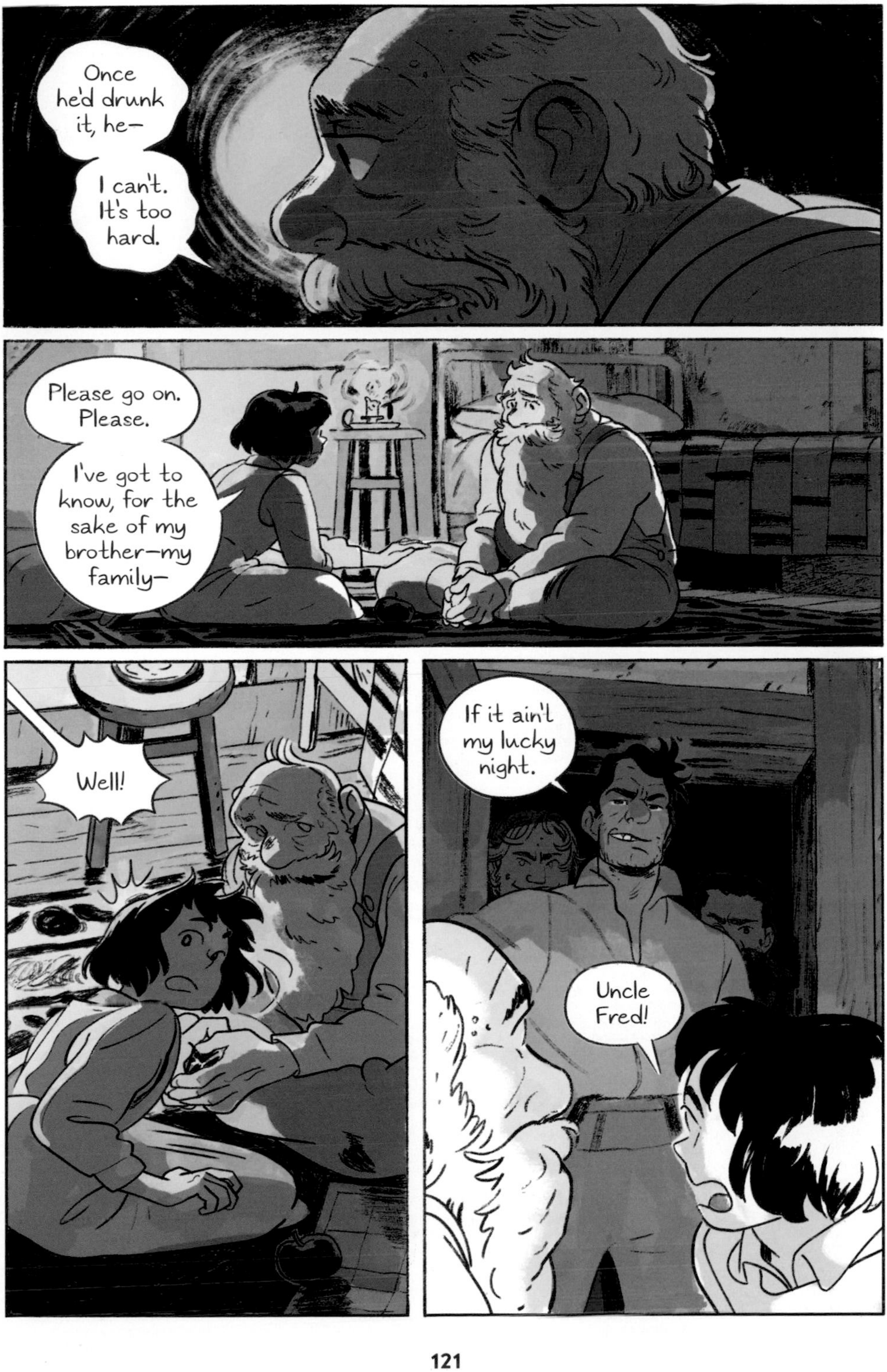

Once he'd drunk it, he—
I can't. It's too hard.
Please go on. Please.
I've got to know, for the sake of my brother—my family—
Well!
If it ain't my lucky night.
Uncle Fred!

First I win big at the poker table, an' now little niece Lucille has come to visit.

It's **Vonceil.** I'm sorry for trespassing. I had to talk to Dell, and—

Vonceil. Ain't that pretty.

See this? She's got a pretty name, too.

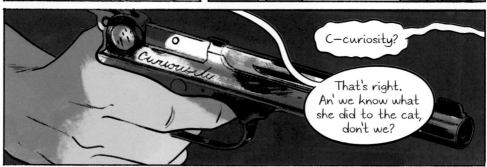

C—curiosity?

That's right. An' we know what she did to the cat, don't we?

Question is, what'll she do about you?

Chapter Seven

Scavengers

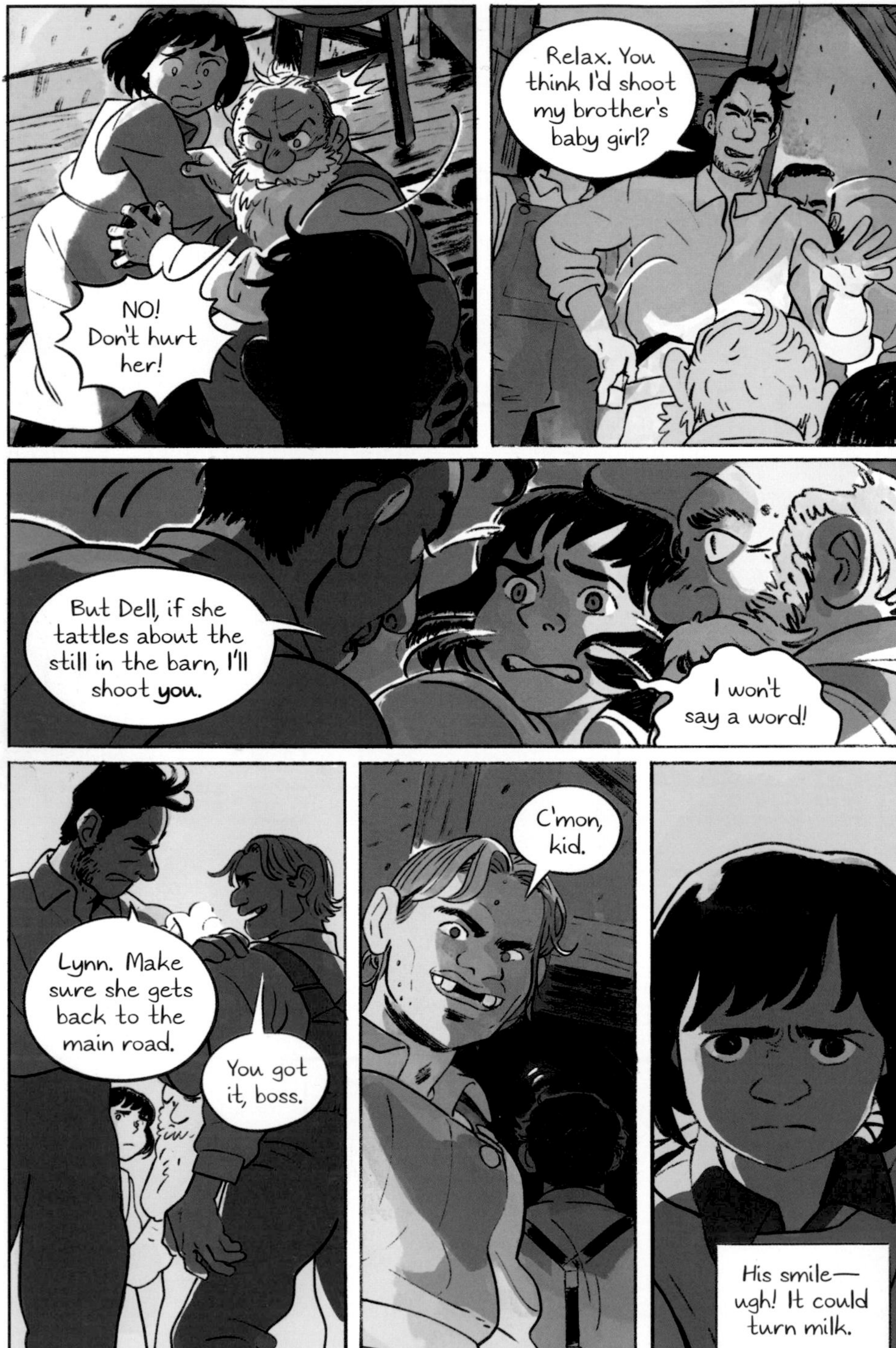
NO! Don't hurt her!
Relax. You think I'd shoot my brother's baby girl?
But Dell, if she tattles about the still in the barn, I'll shoot **you.**
I won't say a word!
Lynn. Make sure she gets back to the main road.
You got it, boss.
C'mon, kid.
His smile— ugh! It could turn milk.

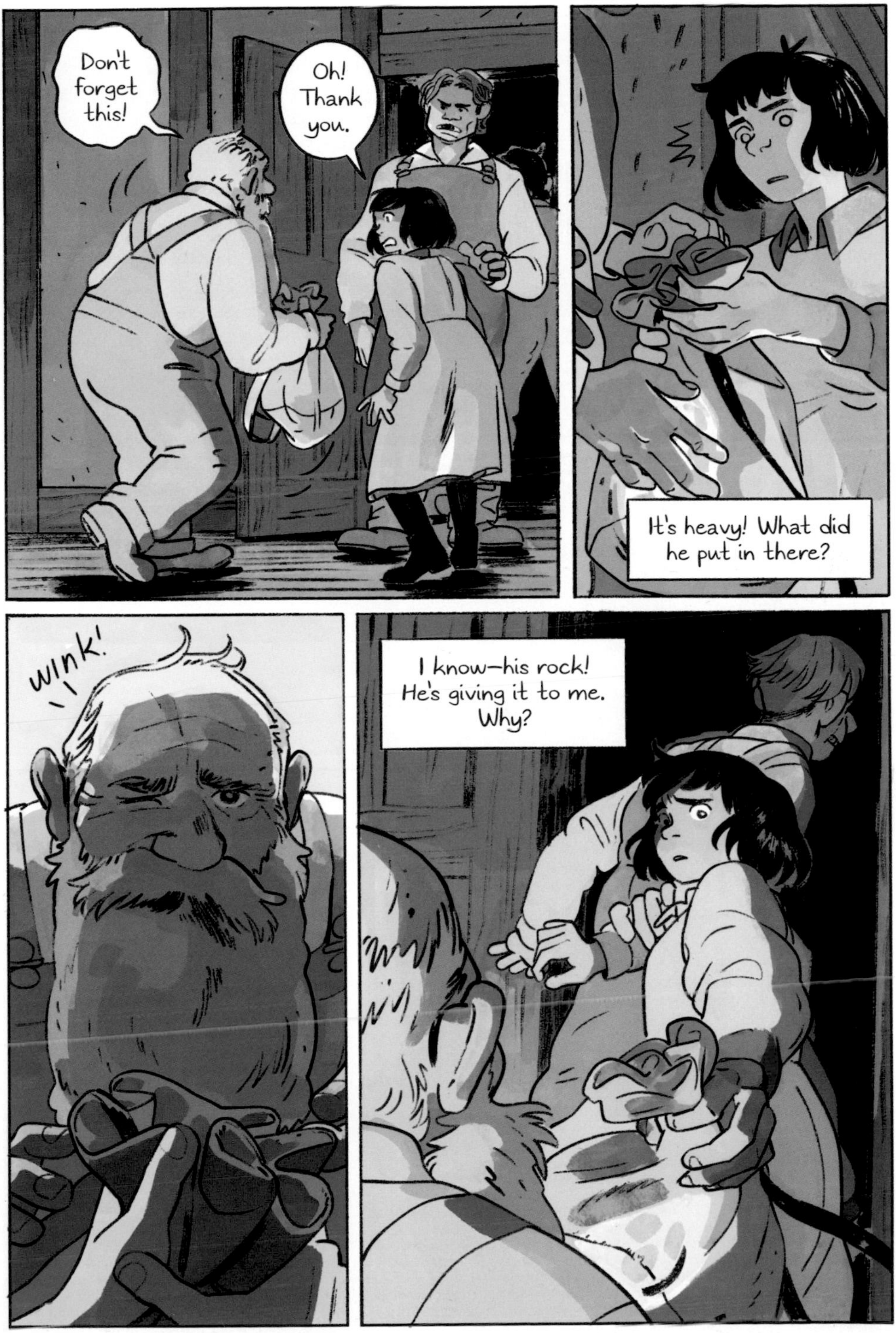

Don't forget this!
Oh! Thank you.
It's heavy! What did he put in there?
WINK!
I know—his rock! He's giving it to me. Why?

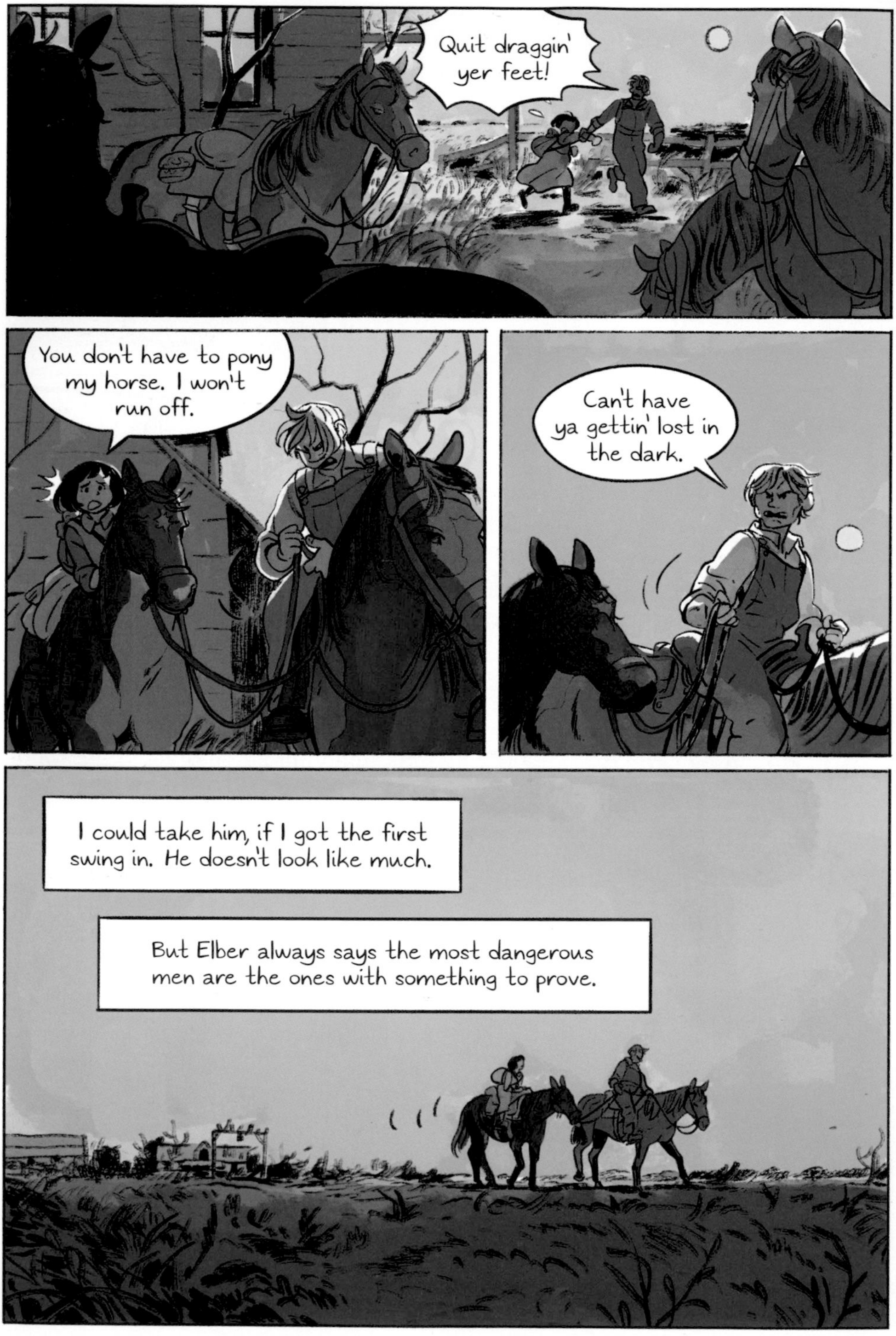
Quit draggin' yer feet!
You don't have to pony my horse. I won't run off.
Can't have ya gettin' lost in the dark.
I could take him, if I got the first swing in. He doesn't look like much.
But Elber always says the most dangerous men are the ones with something to prove.

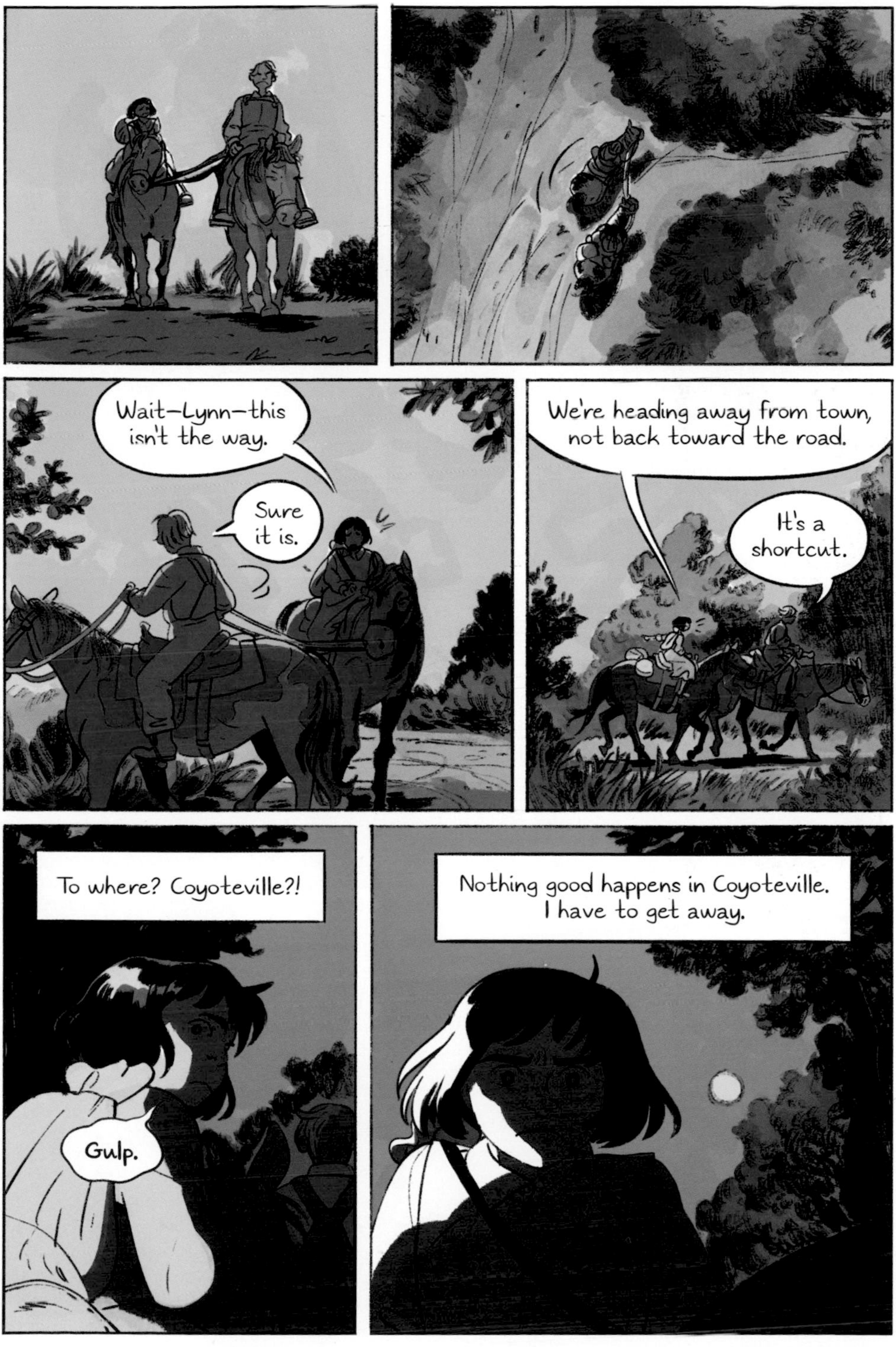
Wait—Lynn—this isn't the way.
Sure it is.
We're heading away from town, not back toward the road.
It's a shortcut.
To where? Coyoteville?!
Gulp.
Nothing good happens in Coyoteville. I have to get away.

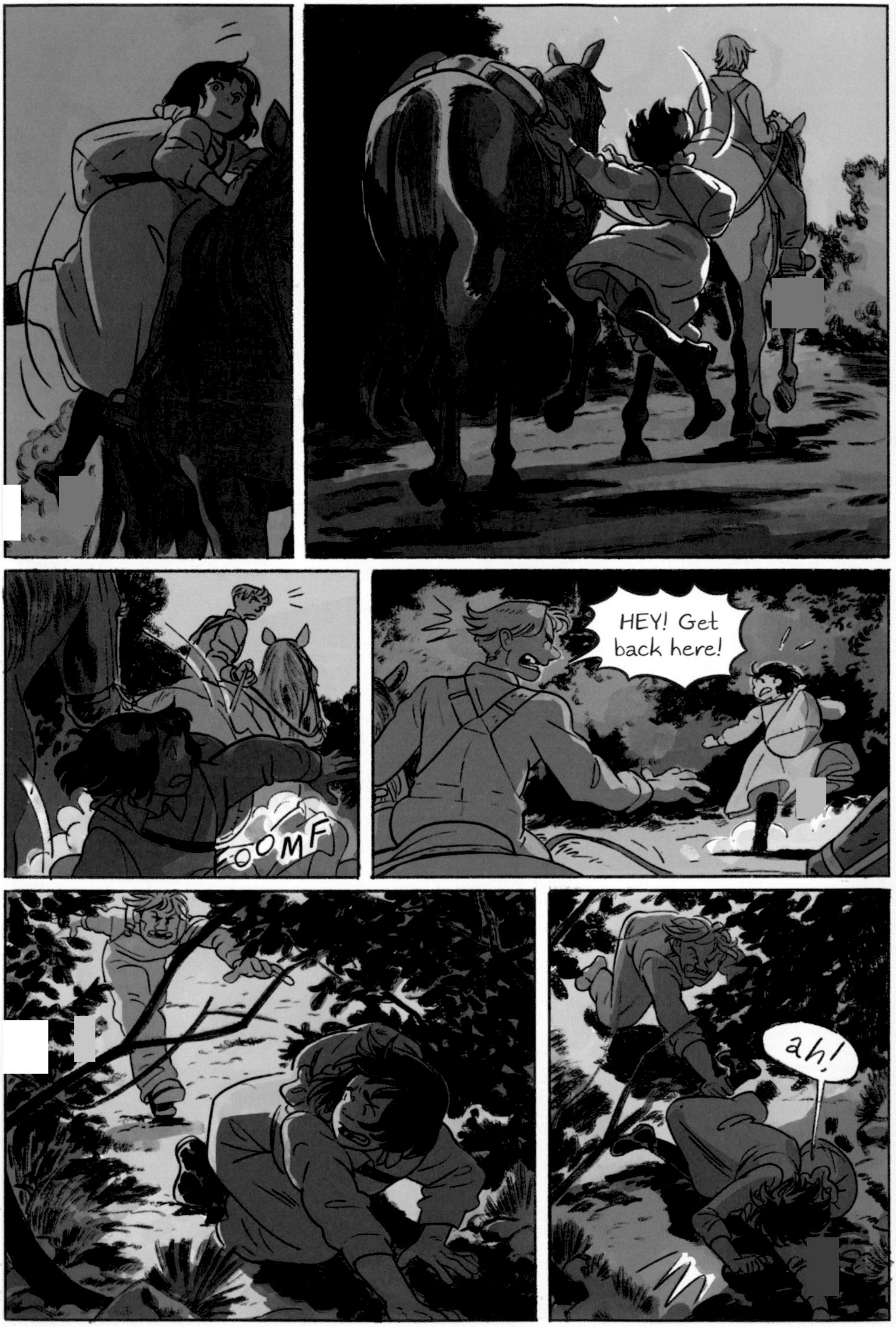
OOMF
HEY! Get back here!
ah!

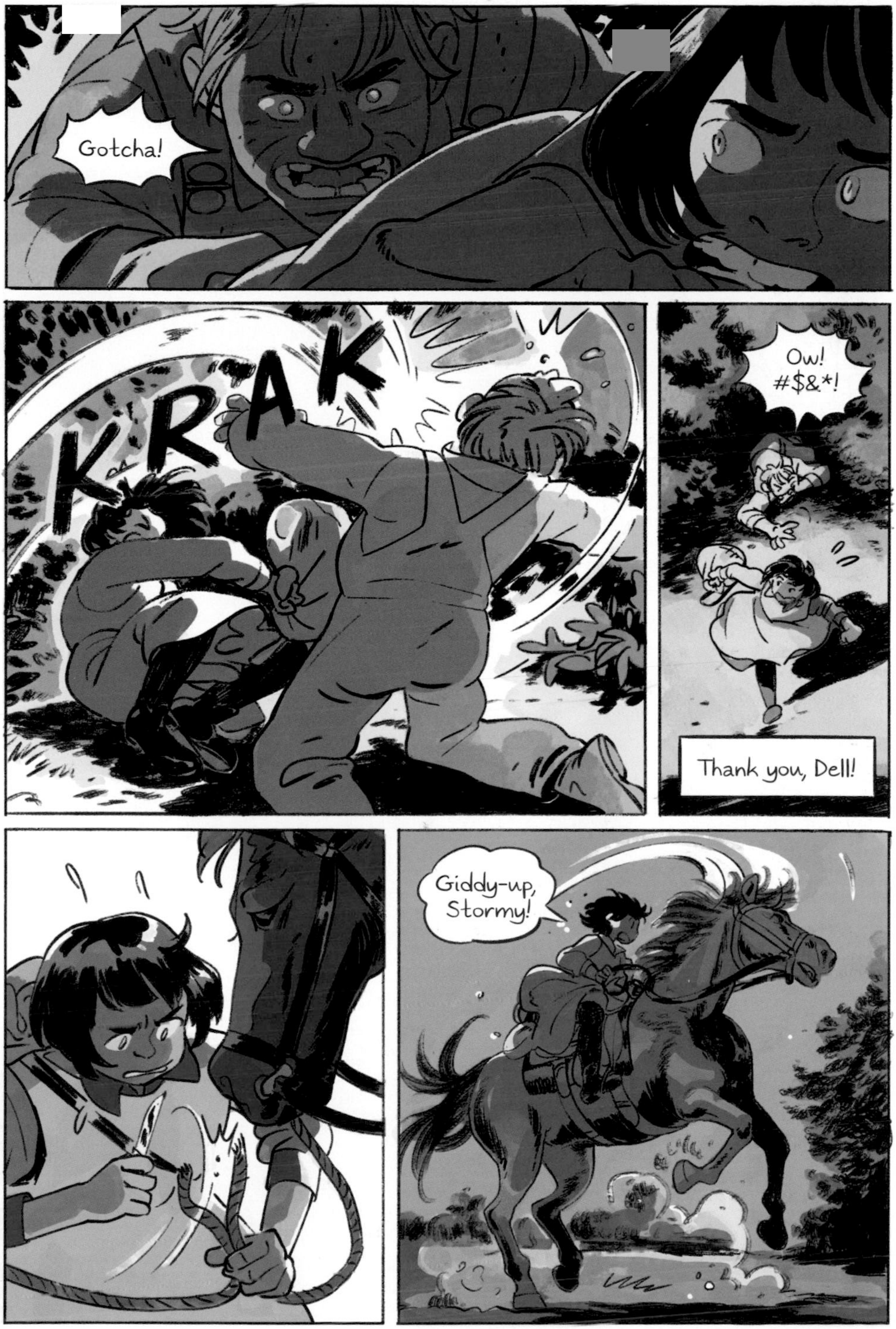
Gotcha!
KRAK
Ow! #$&*!
Thank you, Dell!
Giddy-up, Stormy!

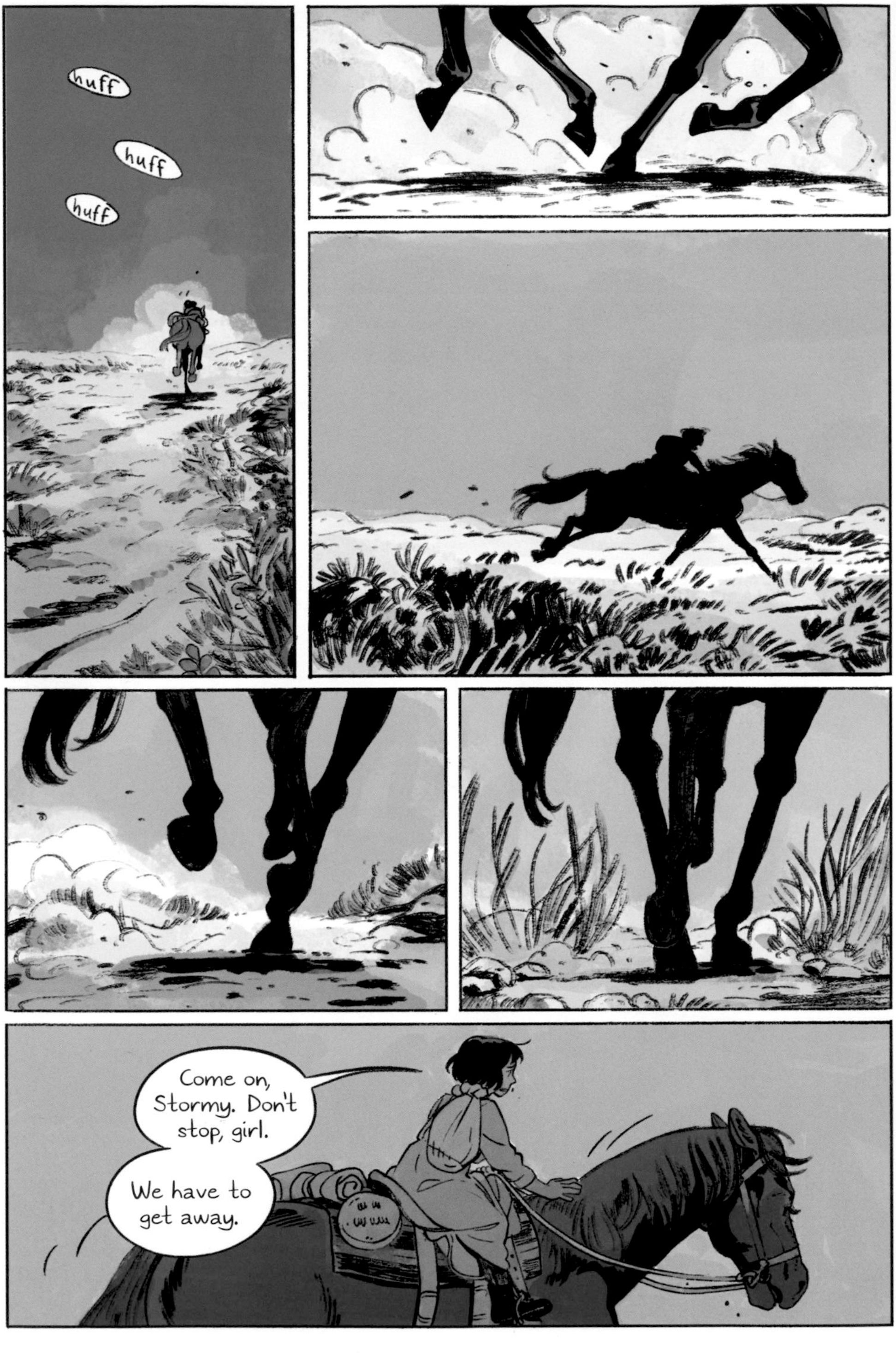
huff
huff
huff
Come on, Stormy. Don't stop, girl.
We have to get away.

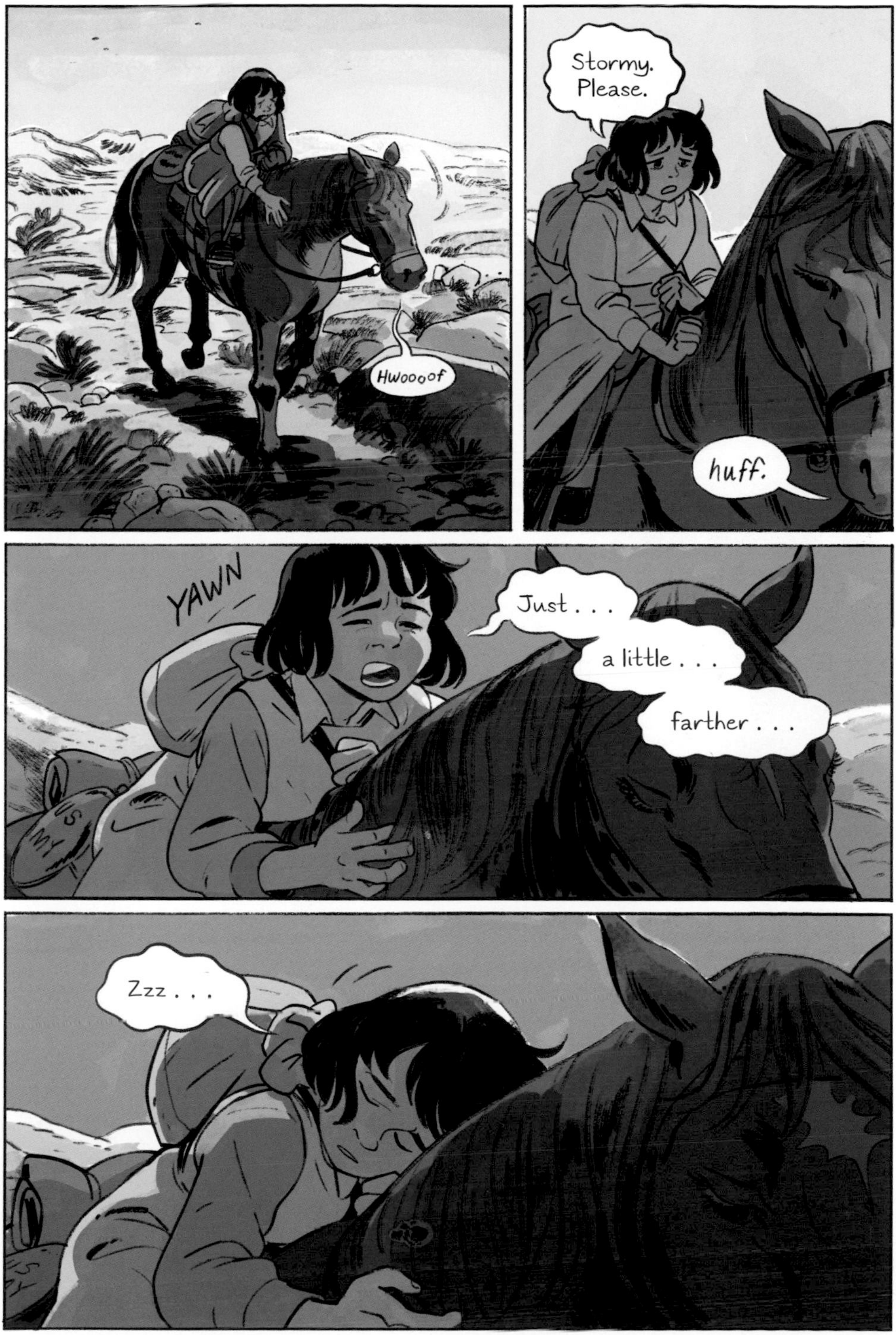
Hwooooof
Stormy. Please.
huff.
YAWN
Just . . .
a little . . .
farther . . .
Zzz . . .

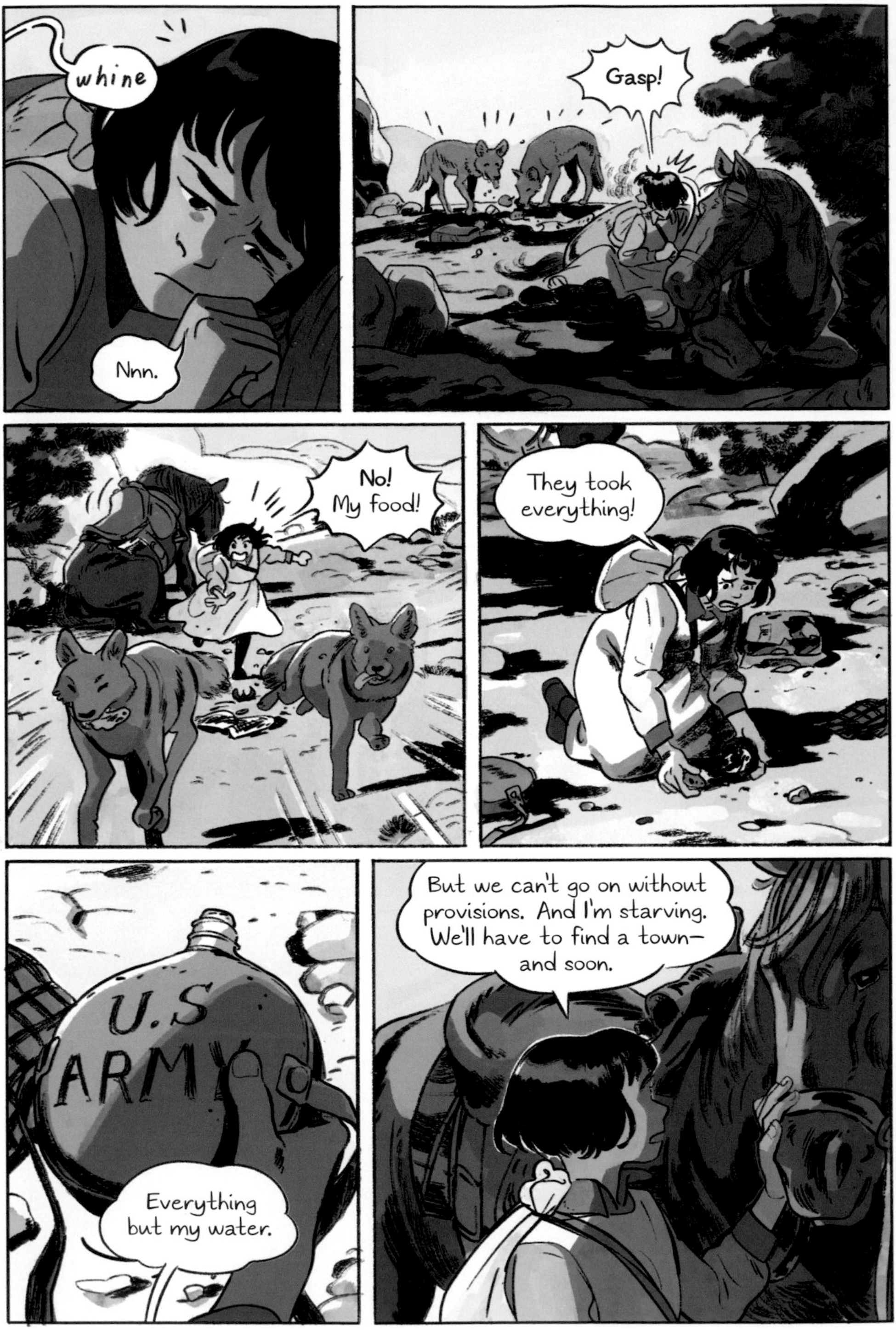
whine
Nnn.
Gasp!
No!
My food!
They took
everything!
U.S
ARMY
Everything
but my water.
But we can't go on without
provisions. And I'm starving.
We'll have to find a town—
and soon.

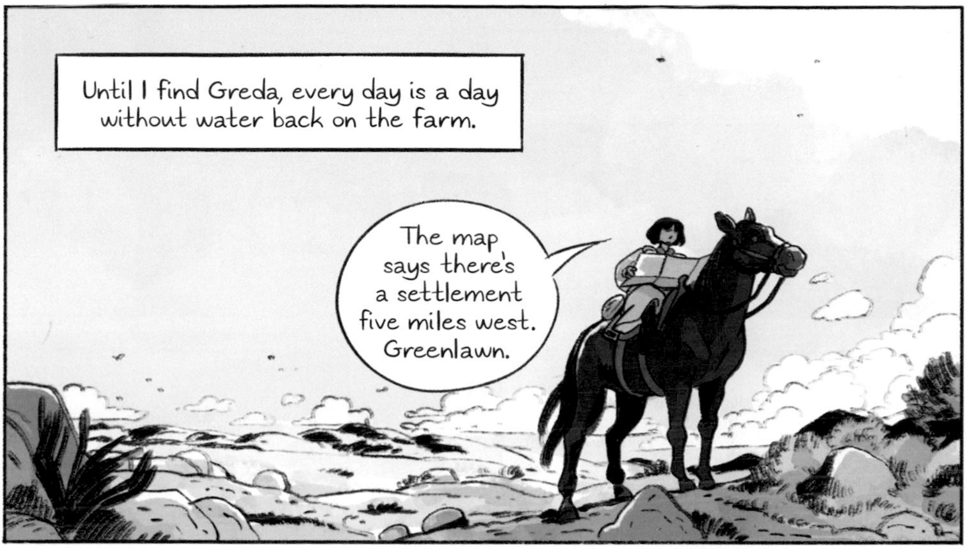
Until I find Greda, every day is a day without water back on the farm.
The map says there's a settlement five miles west. Greenlawn.

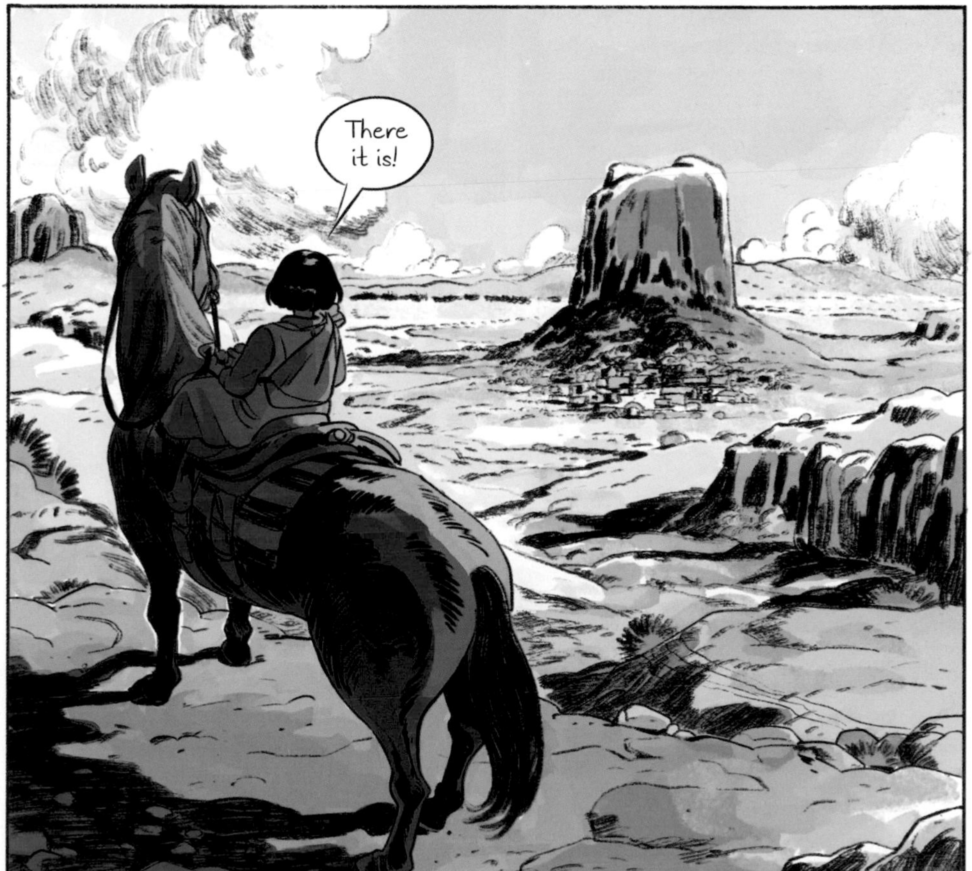
There it is!

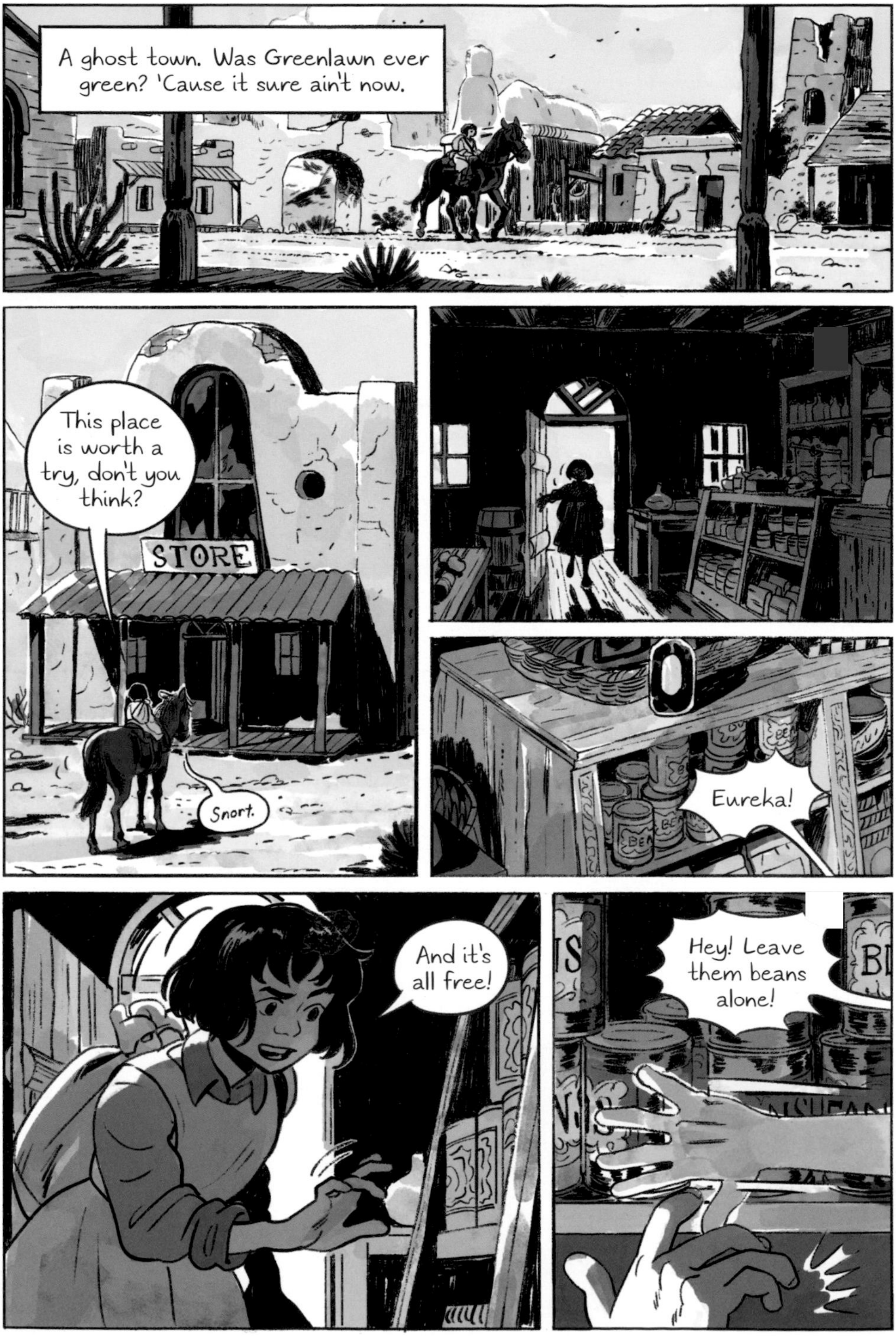
A ghost town. Was Greenlawn ever green? 'Cause it sure ain't now.
This place is worth a try, don't you think?
STORE
Snort.
Eureka!
And it's all free!
Hey! Leave them beans alone!

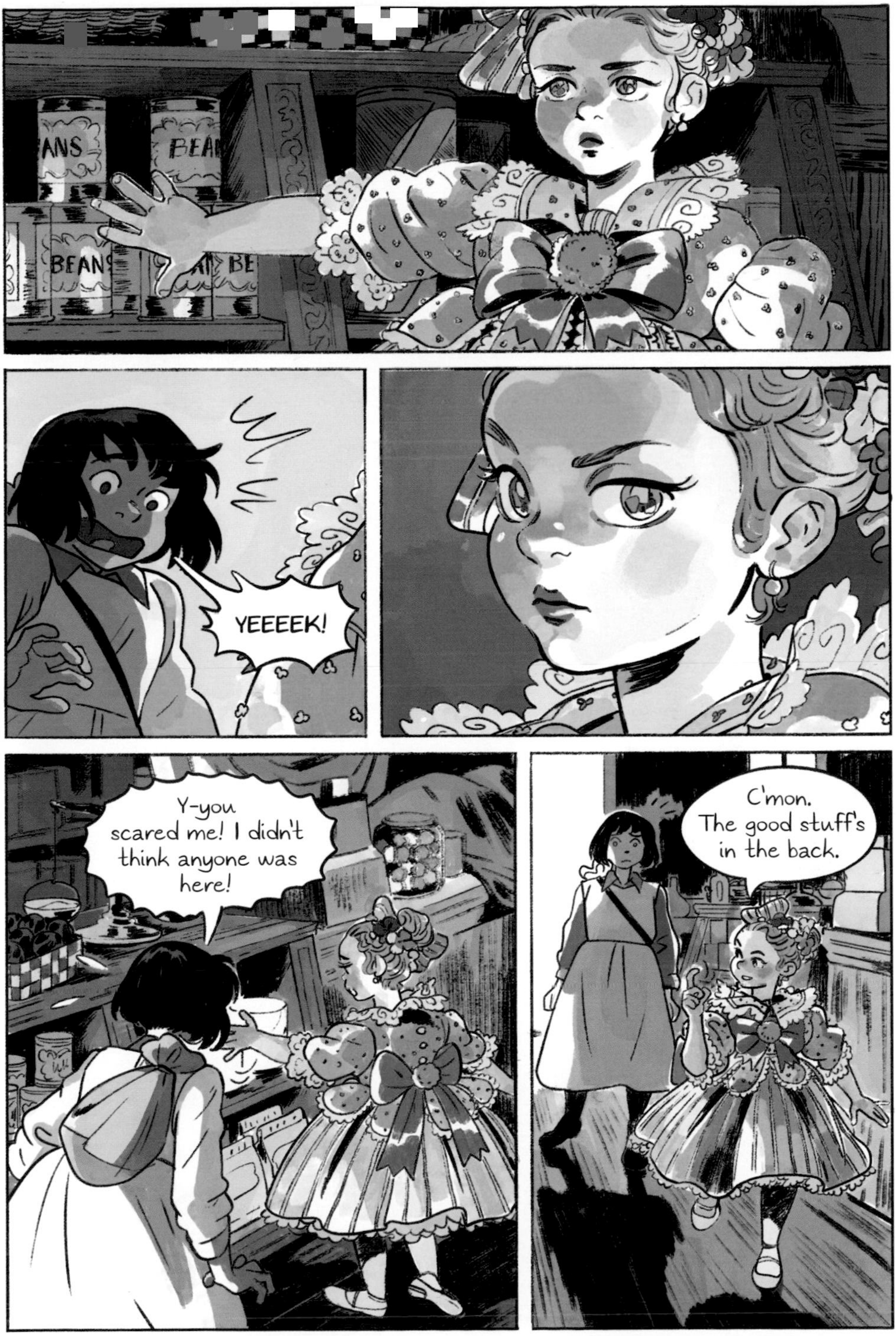
BEANS
YEEEEK!
Y-you scared me! I didn't think anyone was here!
C'mon. The good stuff's in the back.

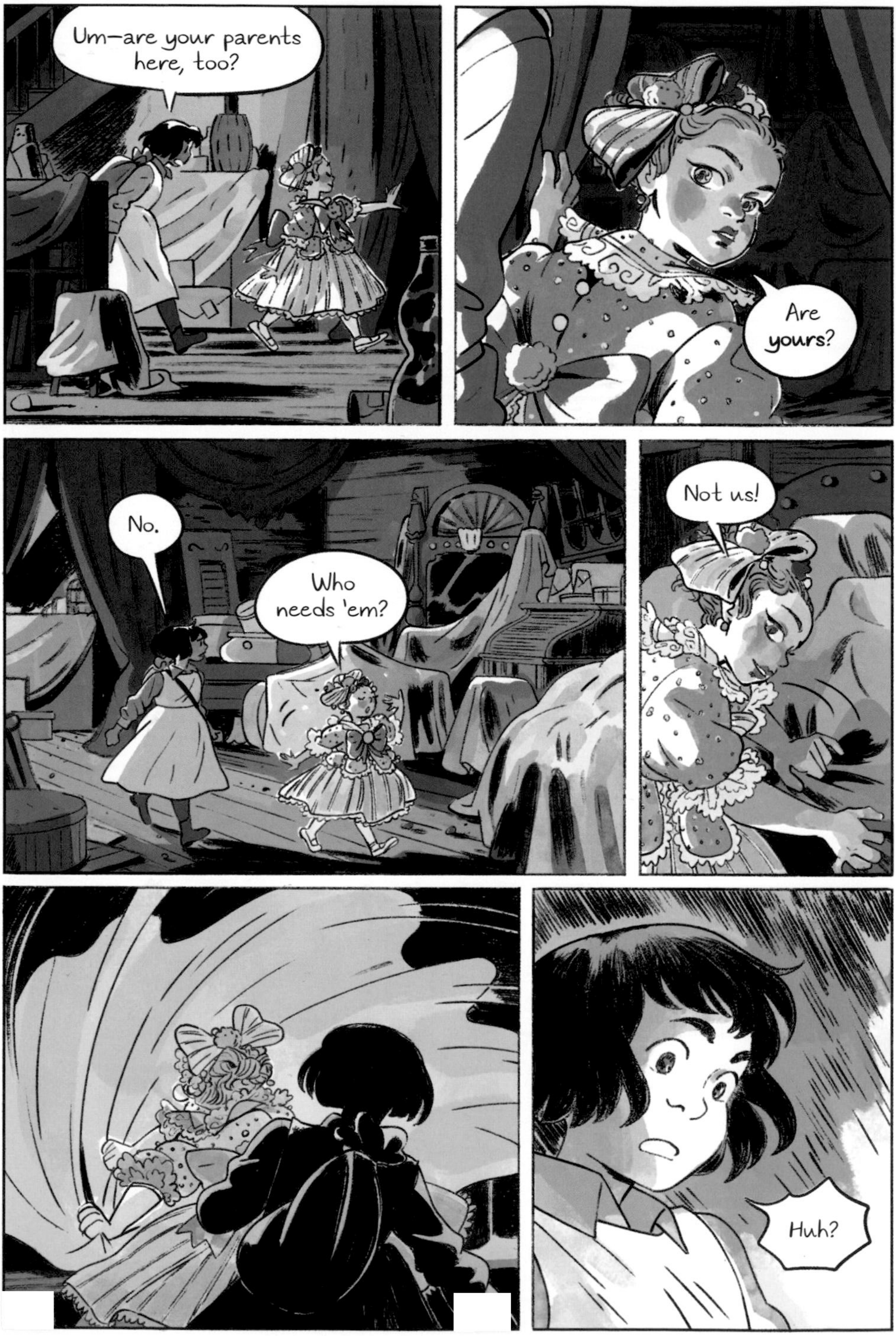
Um—are your parents here, too?
Are **yours**?
No.
Who needs 'em?
Not us!
Huh?

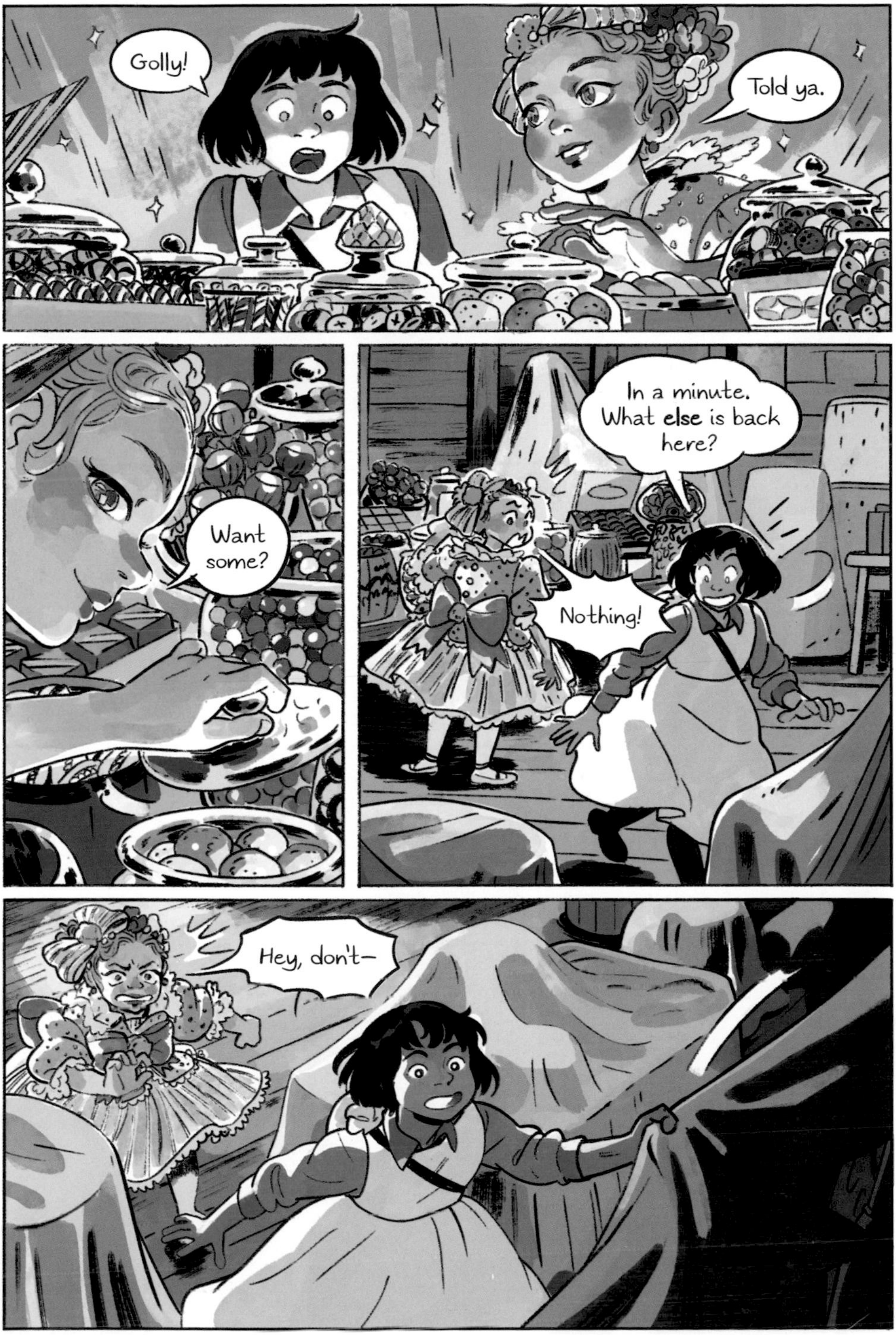
Golly!
Told ya.
Want some?
In a minute. What else is back here?
Nothing!
Hey, don't—

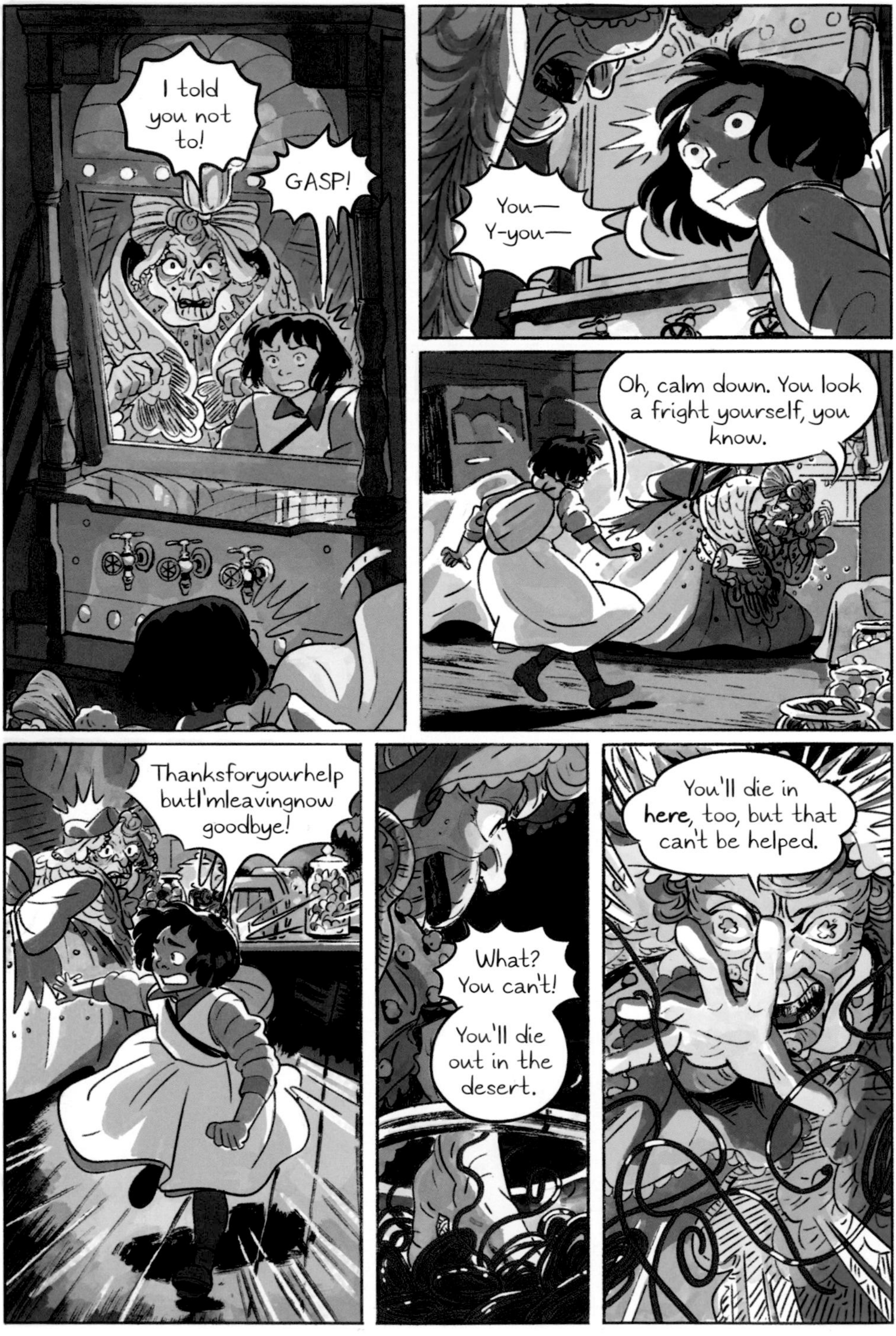
I told you not to!
GASP!
You— Y-you—
Oh, calm down. You look a fright yourself, you know.
Thanksforyourhelp butI'mleavingnow goodbye!
What? You can't!
You'll die out in the desert.
You'll die in **here**, too, but that can't be helped.

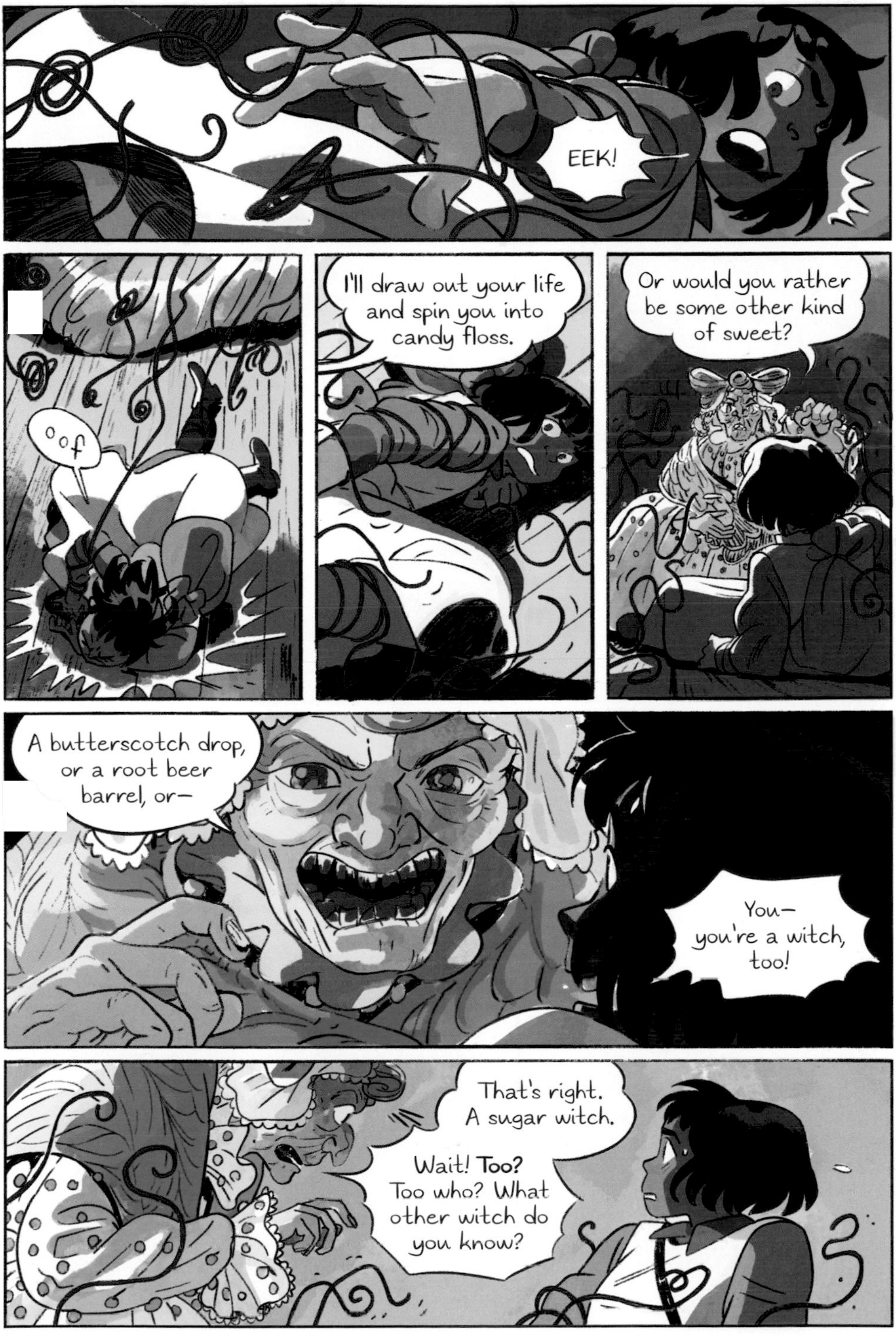

EEK!
oof
I'll draw out your life and spin you into candy floss.
Or would you rather be some other kind of sweet?
A butterscotch drop, or a root beer barrel, or—
You— you're a witch, too!
That's right. A sugar witch.
Wait! **Too?** Too who? What other witch do you know?

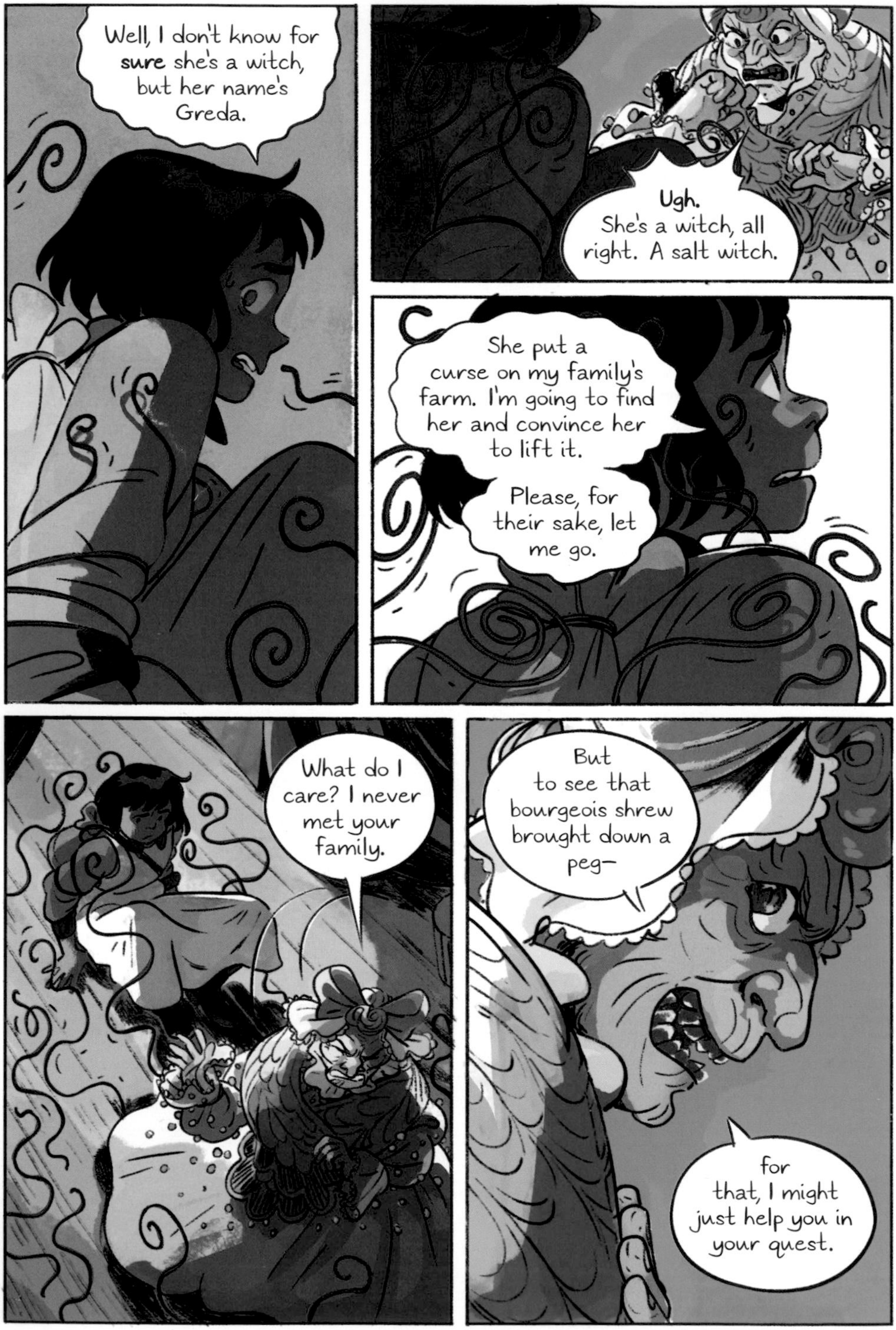
Well, I don't know for **sure** she's a witch, but her name's Greda.
Ugh. She's a witch, all right. A salt witch.
She put a curse on my family's farm. I'm going to find her and convince her to lift it.
Please, for their sake, let me go.
What do I care? I never met your family.
But to see that bourgeois shrew brought down a peg—
for that, I might just help you in your quest.

Chapter Eight

Rock Candy

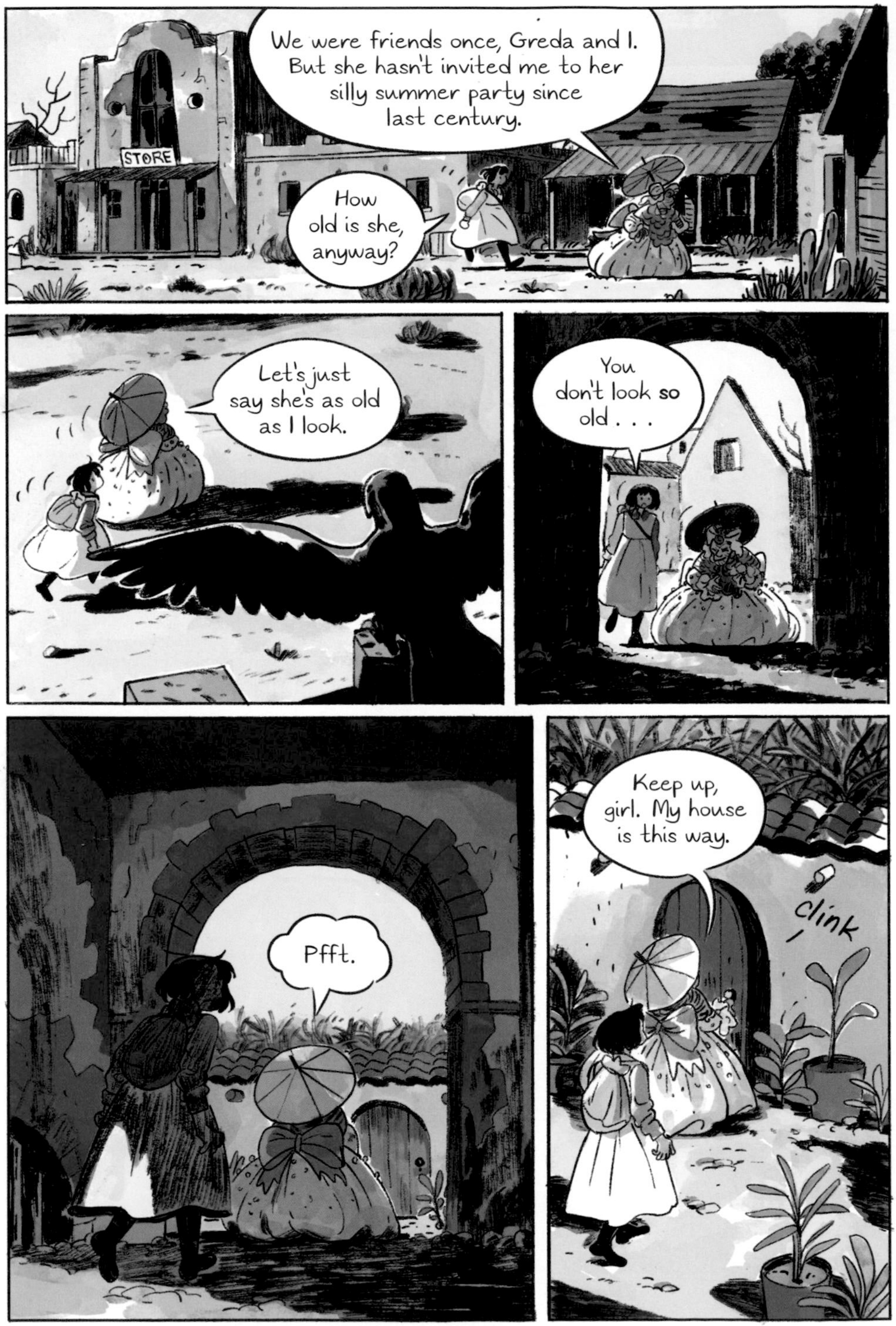
We were friends once, Greda and I. But she hasn't invited me to her silly summer party since last century.
STORE
How old is she, anyway?
Let's just say she's as old as I look.
You don't look **so** old . . .
Pfft.
Keep up, girl. My house is this way.
clink

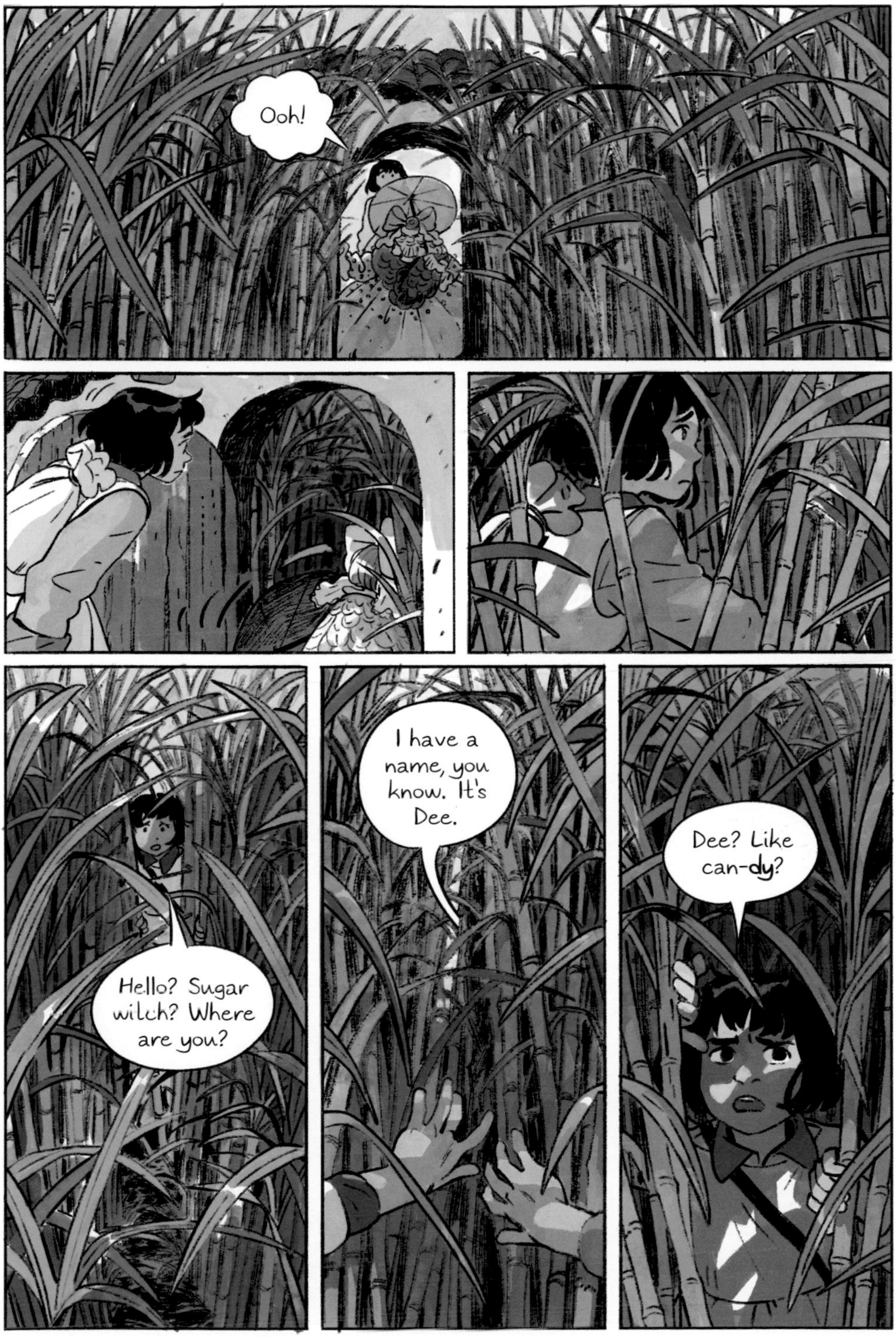
Ooh!
Hello? Sugar witch? Where are you?
I have a name, you know. It's Dee.
Dee? Like can-dy?

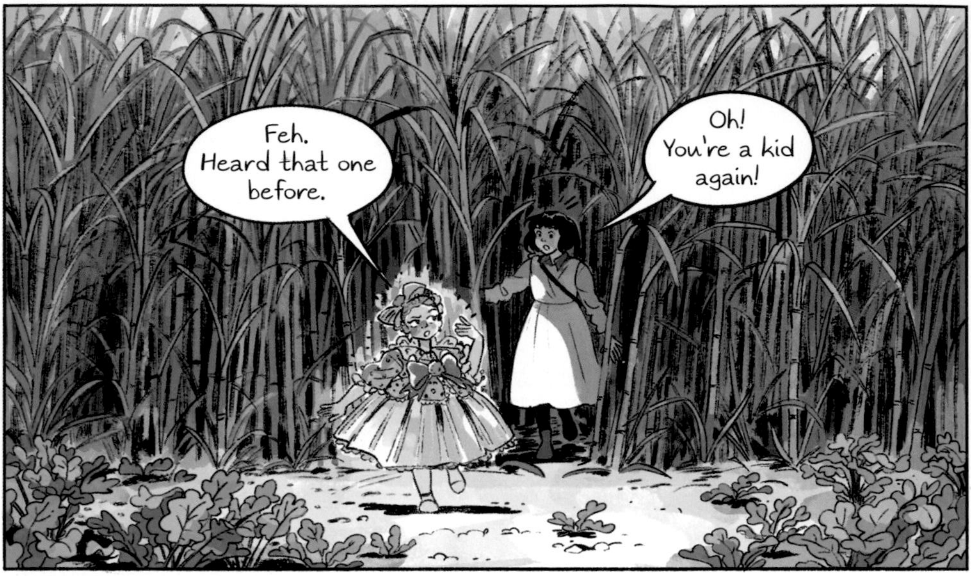
Feh. Heard that one before.
Oh! You're a kid again!

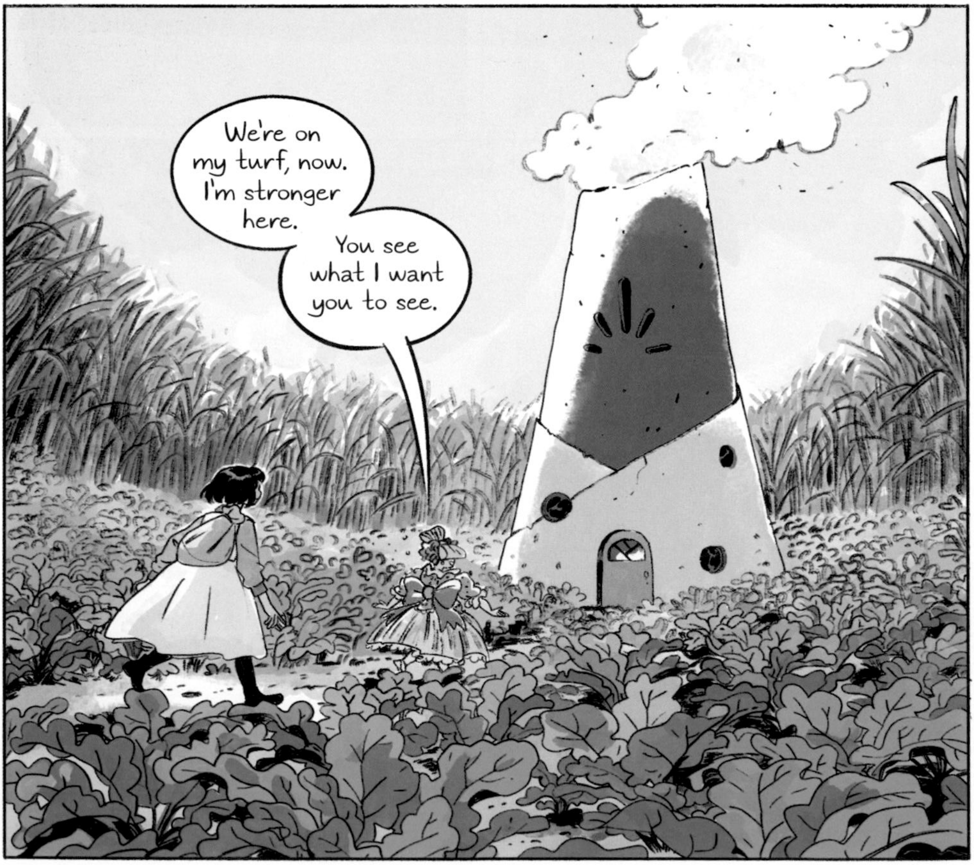
We're on my turf, now. I'm stronger here.
You see what I want you to see.

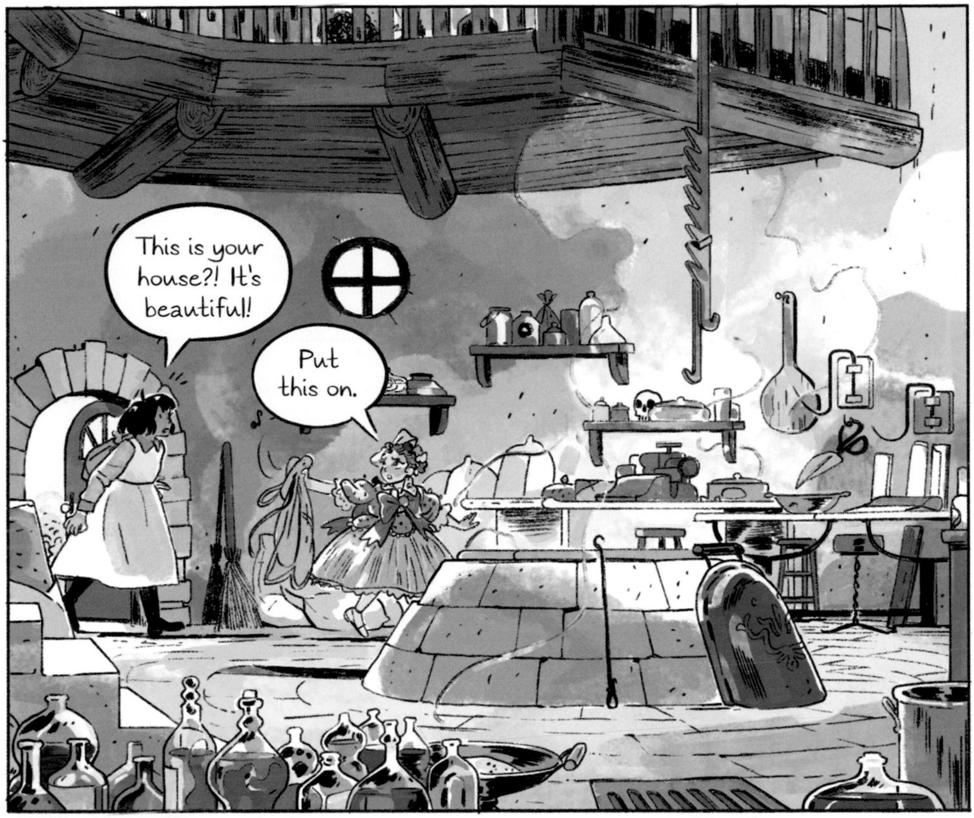
This is your house?! It's beautiful!
Put this on.

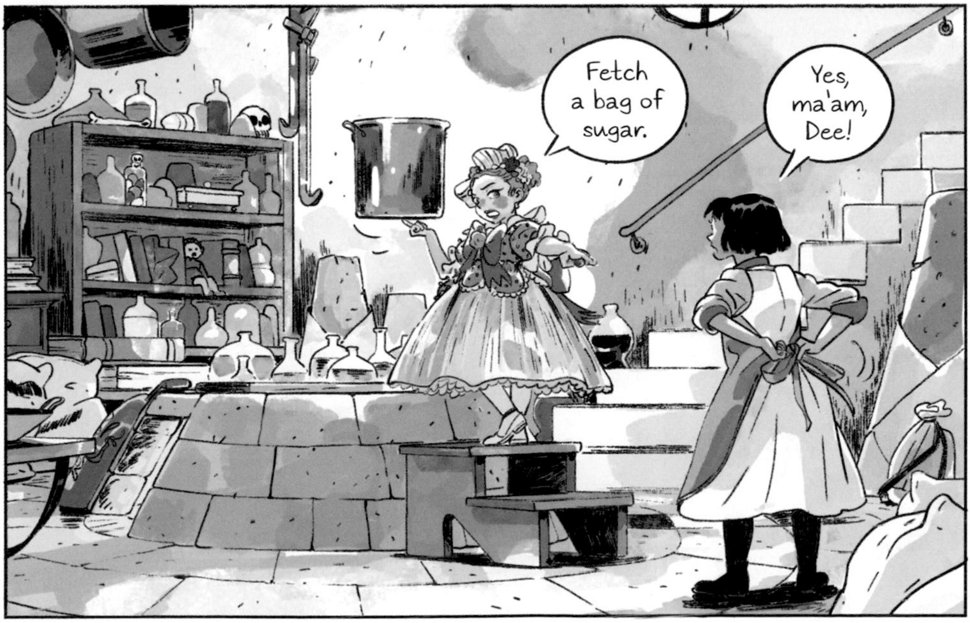
Fetch a bag of sugar.
Yes, ma'am, Dee!

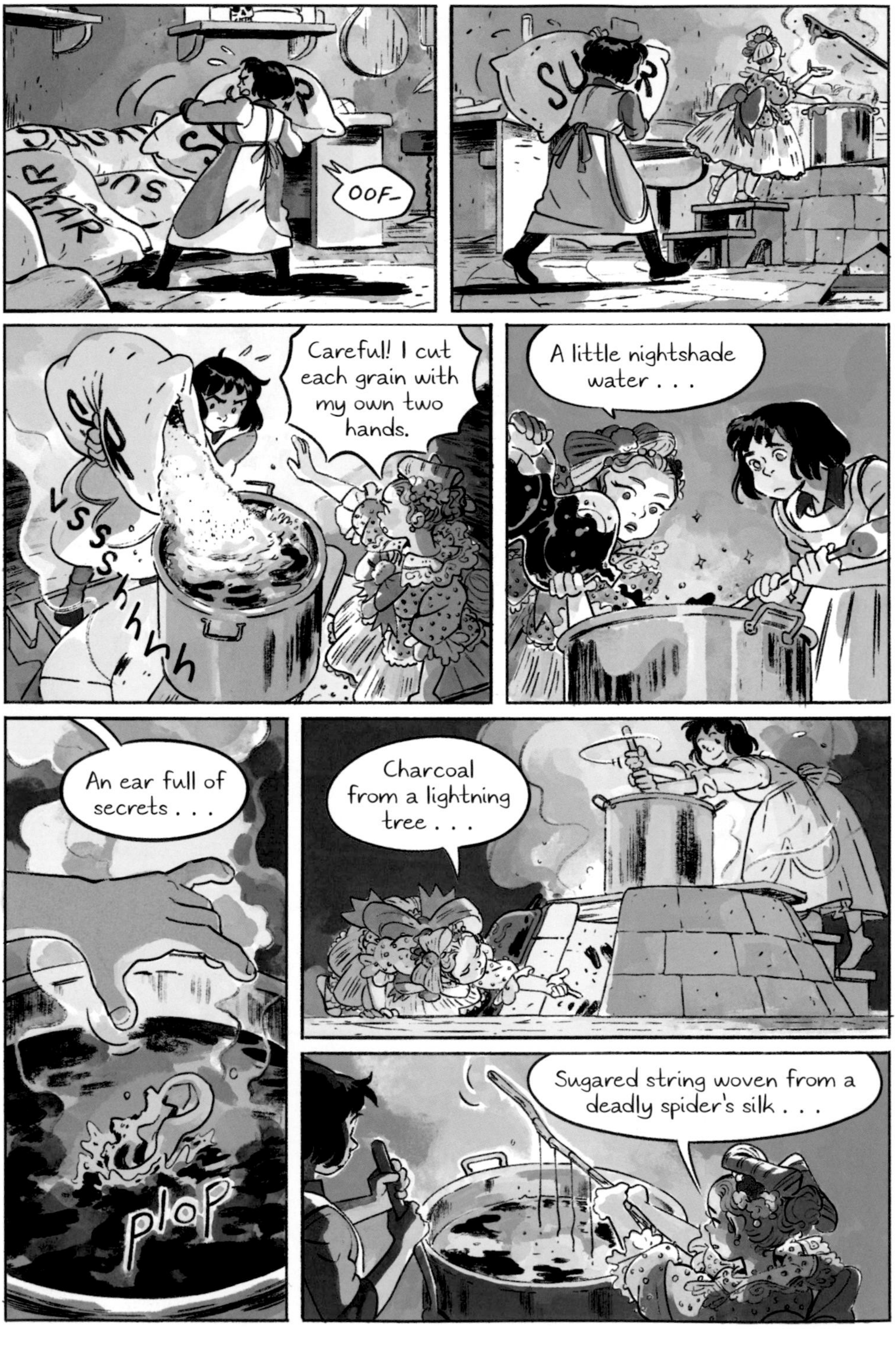
OOF–
Careful! I cut each grain with my own two hands.
VSSSHHHHH
A little nightshade water . . .
An ear full of secrets . . .
plop
Charcoal from a lightning tree . . .
Sugared string woven from a deadly spider's silk . . .

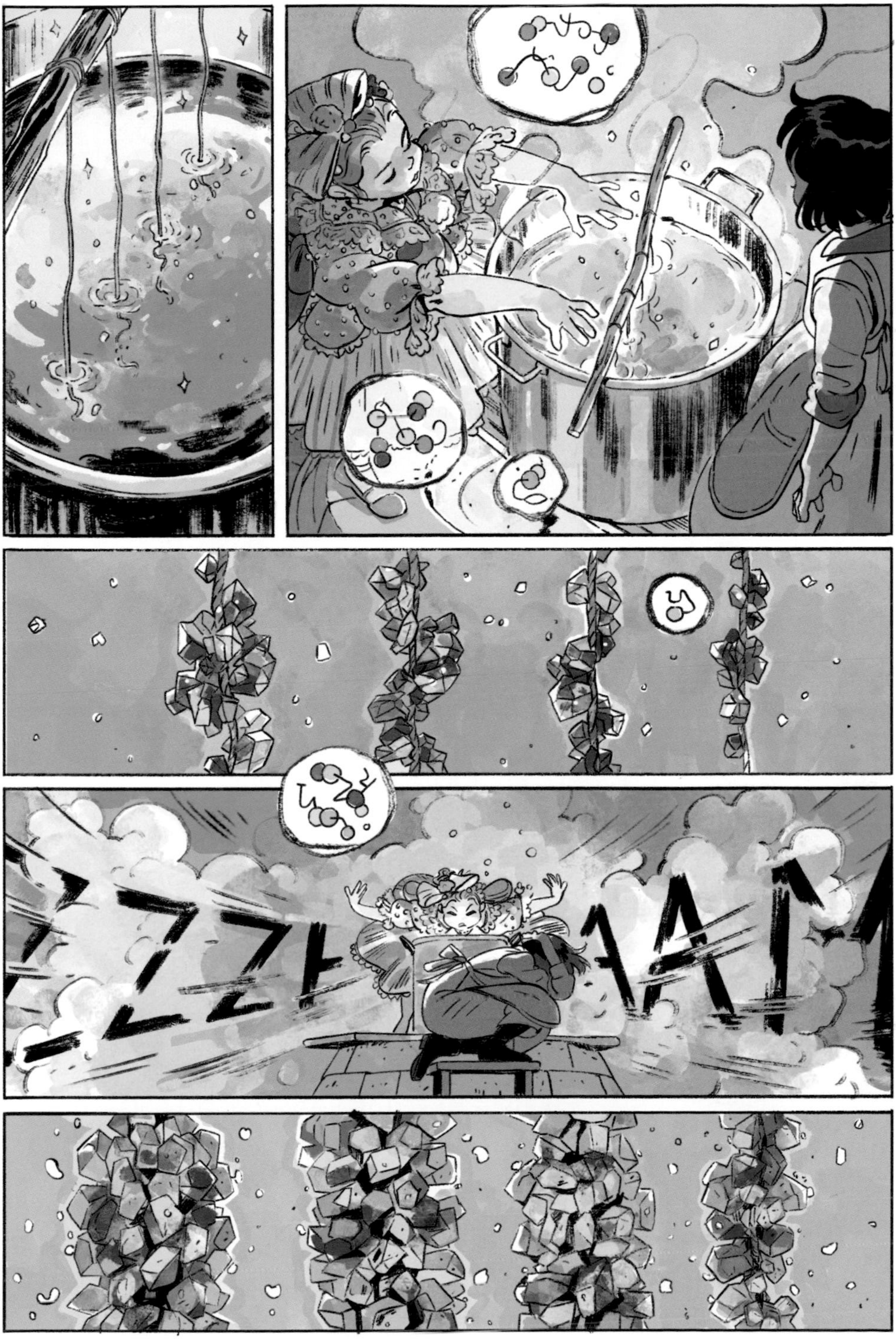

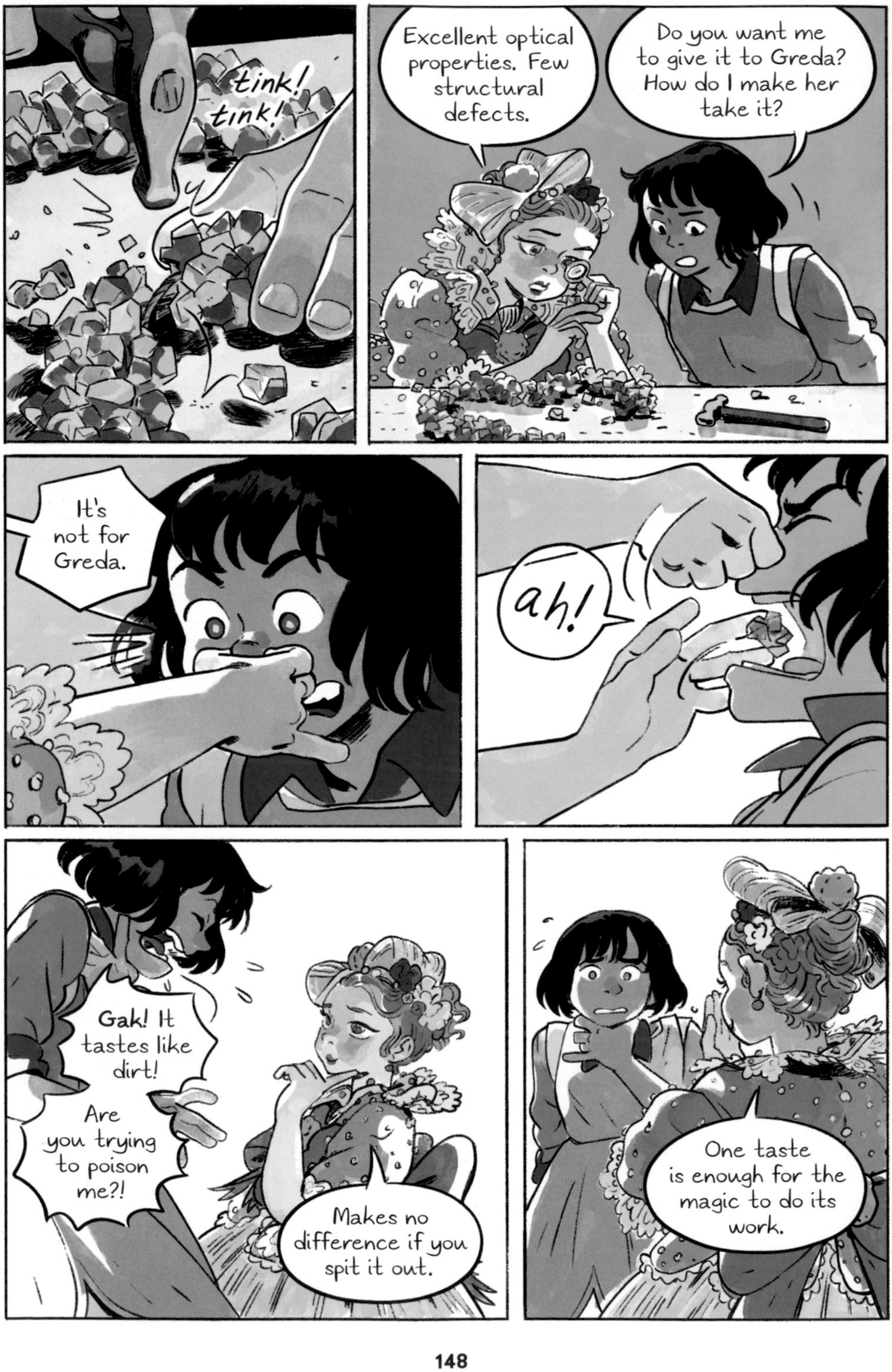
tink!
tink!
Excellent optical properties. Few structural defects.
Do you want me to give it to Greda? How do I make her take it?
It's not for Greda.
ah!
Gak! It tastes like dirt!
Are you trying to poison me?!
Makes no difference if you spit it out.
One taste is enough for the magic to do its work.

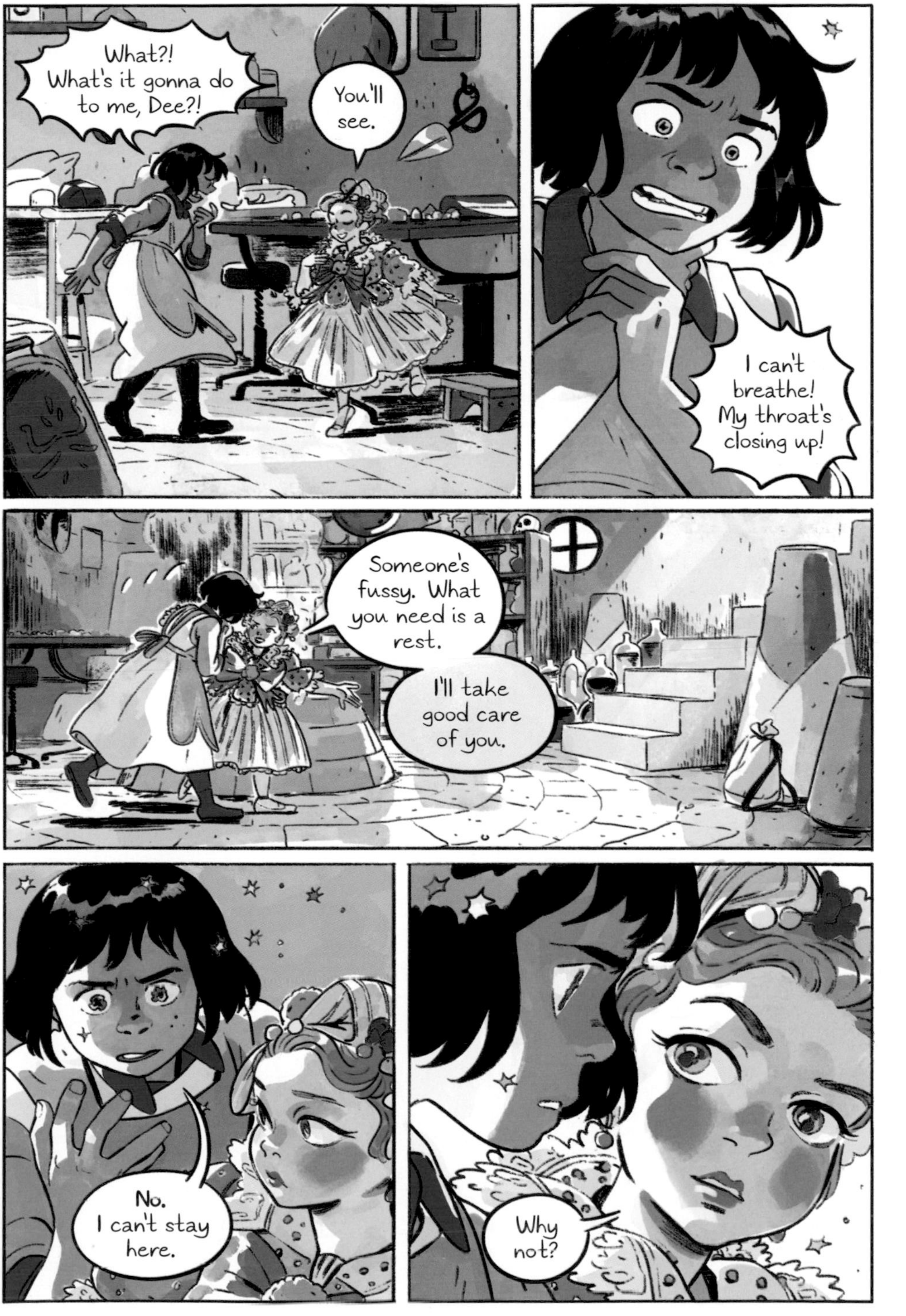
What?! What's it gonna do to me, Dee?!
You'll see.
I can't breathe! My throat's closing up!
Someone's fussy. What you need is a rest.
I'll take good care of you.
No. I can't stay here.
Why not?

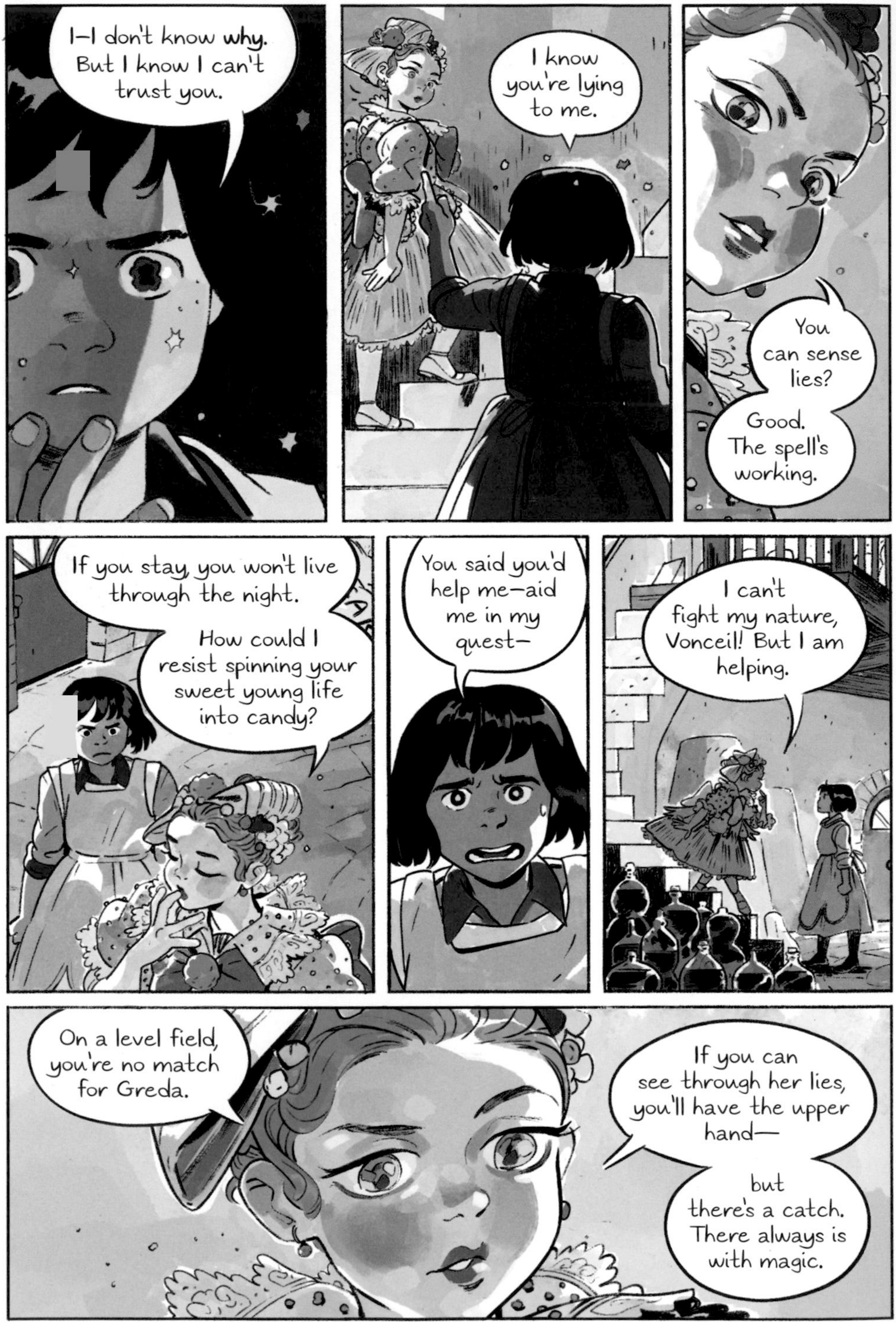
I—I don't know why. But I know I can't trust you.
I know you're lying to me.
You can sense lies?
Good. The spell's working.
If you stay, you won't live through the night.
How could I resist spinning your sweet young life into candy?
You said you'd help me—aid me in my quest—
I can't fight my nature, Vonceil! But I am helping.
On a level field, you're no match for Greda.
If you can see through her lies, you'll have the upper hand—
but there's a catch. There always is with magic.

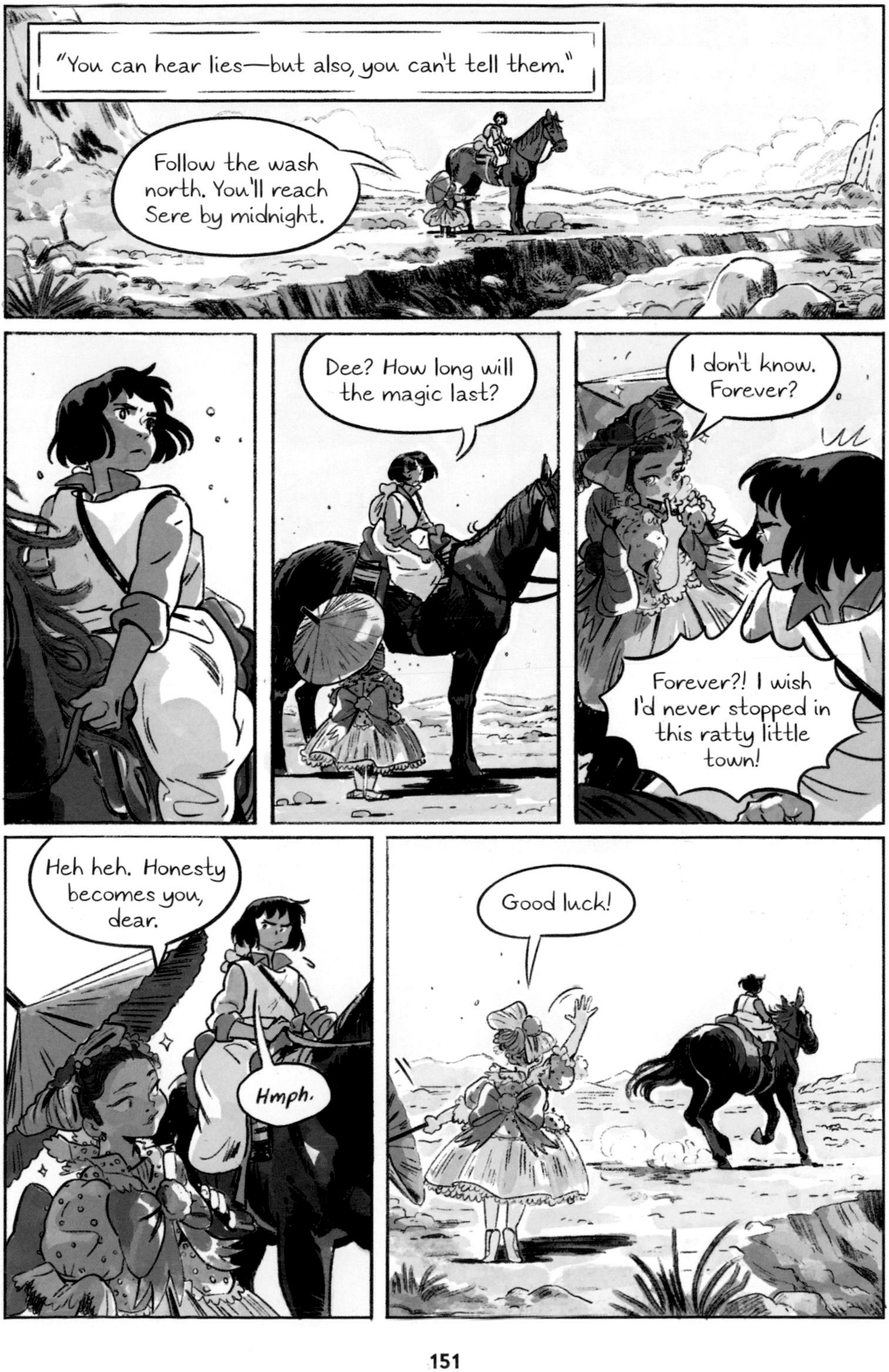
"You can hear lies—but also, you can't tell them."
Follow the wash north. You'll reach Sere by midnight.
Dee? How long will the magic last?
I don't know. Forever?
Forever?! I wish I'd never stopped in this ratty little town!
Heh heh. Honesty becomes you, dear.
Hmph.
Good luck!

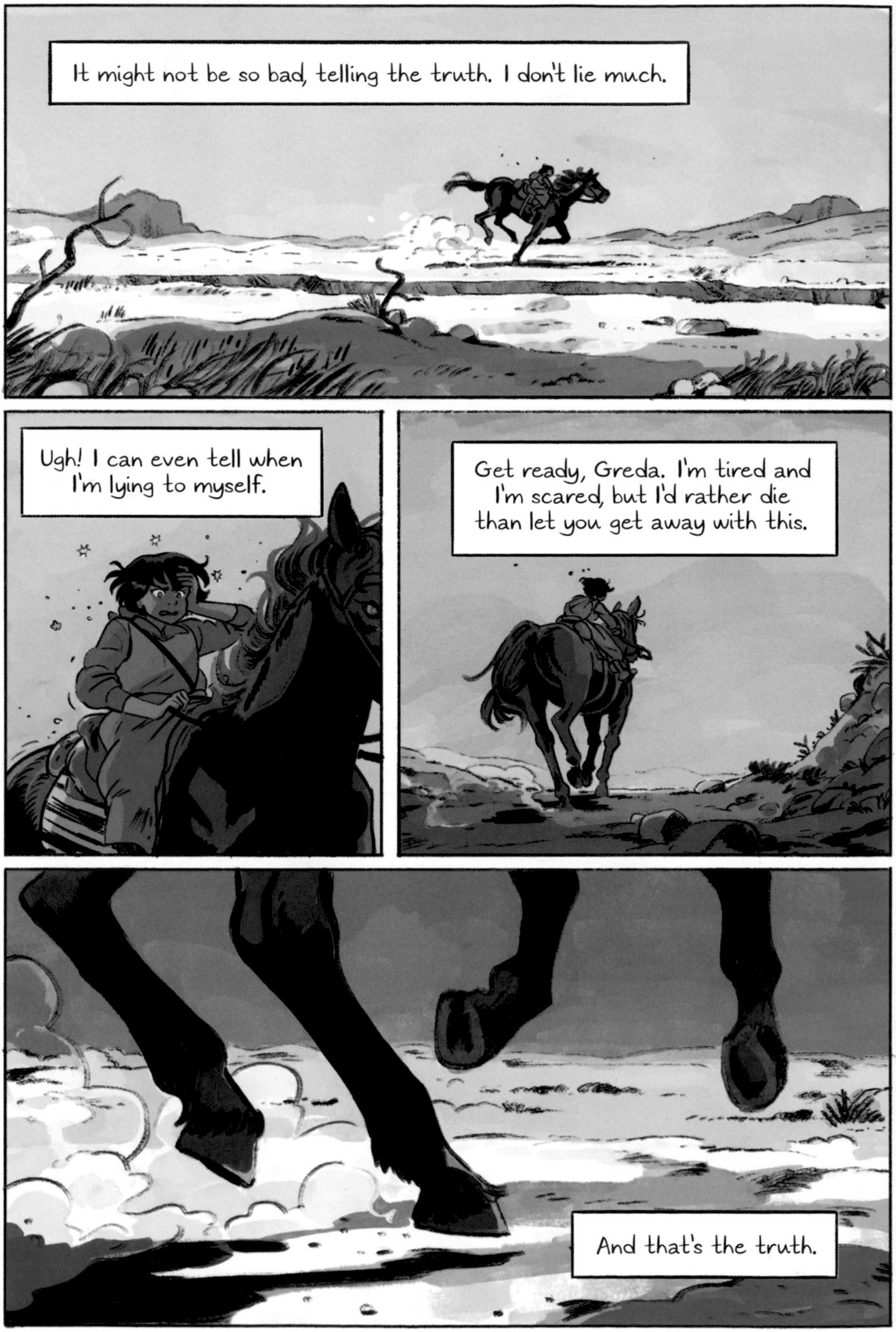
It might not be so bad, telling the truth. I don't lie much.
Ugh! I can even tell when I'm lying to myself.
Get ready, Greda. I'm tired and I'm scared, but I'd rather die than let you get away with this.
And that's the truth.

Chapter Nine

Hospitality

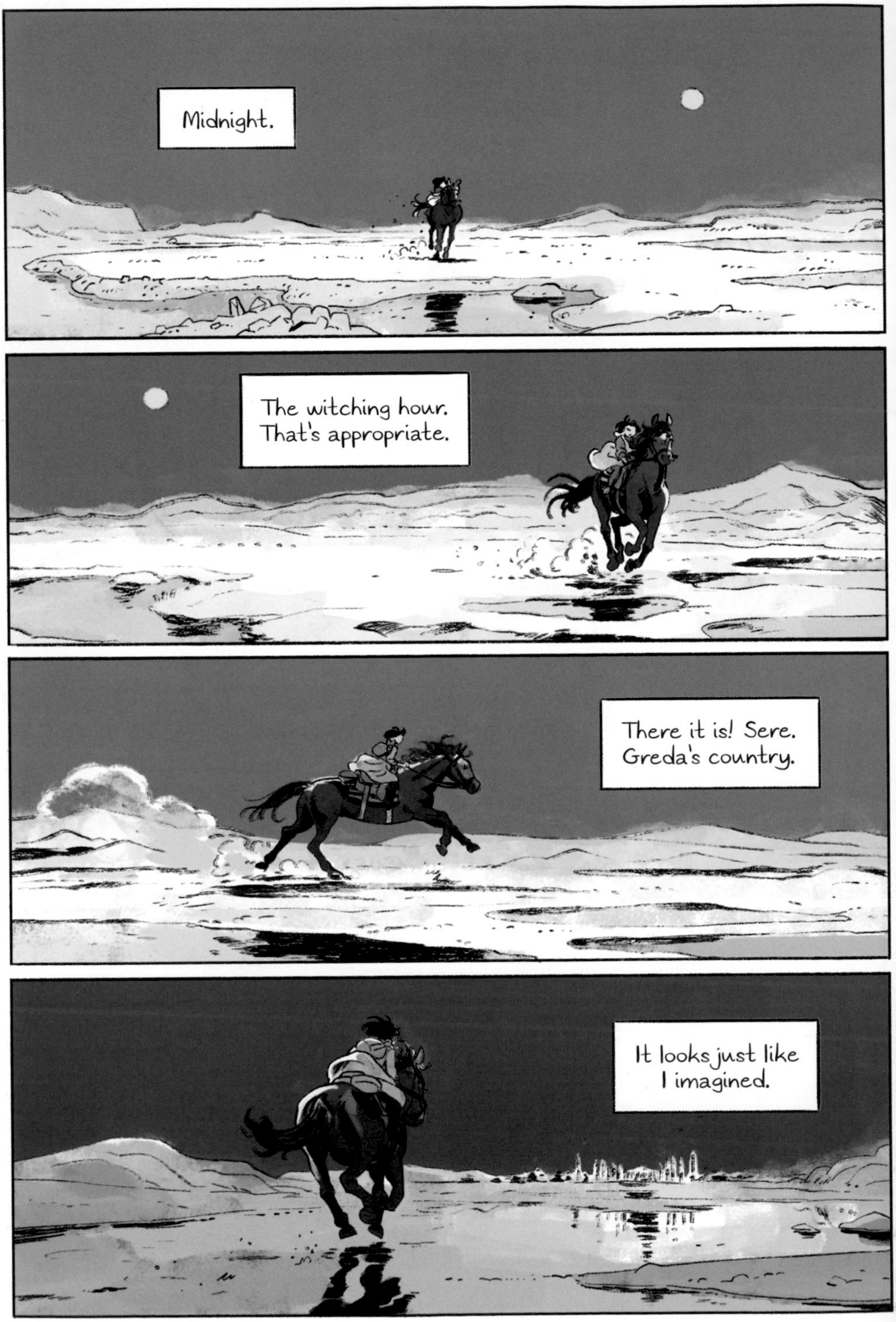
Midnight.
The witching hour. That's appropriate.
There it is! Sere. Greda's country.
It looks just like I imagined.

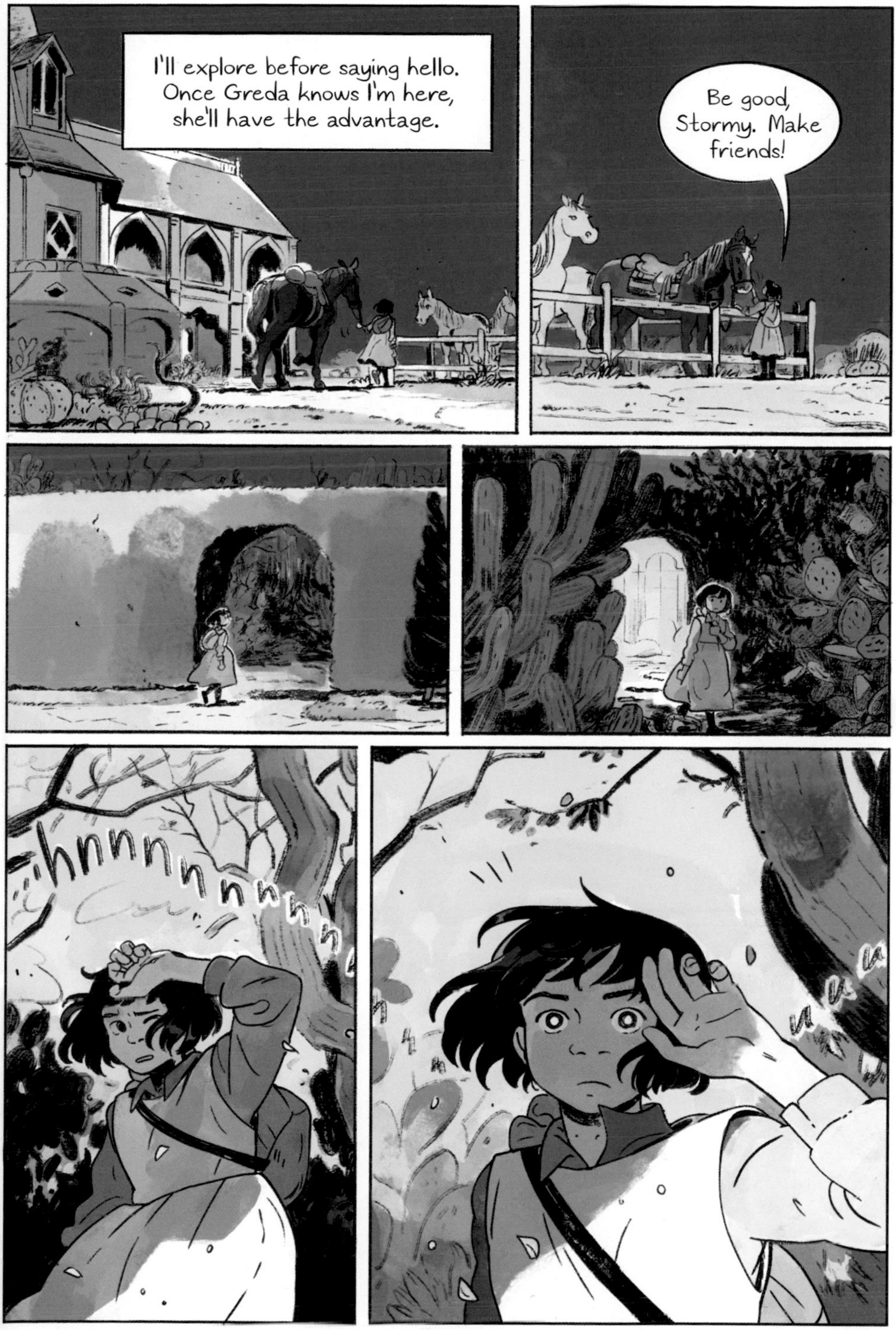
I'll explore before saying hello. Once Greda knows I'm here, she'll have the advantage.
Be good, Stormy. Make friends!
hnnnnnnnnnn

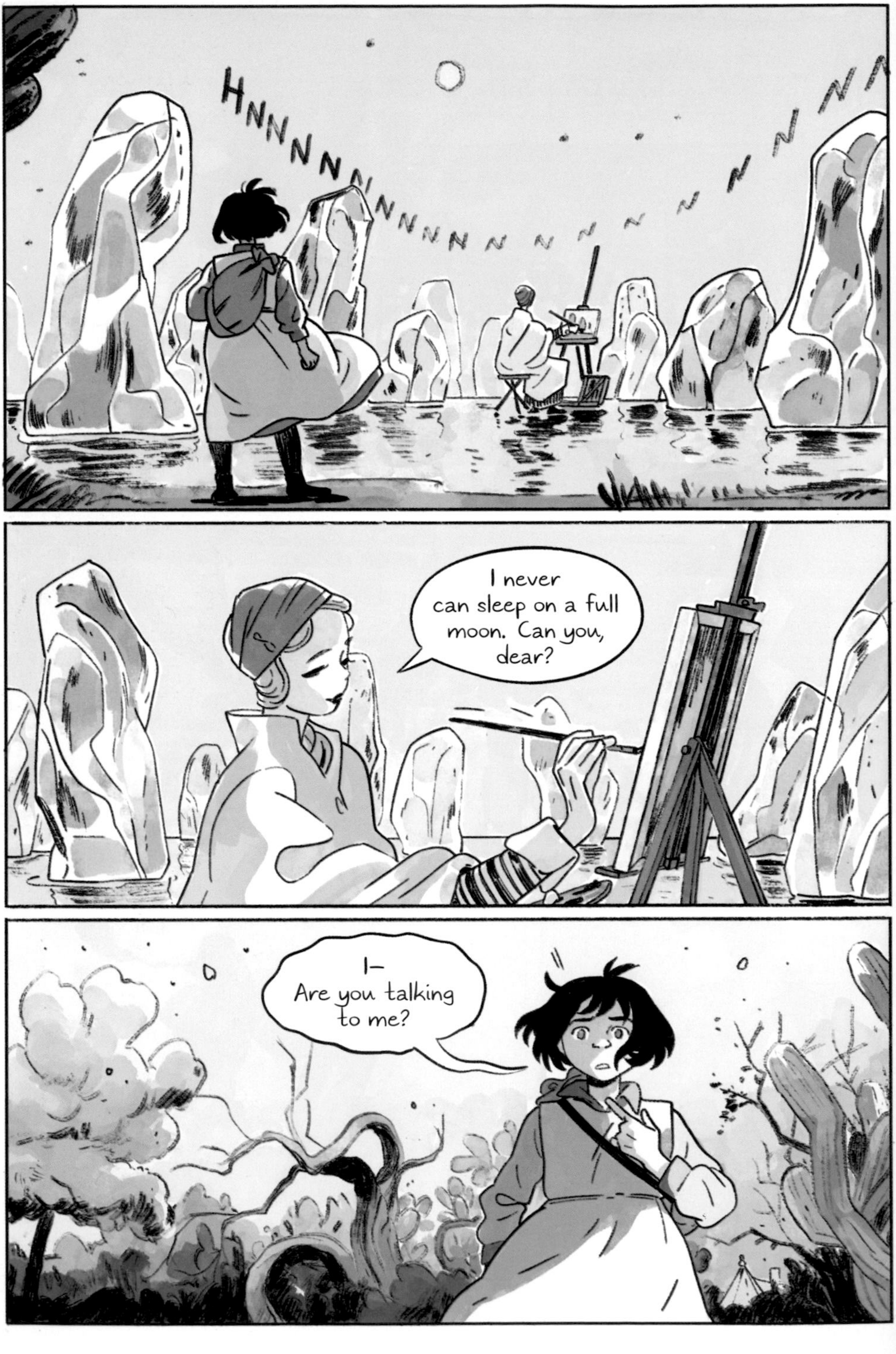
HNNNNNNNNNNNNNNNNNNNNNN
I never can sleep on a full moon. Can you, dear?
I– Are you talking to me?

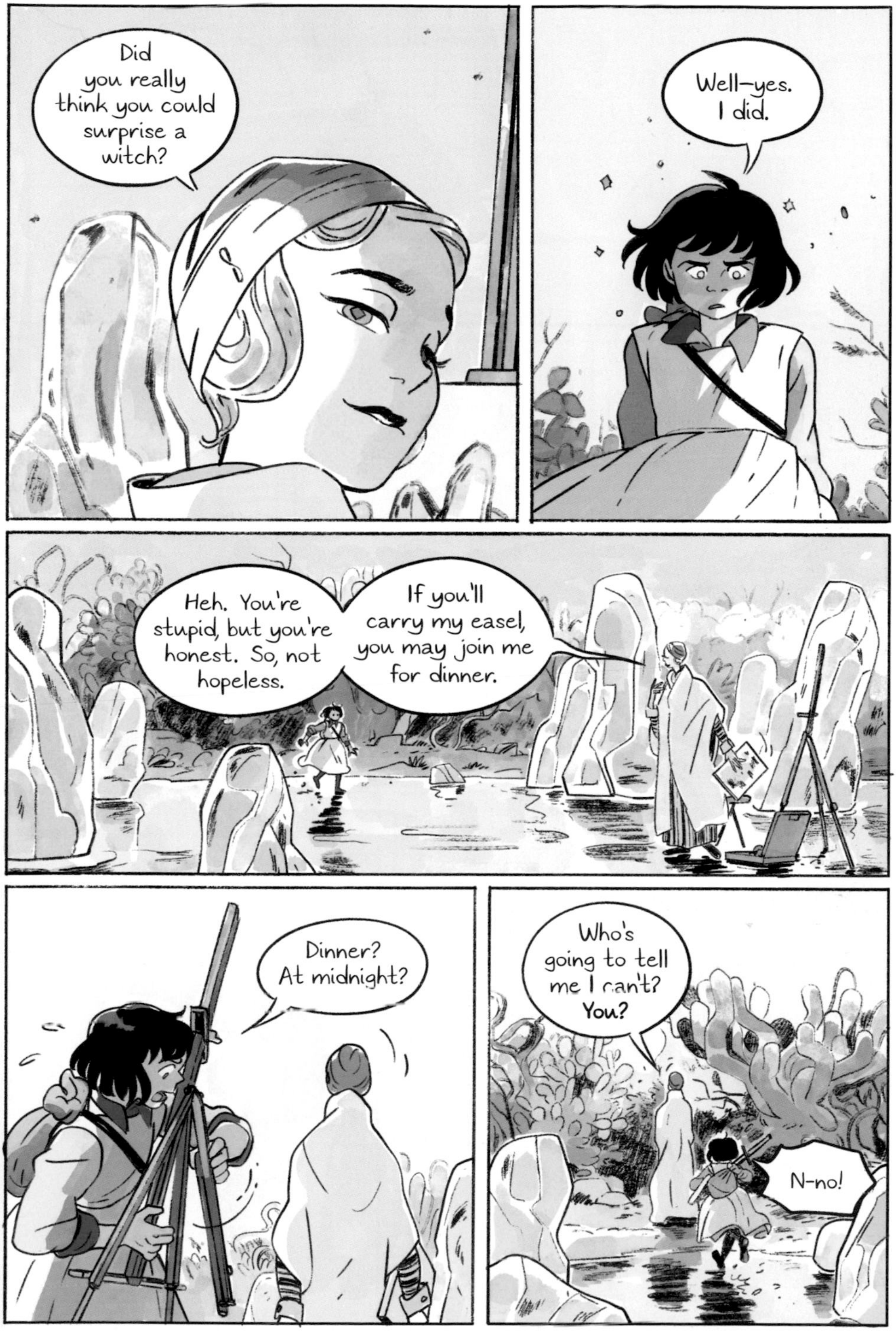

Did you really think you could surprise a witch?
Well—yes. I did.
Heh. You're stupid, but you're honest. So, not hopeless.
If you'll carry my easel, you may join me for dinner.
Dinner? At midnight?
Who's going to tell me I can't? **You?**
N-no!

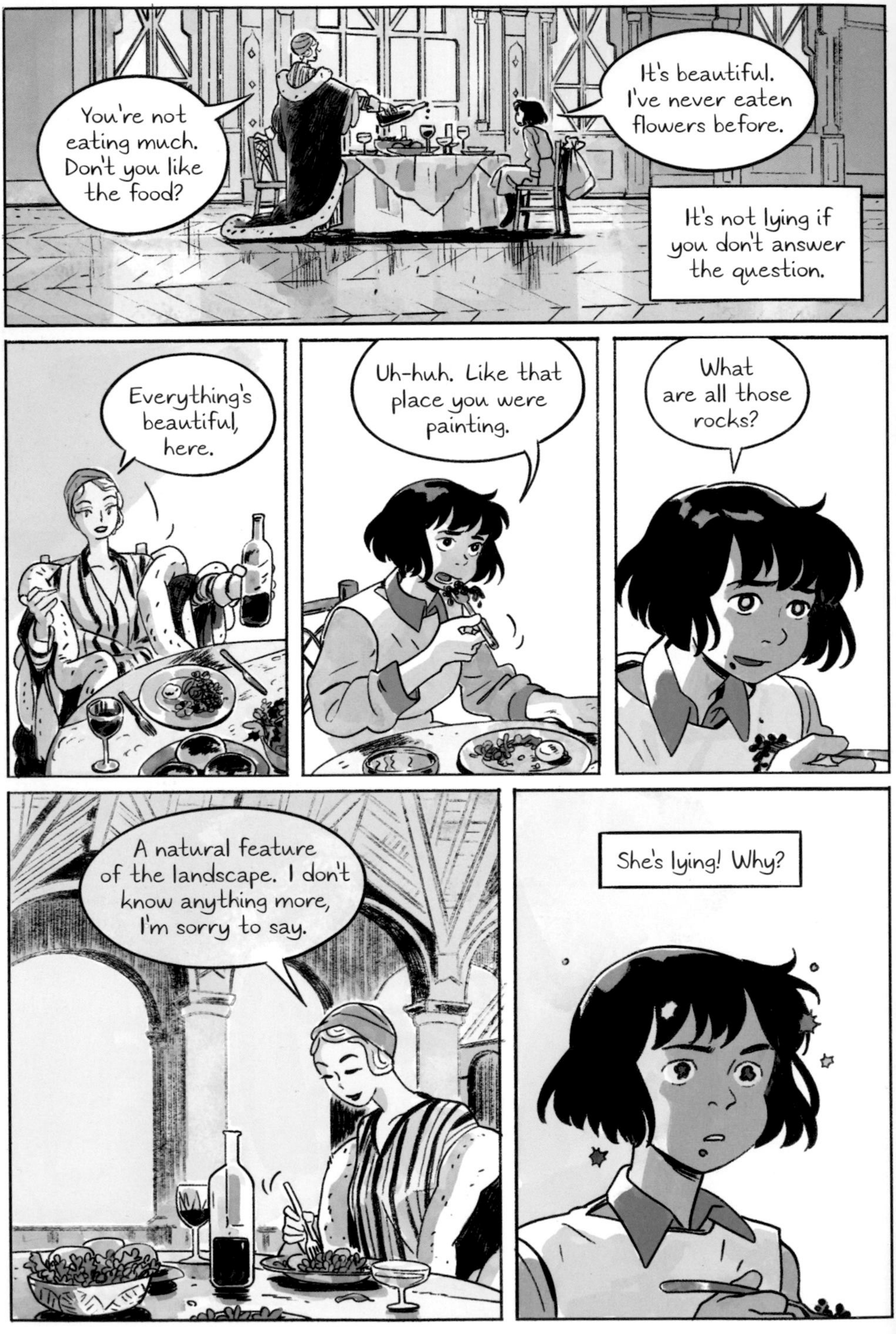
You're not eating much. Don't you like the food?
It's beautiful. I've never eaten flowers before.
It's not lying if you don't answer the question.
Everything's beautiful, here.
Uh-huh. Like that place you were painting.
What are all those rocks?
A natural feature of the landscape. I don't know anything more, I'm sorry to say.
She's lying! Why?

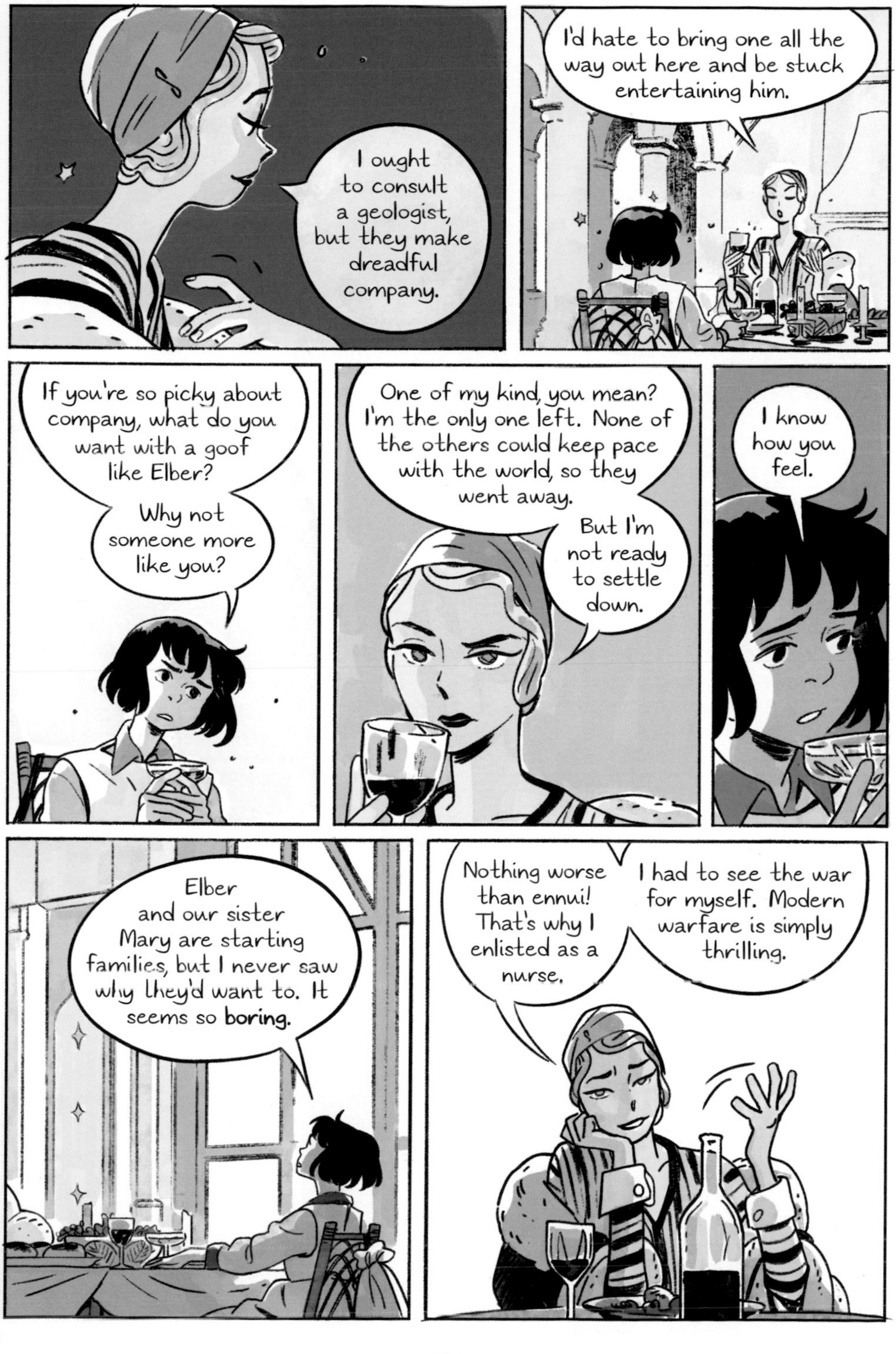
I ought to consult a geologist, but they make dreadful company.
I'd hate to bring one all the way out here and be stuck entertaining him.
If you're so picky about company, what do you want with a goof like Elber?
Why not someone more like you?
One of my kind, you mean? I'm the only one left. None of the others could keep pace with the world, so they went away.
But I'm not ready to settle down.
I know how you feel.
Elber and our sister Mary are starting families, but I never saw why they'd want to. It seems so **boring.**
Nothing worse than ennui! That's why I enlisted as a nurse.
I had to see the war for myself. Modern warfare is simply thrilling.

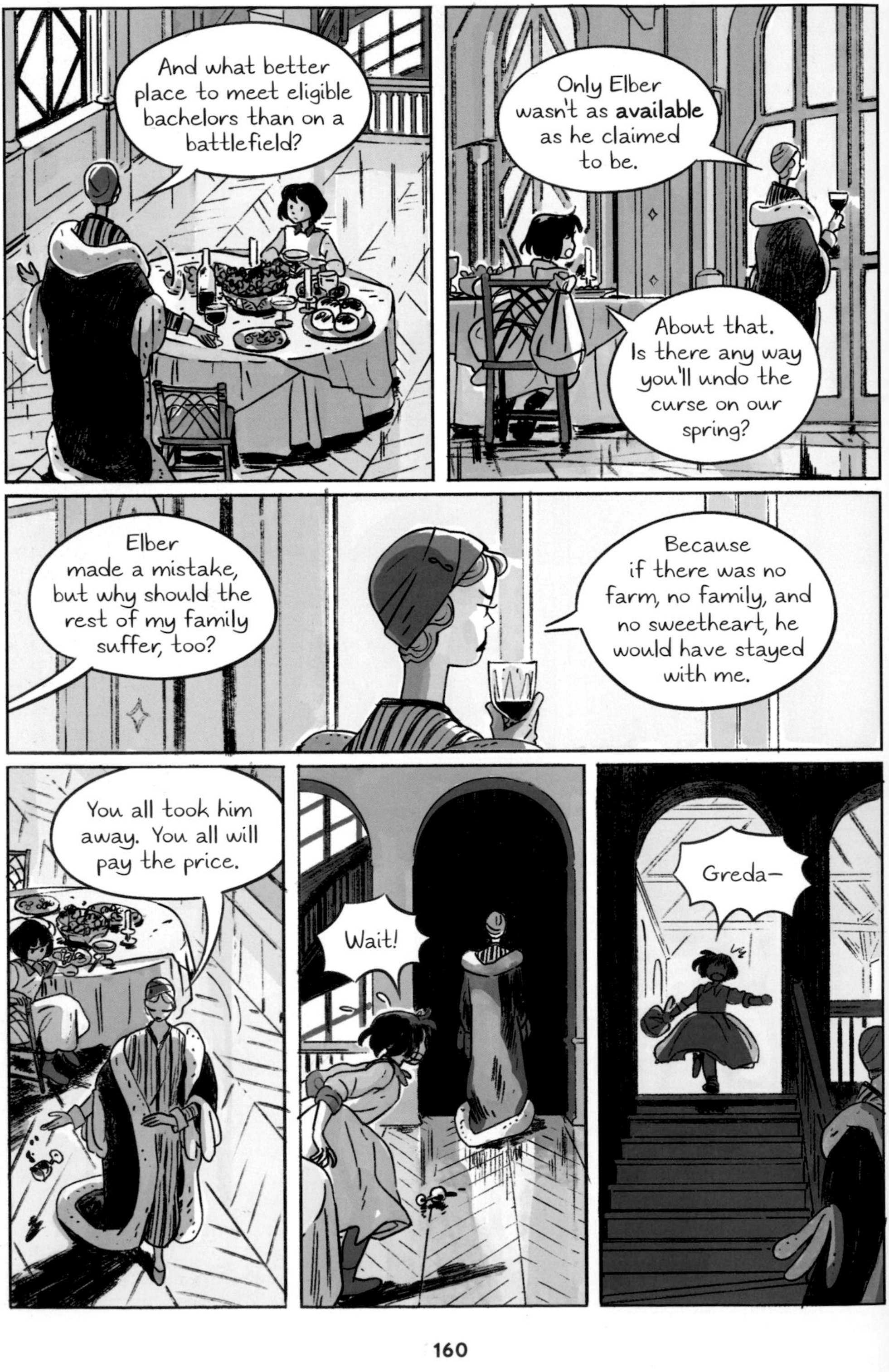
And what better place to meet eligible bachelors than on a battlefield?
Only Elber wasn't as **available** as he claimed to be.
About that. Is there any way you'll undo the curse on our spring?
Elber made a mistake, but why should the rest of my family suffer, too?
Because if there was no farm, no family, and no sweetheart, he would have stayed with me.
You all took him away. You all will pay the price.
Wait!
Greda—

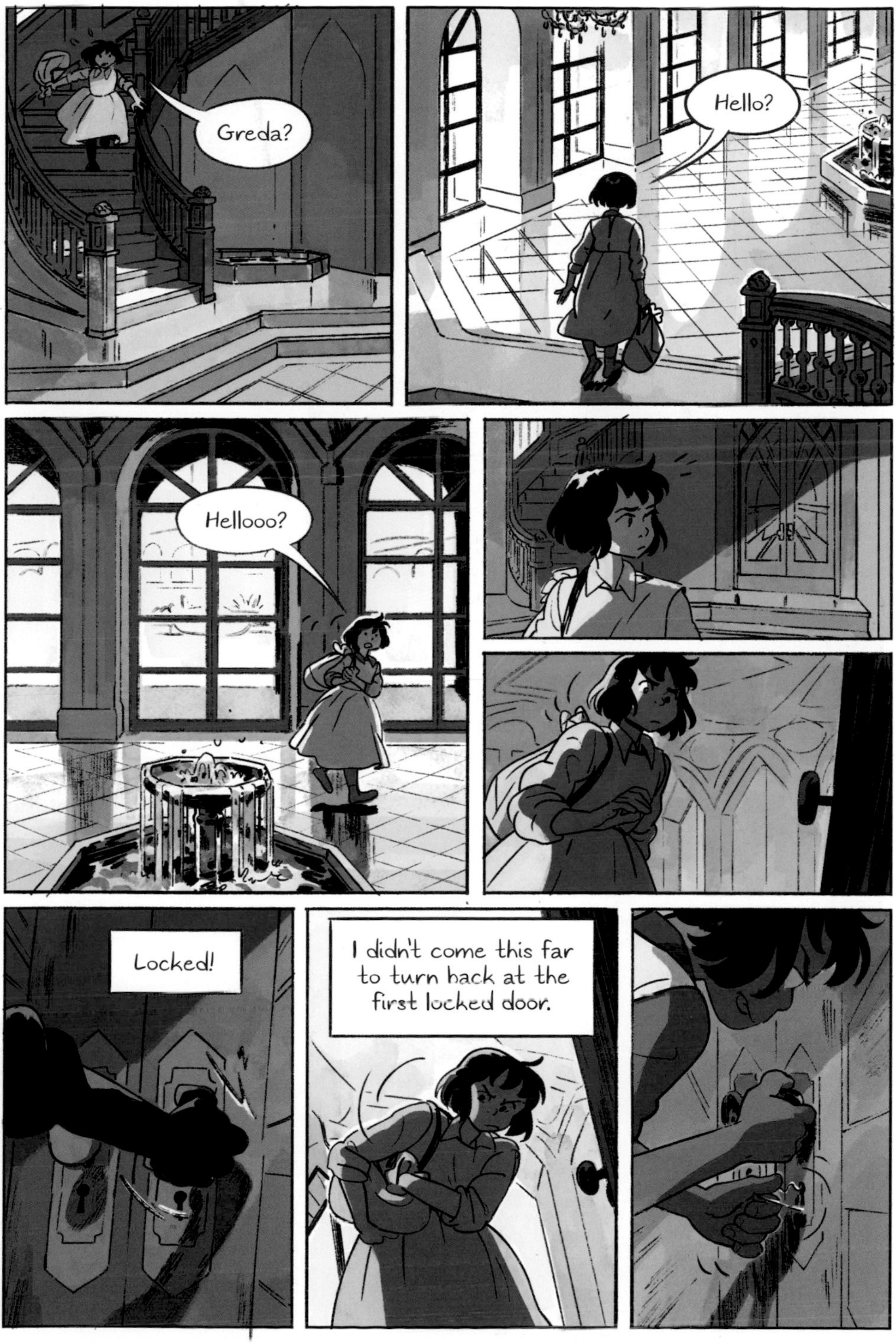
Greda?
Hello?
Hellooo?
Locked!
I didn't come this far to turn back at the first locked door.

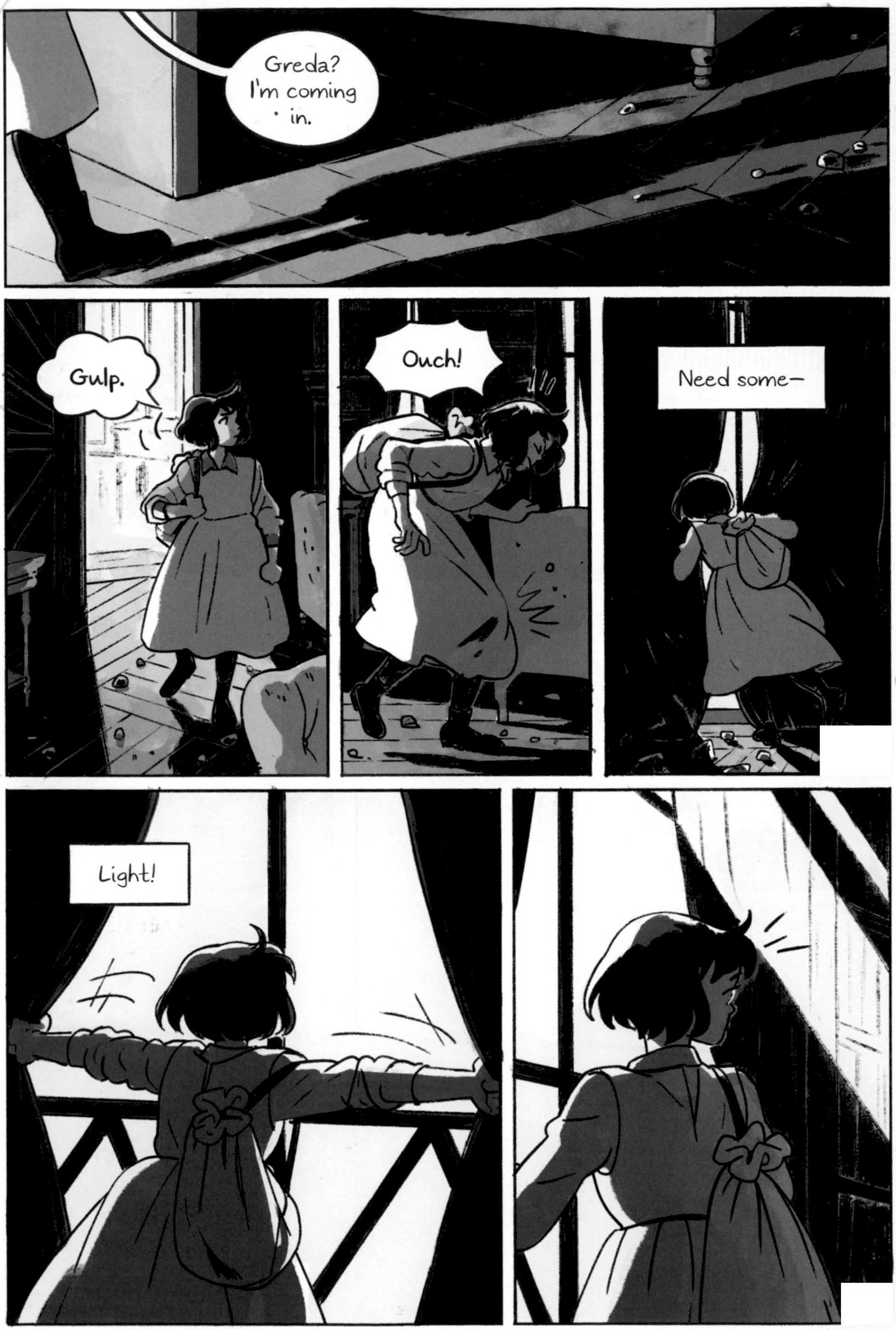
Greda? I'm coming in.
Gulp.
Ouch!
Need some—
Light!

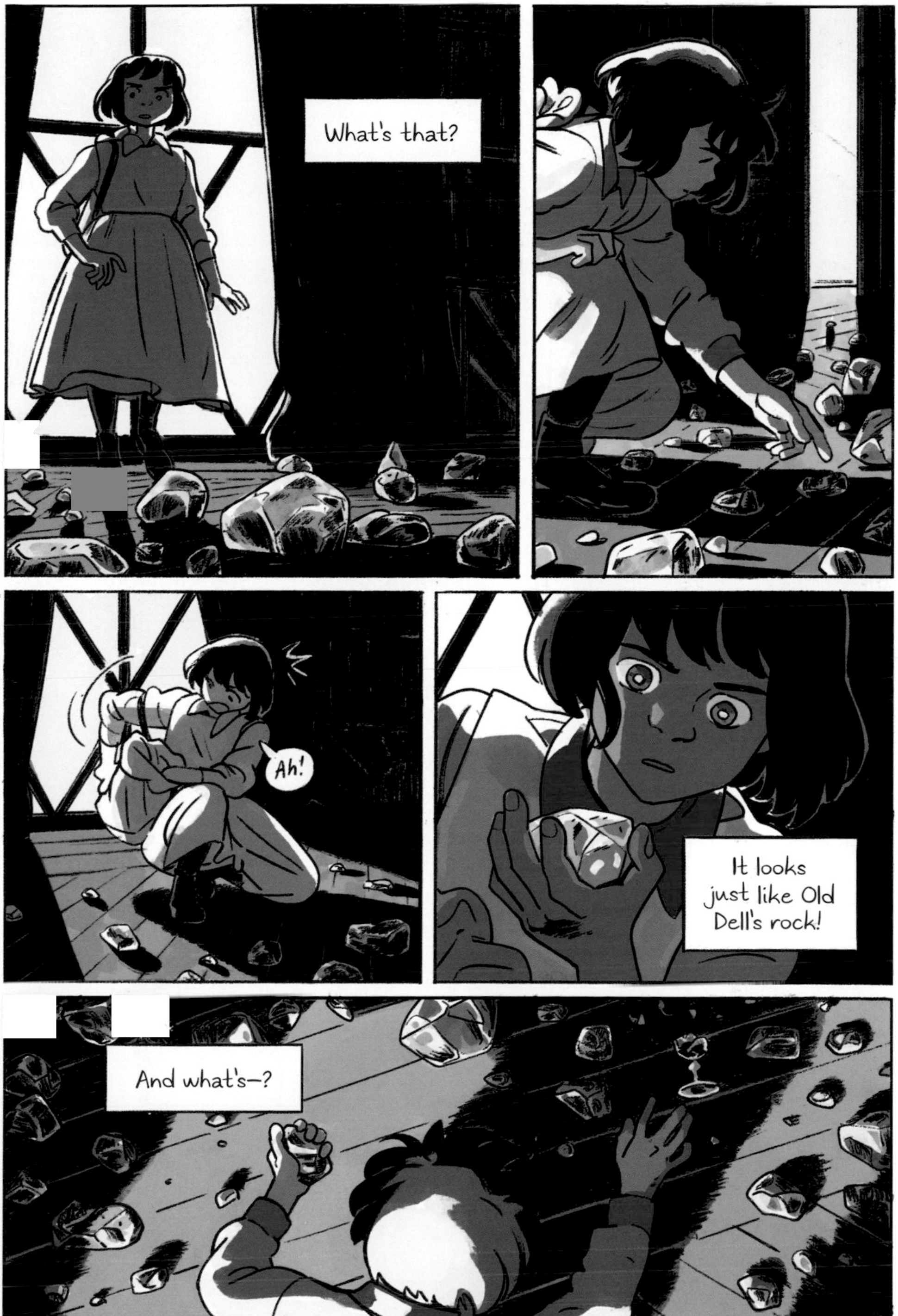
What's that?
Ah!
It looks just like Old Dell's rock!
And what's—?

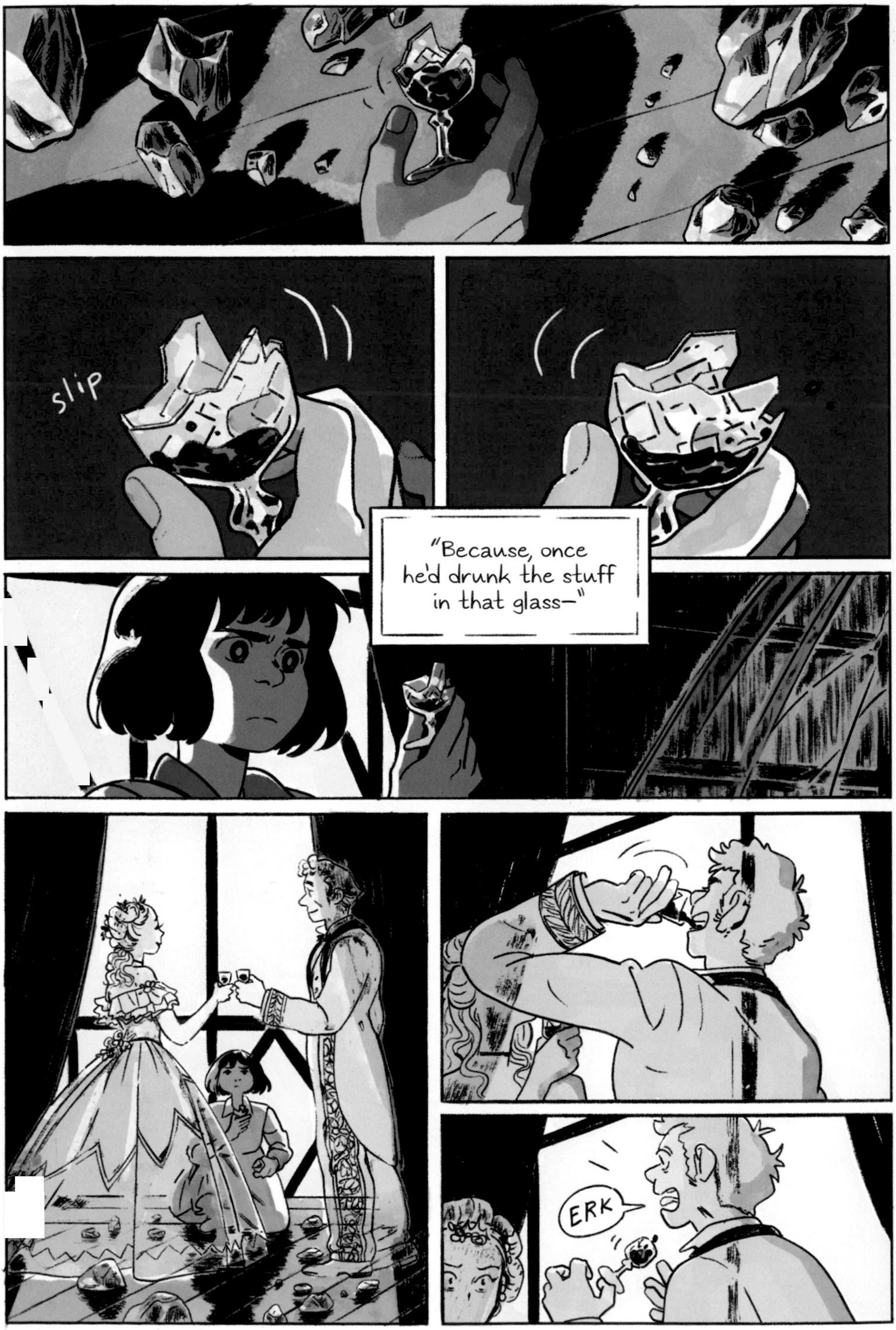
slip
"Because, once he'd drunk the stuff in that glass—"
ERK

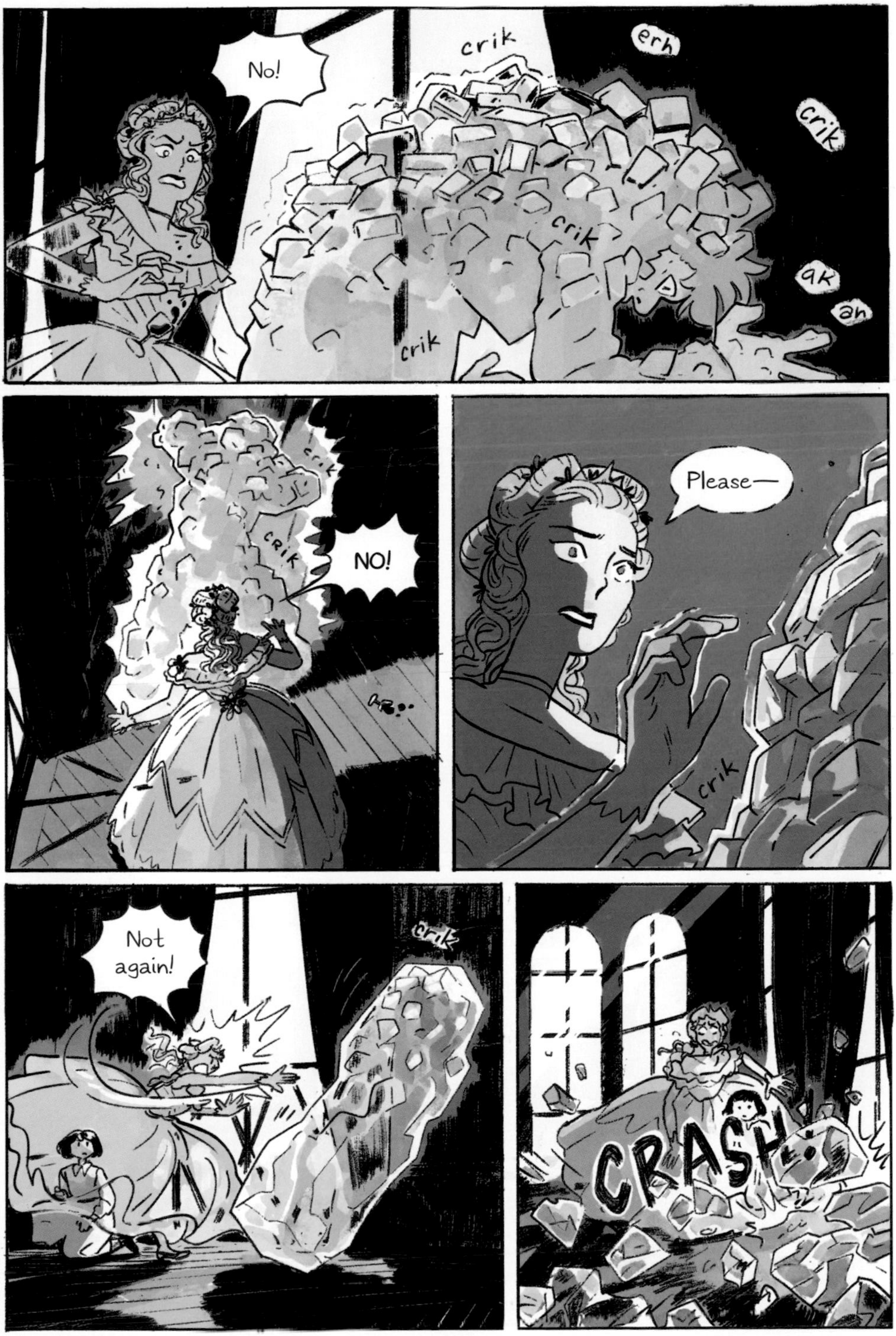
No!
crik
erh
crik
crik
ak
ah
crik
crik
crik
NO!
Please—
crik
Not again!
crik
CRASH

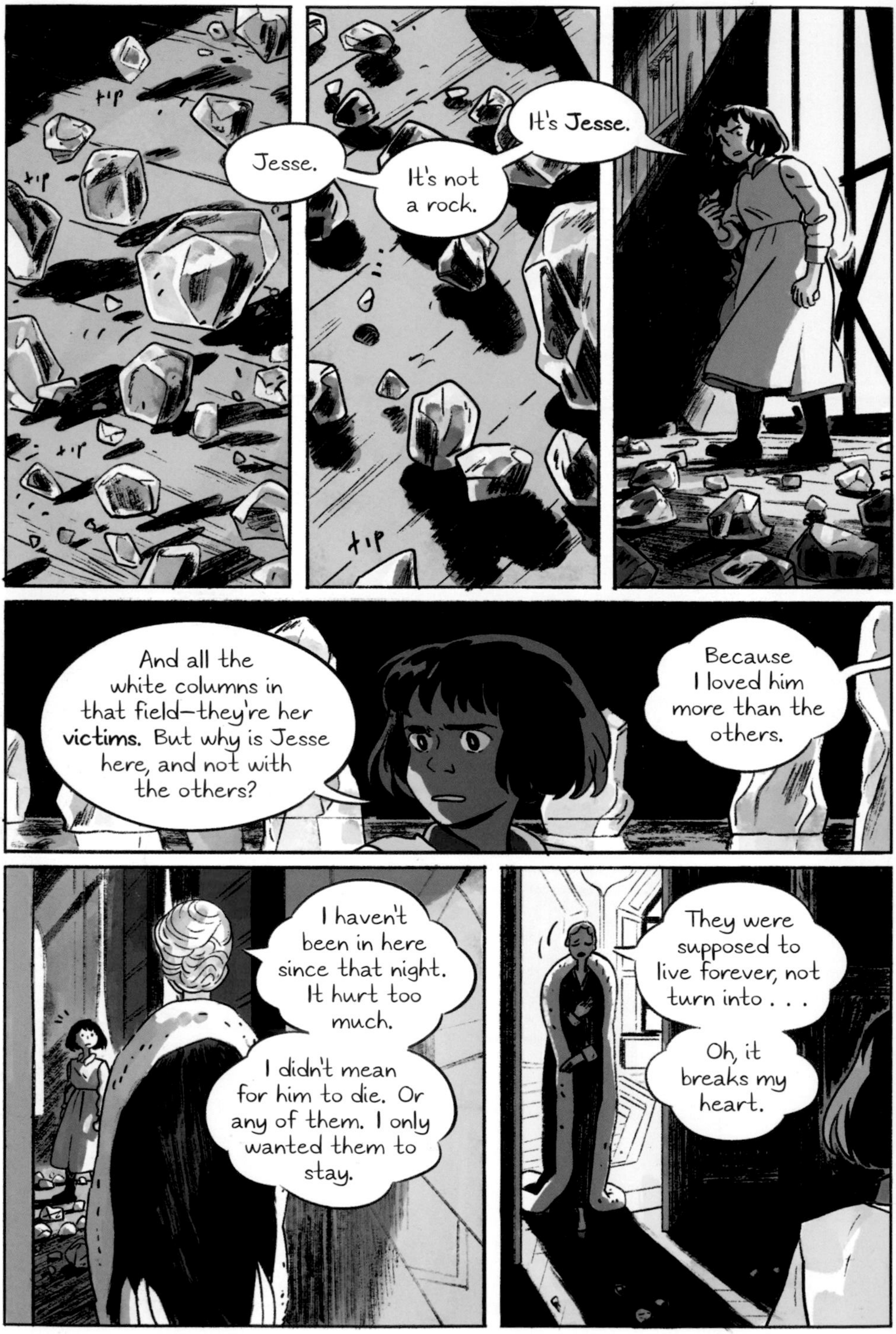

tip
tip
tip
Jesse.
It's not a rock.
It's Jesse.
tip
And all the white columns in that field—they're her victims. But why is Jesse here, and not with the others?
Because I loved him more than the others.
I haven't been in here since that night. It hurt too much.
I didn't mean for him to die. Or any of them. I only wanted them to stay.
They were supposed to live forever, not turn into . . .
Oh, it breaks my heart.

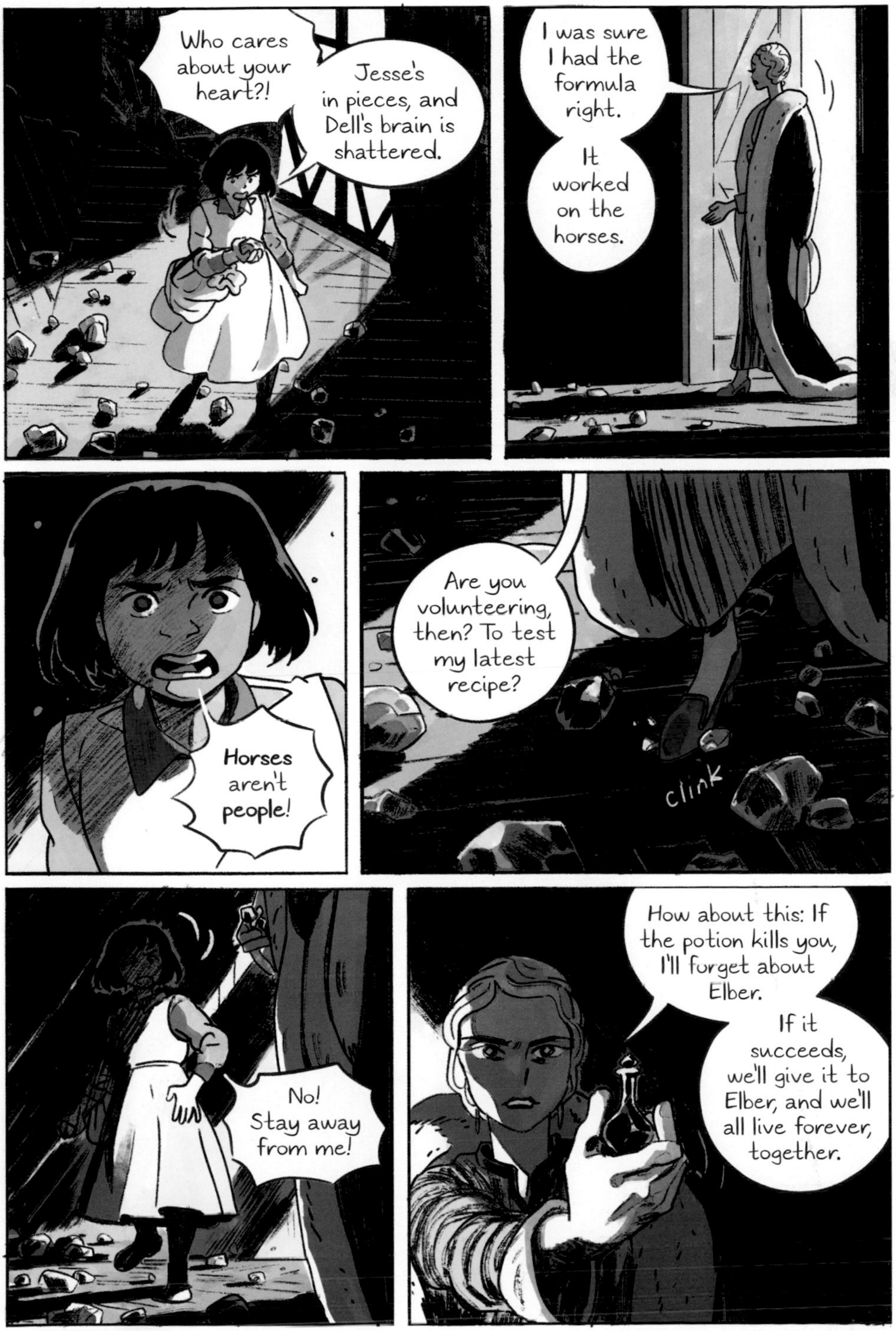
Who cares about your heart?!
Jesse's in pieces, and Dell's brain is shattered.
I was sure I had the formula right.
It worked on the horses.
Horses aren't people!
Are you volunteering, then? To test my latest recipe?
clink
No! Stay away from me!
How about this: If the potion kills you, I'll forget about Elber.
If it succeeds, we'll give it to Elber, and we'll all live forever, together.

No deal. If I drink, whether I live or die, you'll leave Elber alone.

And you'll fix the spring, too.

Pick one, girl. Elber or the spring. You can't have both.

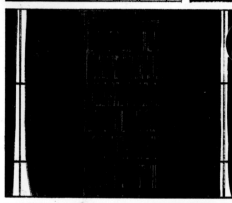

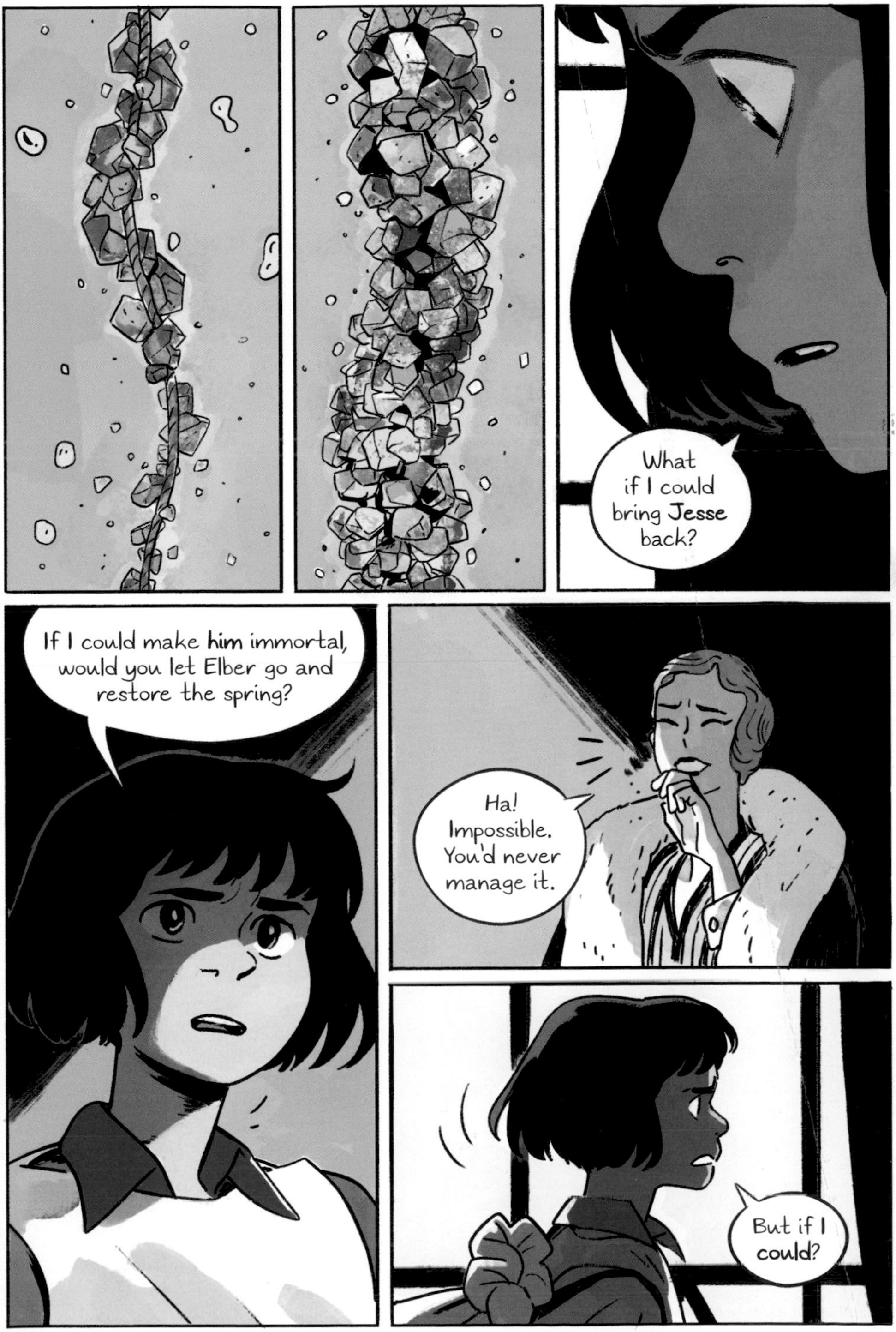
What if I could bring **Jesse** back?
If I could make **him** immortal, would you let Elber go and restore the spring?
Ha! Impossible. You'd never manage it.
But if I **could**?

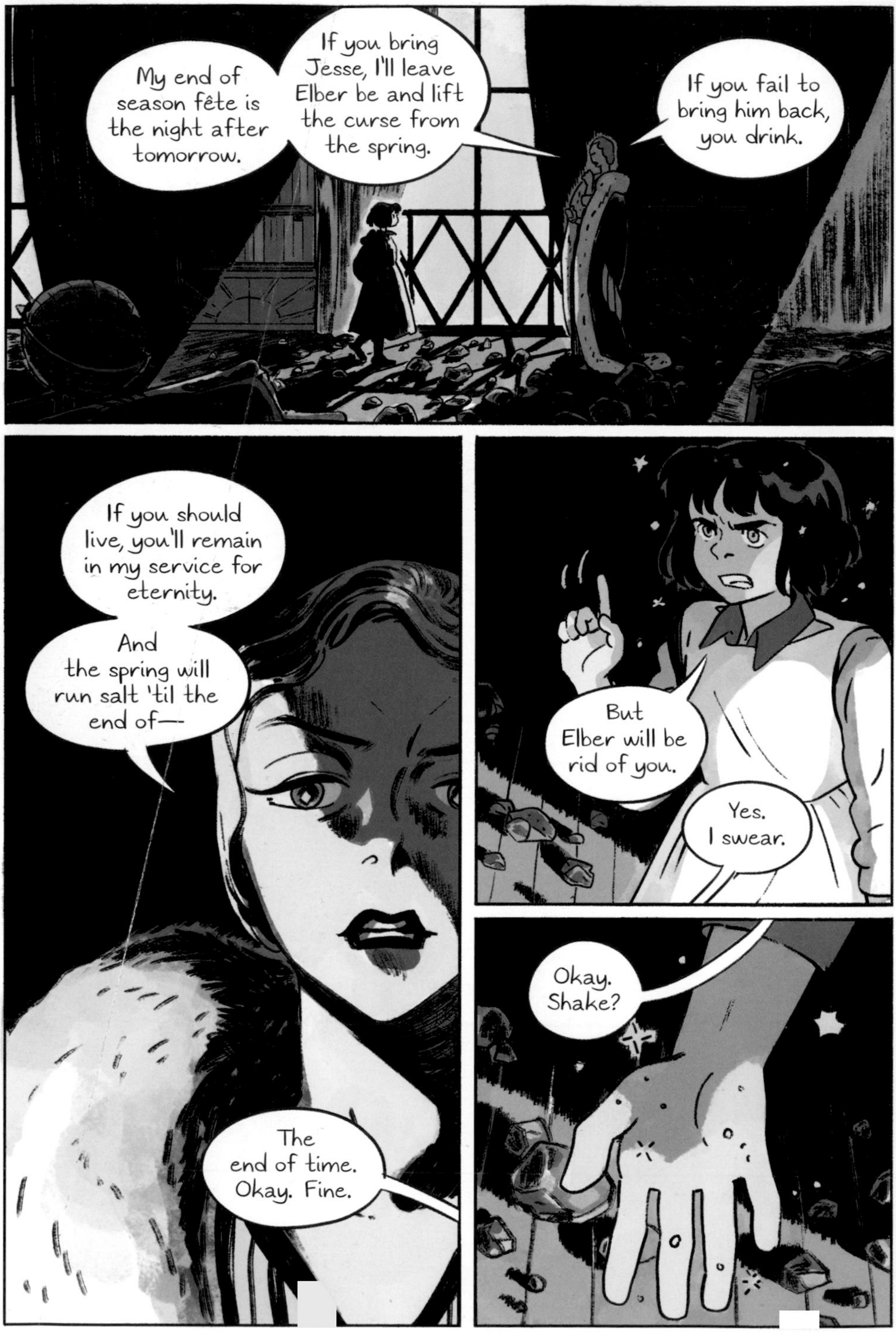

My end of season fête is the night after tomorrow.
If you bring Jesse, I'll leave Elber be and lift the curse from the spring.
If you fail to bring him back, you drink.
If you should live, you'll remain in my service for eternity.
And the spring will run salt 'til the end of—
But Elber will be rid of you.
Yes. I swear.
The end of time. Okay. Fine.
Okay. Shake?

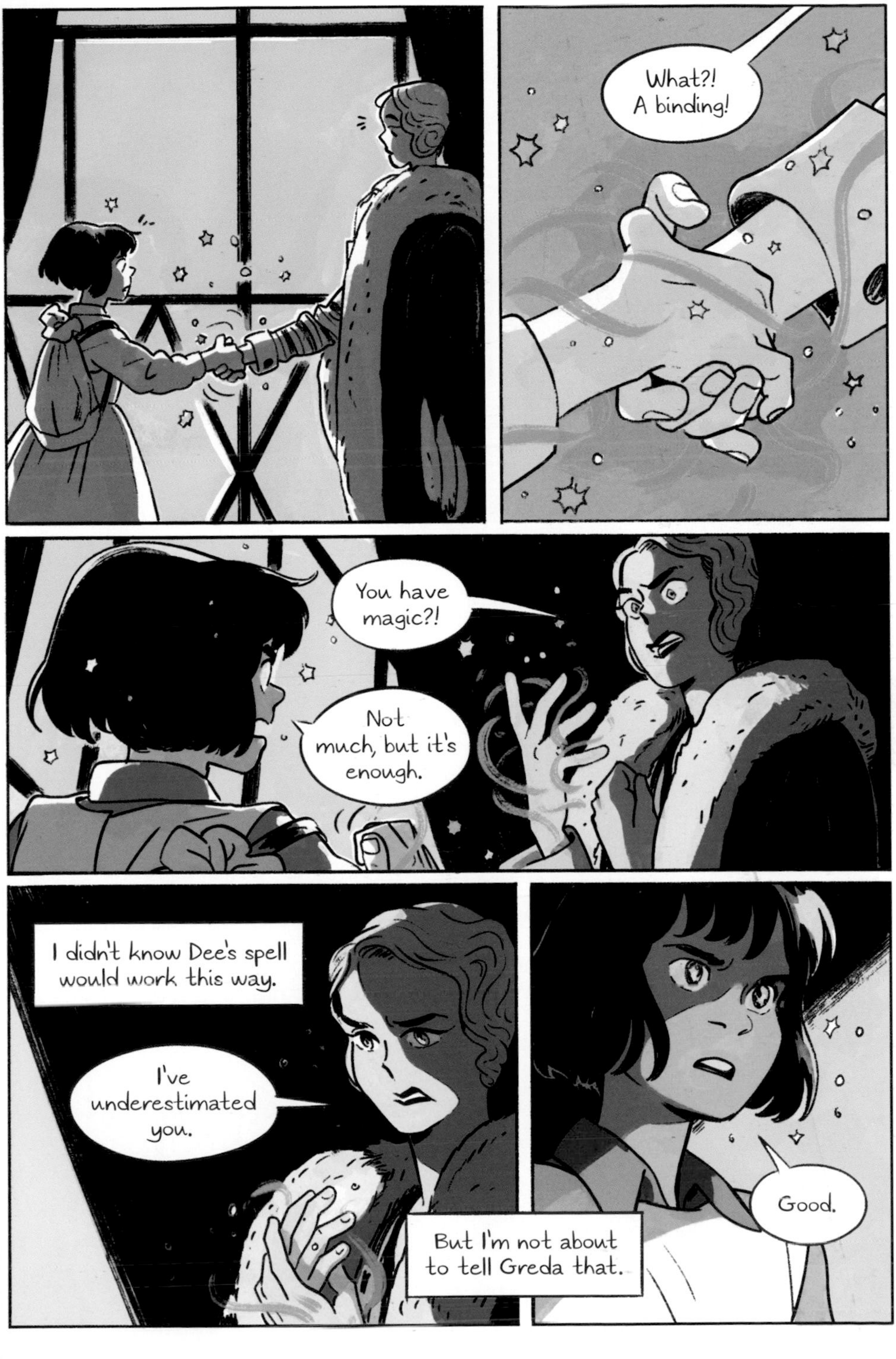
What?! A binding!
You have magic?!
Not much, but it's enough.
I didn't know Dee's spell would work this way.
I've underestimated you.
But I'm not about to tell Greda that.
Good.

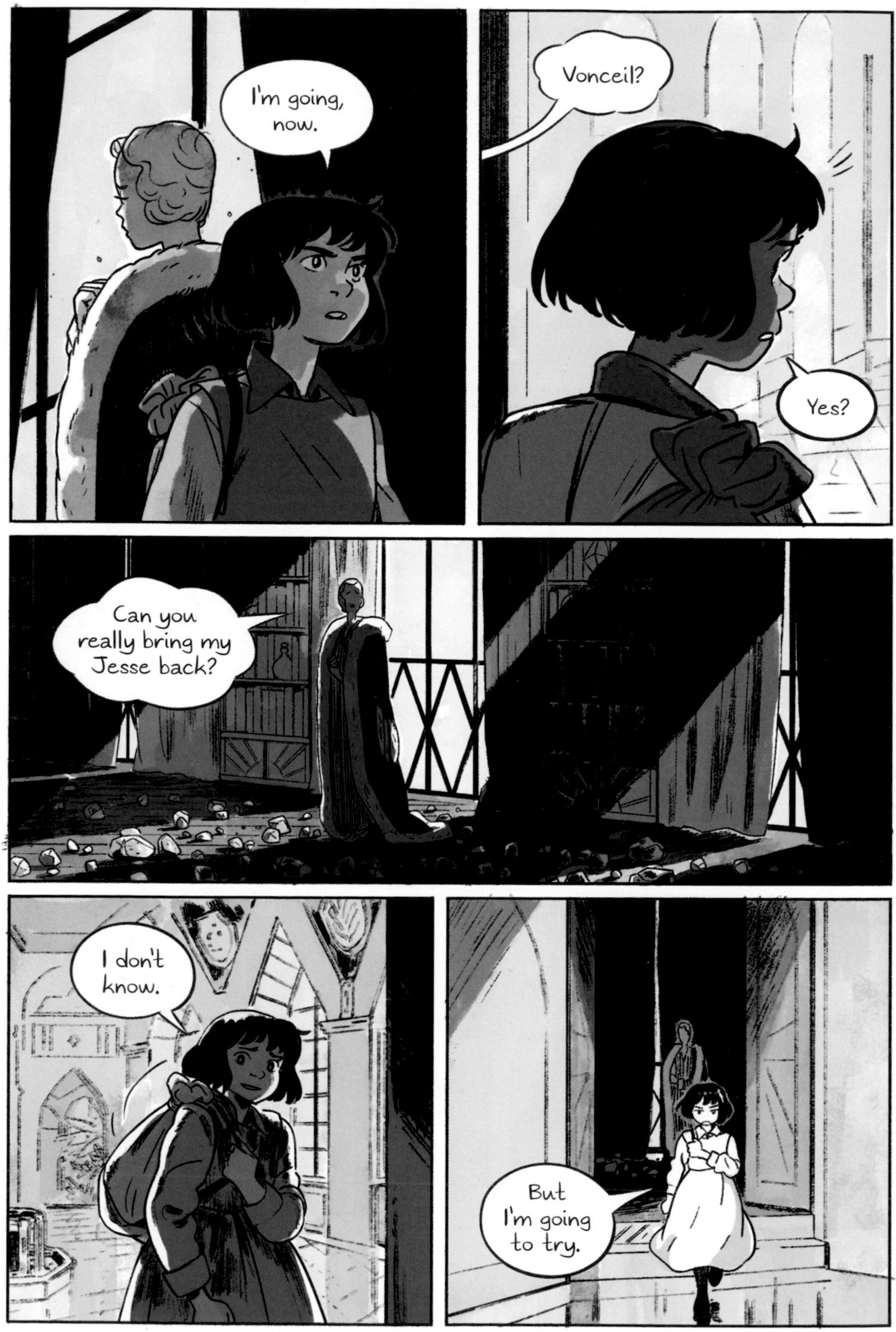
I'm going, now.
Vonceil?
Yes?
Can you really bring my Jesse back?
I don't know.
But I'm going to try.

Chapter Ten

The Magic of Tears

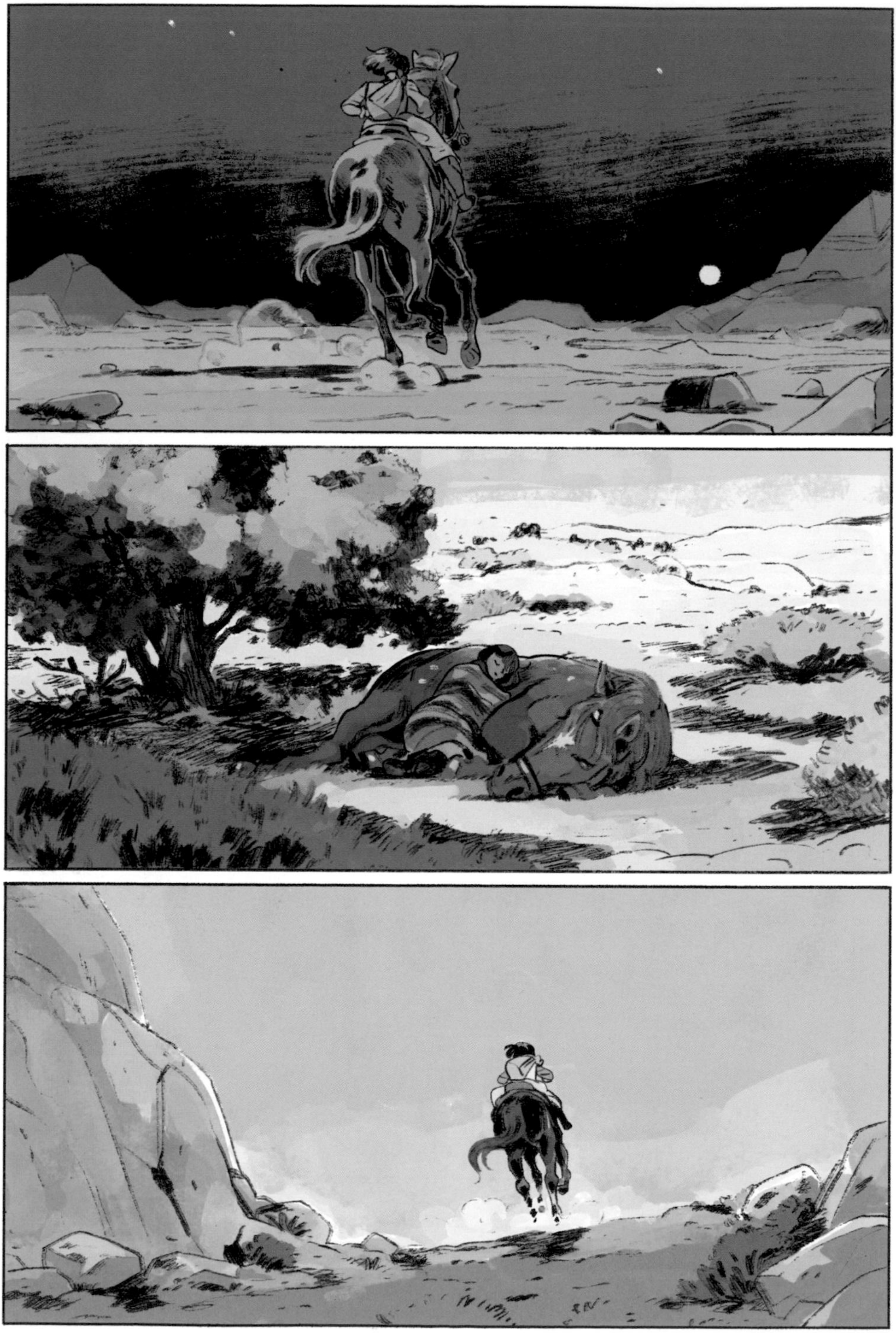

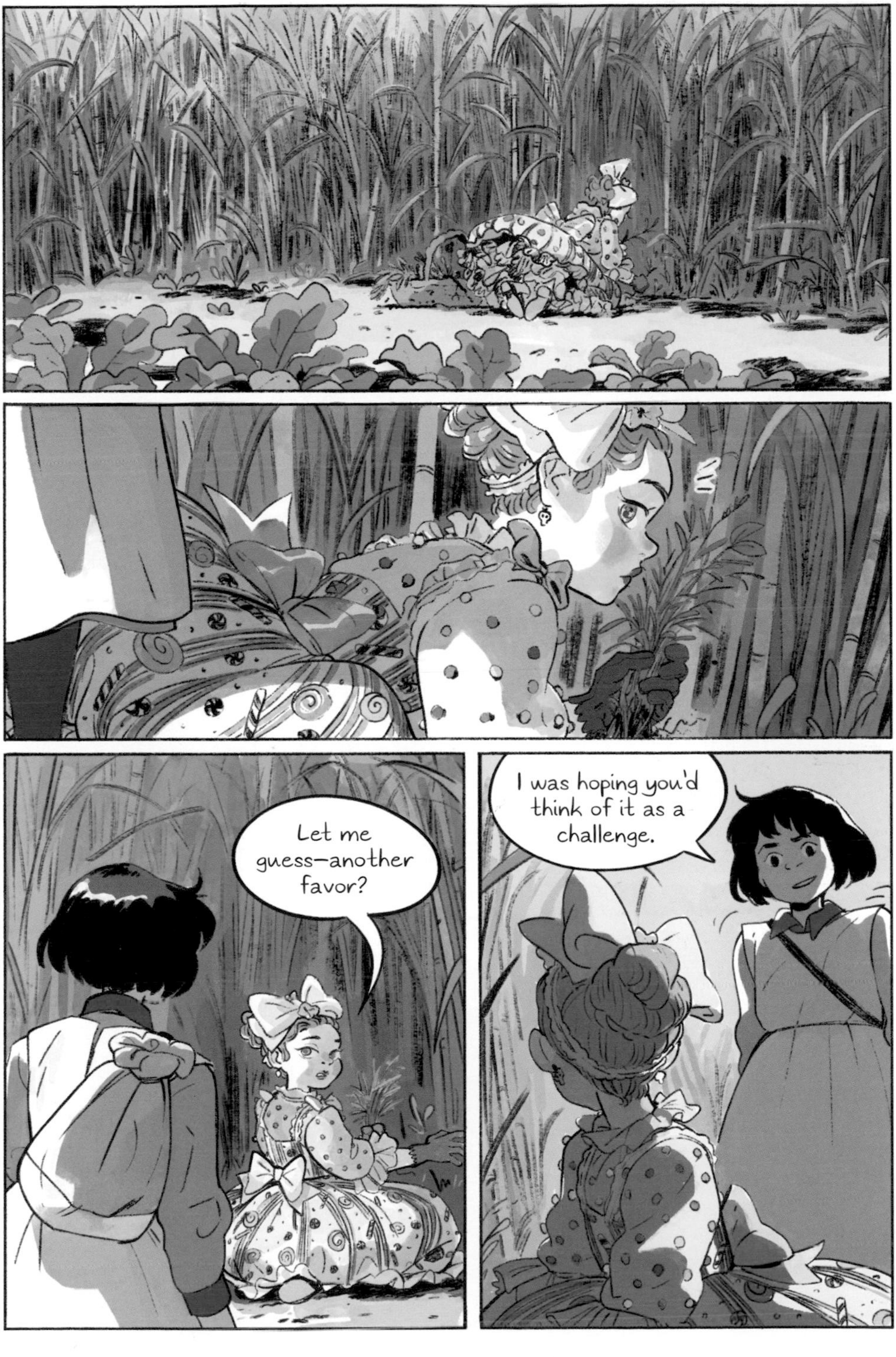
Let me guess—another favor?
I was hoping you'd think of it as a challenge.

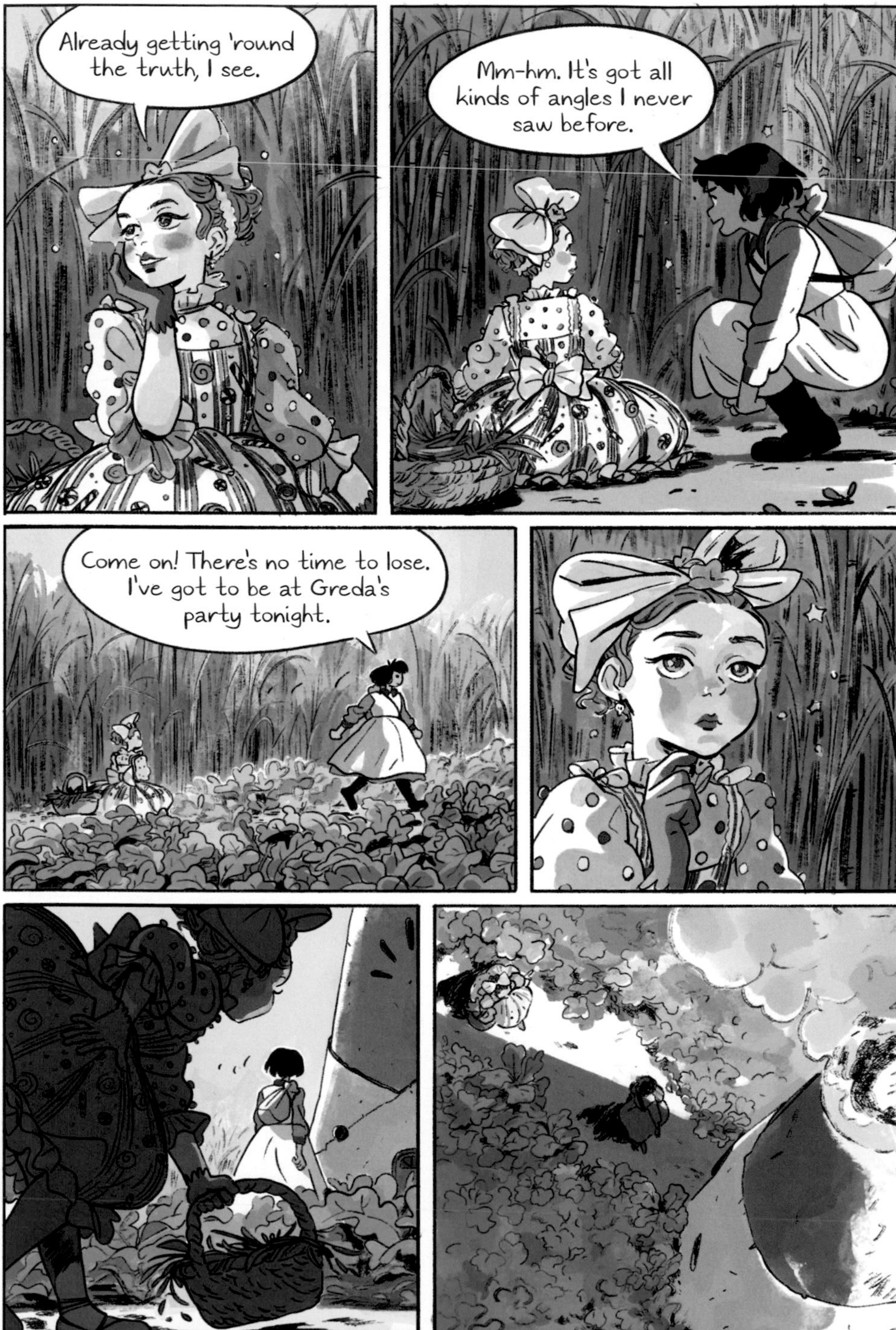
Already getting 'round the truth, I see.
Mm-hm. It's got all kinds of angles I never saw before.
Come on! There's no time to lose. I've got to be at Greda's party tonight.

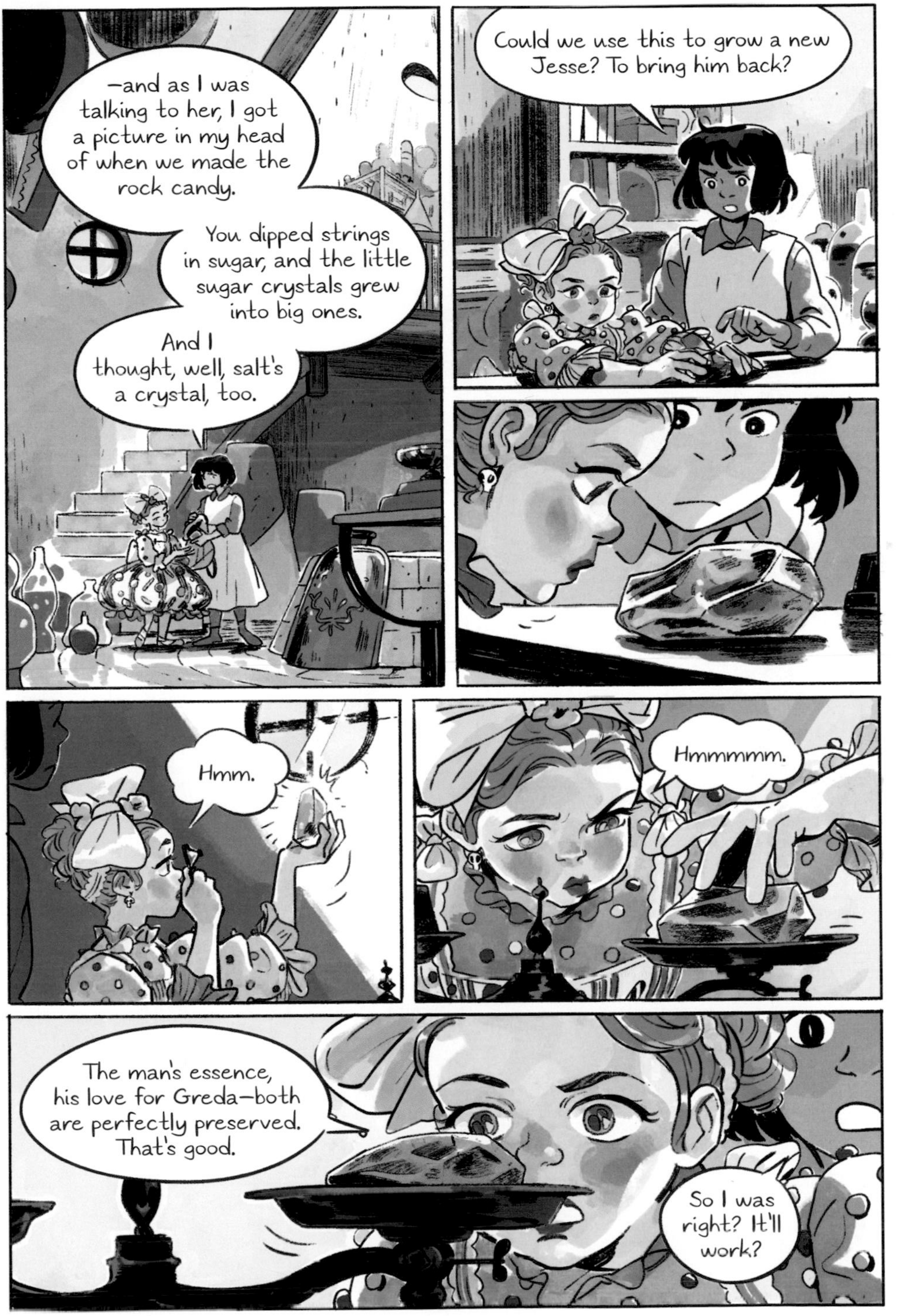
—and as I was talking to her, I got a picture in my head of when we made the rock candy.
You dipped strings in sugar, and the little sugar crystals grew into big ones.
And I thought, well, salt's a crystal, too.
Could we use this to grow a new Jesse? To bring him back?
Hmm.
Hmmmmm.
The man's essence, his love for Greda—both are perfectly preserved. That's good.
So I was right? It'll work?

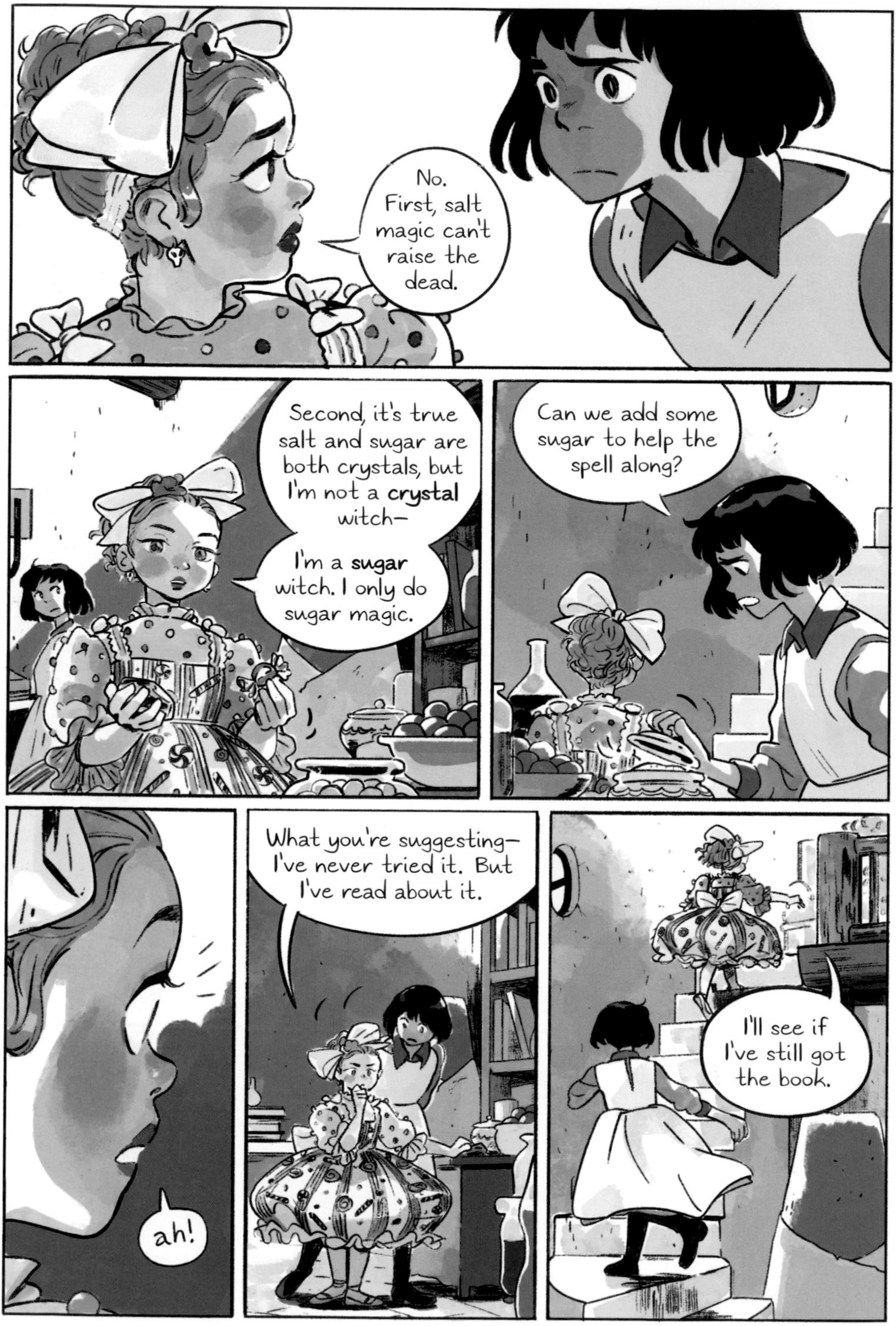
No. First, salt magic can't raise the dead.
Second, it's true salt and sugar are both crystals, but I'm not a **crystal** witch—
I'm a **sugar** witch. I only do sugar magic.
Can we add some sugar to help the spell along?
ah!
What you're suggesting— I've never tried it. But I've read about it.
I'll see if I've still got the book.

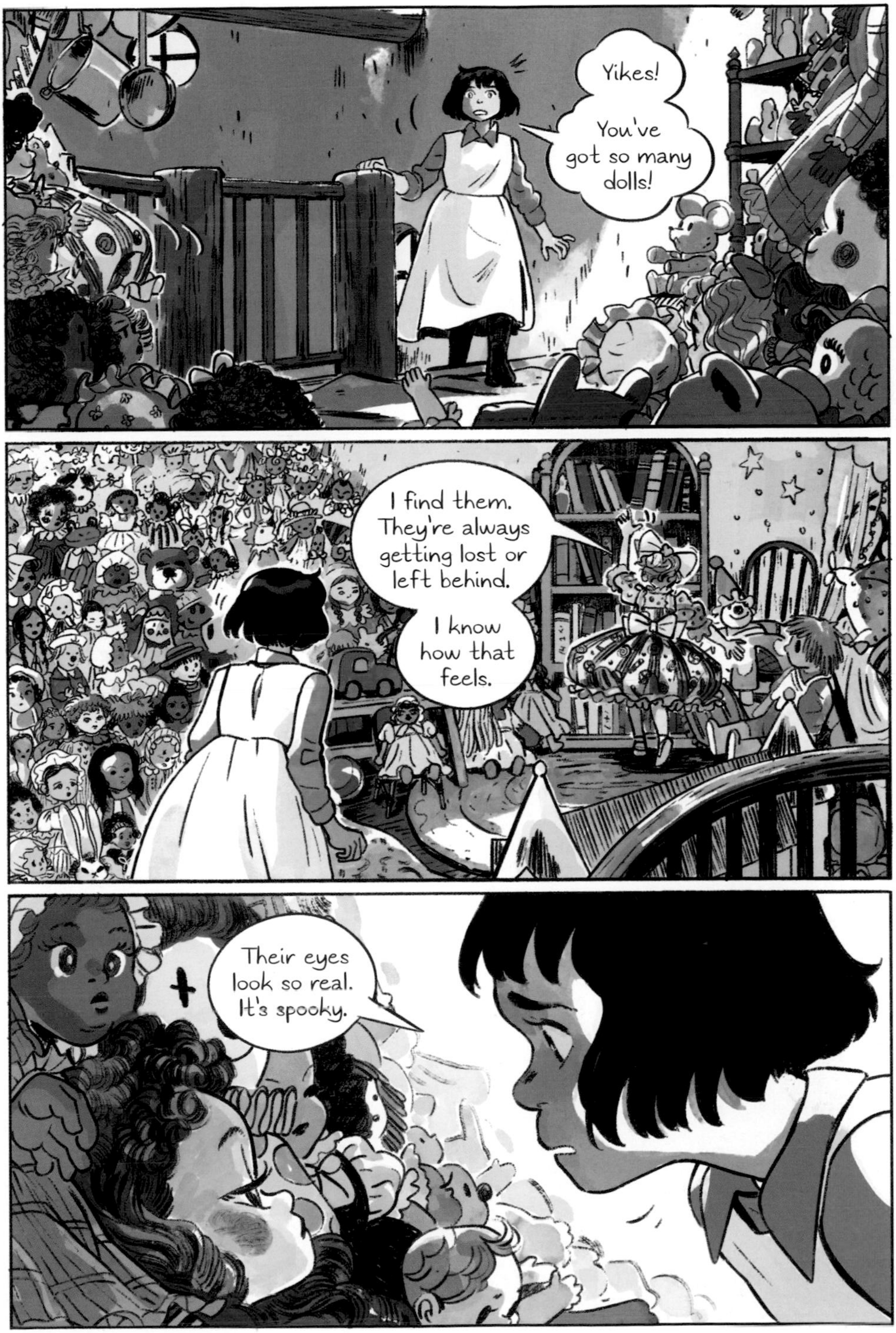
Yikes!
You've got so many dolls!
I find them. They're always getting lost or left behind.
I know how that feels.
Their eyes look so real. It's spooky.

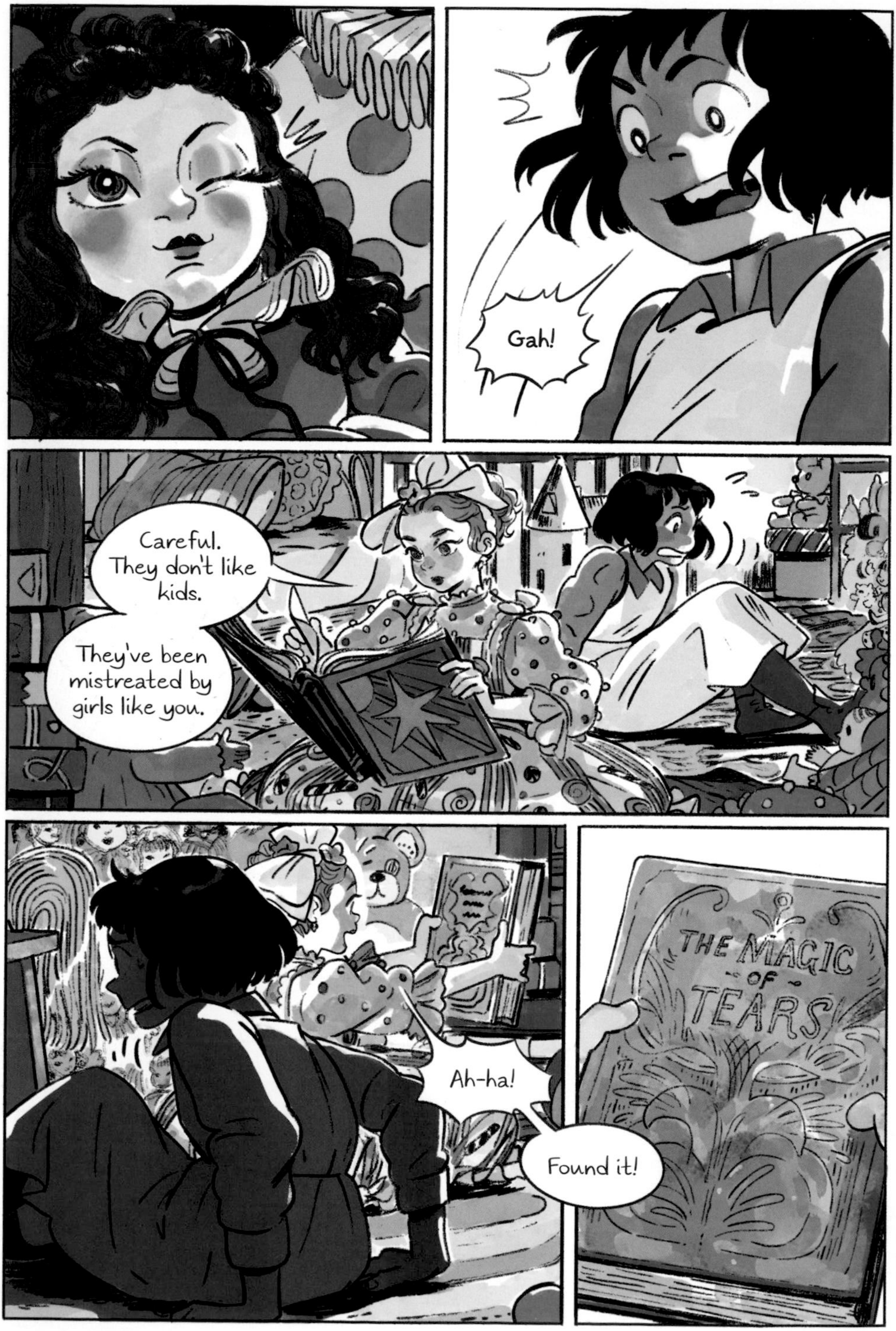
Gah!
Careful. They don't like kids.
They've been mistreated by girls like you.
Ah-ha!
Found it!
THE MAGIC OF TEARS

Tears? But aren't they salty?

They're salty **and** sweet. They make powerful magic, but the methods are rarely used.

How come?

They require a great sacrifice.

What . . . what kind of sacrifice?

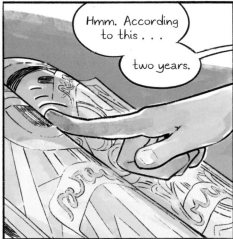

Hmm. According to this . . .

two years.

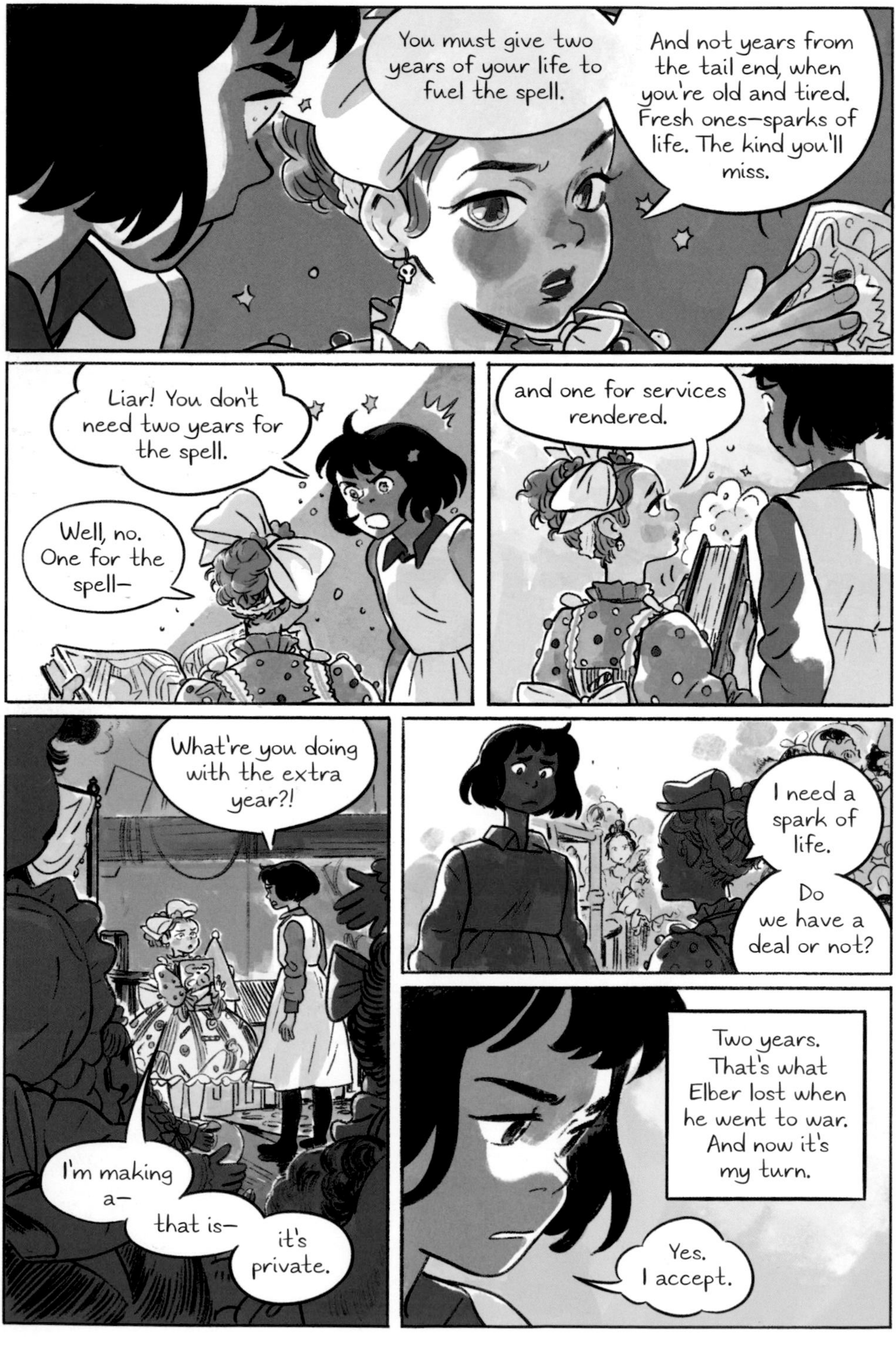
You must give two years of your life to fuel the spell.
And not years from the tail end, when you're old and tired. Fresh ones—sparks of life. The kind you'll miss.
Liar! You don't need two years for the spell.
Well, no. One for the spell—
and one for services rendered.
What're you doing with the extra year?!
I'm making a—
that is—
it's private.
I need a spark of life.
Do we have a deal or not?
Two years. That's what Elber lost when he went to war. And now it's my turn.
Yes. I accept.

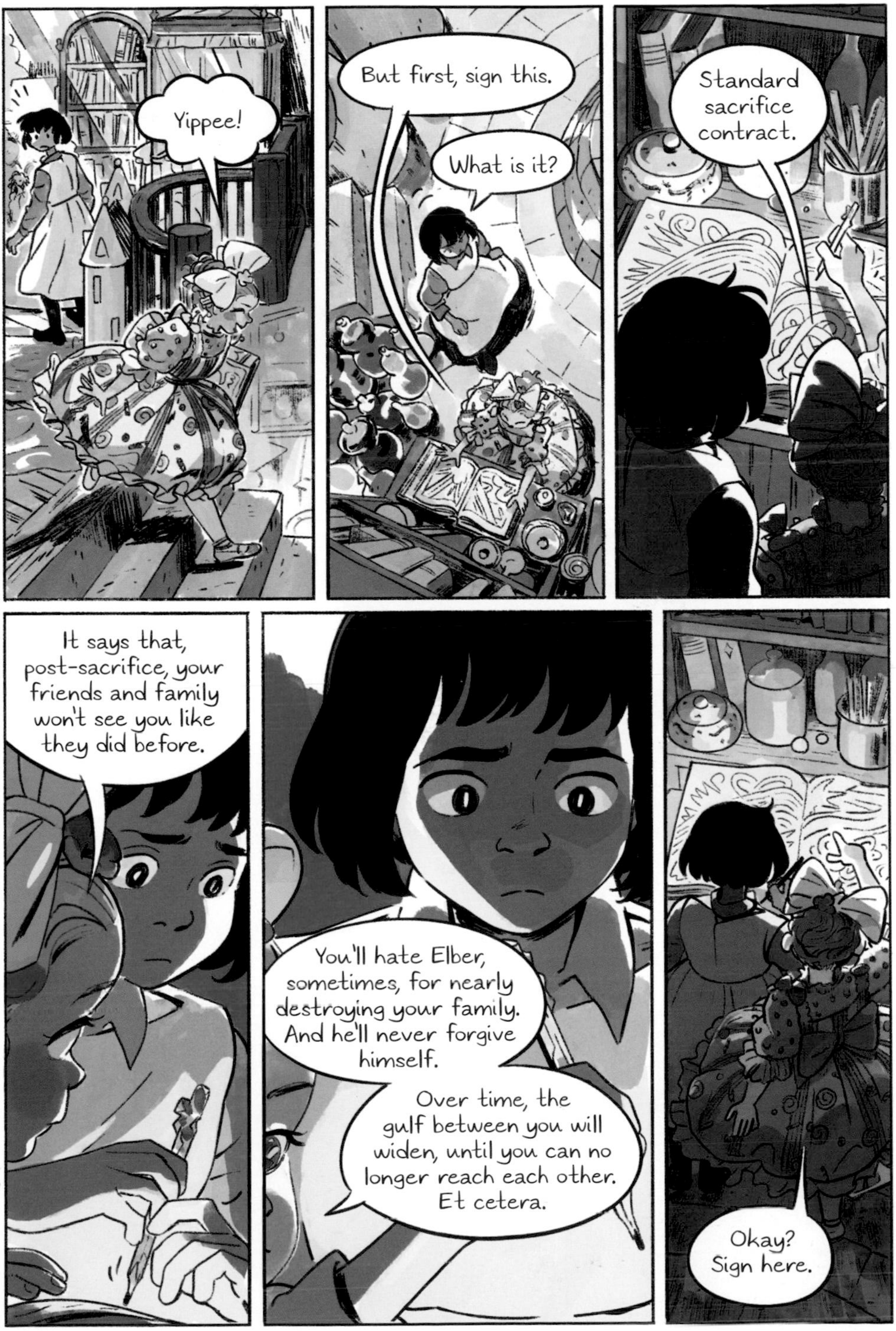
Yippee!
But first, sign this.
What is it?
Standard sacrifice contract.
It says that, post-sacrifice, your friends and family won't see you like they did before.
You'll hate Elber, sometimes, for nearly destroying your family. And he'll never forgive himself.
Over time, the gulf between you will widen, until you can no longer reach each other. Et cetera.
Okay? Sign here.

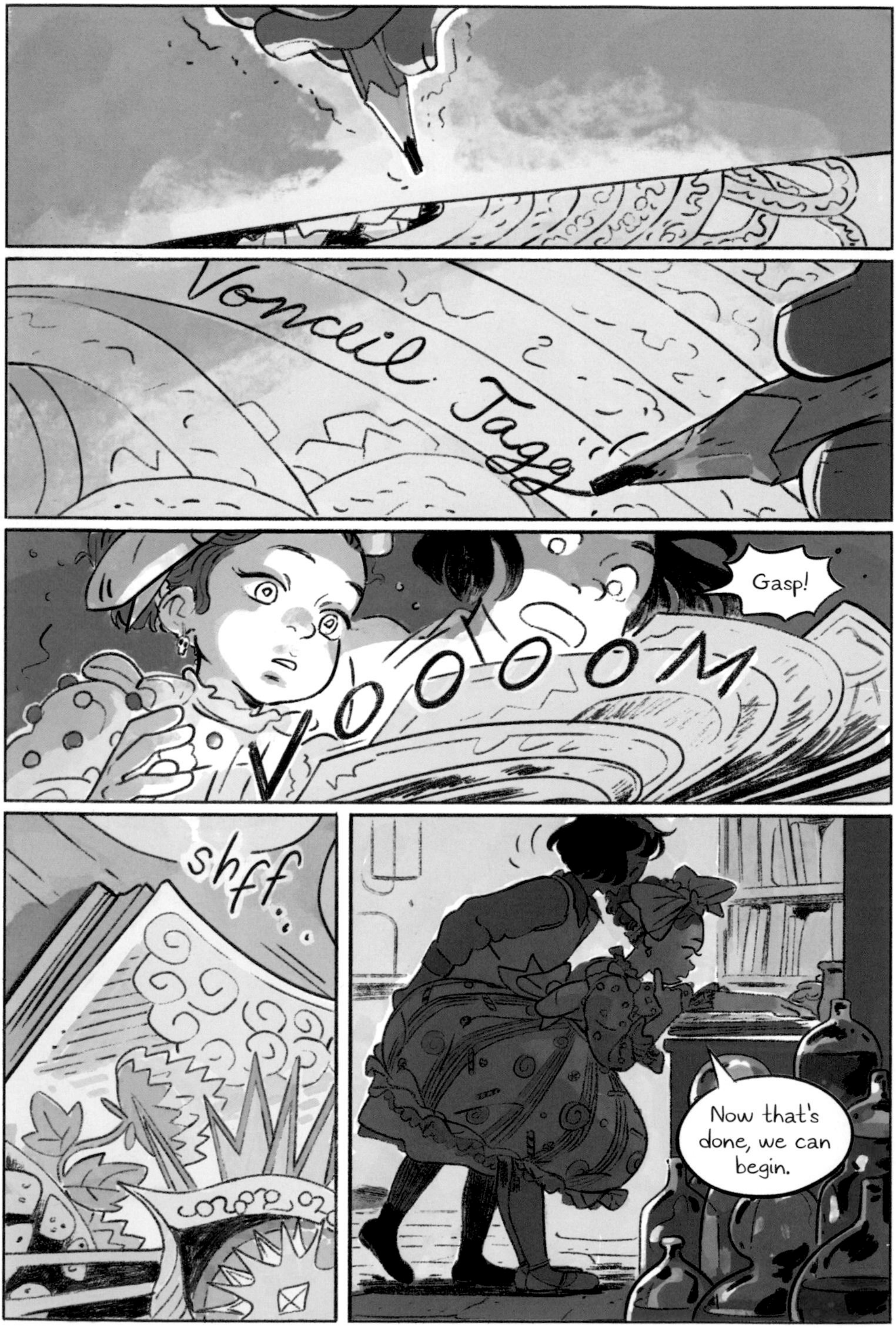
Voncil Jagg
Gasp!
VOOOOOM
shff...
Now that's done, we can begin.

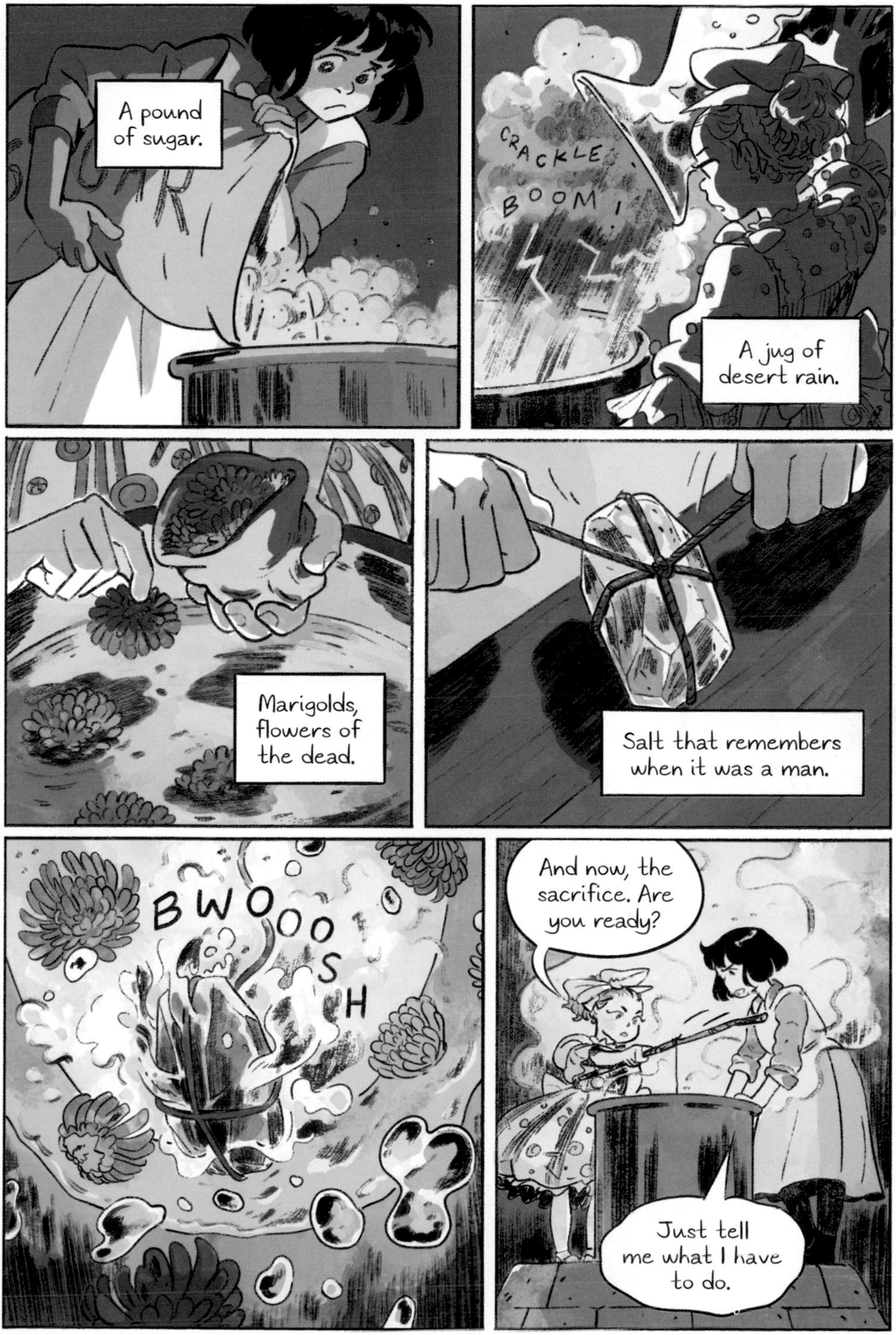
A pound of sugar.
CRACKLE
BOOM!
A jug of desert rain.
Marigolds, flowers of the dead.
Salt that remembers when it was a man.
BWOOOOSH
And now, the sacrifice. Are you ready?
Just tell me what I have to do.

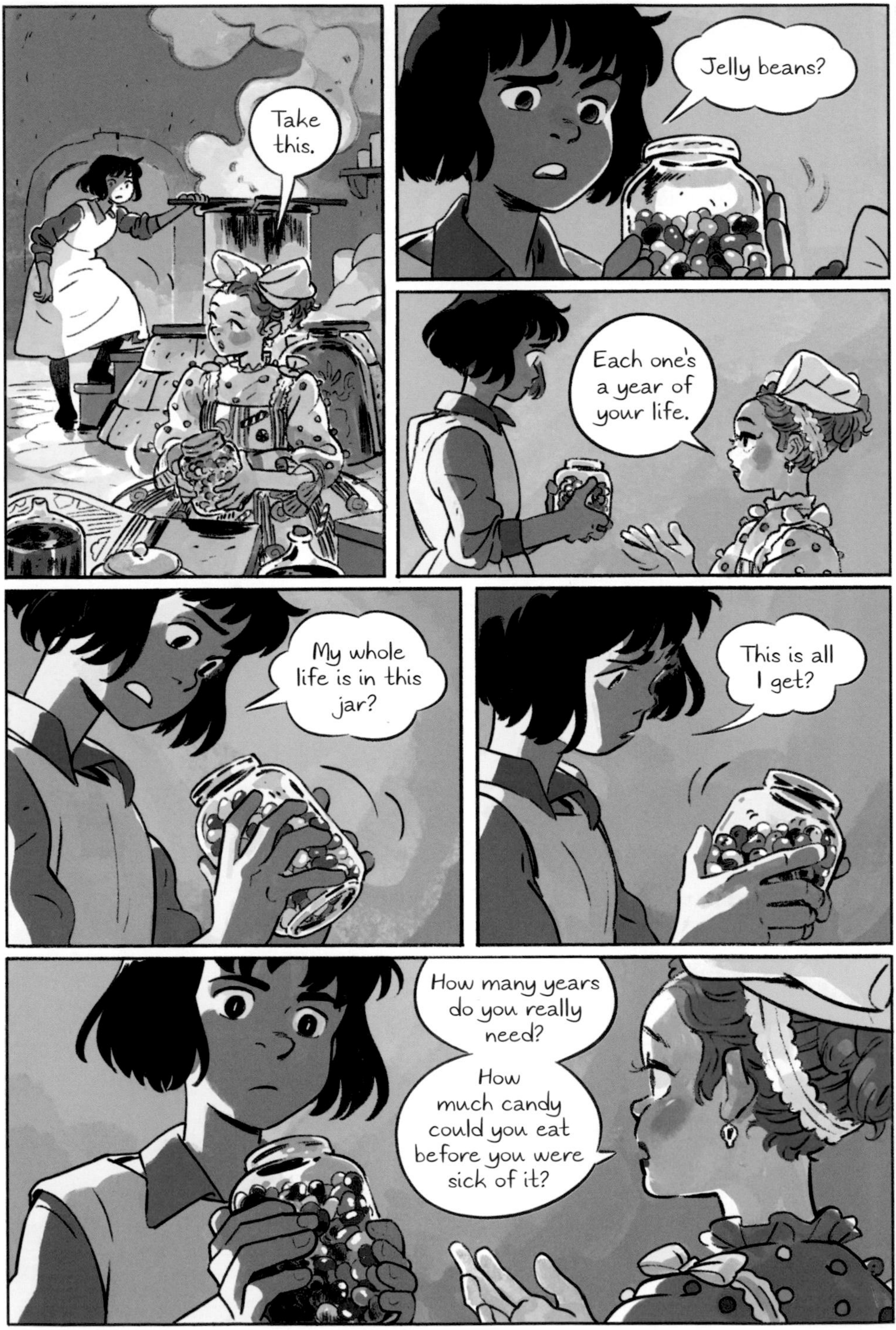
Take this.
Jelly beans?
Each one's a year of your life.
My whole life is in this jar?
This is all I get?
How many years do you really need?
How much candy could you eat before you were sick of it?

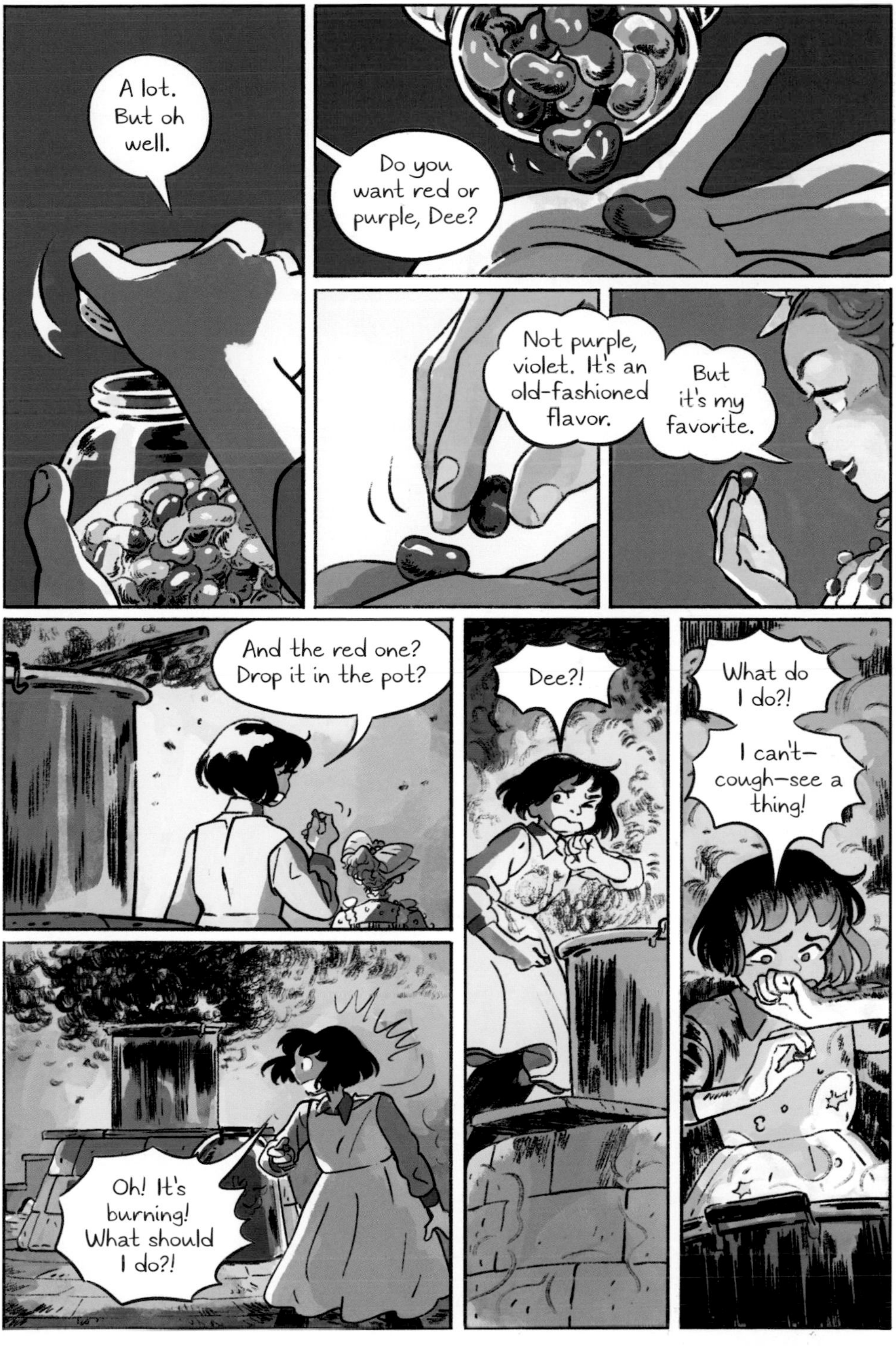
A lot. But oh well.
Do you want red or purple, Dee?
Not purple, violet. It's an old-fashioned flavor.
But it's my favorite.
And the red one? Drop it in the pot?
Dee?!
What do I do?!
I can't—cough—see a thing!
Oh! It's burning! What should I do?!

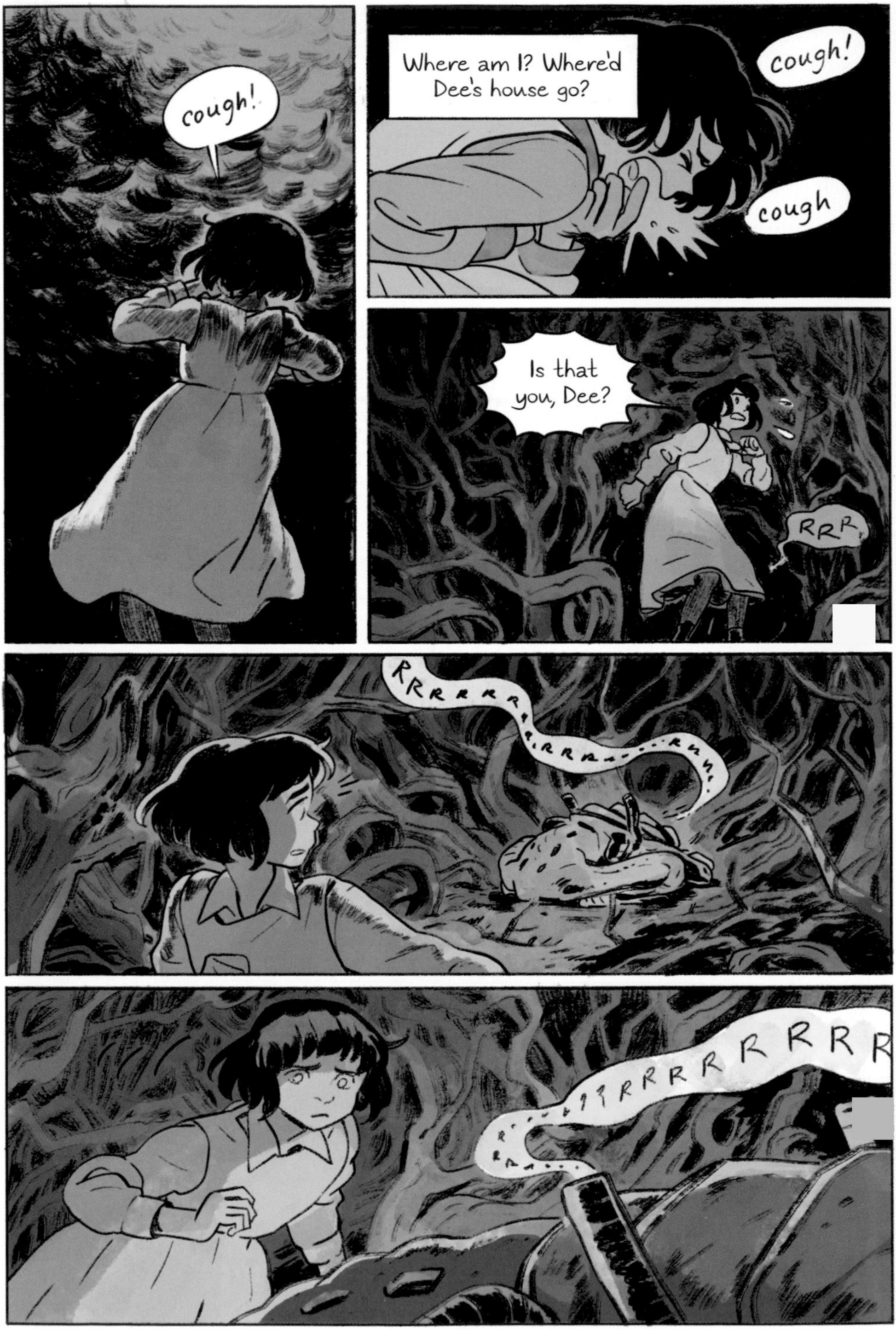
cough!
Where am I? Where'd Dee's house go?
cough!
cough
Is that you, Dee?
RRR
RRRRRRRRRRRrrrr
RRRRRRRRRRR

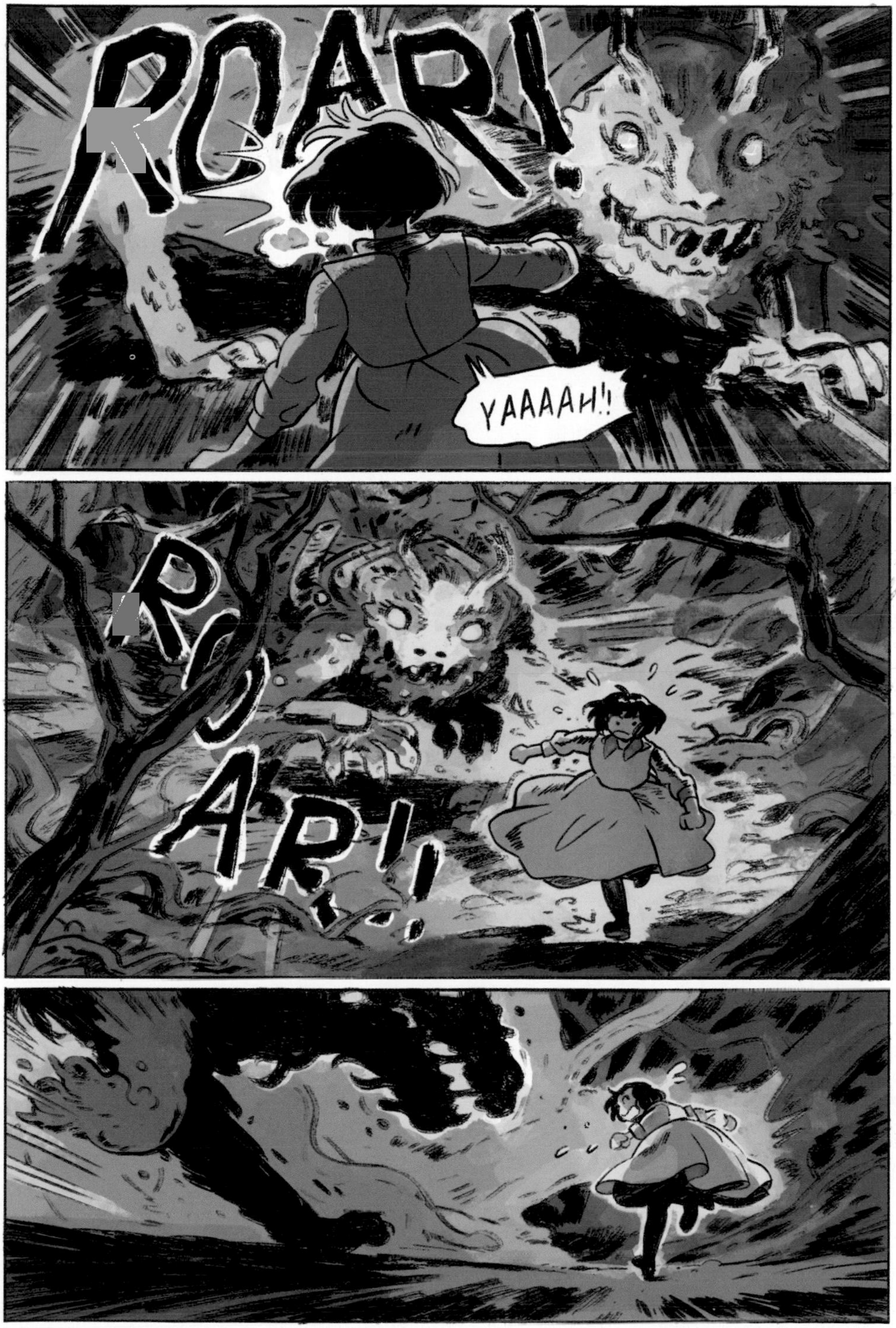
ROAR!
YAAAAH!!
ROAR!!

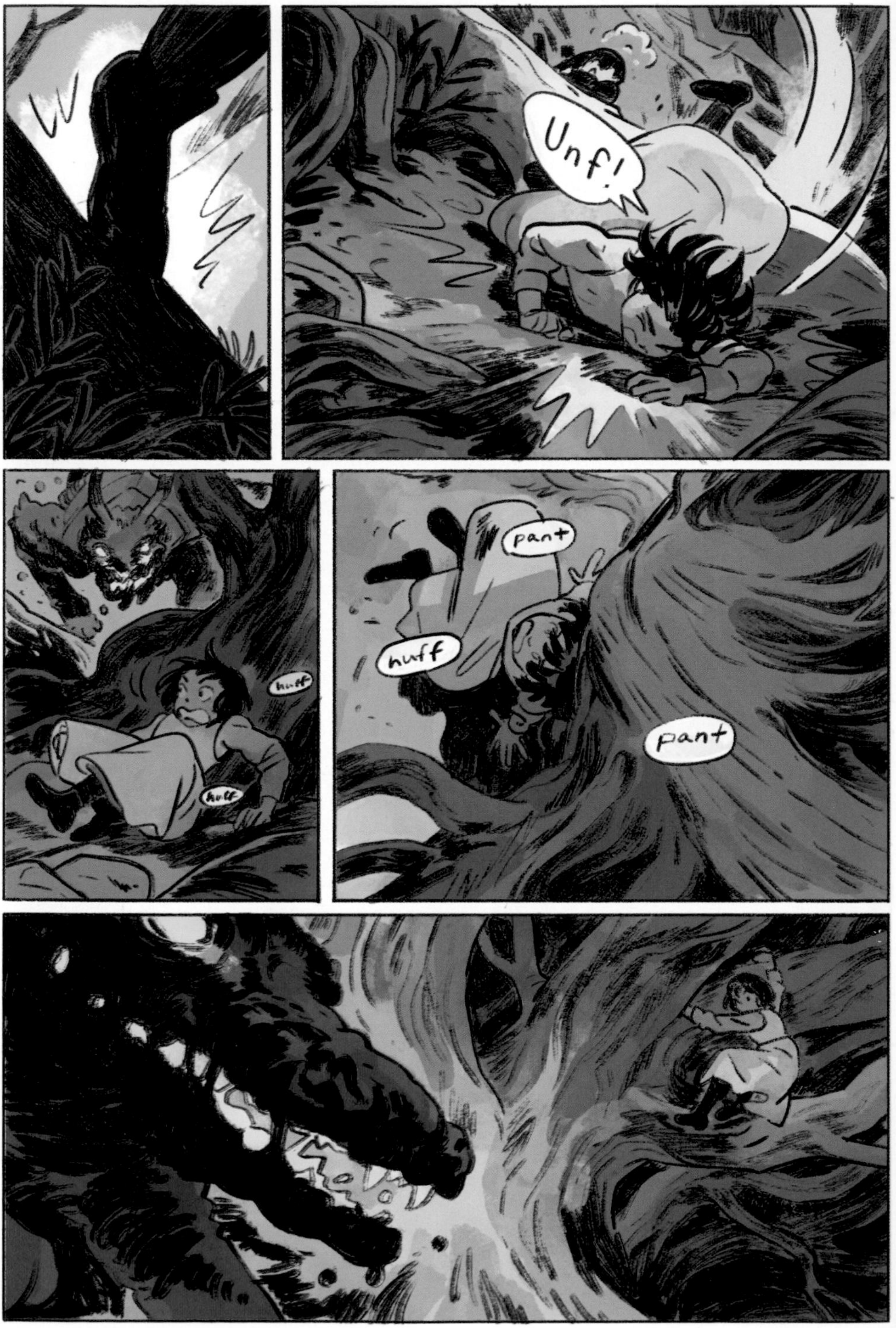
Unf!
pant
huff
huff
huff
pant

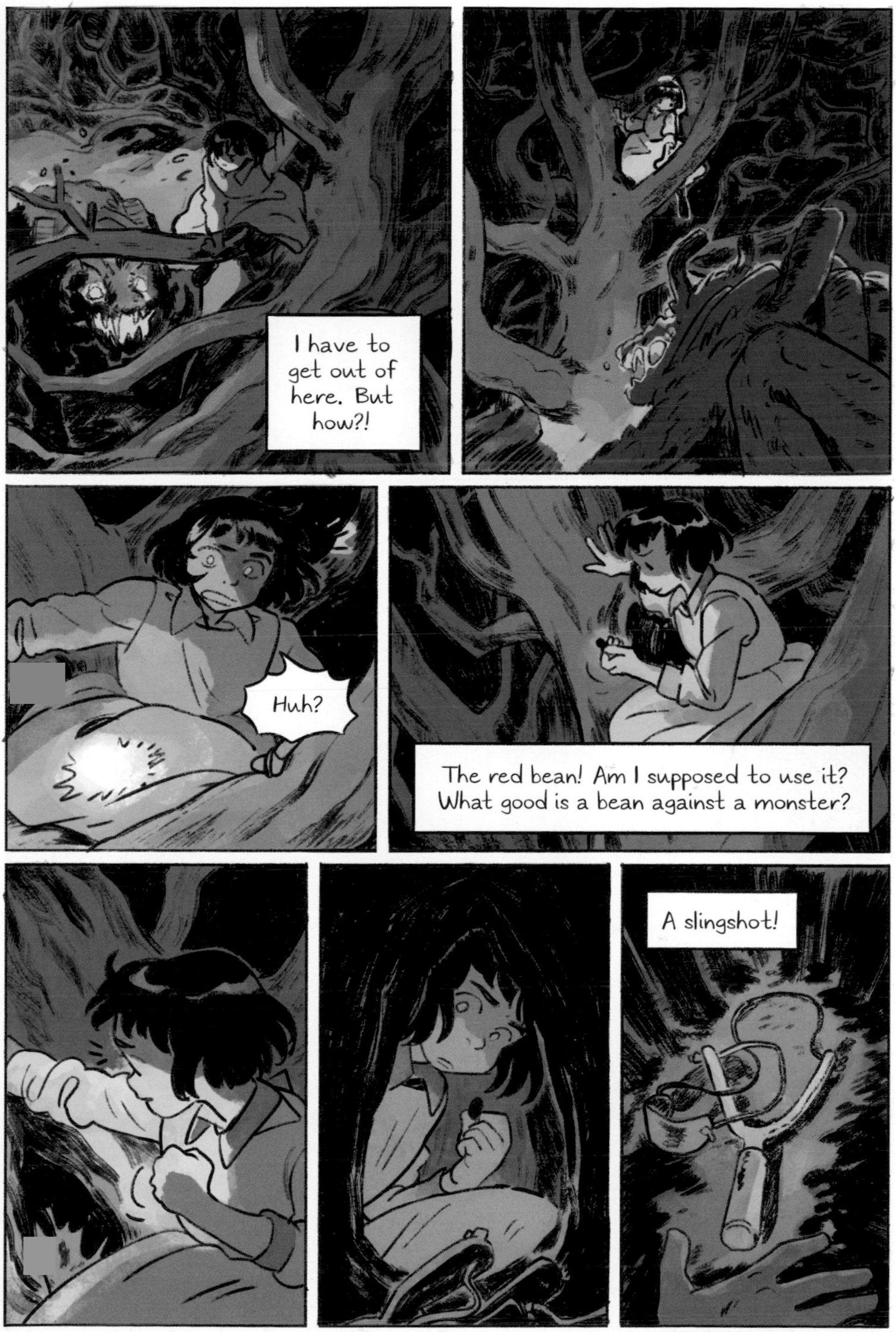
I have to get out of here. But how?!
Huh?
The red bean! Am I supposed to use it? What good is a bean against a monster?
A slingshot!

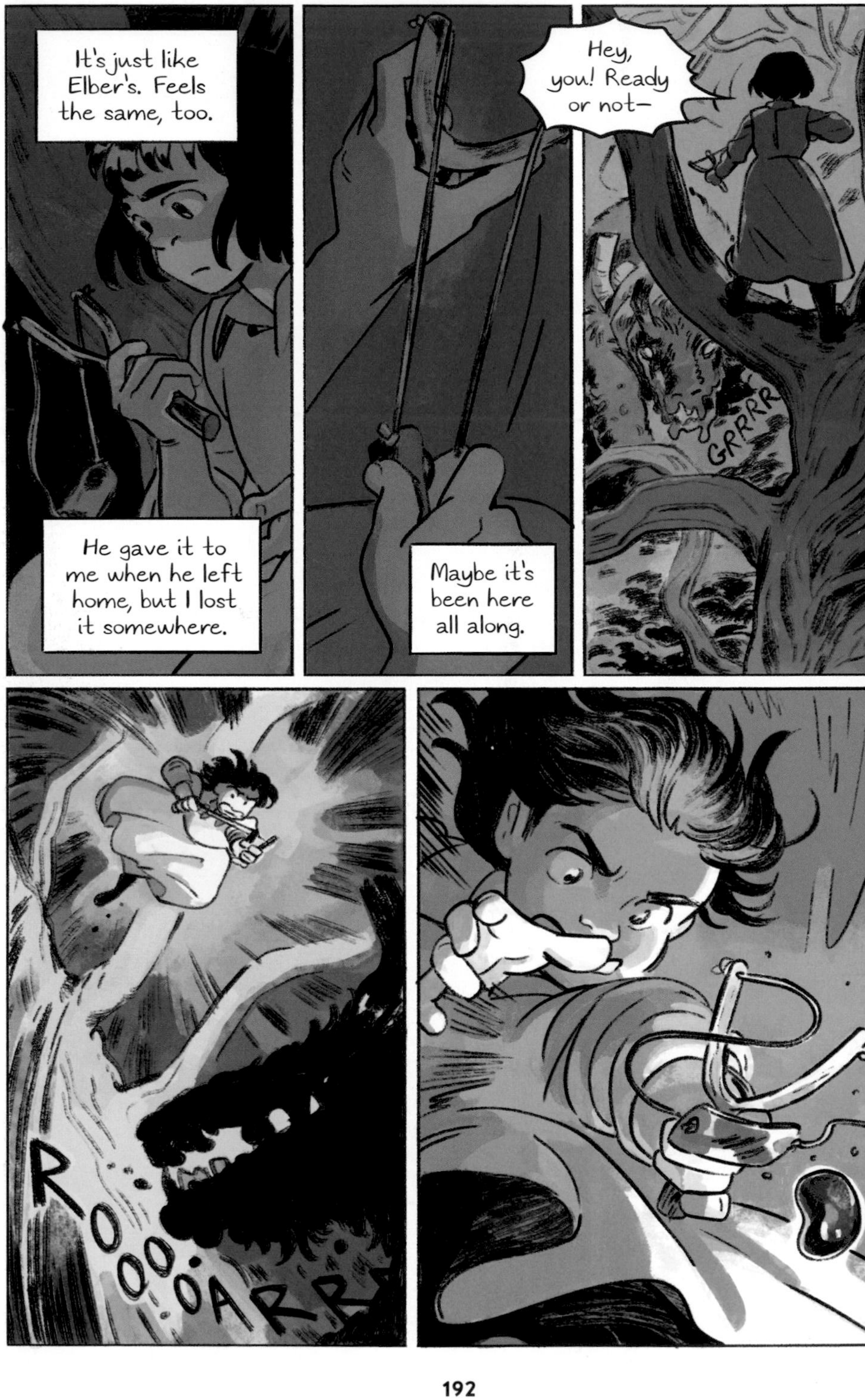
It's just like Elber's. Feels the same, too.
He gave it to me when he left home, but I lost it somewhere.
Maybe it's been here all along.
Hey, you! Ready or not—
GRRRR
ROOOOOARR

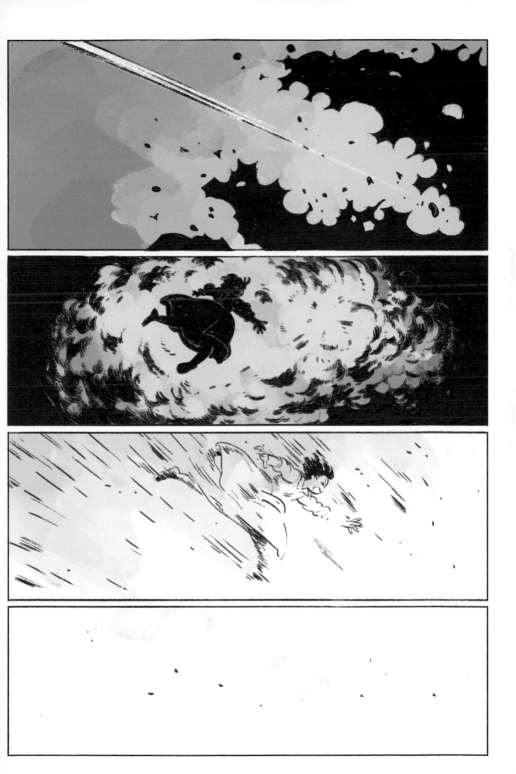

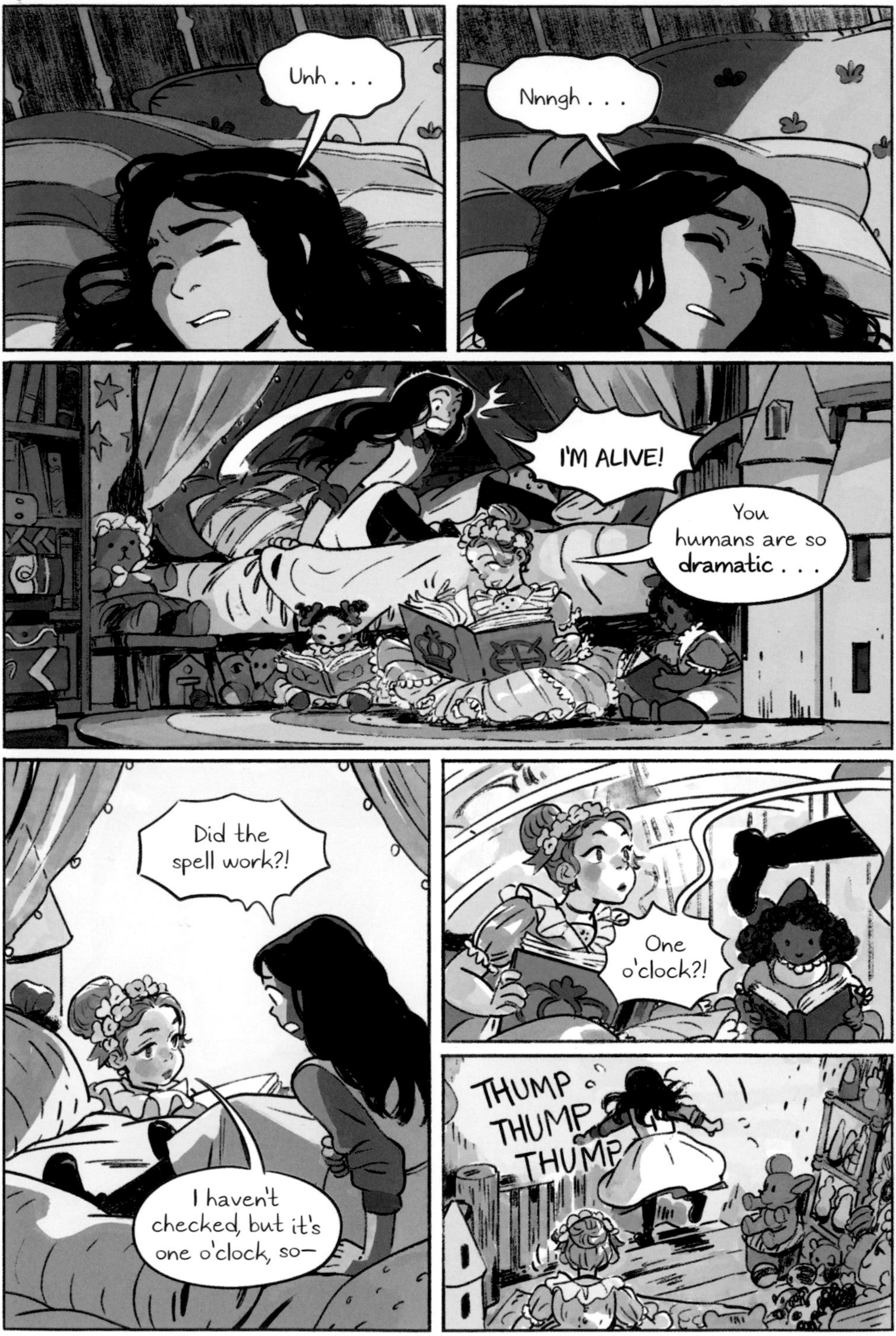
Unh . . .
Nnngh . . .
I'M ALIVE!
You humans are so **dramatic** . . .
Did the spell work?!
I haven't checked, but it's one o'clock, so—
One o'clock?!
THUMP THUMP THUMP

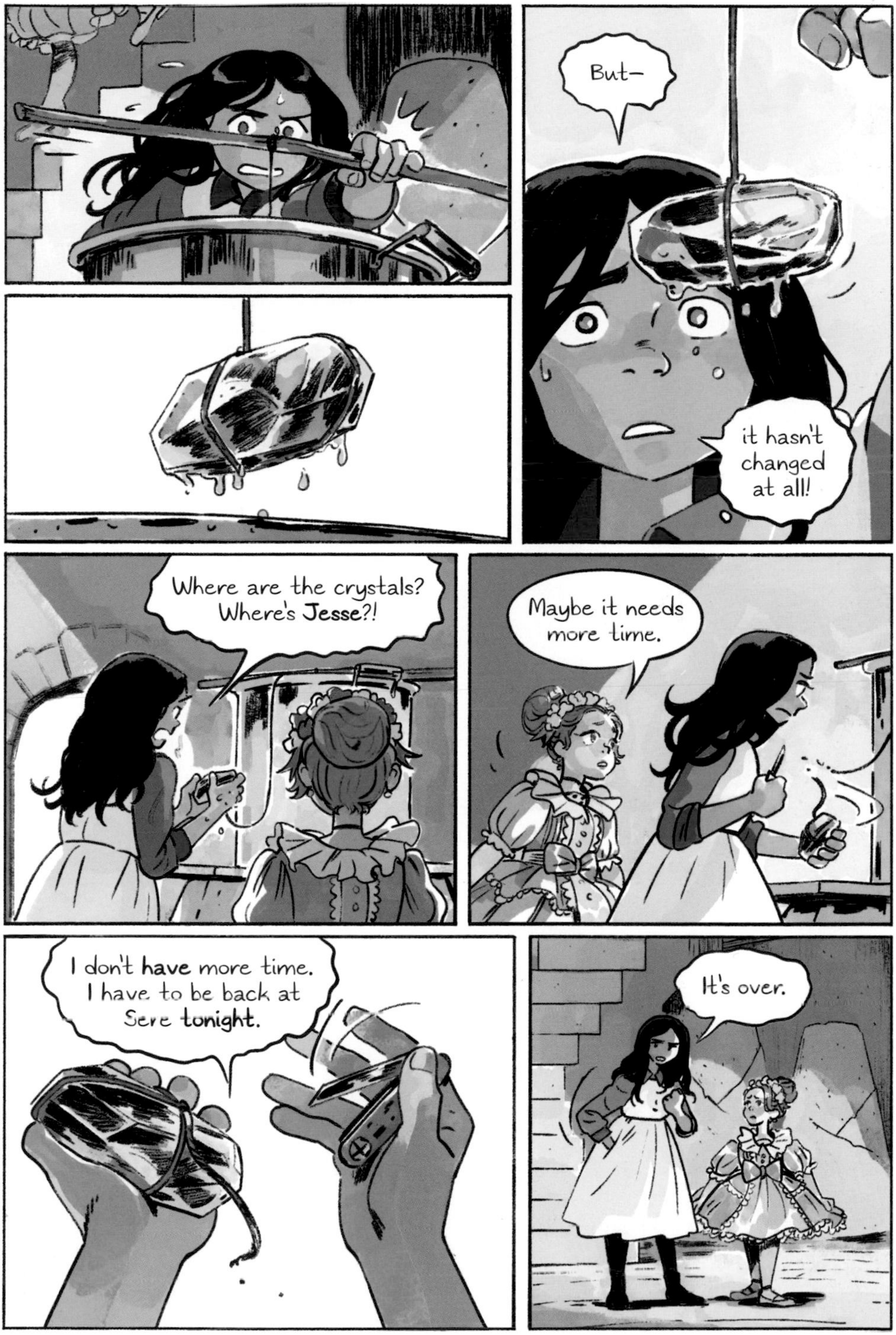
But–
it hasn't changed at all!
Where are the crystals? Where's **Jesse**?!
Maybe it needs more time.
I don't **have** more time. I have to be back at Sere **tonight**.
It's over.

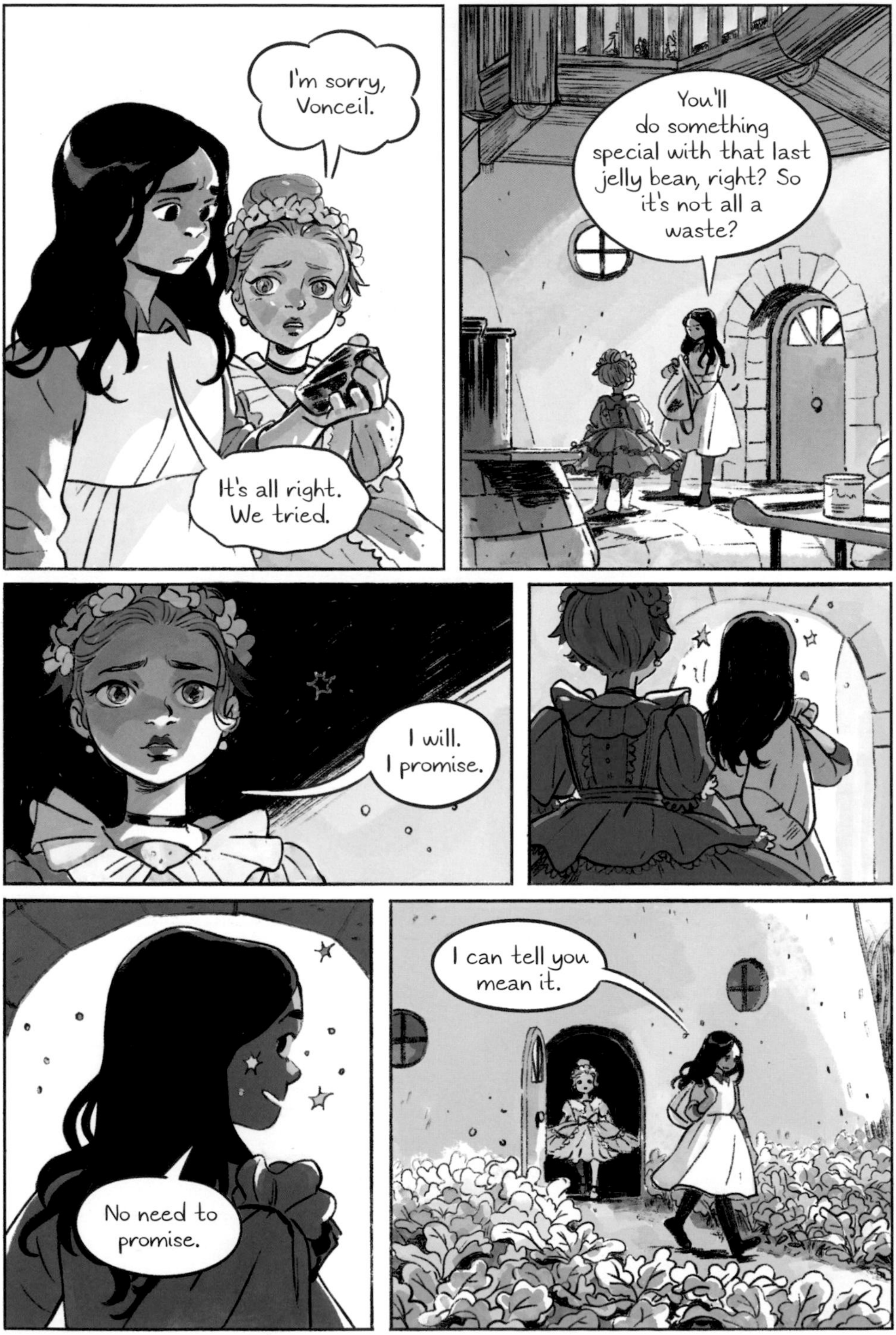
I'm sorry, Vonceil.
It's all right. We tried.
You'll do something special with that last jelly bean, right? So it's not all a waste?
I will. I promise.
No need to promise.
I can tell you mean it.

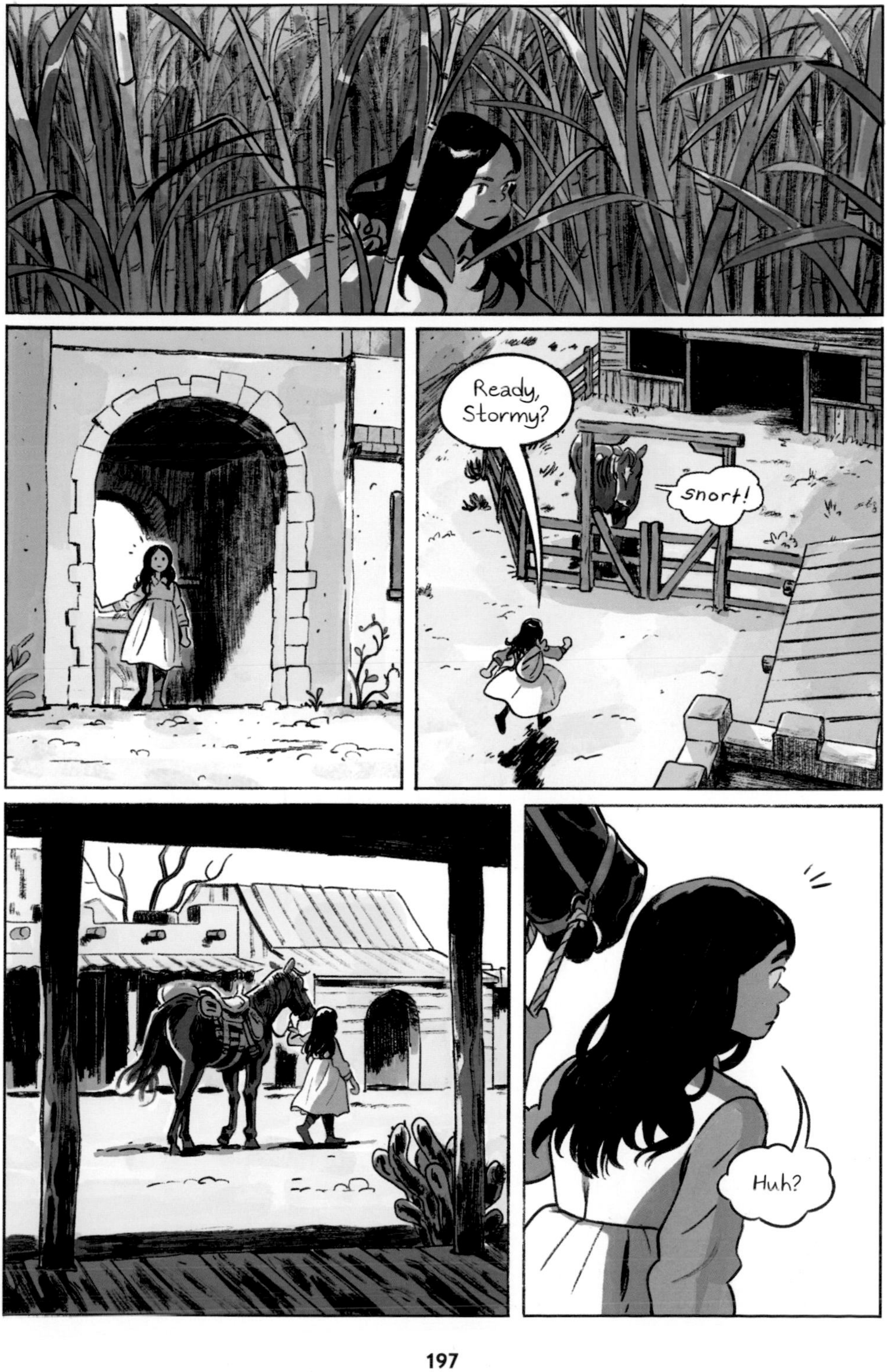
Ready, Stormy?
snort!
Huh?

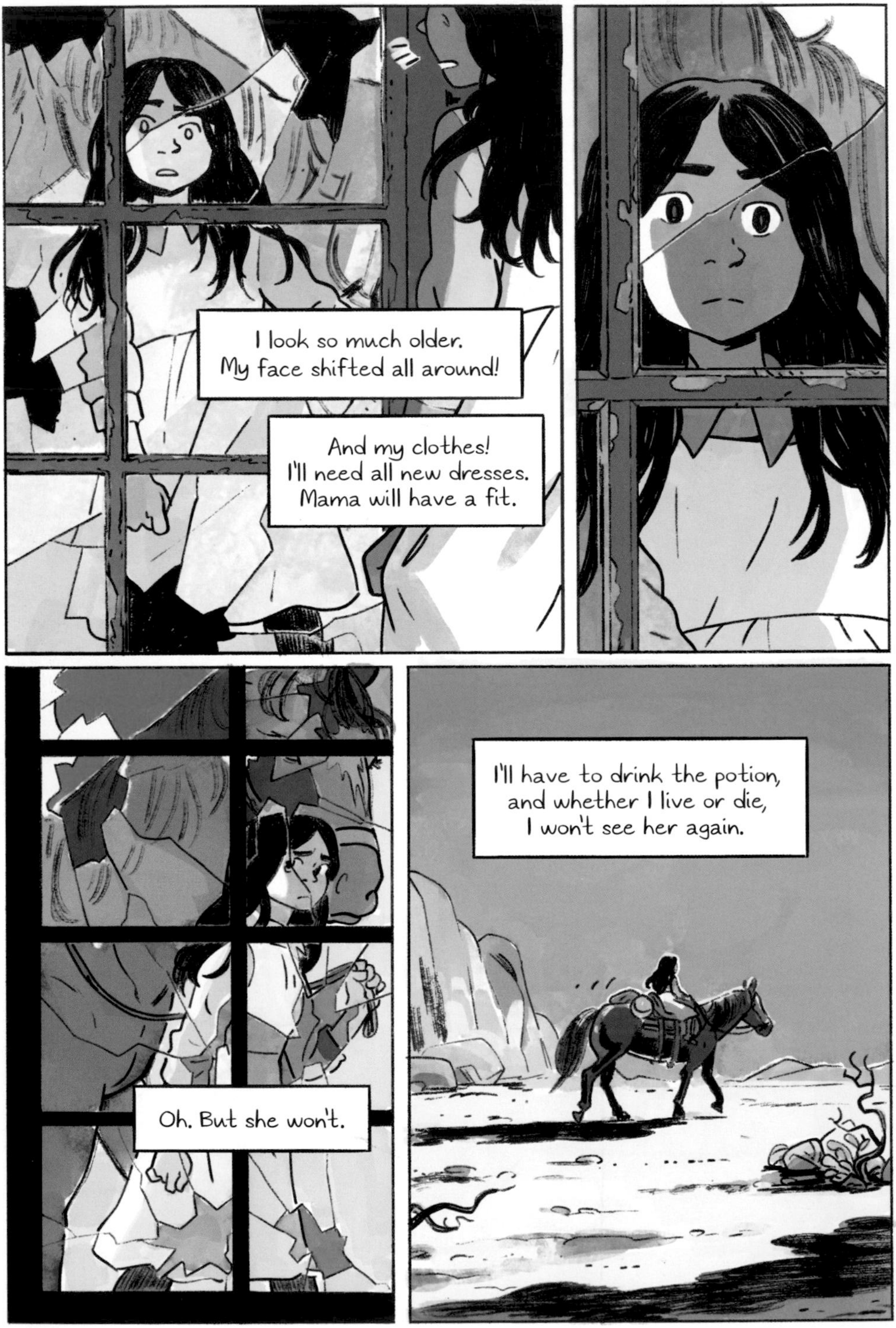
I look so much older.
My face shifted all around!
And my clothes!
I'll need all new dresses.
Mama will have a fit.
Oh. But she won't.
I'll have to drink the potion,
and whether I live or die,
I won't see her again.

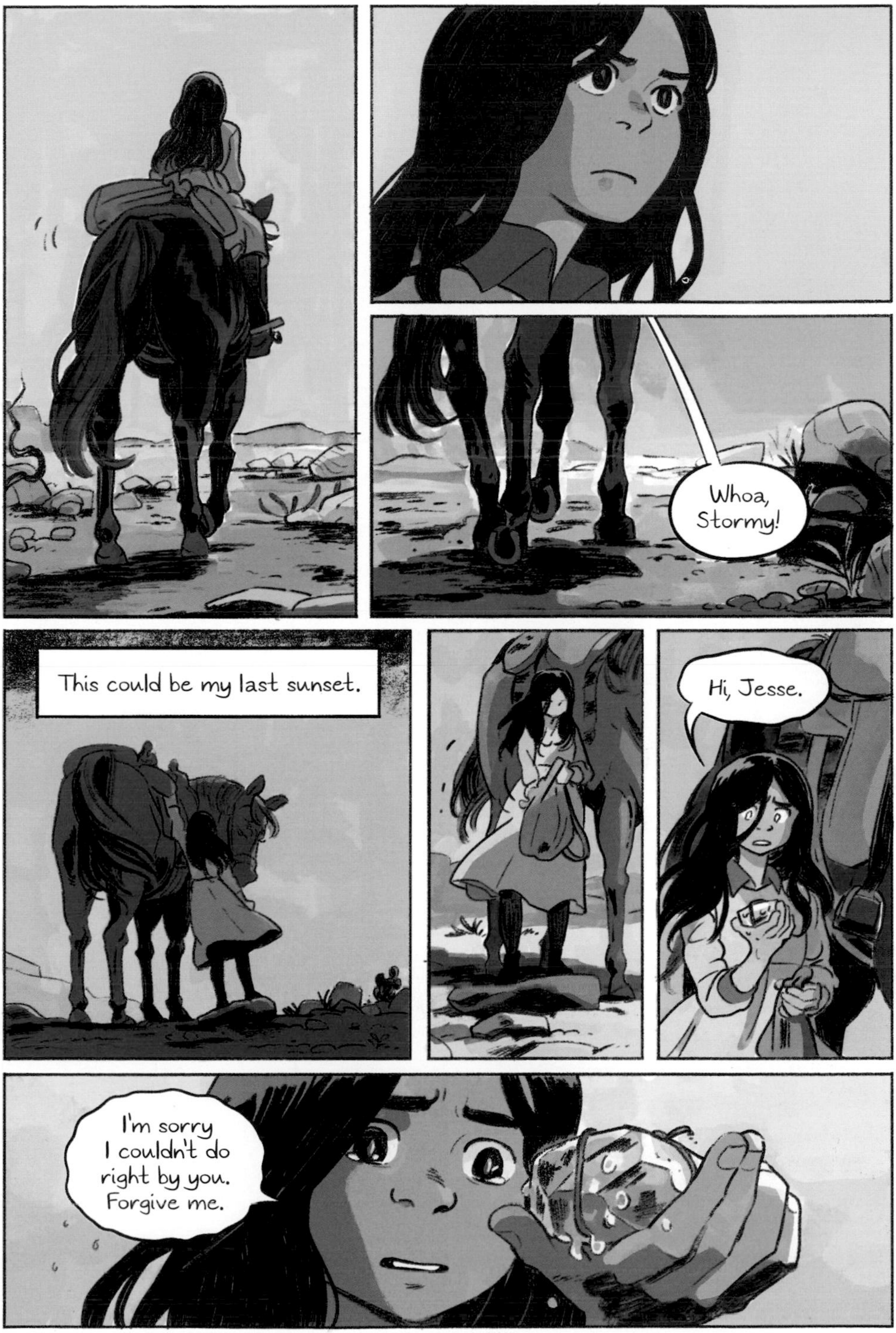
Whoa,
Stormy!
This could be my last sunset.
Hi, Jesse.
I'm sorry
I couldn't do
right by you.
Forgive me.

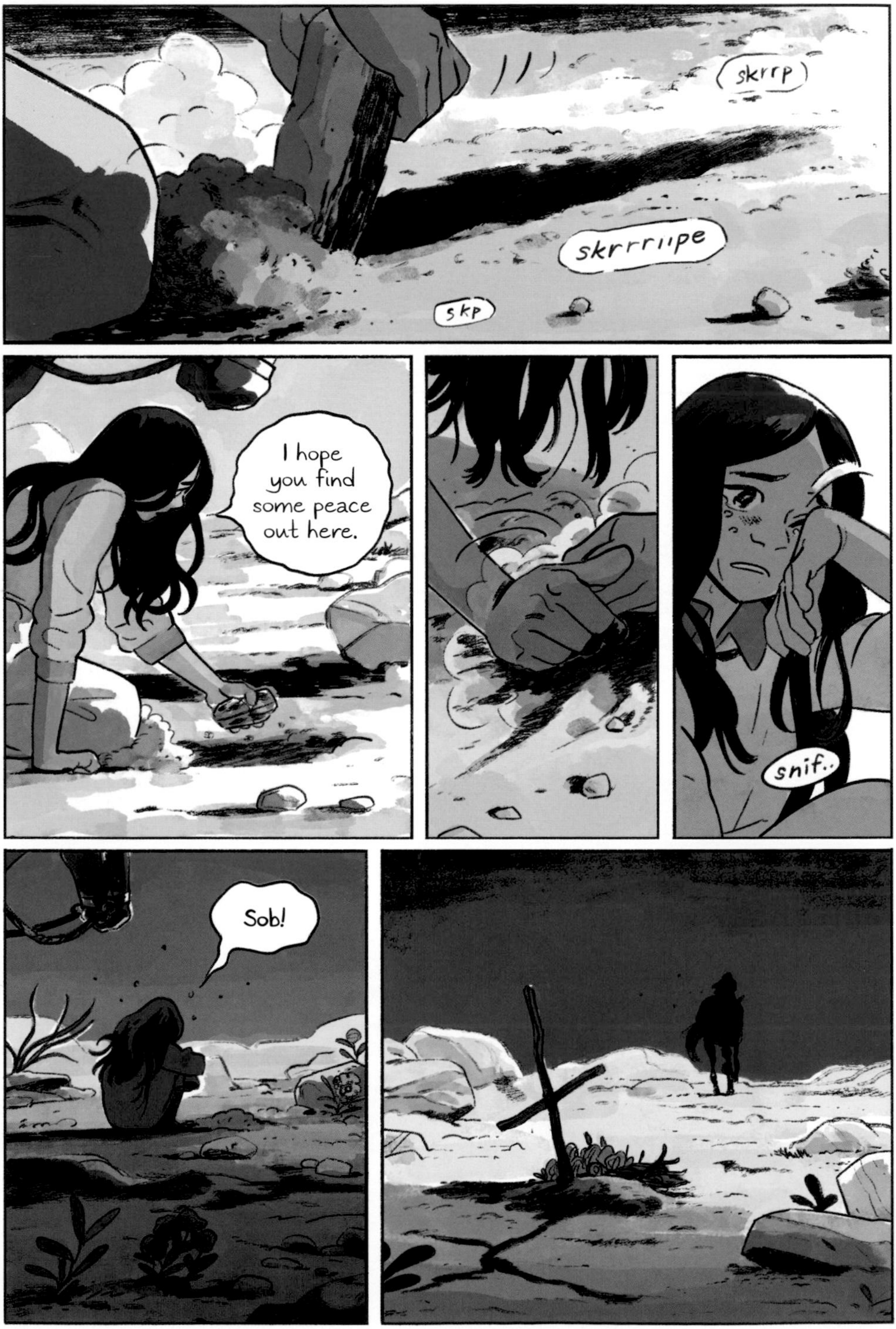
skrrp
skrrriipe
skp
I hope you find some peace out here.
snif..
Sob!

Chapter Eleven

An Uninvited Guest

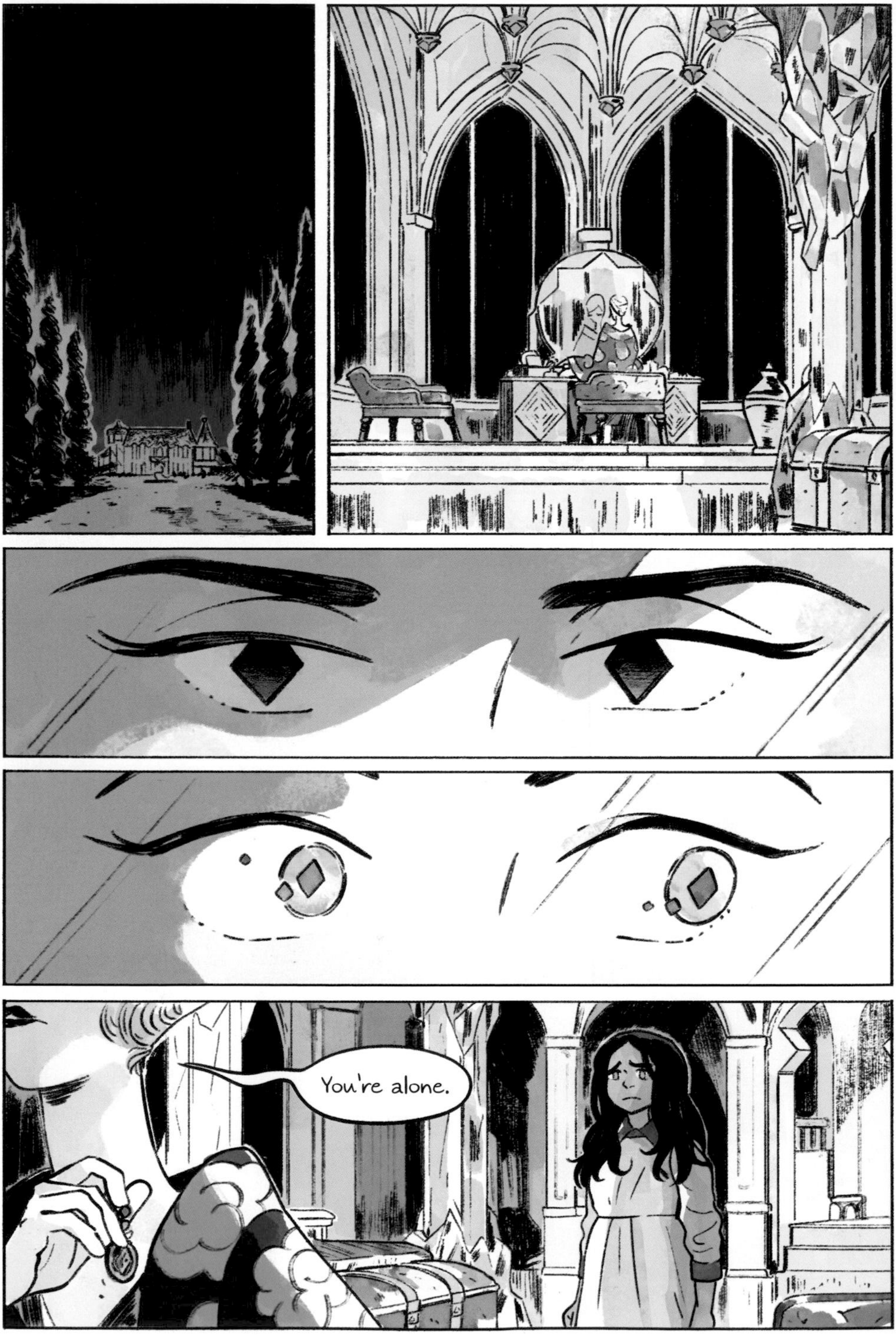
You're alone.

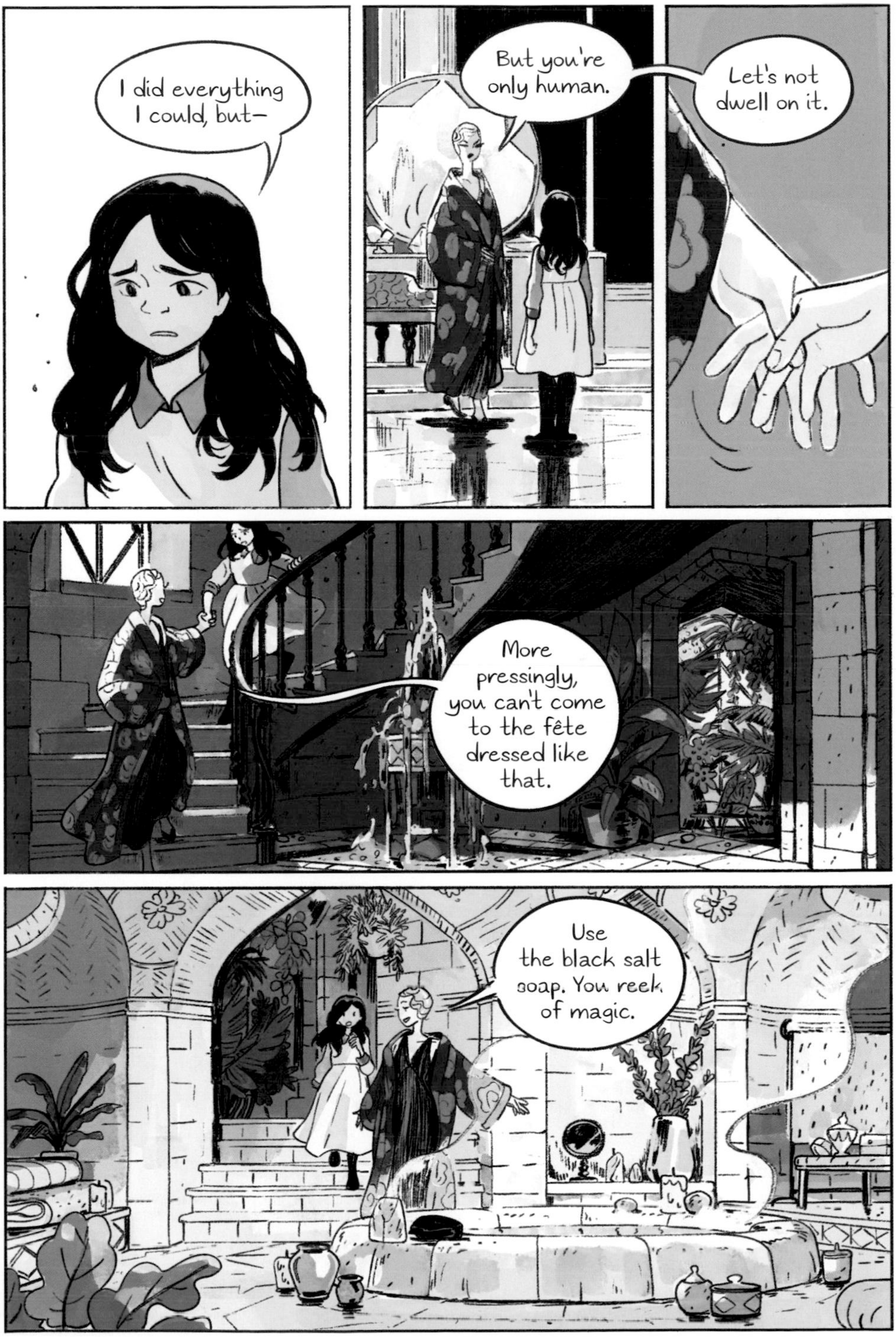
I did everything I could, but—
But you're only human.
Let's not dwell on it.
More pressingly, you can't come to the fête dressed like that.
Use the black salt soap. You reek of magic.

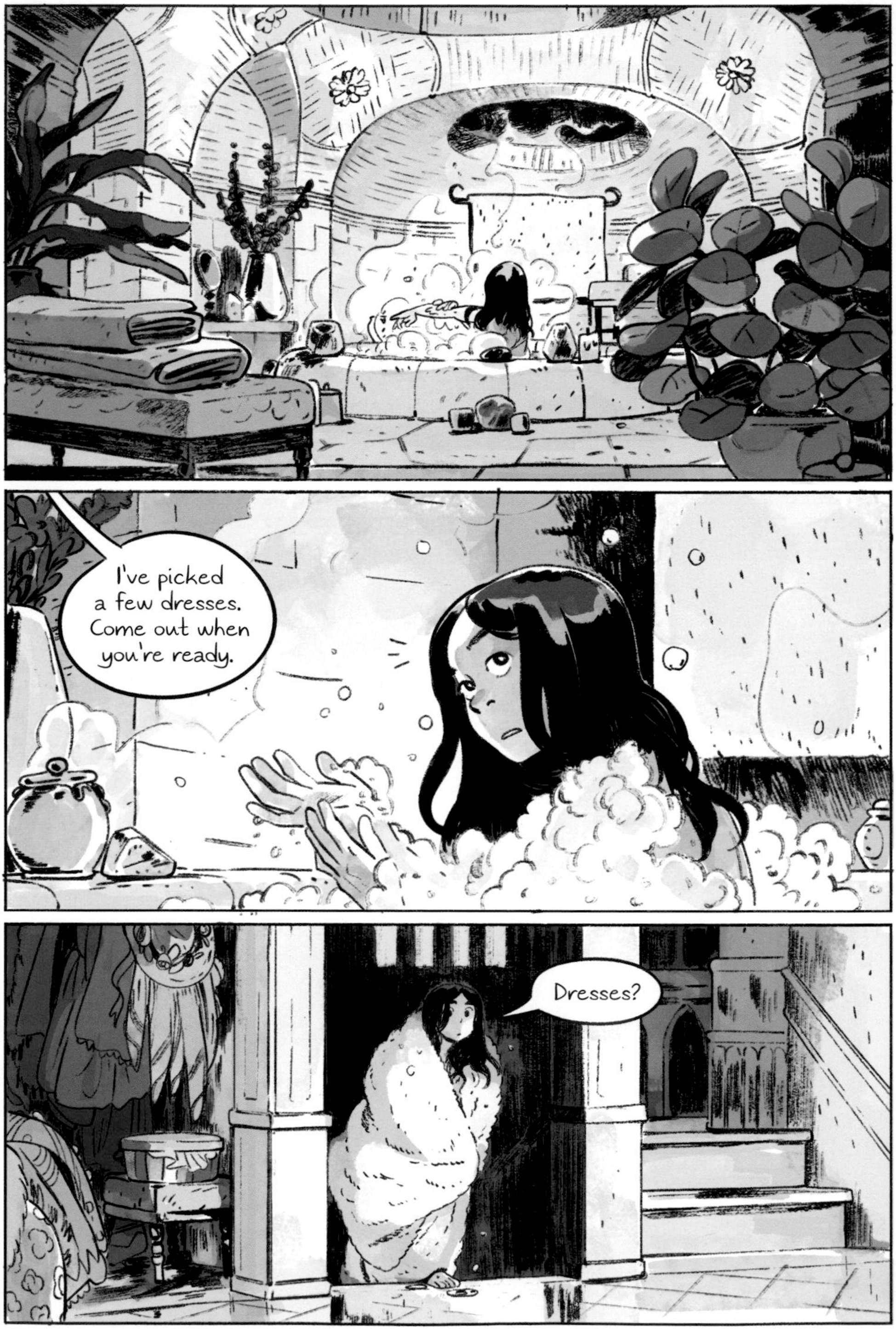

I've picked a few dresses. Come out when you're ready.
Dresses?

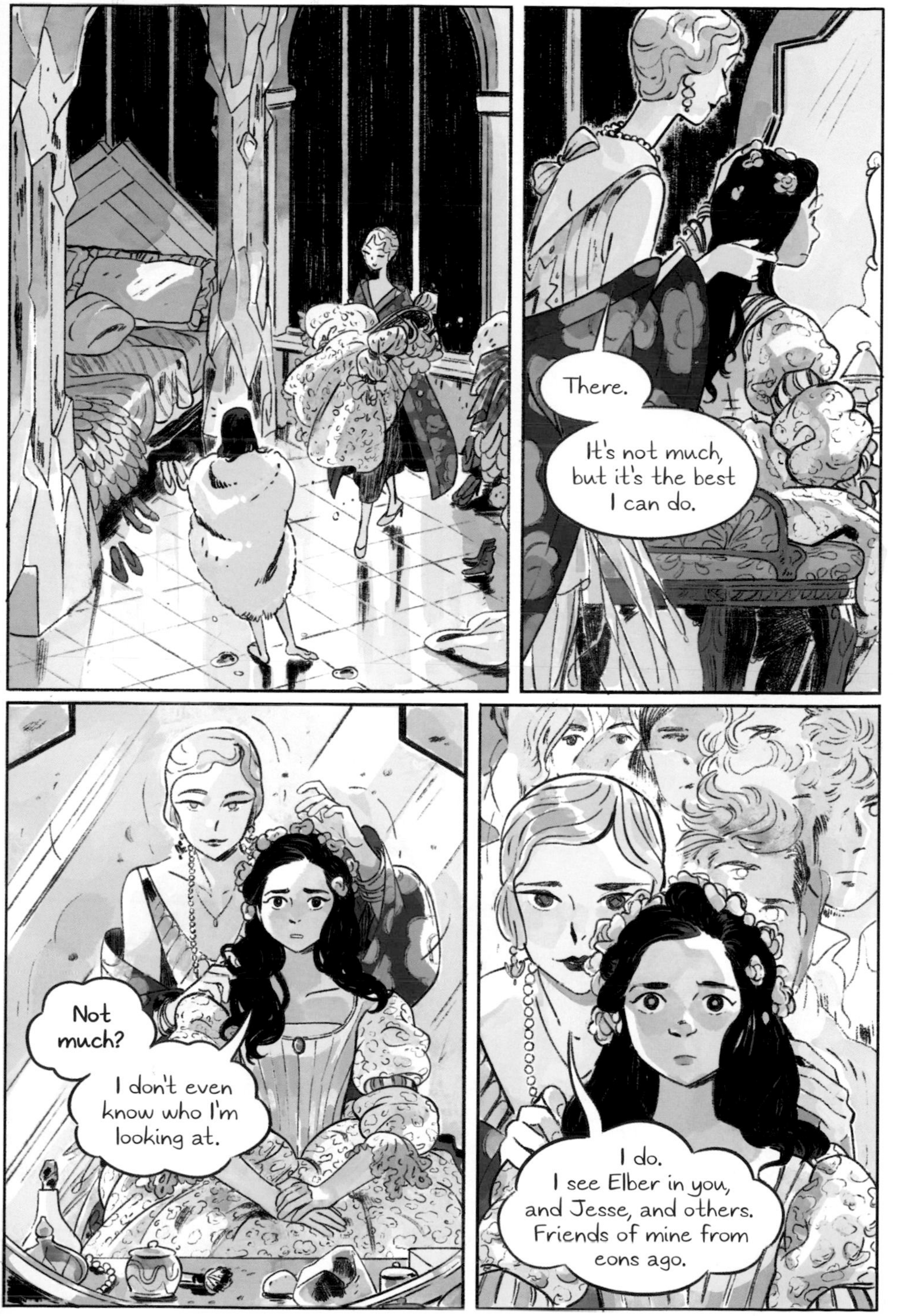
There.
It's not much, but it's the best I can do.
Not much?
I don't even know who I'm looking at.
I do. I see Elber in you, and Jesse, and others. Friends of mine from eons ago.

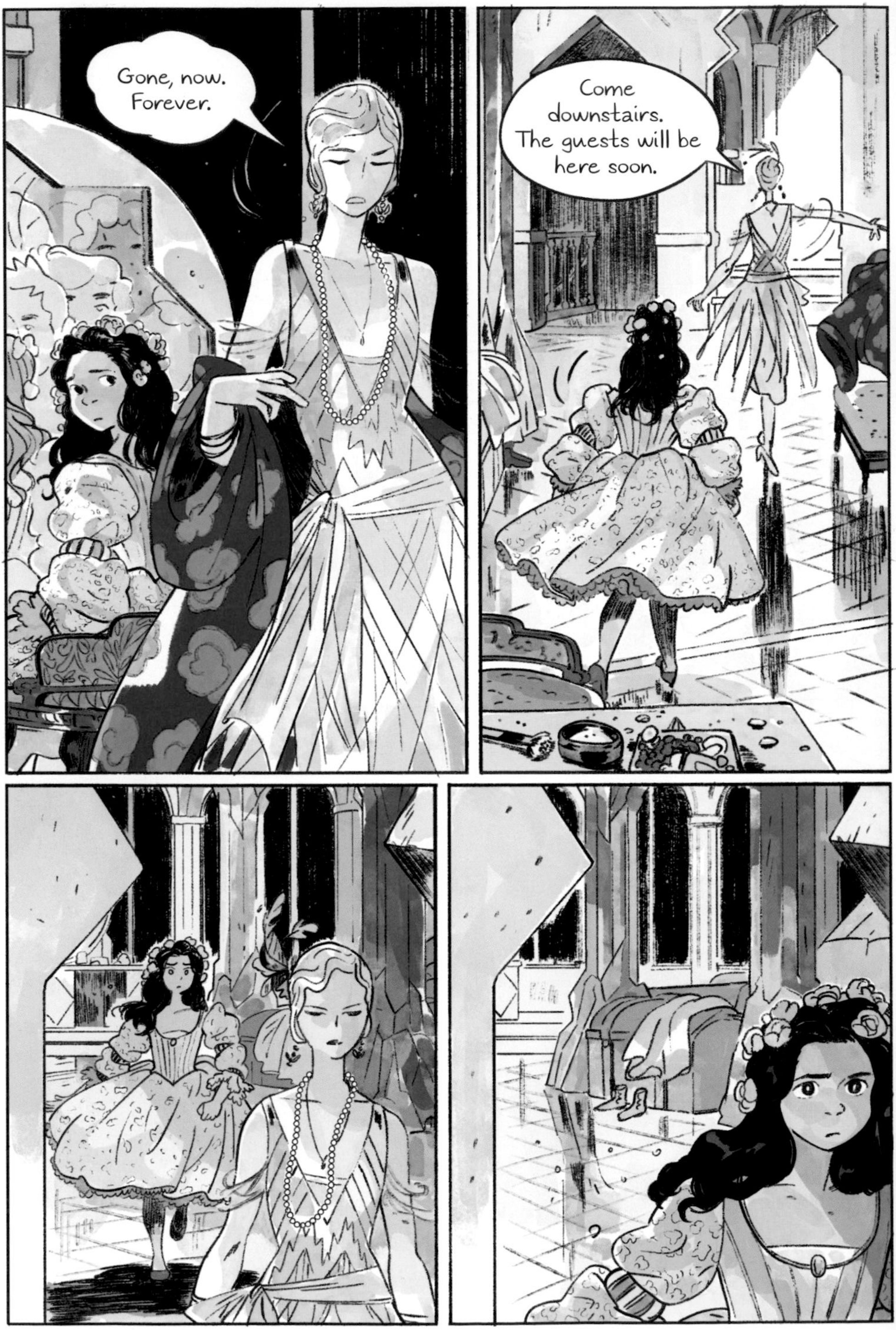
Gone, now.
Forever.
Come downstairs.
The guests will be here soon.

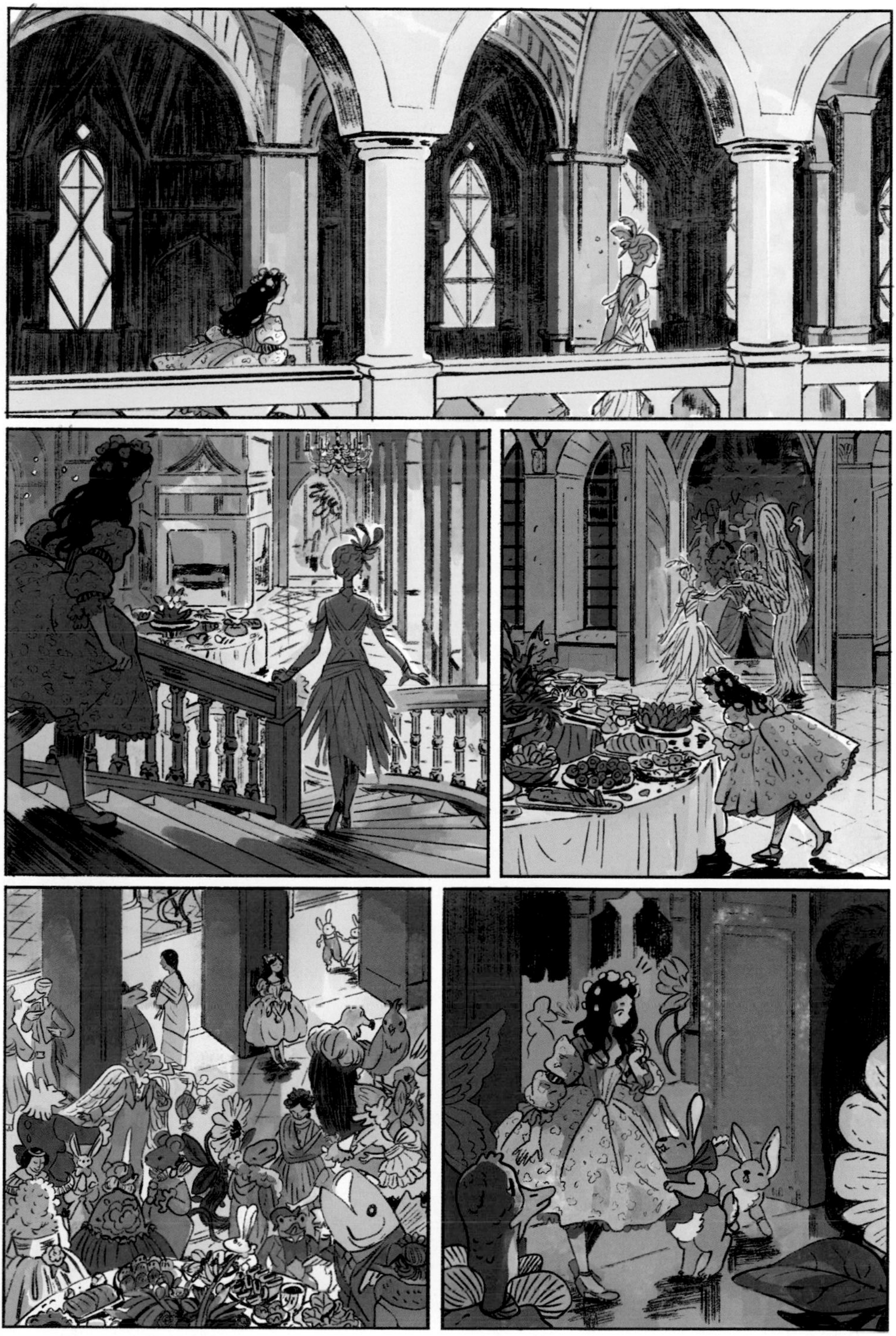

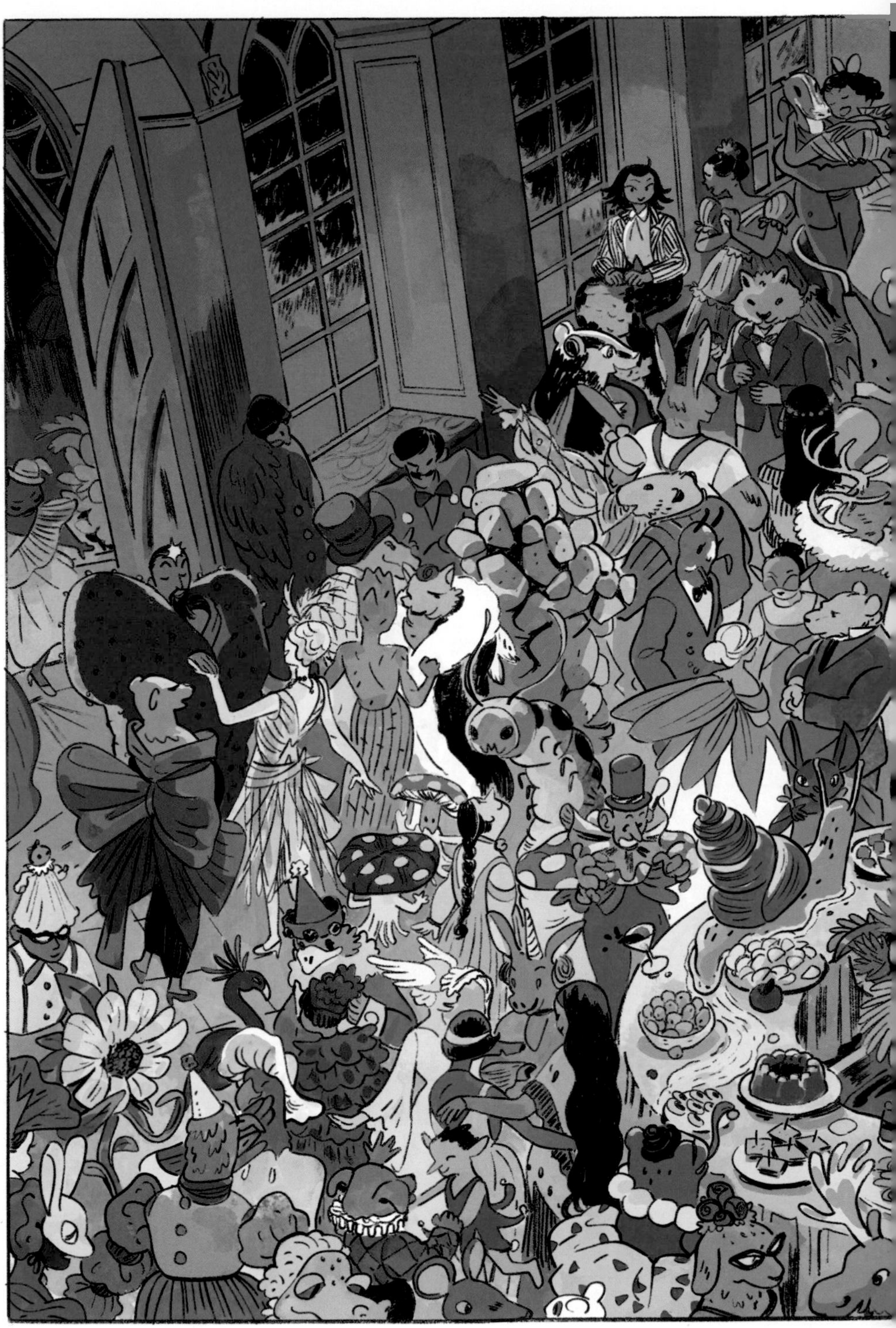

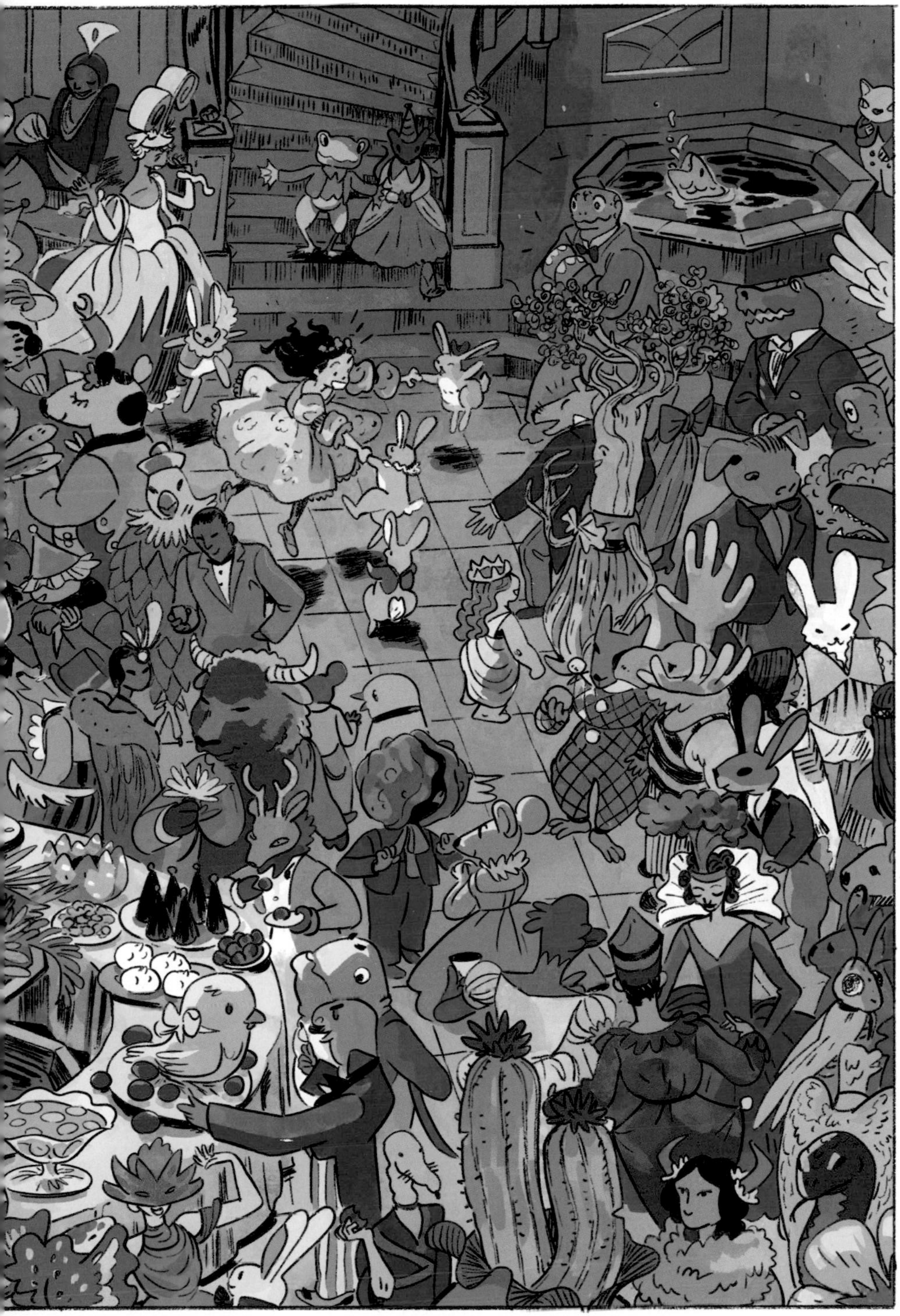

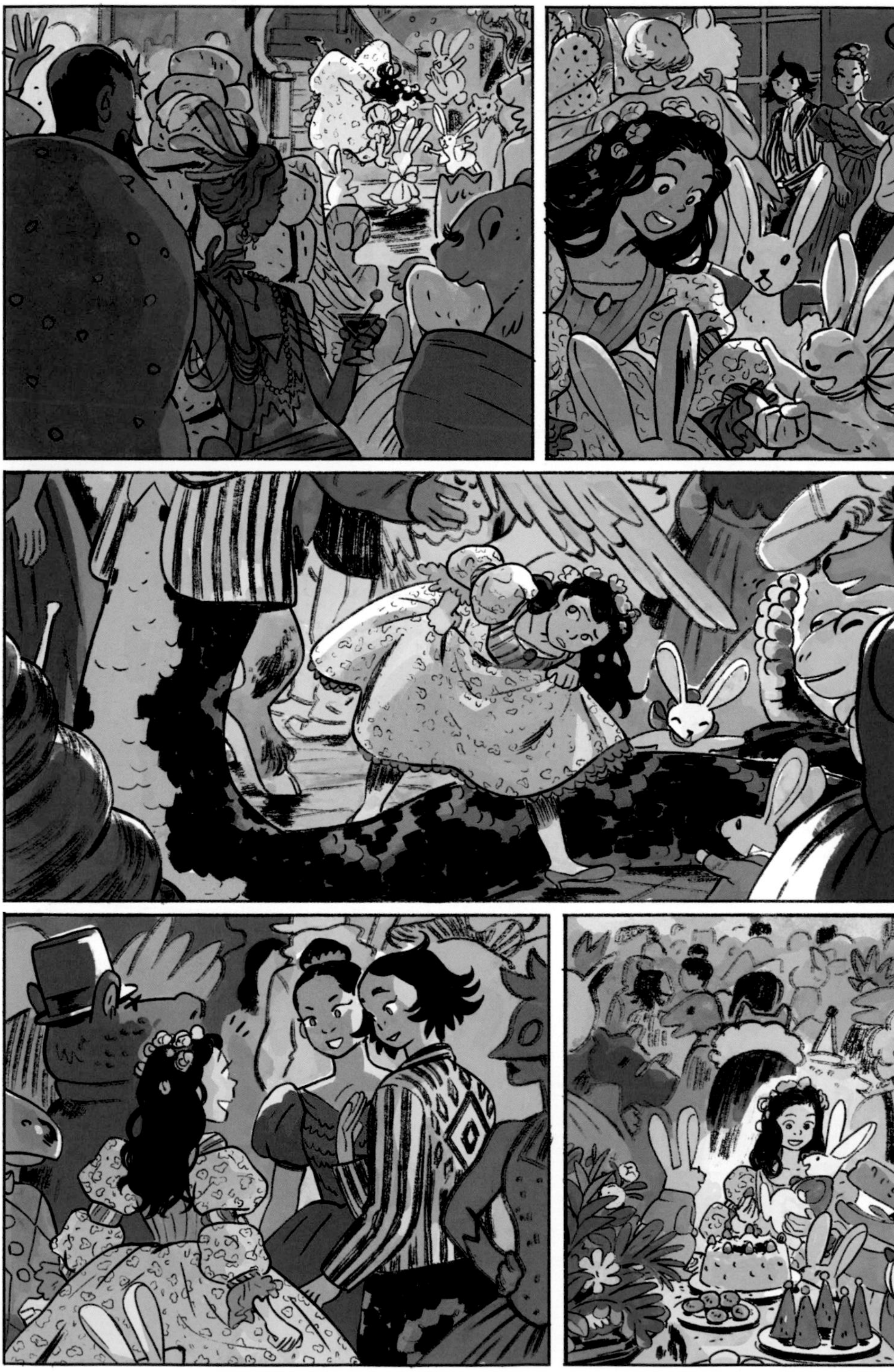

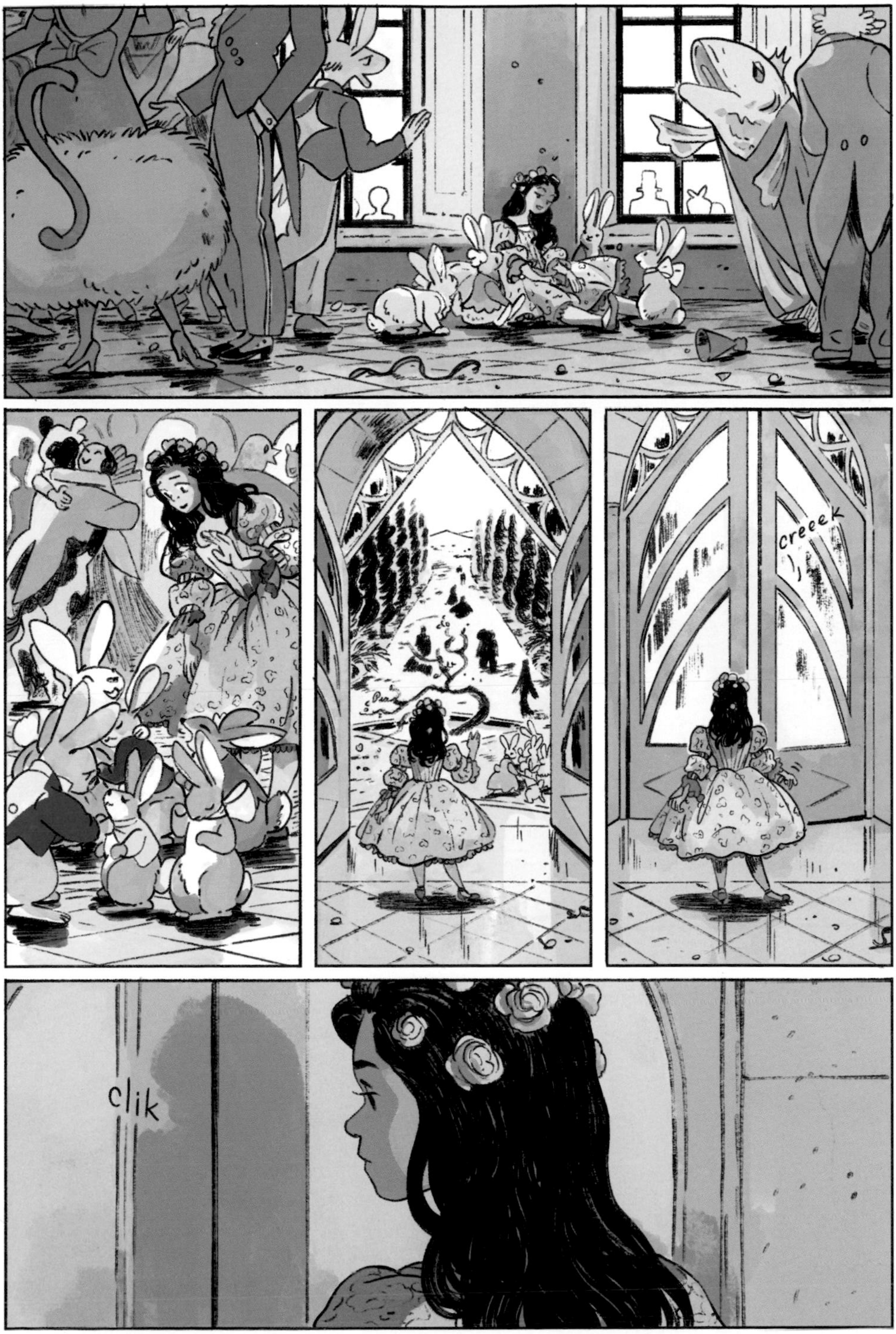
creeek
clik

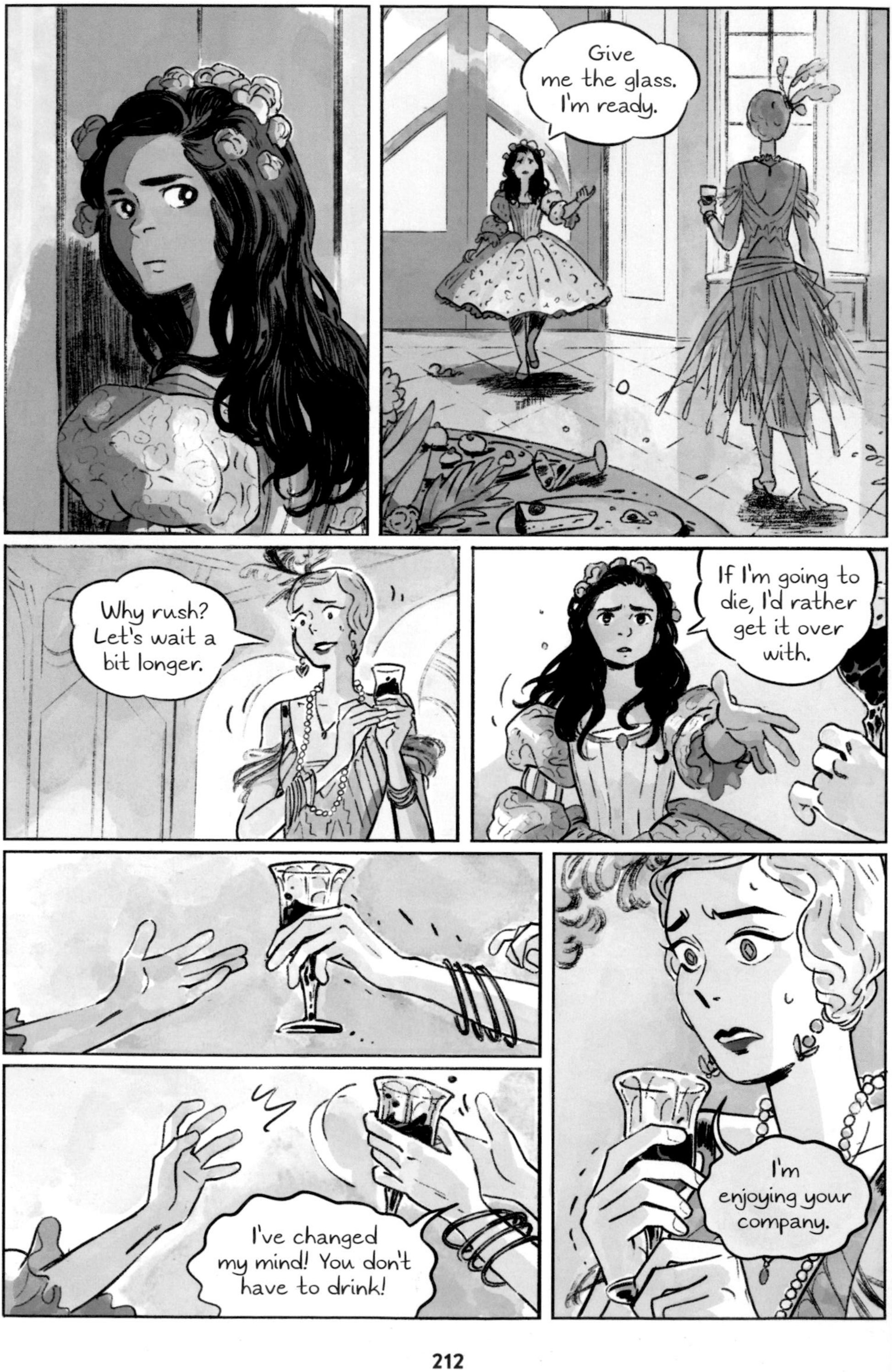
Give me the glass. I'm ready.
Why rush? Let's wait a bit longer.
If I'm going to die, I'd rather get it over with.
I've changed my mind! You don't have to drink!
I'm enjoying your company.

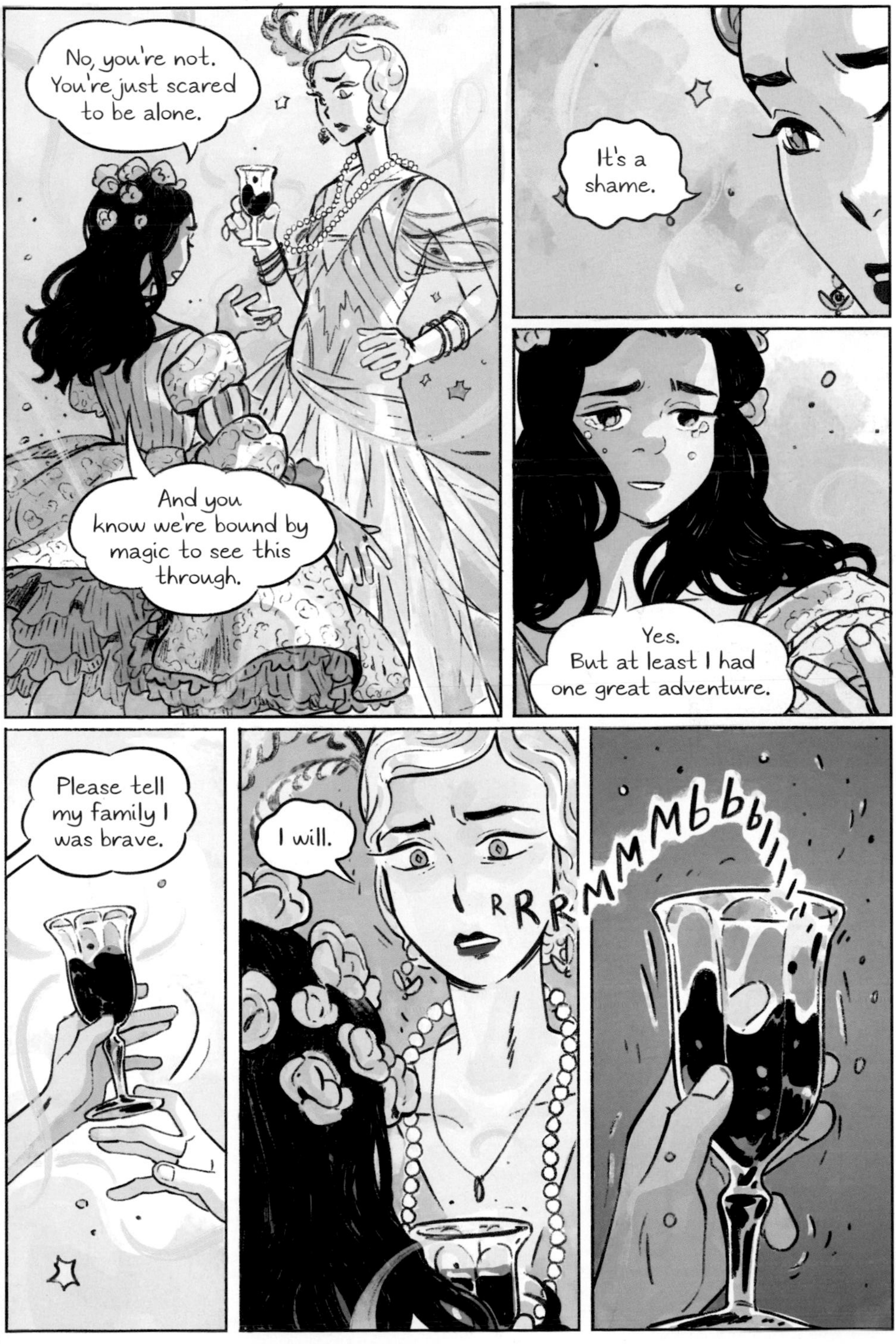
No, you're not. You're just scared to be alone.
And you know we're bound by magic to see this through.
It's a shame.
Yes. But at least I had one great adventure.
Please tell my family I was brave.
I will.
RRRMMMMbbb!!!

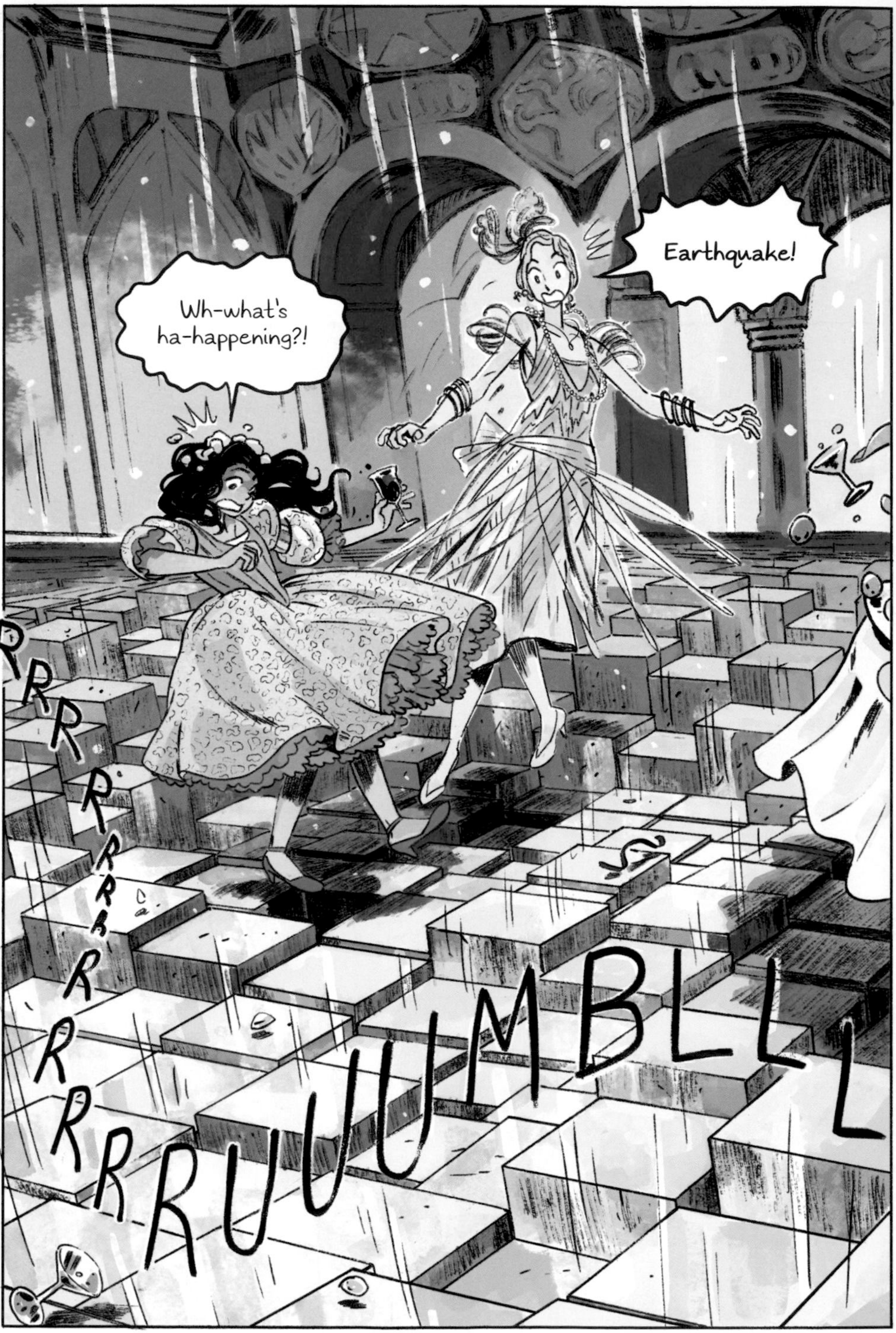

Wh-what's ha-happening?!
Earthquake!
RRRRRRRRRRRRRRUUUUMBLLL

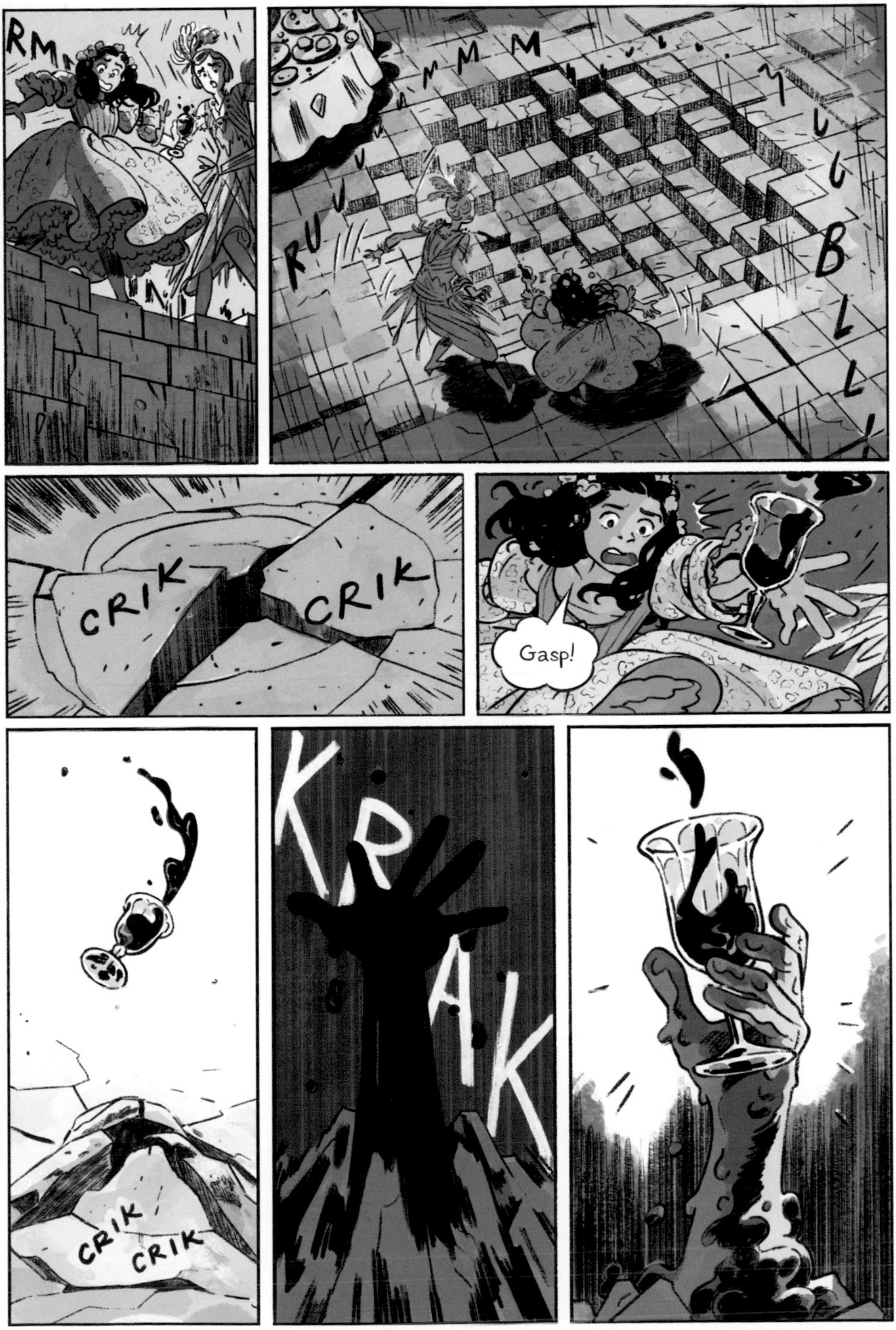
RM
RUUUNMMMM
MUGBLLL
CRIK CRIK
Gasp!
CRIK CRIK
KRAK

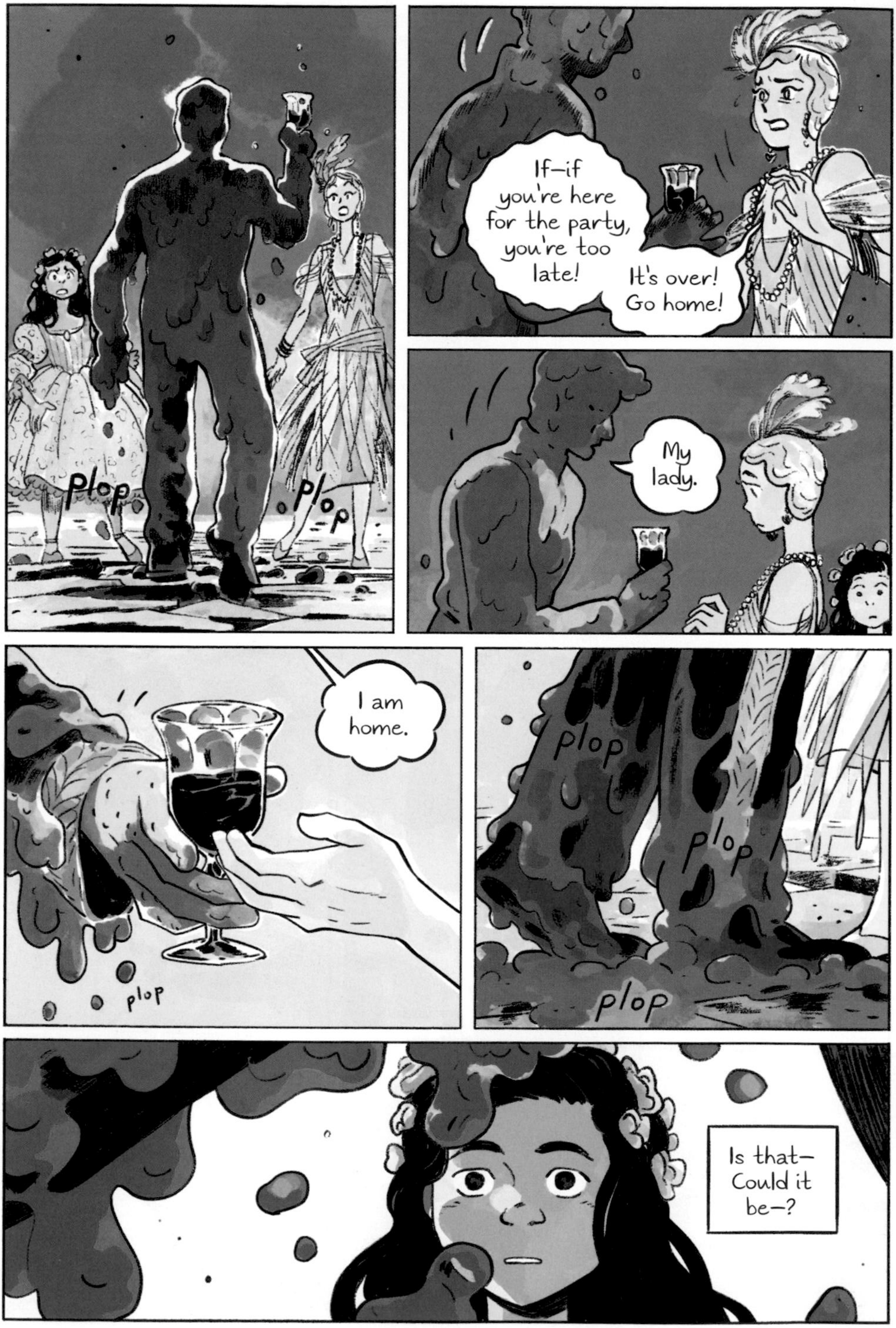
plop
plop
If—if you're here for the party, you're too late!
It's over! Go home!
My lady.
I am home.
plop
plop
plop
plop
Is that— Could it be—?

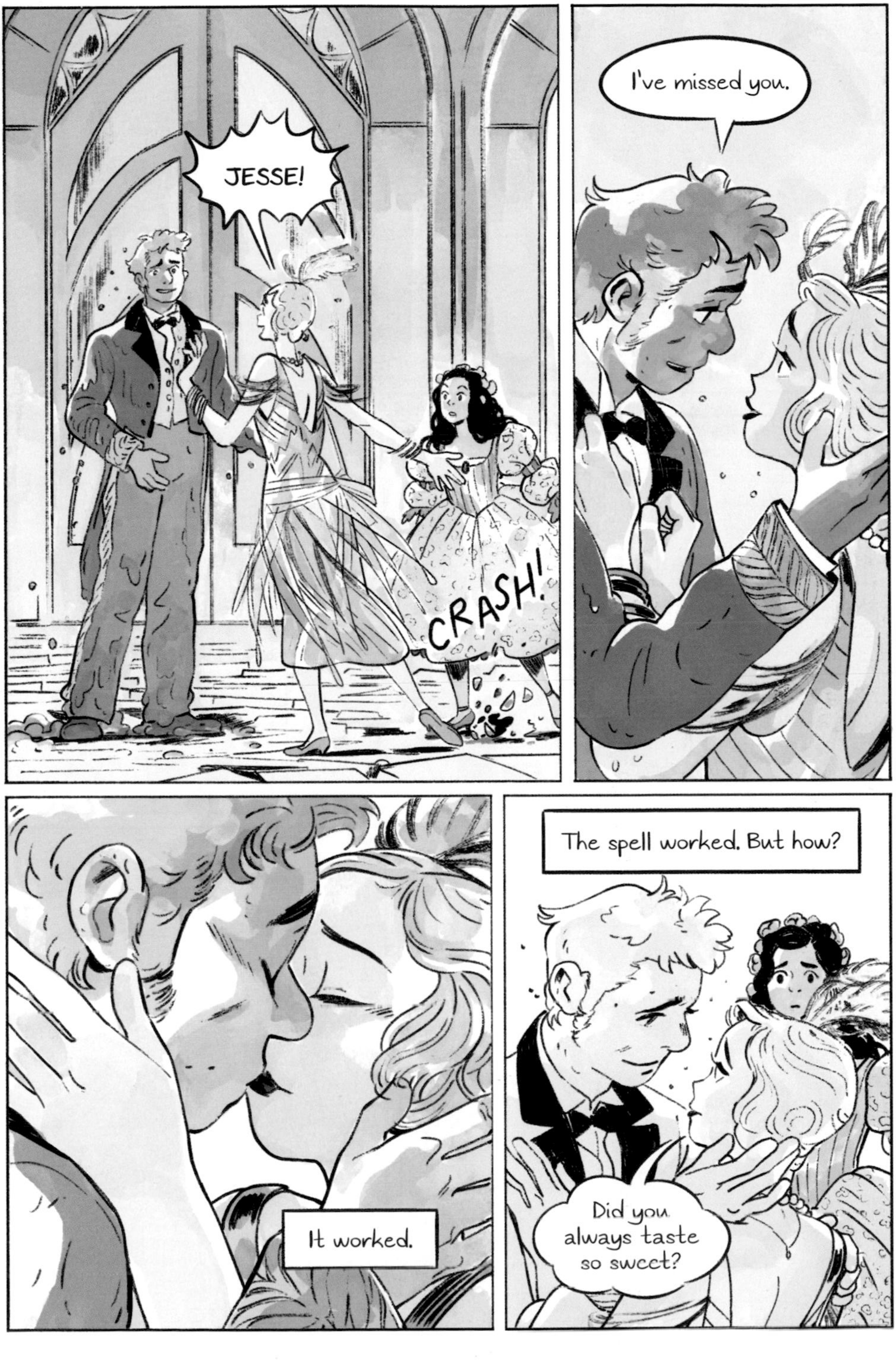
JESSE!
CRASH!
I've missed you.
It worked.
The spell worked. But how?
Did you always taste so swcct?

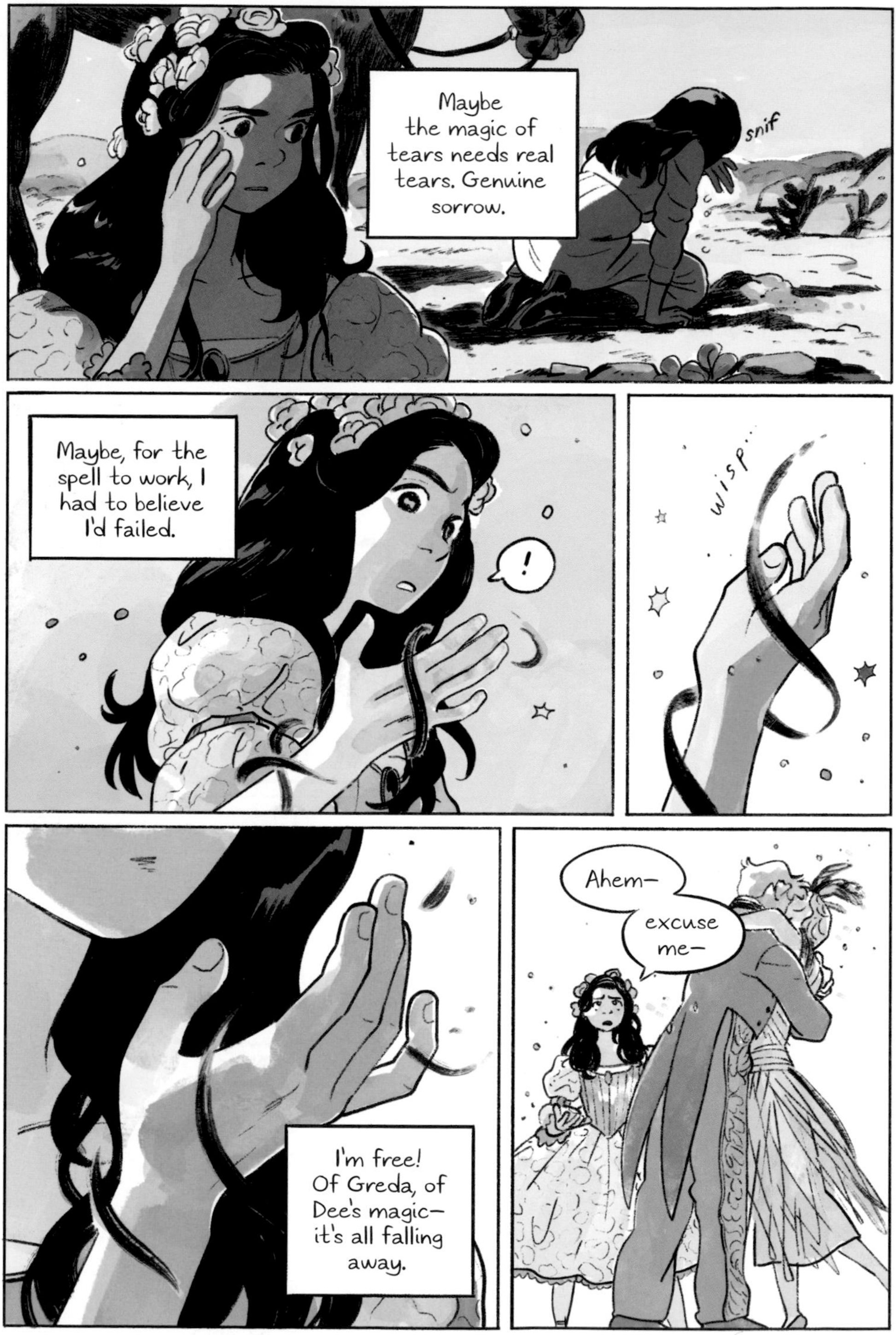
Maybe the magic of tears needs real tears. Genuine sorrow.
snif
Maybe, for the spell to work, I had to believe I'd failed.
!
wisp...
I'm free! Of Greda, of Dee's magic— it's all falling away.
Ahem—
excuse me—

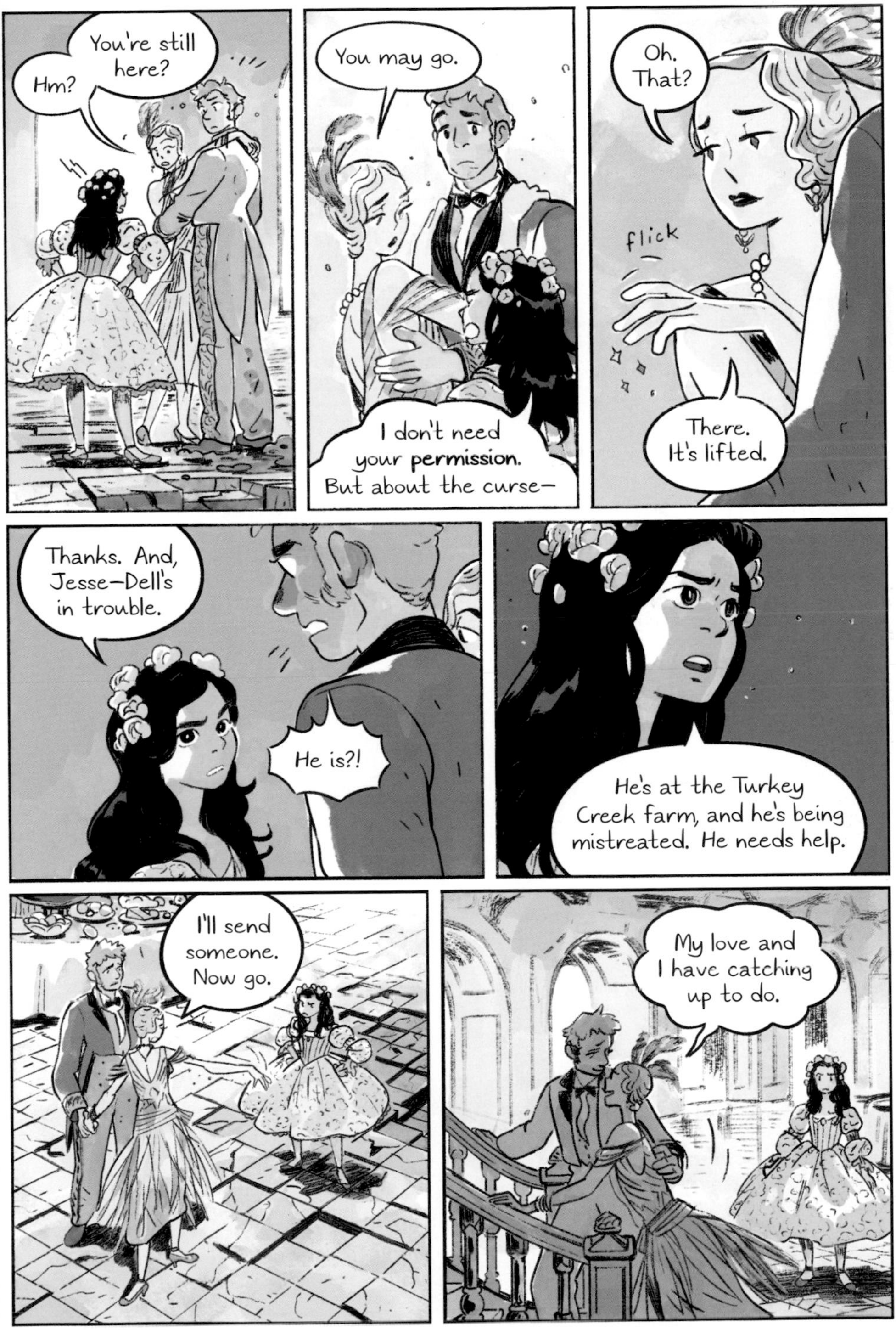
Hm?
You're still here?
You may go.
I don't need your **permission.** But about the curse—
flick
Oh. That?
There. It's lifted.
Thanks. And, Jesse-Dell's in trouble.
He is?!
He's at the Turkey Creek farm, and he's being mistreated. He needs help.
I'll send someone. Now go.
My love and I have catching up to do.

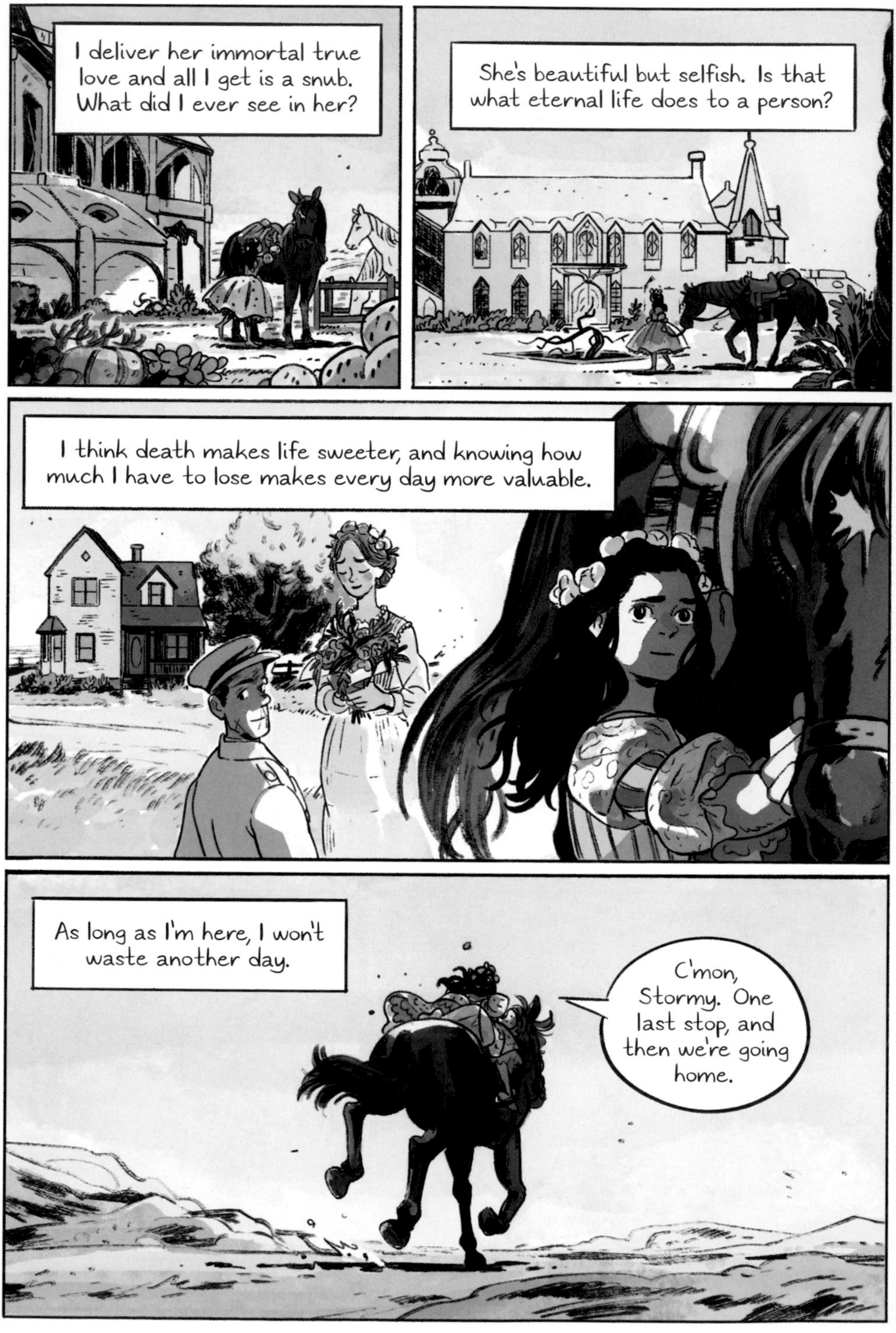
I deliver her immortal true love and all I get is a snub. What did I ever see in her?
She's beautiful but selfish. Is that what eternal life does to a person?
I think death makes life sweeter, and knowing how much I have to lose makes every day more valuable.
As long as I'm here, I won't waste another day.
C'mon, Stormy. One last stop, and then we're going home.

Chapter Twelve

About Time

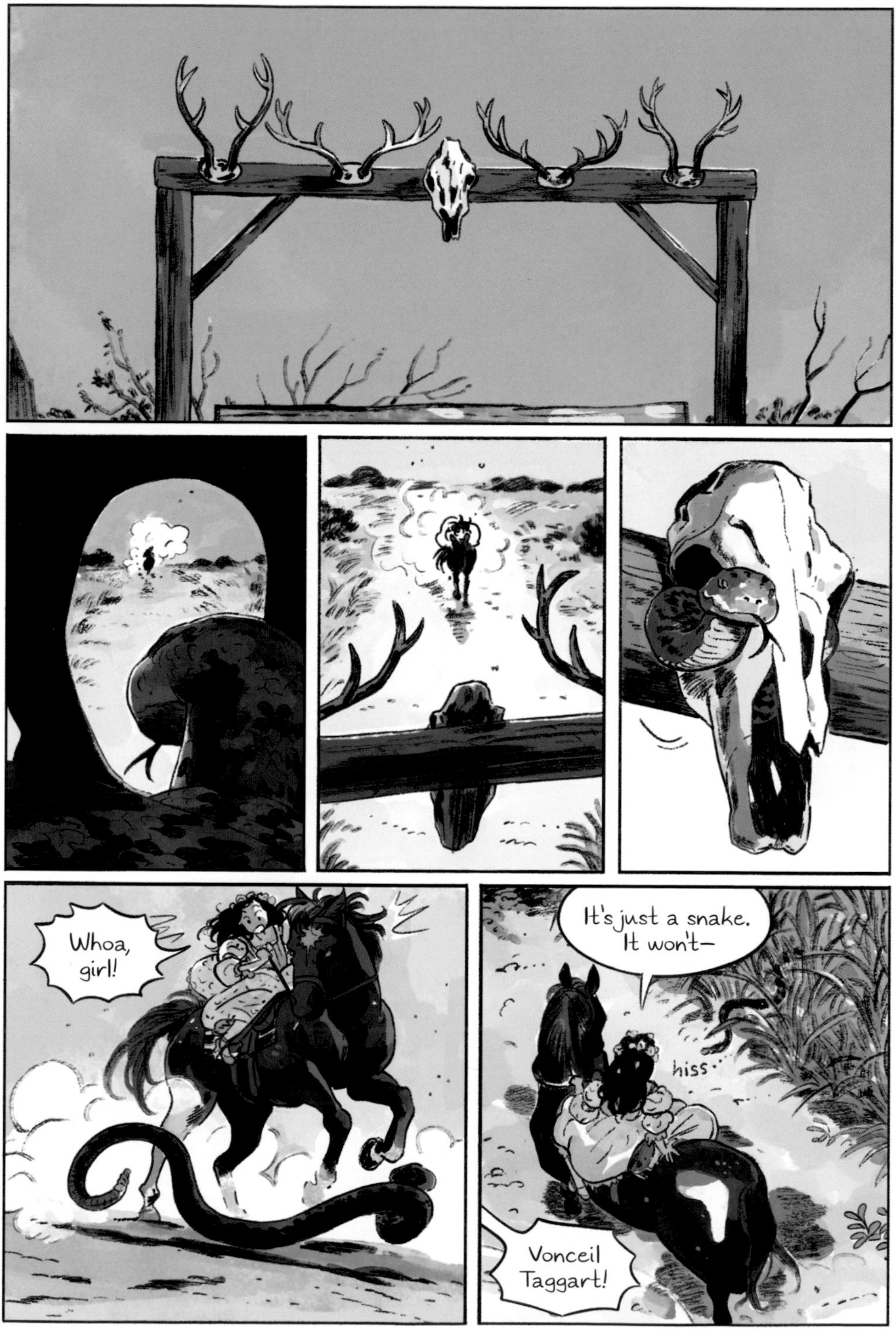
Whoa, girl!
It's just a snake. It won't—
hiss...
Vonceil Taggart!

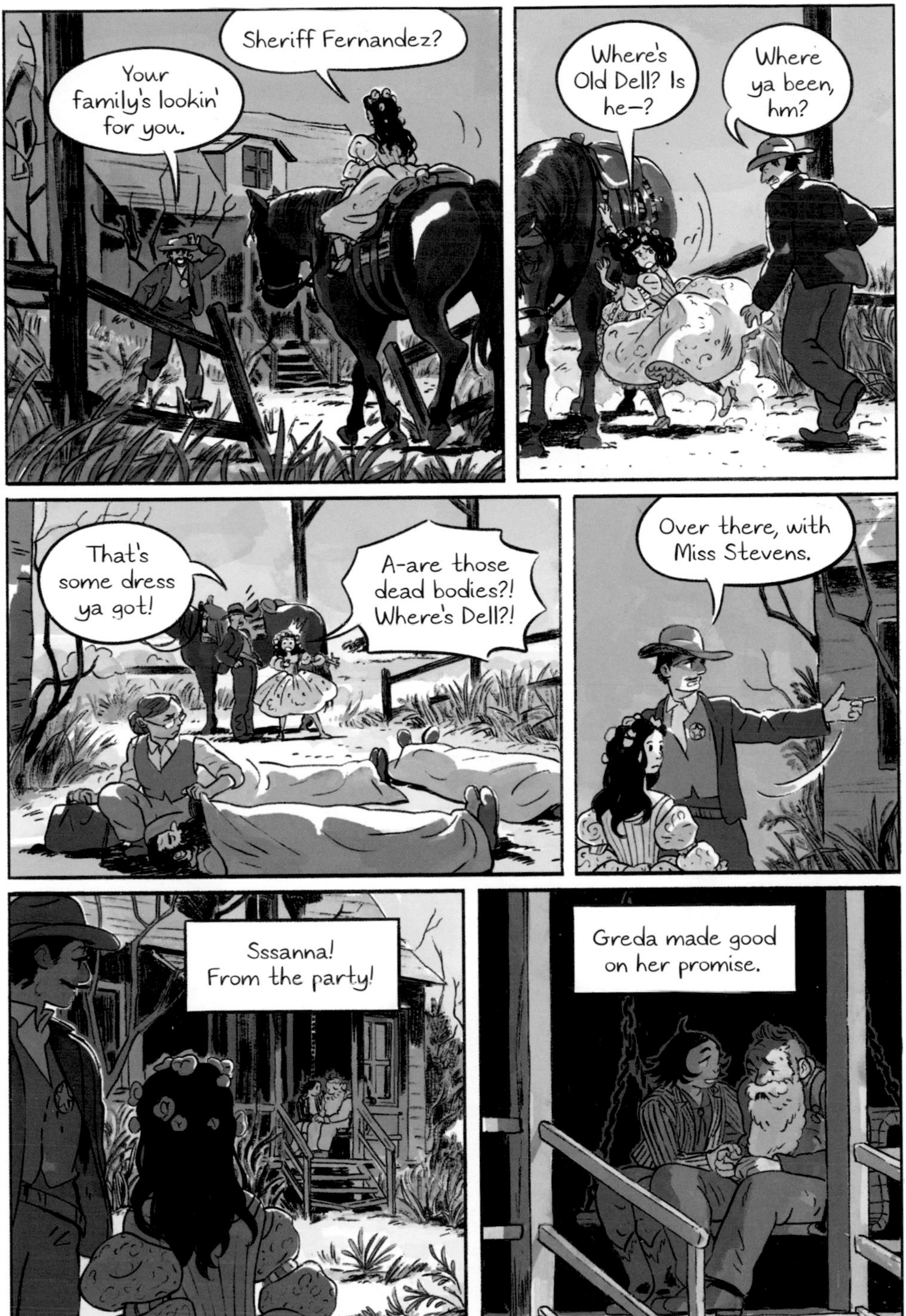
Sheriff Fernandez?
Your family's lookin' for you.
Where's Old Dell? Is he—?
Where ya been, hm?
That's some dress ya got!
A-are those dead bodies?! Where's Dell?!
Over there, with Miss Stevens.
Sssanna! From the party!
Greda made good on her promise.

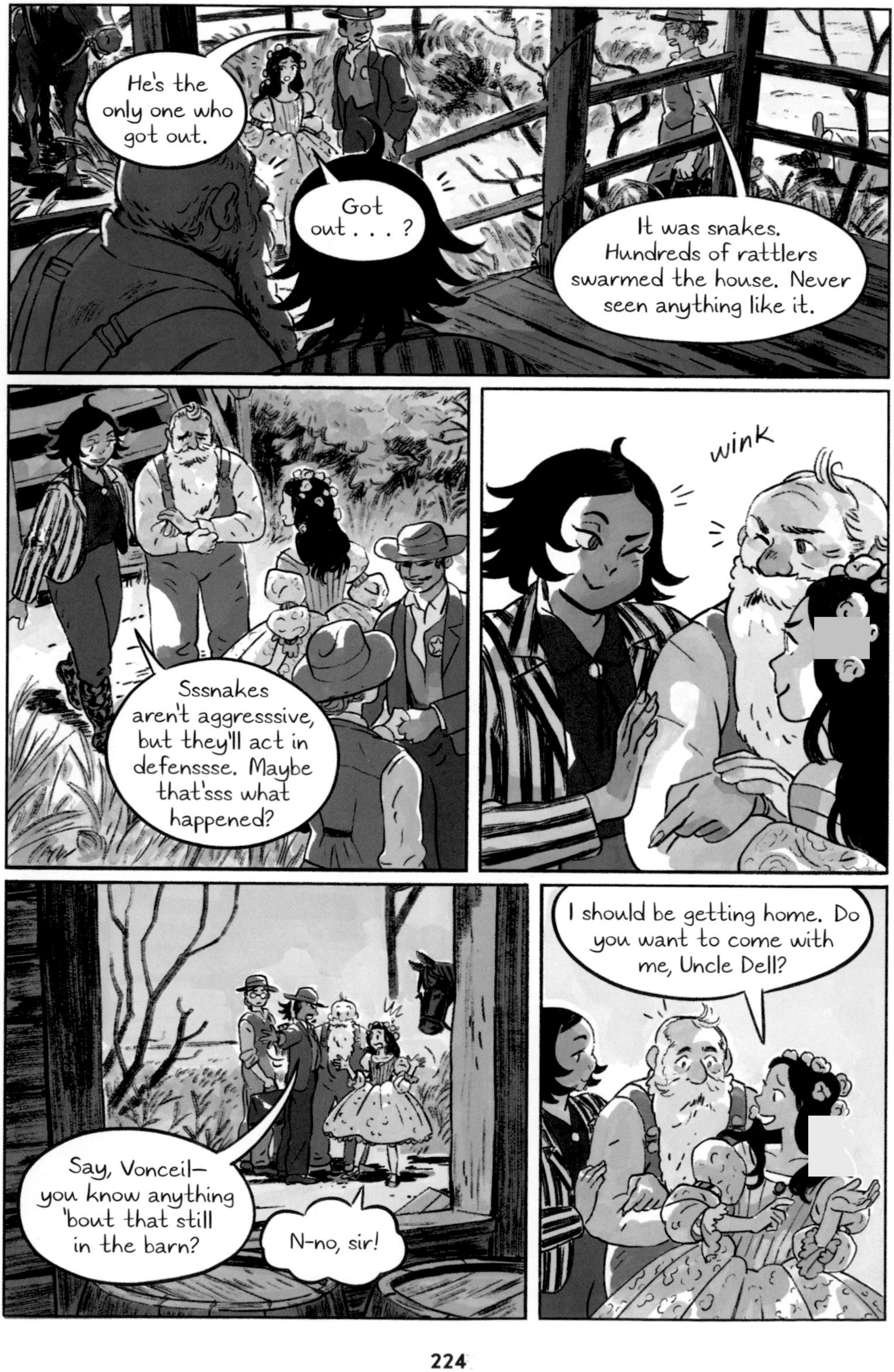
He's the only one who got out.
Got out . . . ?
It was snakes. Hundreds of rattlers swarmed the house. Never seen anything like it.
Sssnakes aren't aggresssive, but they'll act in defenssse. Maybe that'sss what happened?
wink
Say, Vonceil— you know anything 'bout that still in the barn?
N-no, sir!
I should be getting home. Do you want to come with me, Uncle Dell?

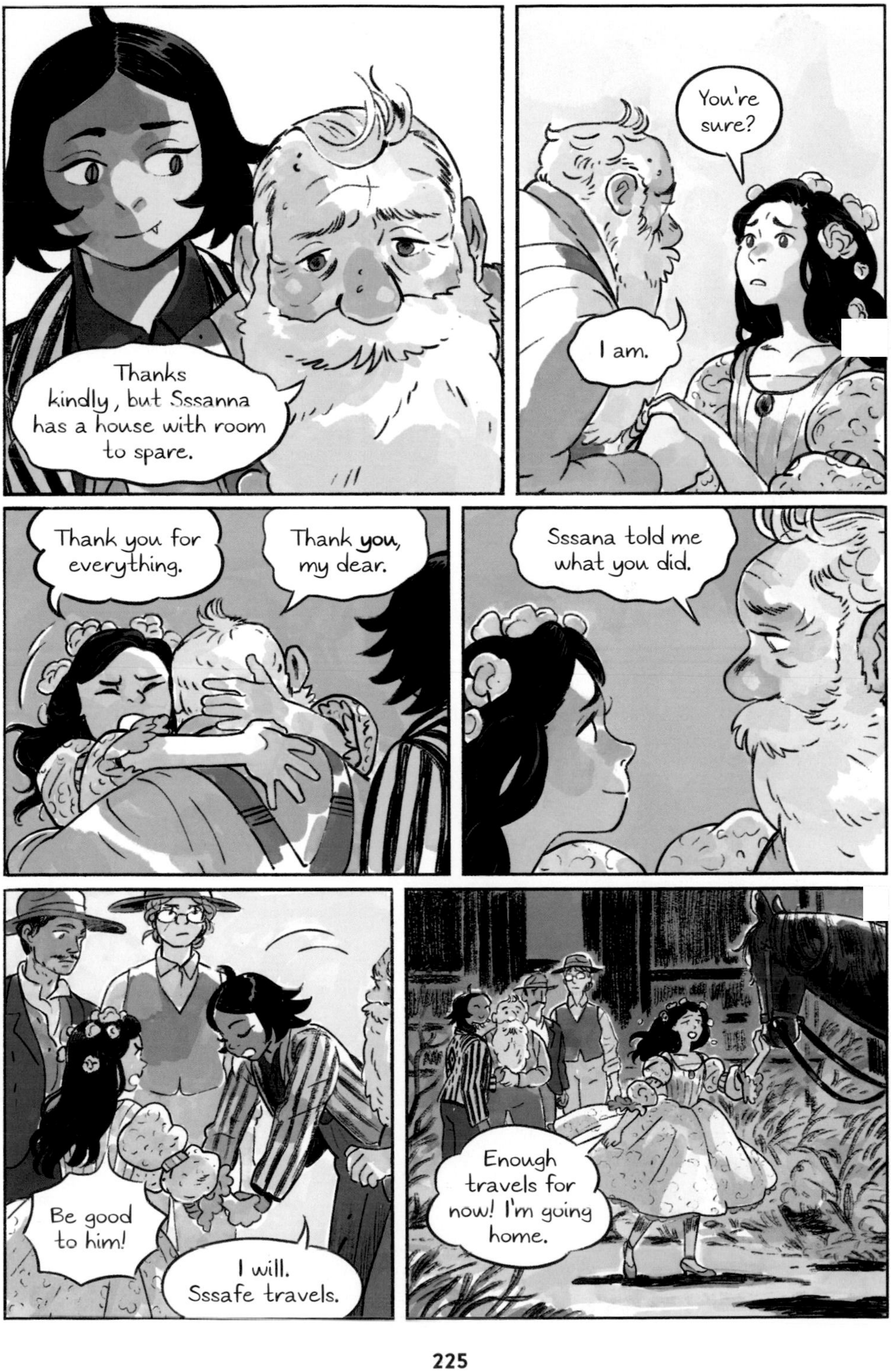
Thanks kindly, but Sssanna has a house with room to spare.
You're sure?
I am.
Thank you for everything.
Thank **you**, my dear.
Sssana told me what you did.
Be good to him!
I will. Sssafe travels.
Enough travels for now! I'm going home.

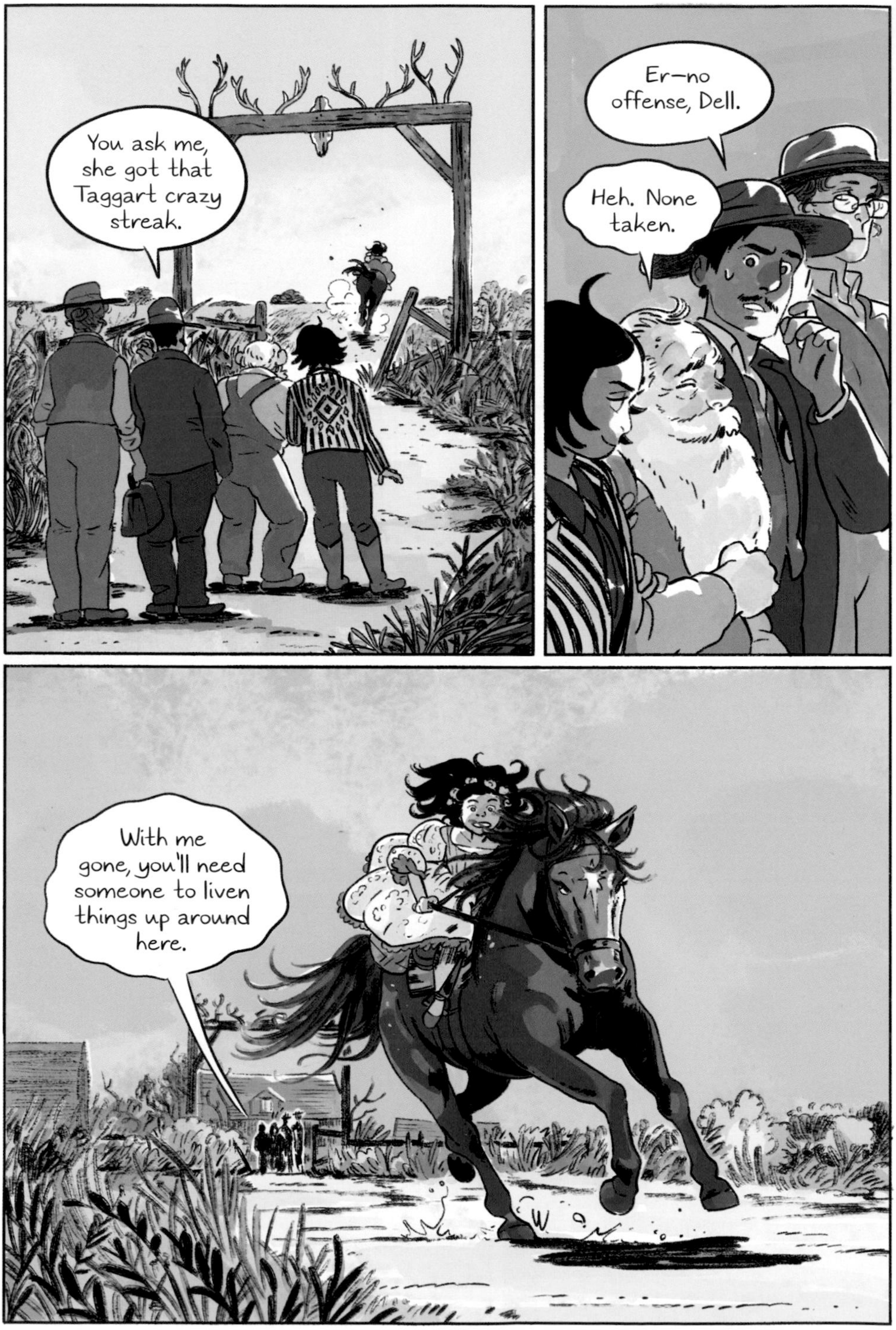
You ask me, she got that Taggart crazy streak.
Er—no offense, Dell.
Heh. None taken.
With me gone, you'll need someone to liven things up around here.

Epilogue

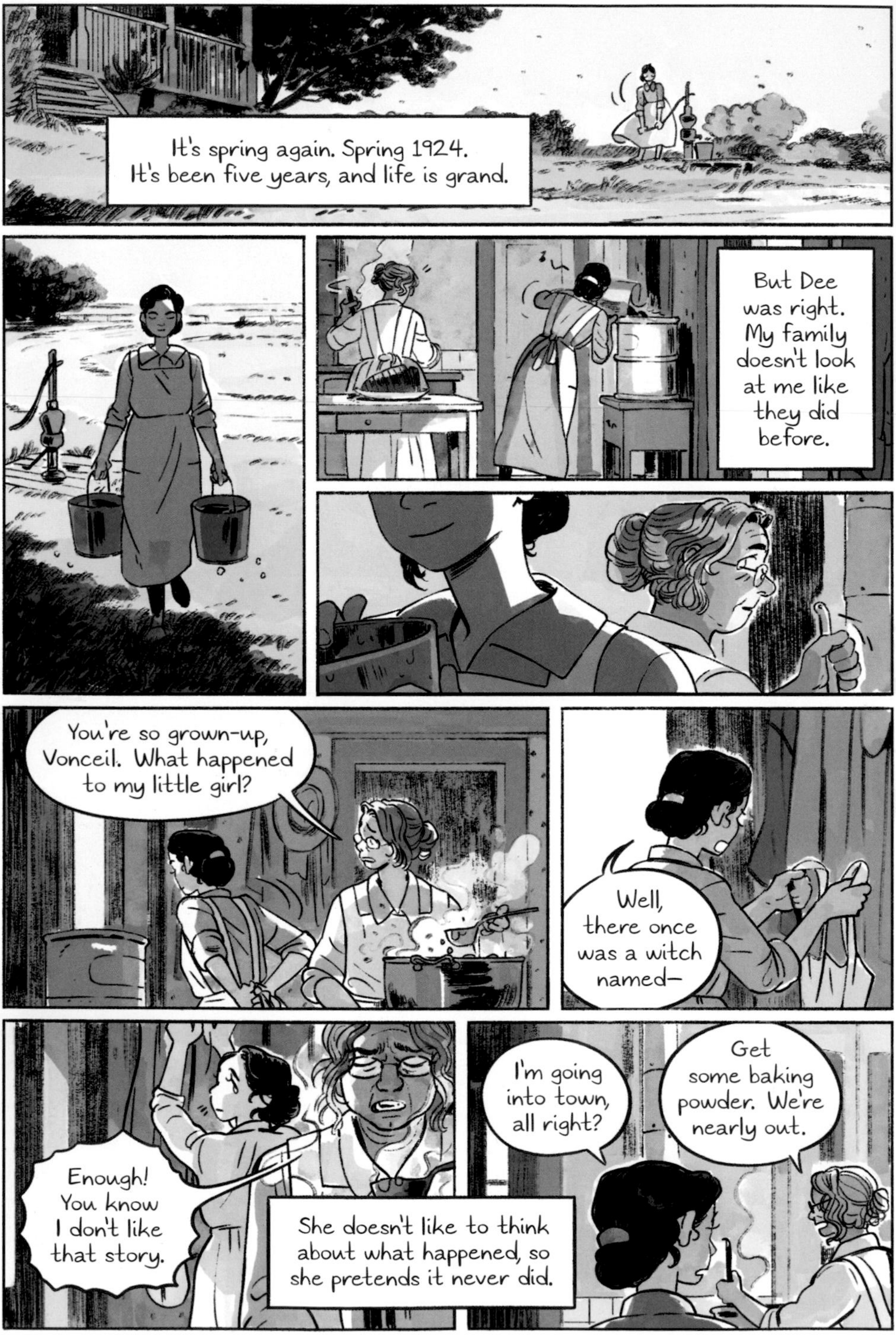
It's spring again. Spring 1924.
It's been five years, and life is grand.
But Dee was right. My family doesn't look at me like they did before.
You're so grown-up, Vonceil. What happened to my little girl?
Well, there once was a witch named–
Enough! You know I don't like that story.
She doesn't like to think about what happened, so she pretends it never did.
I'm going into town, all right?
Get some baking powder. We're nearly out.

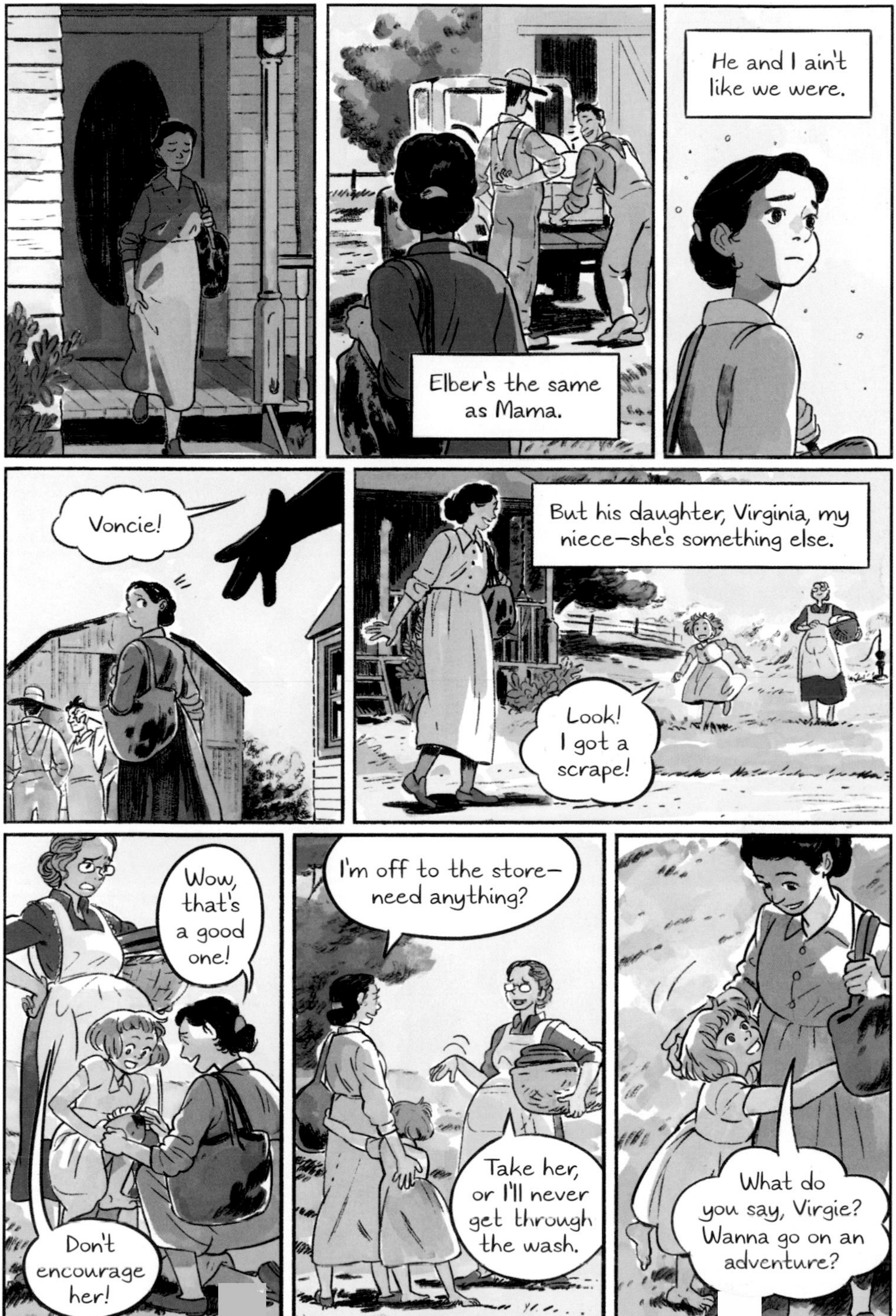
Elber's the same as Mama.
He and I ain't like we were.
Voncie!
But his daughter, Virginia, my niece—she's something else.
Look! I got a scrape!
Wow, that's a good one!
Don't encourage her!
I'm off to the store—need anything?
Take her, or I'll never get through the wash.
What do you say, Virgie? Wanna go on an adventure?

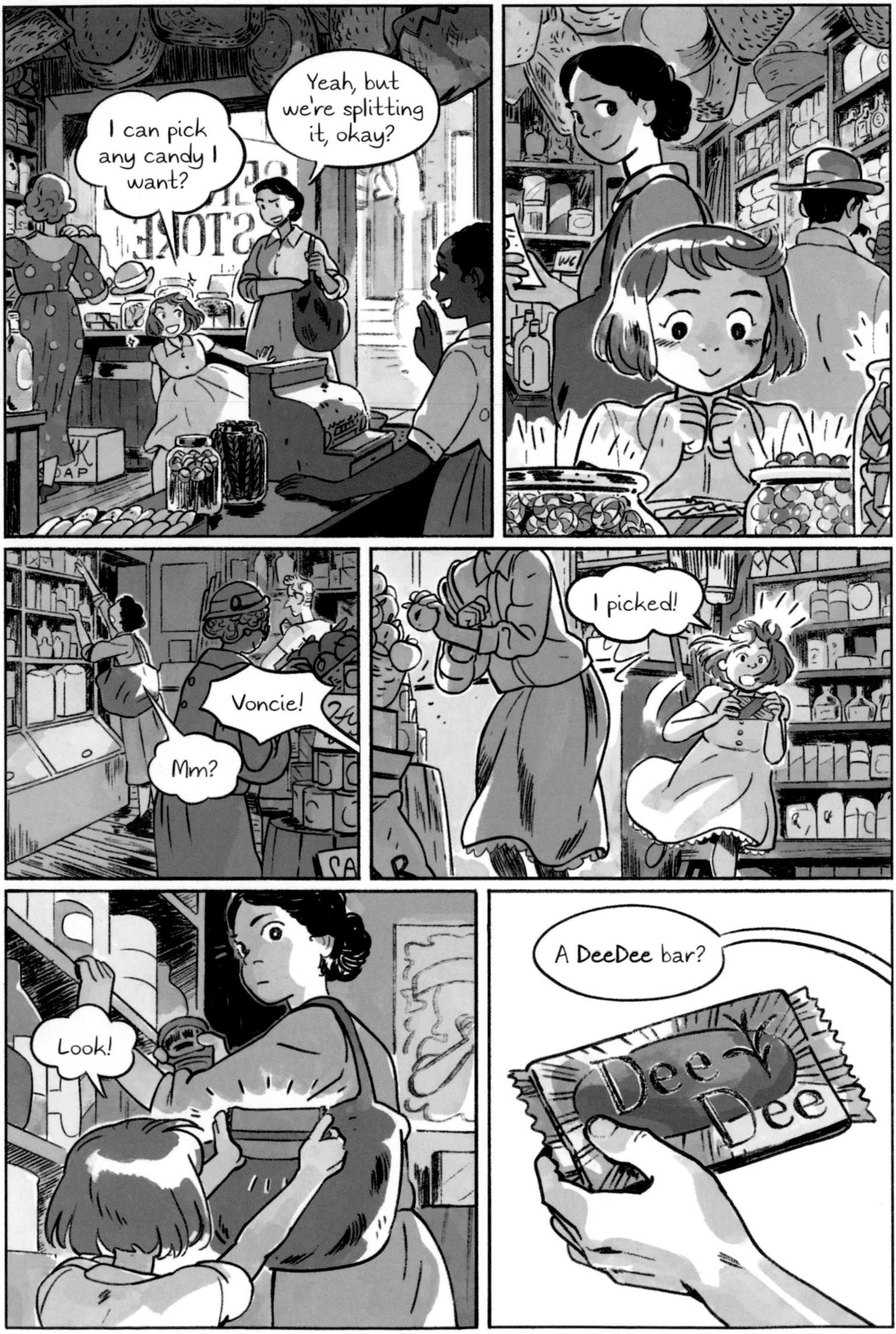
I can pick any candy I want?
Yeah, but we're splitting it, okay?
STORE
Voncie!
Mm?
I picked!
Look!
A DeeDee bar?
Dee Dee

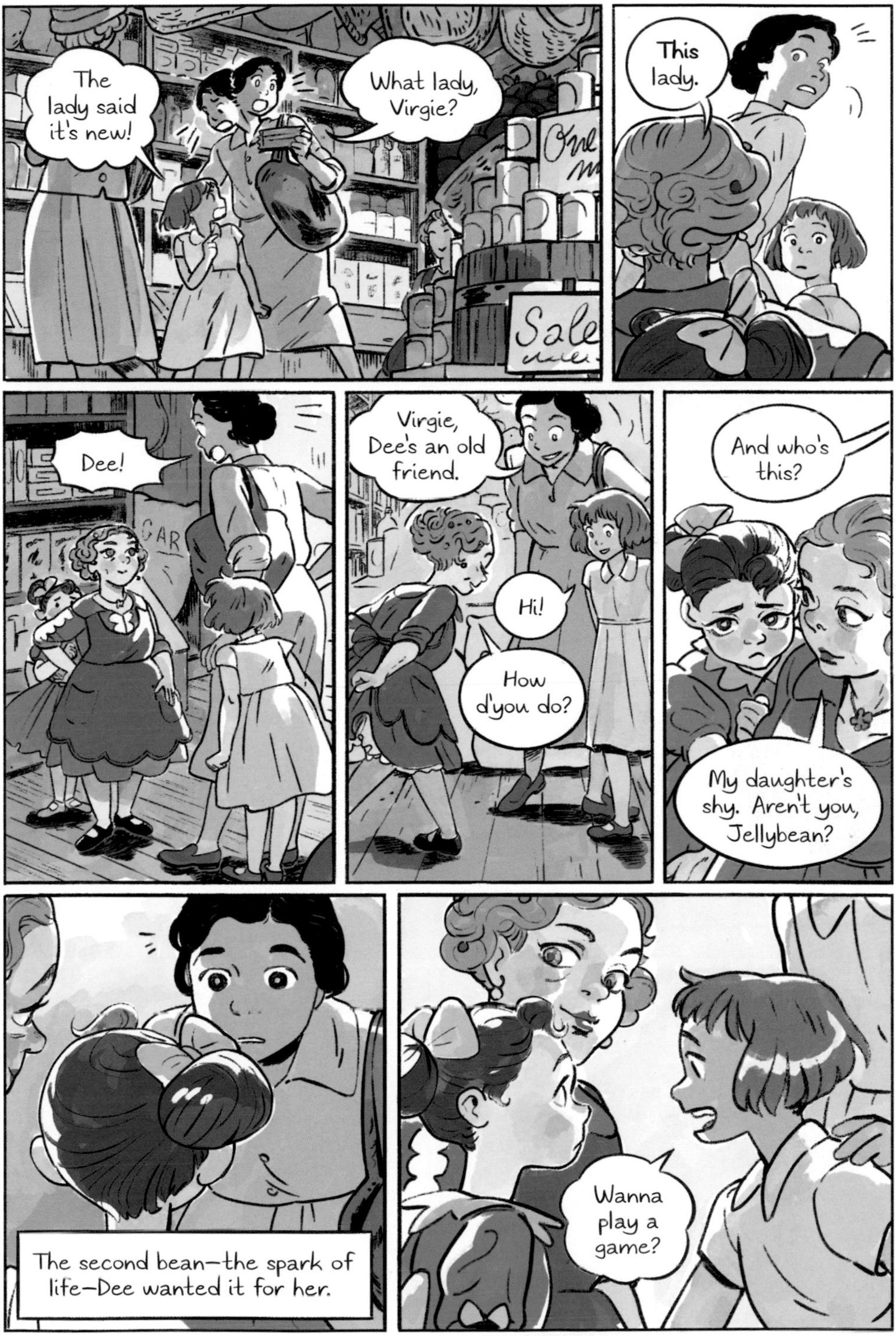

The lady said it's new!
What lady, Virgie?
One
Sale
This lady.
Dee!
GAR
Virgie, Dee's an old friend.
Hi!
How d'you do?
And who's this?
My daughter's shy. Aren't you, Jellybean?
The second bean—the spark of life—Dee wanted it for her.
Wanna play a game?

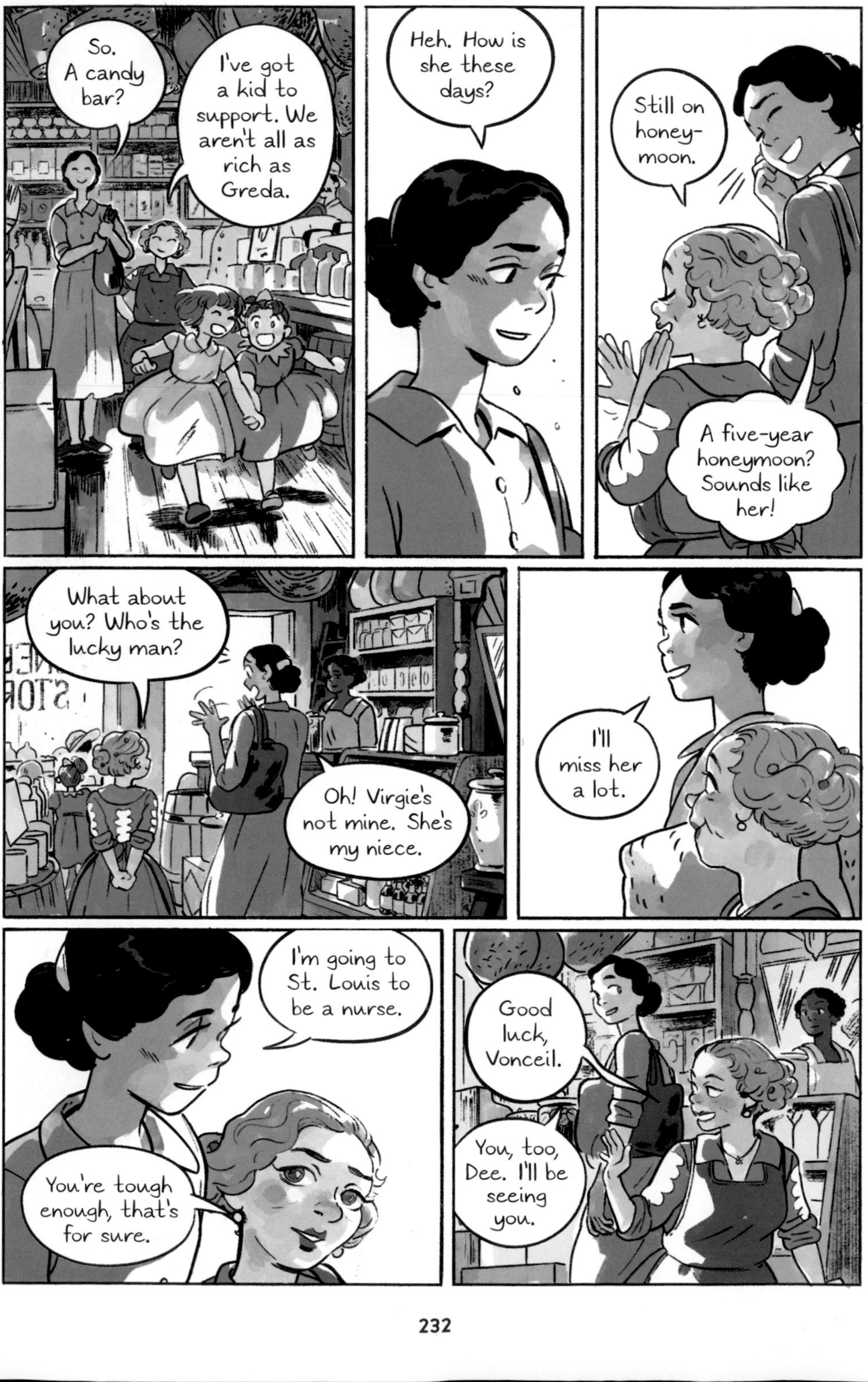

So. A candy bar?
I've got a kid to support. We aren't all as rich as Greda.
Heh. How is she these days?
Still on honey-moon.
A five-year honeymoon? Sounds like her!
What about you? Who's the lucky man?
Oh! Virgie's not mine. She's my niece.
I'll miss her a lot.
I'm going to St. Louis to be a nurse.
You're tough enough, that's for sure.
Good luck, Vonceil.
You, too, Dee. I'll be seeing you.

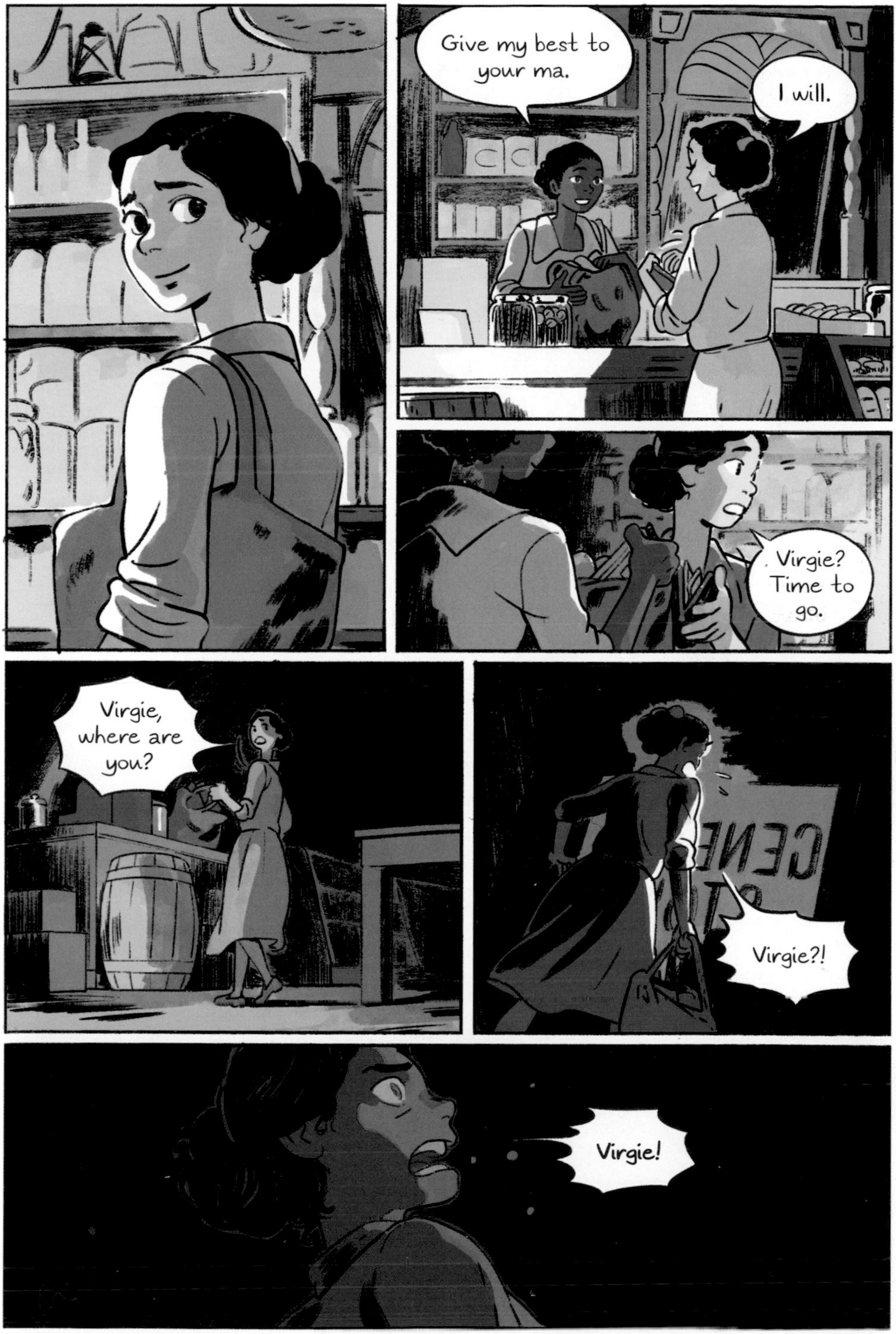
Give my best to your ma.
I will.
Virgie? Time to go.
Virgie, where are you?
Virgie?!
Virgie!

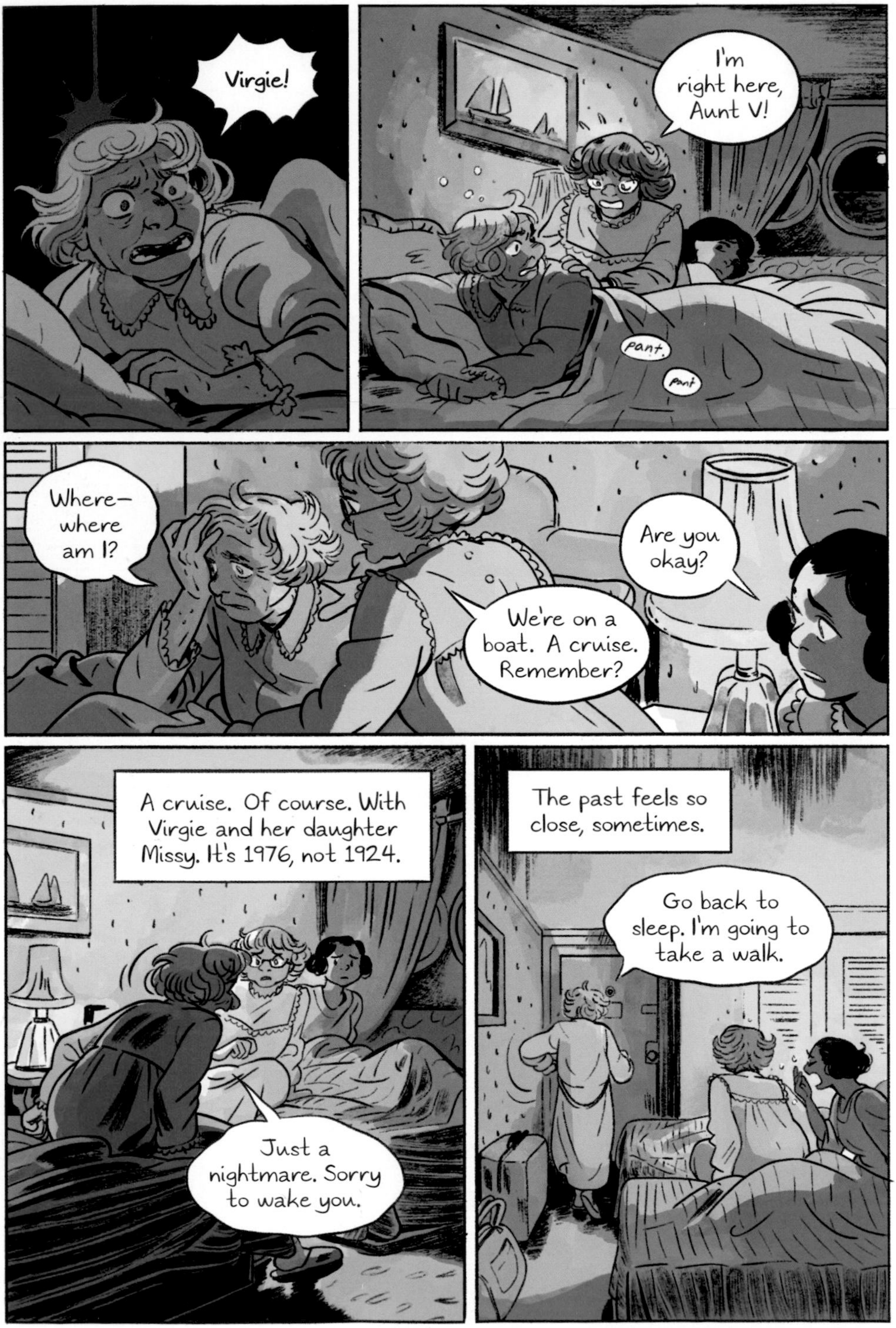
Virgie!
I'm right here, Aunt V!
pant.
pant
Where— where am I?
Are you okay?
We're on a boat. A cruise. Remember?
A cruise. Of course. With Virgie and her daughter Missy. It's 1976, not 1924.
Just a nightmare. Sorry to wake you.
The past feels so close, sometimes.
Go back to sleep. I'm going to take a walk.

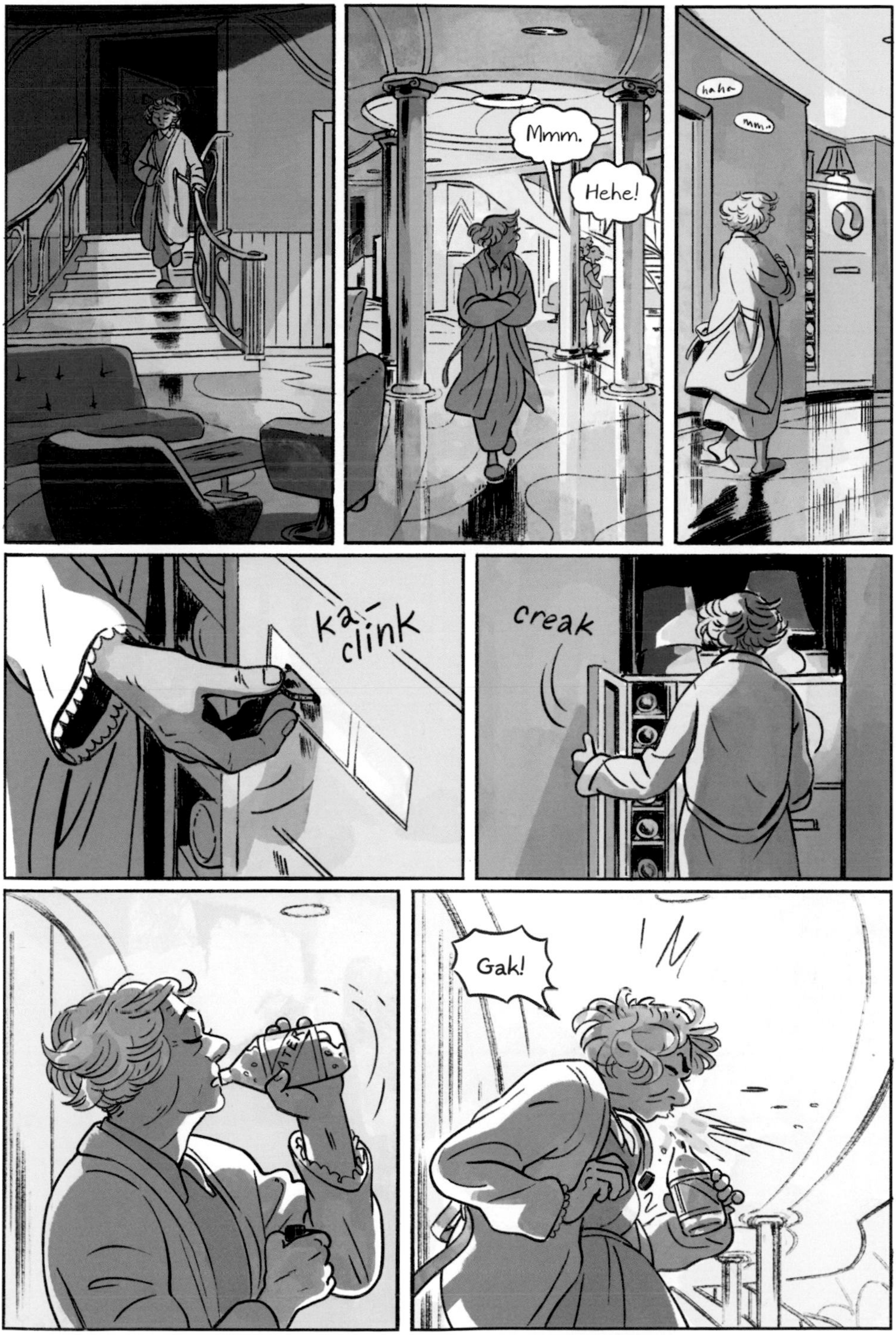
Mmm.
Hehe!
haha
mm..
ka-clink
creak
Gak!

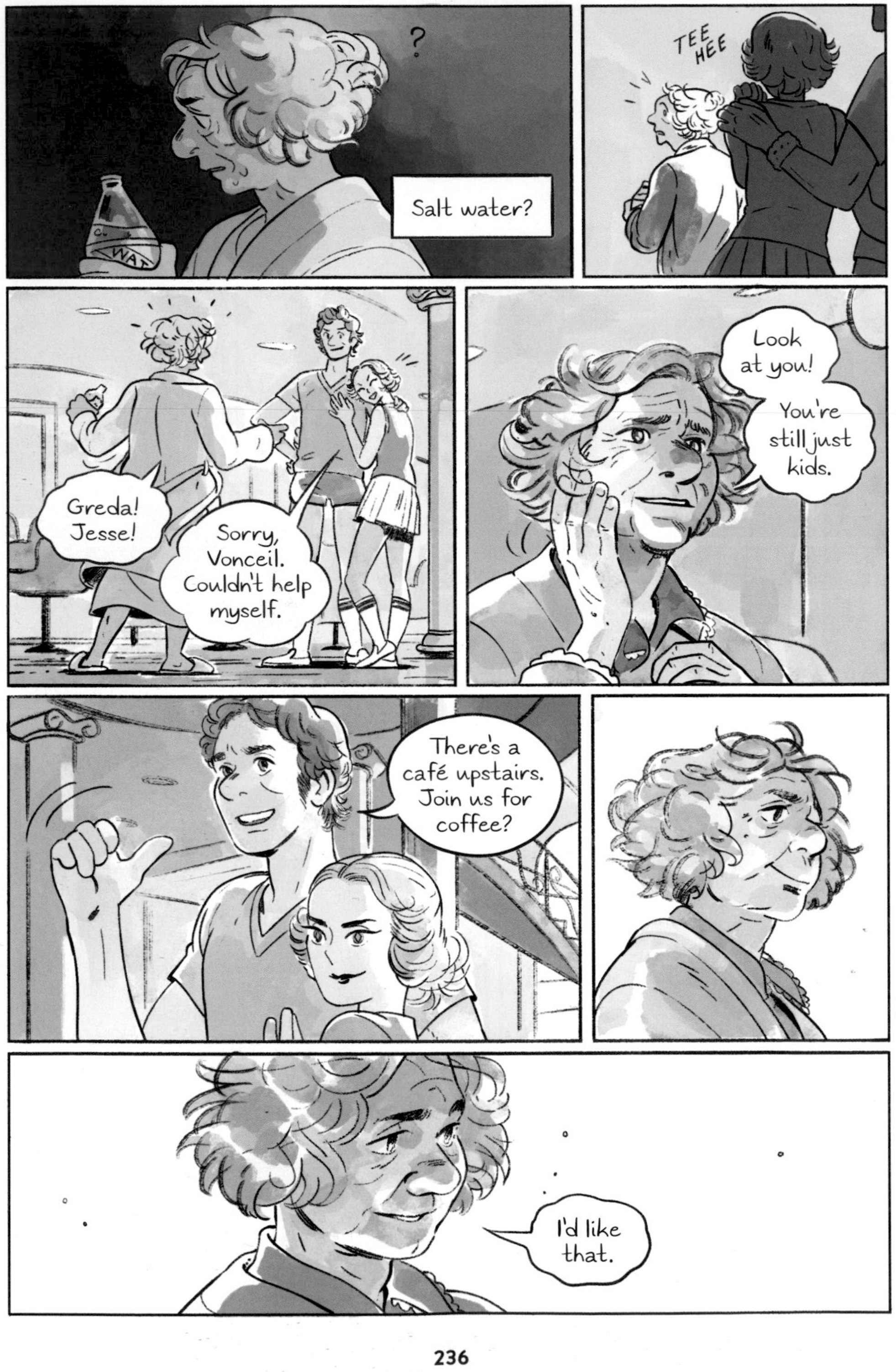
?
Salt water?
TEE HEE
Greda! Jesse!
Sorry, Vonceil. Couldn't help myself.
Look at you!
You're still just kids.
There's a café upstairs. Join us for coffee?
I'd like that.

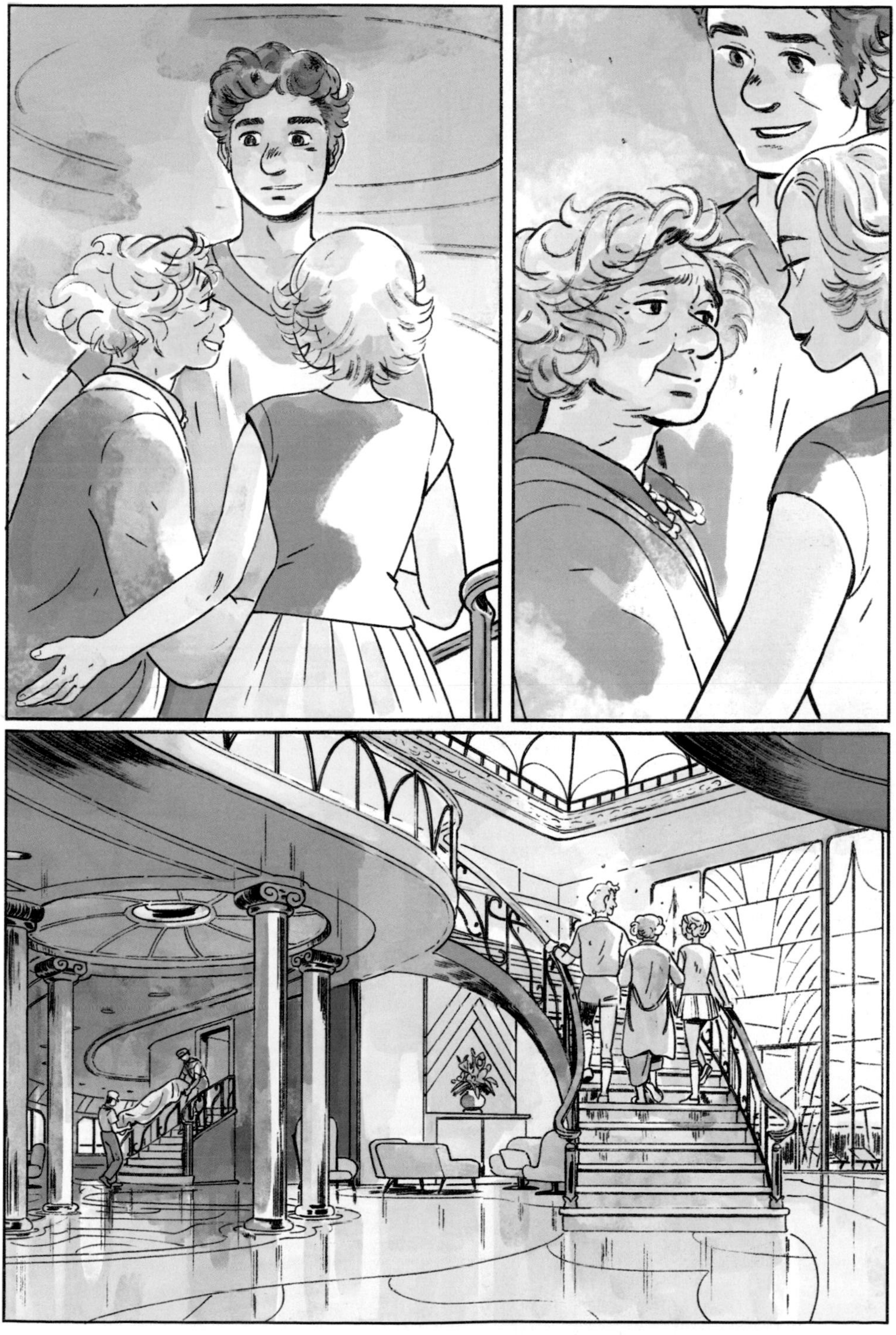

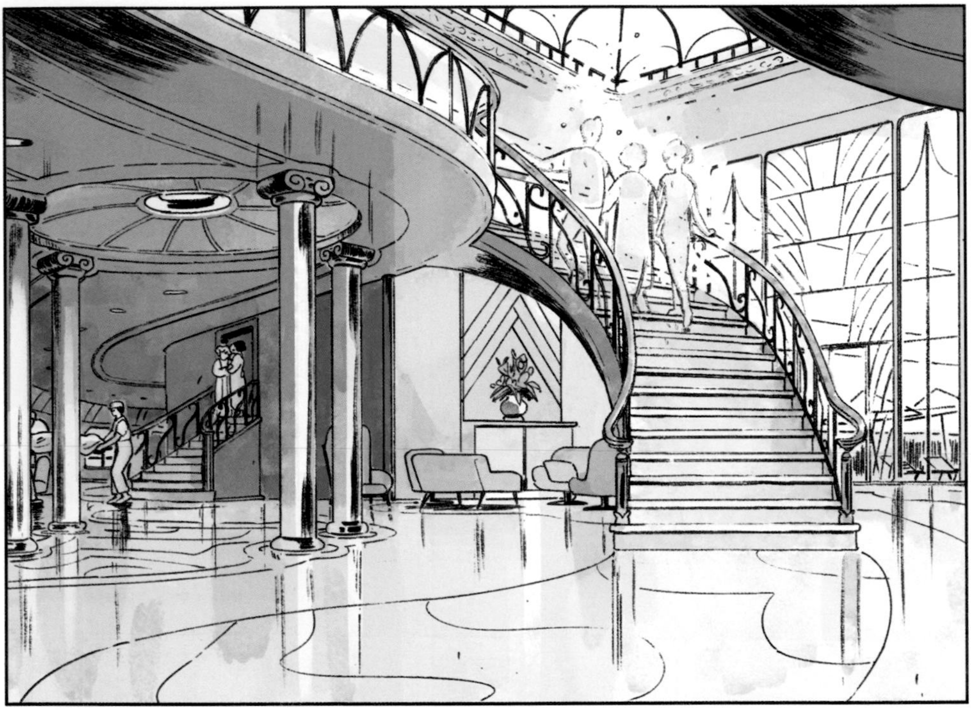

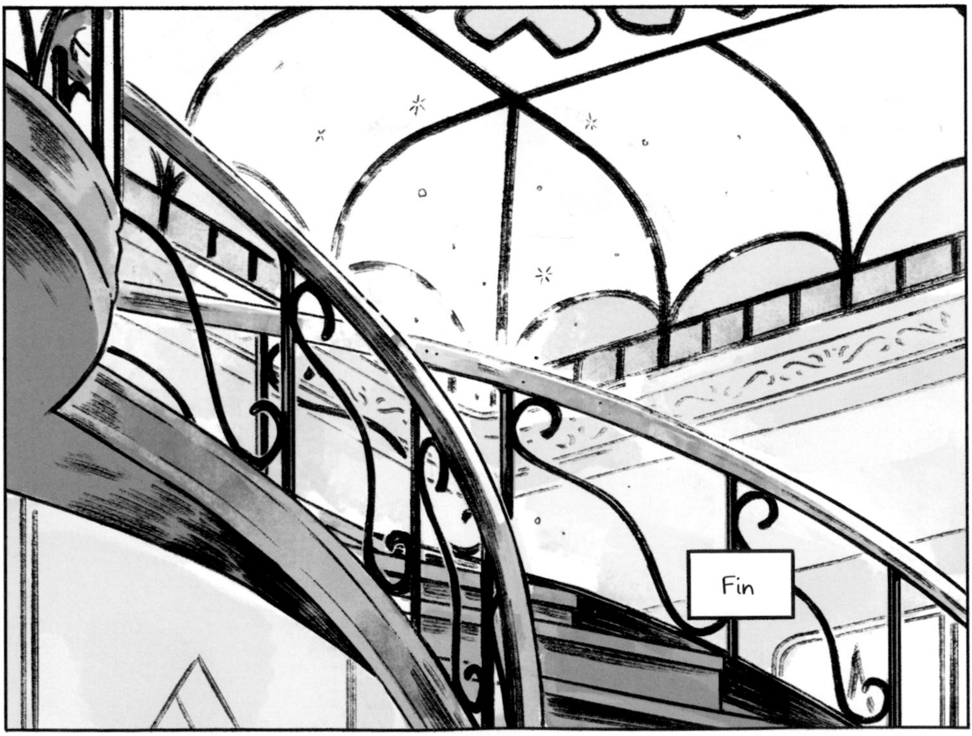
Fin